REMNANTS

Broken Galaxy Book Five

Phil Huddleston

CONTENTS

Broken Galaxy Book Five: *Remnants*
by Phil Huddleston

ISBN eBook: 978-1-7372142-0-5
ISBN Paperback: 978-1-7372142-1-2
ISBN Hardcover:

Cover Art by Ad Astra Book Covers
adastrabookcovers@gmail.com

FROM EARLIER BOOKS

Broken Galaxy - The name used to describe the state of affairs in the Orion Arm of the Milky Way. The ancient Golden Empire lasted for twenty thousand years; but two thousand years ago it collapsed, throwing the Arm into a Dark Age from which it is still recovering.

Goblins - Sentient AI lifeforms, usually androids, originating from the Stalingrad system 1,275 light years from Earth. Recently signed a Treaty of Alliance with Humans. As a result of the Treaty, Goblins obtained title to the planet Venus in the Sol System.

Jim Carter - U.S. Marine turned mercenary pilot turned semi-retired hermit turned space pilot. Fought in the African Wars on Earth. Fought at the Battle of Dutch Harbor. Fought in the Singheko War as CAG (Commander Attack Group) for the EDF (Earth Defense Force). After the Battle of Dekanna, left the EDF to care for his dying wife, Admiral Rita Page.

Bonnie Page - Ex-Air Force fighter pilot; first the lover of Jim Carter, later the lover of Rita Page. Fought in the Singheko War. After the capture of Rita Page by the Singheko, assumed command of the EDF as Fleet Admiral. Currently married to Luke Powell, captain of the destroyer *Dragon*.

Rita Page - A clone created by the renegade sentient starship *Jade* with the dual memories, knowledge, and feelings of both Jim Carter and Bonnie Page. As a result of her dual consciousness, she was in love with both Jim and Bonnie. Took Bonnie's last name since she was not created with one of her own. Served as Fleet Admiral of the EDF until captured by the Singheko; poisoned herself to prevent military secrets from falling into the hands of the enemy. Unable to survive as a biological being, Rita was scanned into Goblin form after the Battle of Dekanna.

Tika - a Goblin who assisted Humans in the Singheko Wars, saving their fleet from destruction. As Rita Page was dying, Tika transferred Rita's consciousness into a Goblin android body.

Rachel Gibson - former XO of the destroyer *Dragon.* Awarded the Navy Cross for her actions at the Battle of Dekanna. Promoted as Flag Aide to Admiral Bonnie Page.

Oliver "Ollie" Coston - Marine Major who penetrated the Singheko as an undercover operative during the Singheko Wars. After the surrender of the Singheko, Ollie was promoted to Lieutenant Colonel and assigned as Security Officer to the Human Embassy on Singheko.

Tatiana Powell - A half-English, half-Ukrainian woman arrested by the Ukrainian police for drug smuggling. During the Singheko invasion, she was handed over to them as they were filling their slave ships with Human prisoners. Imprisoned in a large wire cage on a slave ship sent to the planet Deriko along with 12,000 other Human prisoners. After arrival at Deriko, initiated a slave rebellion and pushed the Singheko off the planet. Recruited into the EDF as Admiral of Ground Forces.

Luke Powell - father of Tatiana Powell and husband of Admiral Bonnie Page. Saved the EDF flagship *Merkkessa* in the last minutes of the Battle of Dekanna by inserting his wrecked destroyer *Dragon* between the enemy and the *Merkkessa.* Awarded the Navy Cross.

Gillian Carter Rodgers - sister of Jim Carter. Currently acting as foster mother of Jim and Rita's daughter Imogen.

Mark Rodgers - A former General in the U.S. Army. Husband of Jim Carter's sister Gillian.

PROLOGUE

Packet Boat *Donkey*
Enroute to Stalingrad System

Rita came back to herself. It was dark. She didn't know where she was.

The last thing she remembered was sitting in the Singheko shuttle, on her way to be tortured and killed by the enemy.

The poison. I made Stephanie give me poison. Why am I alive?

She realized she had another hazy memory. Jim, standing over her in a hospital room. And another vague memory of waking in a shuttle, with Jim lying beside her, holding her.

How could that be?

She tried to speak. But something was wrong. She couldn't feel her tongue. It was as if she had no tongue. She panicked.

I'm losing my mind!

Suddenly she felt a touch. A hand on her shoulder, then moving down to take her hand. She heard a voice.

"Easy, Rita. Take it easy. Everything is OK. You're safe."

Jim.

That's Jim.

She tried to speak again. This time, somehow, it worked. She heard her voice.

"Where..."

But it wasn't really her voice. It was close; it was almost her voice. But something was different. And she couldn't feel her tongue.

"Where..."

"You're safe, Rita. Everything is alright. We're both safe.

We're going to Stalingrad right now - you're going to need some rehabilitation. Then we'll go to Earth to get Imogen. Then we're going to explore the Universe together. Just relax. I'll tell you all about it."

CHAPTER ONE

Stree Prime
2,000 Lights from Stalingrad

"Right there," said the kneeling Stree monk, Tarilli. He pointed in the holotank to a strange set of structures. The largest was a flat, ringlike structure that went completely around a K0-class star. Dozens of other smaller disk-like structures were also present in the system.

"Since our last war with the Goblins two hundred years ago, they've expanded their Dyson swarm significantly. You can see they've completed the Dyson Ring around the star and added another dozen habitat disks."

Great Prophet Videlli stared at the holo, then turned to High Admiral Sojatta. Prostrated on the main floor below the throne, his head bowed, Sojatta waited for the Word that would lead him to Enlightenment.

"Life without the biology of Creation is blasphemy," spoke Videlli. "It cannot be allowed to exist. We cannot let these Goblins continue to grow their population. We will wipe them from the Universe. It is the Word Ordained."

High Admiral Sojatta nodded, being careful not to bring his head up high enough to meet the eyes of the Great Prophet. Only another priest or monk could meet the eyes of Great Prophet Videlli. For anyone else, it was a sentence of death.

"It is the Word Ordained," Sojatta repeated. "Praise be to the Word."

The monk Tarilli, kneeling on the floor, spoke again.

"There is a complication. The blasphemy of the Goblins

is aided by several species of biologicals, who have allied with them. They call themselves variously Dariama, Human, Bagrami, and Taegu."

Great Prophet Videlli looked at Tarilli kneeling before him.

"We cannot allow any biological species to exist which might help the blasphemers. Which are the most aggressive among these biologicals?"

"The Humans, O Word of Prophecy," Tarilli responded. "They have just completed a war with two other species, the Singheko and the Nidarians. Although the Humans won the war, their fleet was devastated by their last battles. They have little capacity for resistance at this point."

The monk switched the holotank to display a rather beautiful blue and white planet. "They reside on this planet, which they call Earth."

Great Prophet Videlli turned back to his High Admiral.

"For two hundred years, we have prepared for the destruction of the Goblins. At last we are ready. We will destroy any who stand in our way. Wipe all of the biologicals who have allied with this blasphemy. And any others who might pose a threat to our war against the Goblins. It is the Word Ordained."

High Admiral Sojatta nodded once more.

"It is the Word Ordained," Sojatta repeated in the timeless mantra. "Praise be to the Word."

CHAPTER TWO

Stalingrad System
Dyson Ring

"Don't be afraid," said Tika. "You can do this."

Rita closed her eyes. She tried to take a deep breath.

Then she remembered.

She was now an android.

And androids don't breathe. Not really. Oh, they can make their chest move up and down. And it looks like they're breathing.

But they're not. She still had a lot to process about her new body.

"OK. I'll try once more."

She was in a training room, lying on her back in a bunk. Her eyes were closed.

She had been a Goblin for three weeks. She had a lot to learn.

With an effort, she tried once again to focus on switching. Tika had explained to her that she could move her consciousness from one form to another. She could switch between android bodies as she wished.

But she would have to learn to control it. And that was the problem. The entire concept scared the hell out of her.

Alternate bodies. Who could have imagined such a thing? This is scary.

But I have to learn how to do it.

"Let your mind float free. Try to perceive a doorway. You should be able to find it just by thinking about it. Reach out for it."

Rita focused. She tried to imagine what Tika was saying.

A doorway. Close to me. All I have to do is find it.

This is crazy.

No, this is way, way beyond crazy.

Letting her mind float free, as Tika had suggested, she felt in her perceptive space for the door...

Slowly, she became aware of it. It seemed to be standing to her right side, a few yards away.

<I can see it> she transmitted to Tika, using her radio voice.

<Good. What does it look like?>

<A large wooden door, like something you'd see in an old castle>

<Good. We all perceive our doors based on our own history and experience. So you perceive it in your own way. That's fine. Try to open it. Desire it to open. Wish it open>

Rita concentrated. She willed the door to open. Slowly, with a creak, it began to move.

<It's working. The door is opening!>

<Excellent. What do you see behind it?>

<There's a body. Just standing there>

<That's the avatar for the other body. Now...imagine a pipe between you and that body. Imagine water flowing down that pipe. You have to desire to move into that body. Think about water flowing down a pipe>

<I'm afraid>

<Don't be afraid. If something goes wrong, you'll just wake up here in your old body. No worries>

<I'm still afraid. I just can't imagine leaving my body for another one...>

<That's the old Human in you talking. You're not a Human anymore. You're a Goblin now. You have to learn how to do this. Even our small children can do it. Don't be afraid>

Rita opened her eyes, looked at the cool white ceiling, and pressed them tight shut again. She relaxed, letting her mind float free. She could see the door, standing open in her mind. Behind the door was a body. It stood waiting, inert.

All I have to do is imagine a pipe. Imagine water flowing down that pipe. I have to desire to move into that body.

Move, dammit!

No, that's not the way. Getting upset won't help.

Relax. Just imagine water flowing down the pipe.

There was a strange feeling. It felt as if someone had poured a bucket of warm water over her, covering her from head to toe. It wasn't a bad feeling at all.

She opened her eyes.

She wasn't in the training room anymore. She was in a large space, lying on a bunk. There were dozens of other android bodies lying in bunks all around her. All of them were inert, just lying there. She was the only one awake.

She called excitedly to Tika.

<I switched! I did it!>

Portsmouth, UK
Sol System

"...and that's the secret of life."

The barman was a couple of yards away, wiping glasses. He turned and stared at Luke.

"What?"

"I said, that's the secret of life," Luke repeated.

"What's the secret of life?" asked the barman.

"*Move Your Ass.*"

The barman gave Luke a sour smile. "That's the secret of life? Move your ass?"

"Yep," said Luke, slurring his words a bit.

"If you say so, Captain."

Luke Powell nodded in satisfaction. He lifted his glass and knocked back another pint of dark. Putting the empty glass back on the bar with a thump, he pointed to it, and the barman refilled it.

"No, I'm serious, Tommy. Think about it. From the time you're born until the day you die. *Move your ass*. That's the secret. Those who get up off their ass and do something useful are happy. And those who sit around on their butts goofing off and wasting time are miserable. All you gotta do to be happy is get up off your butt and move your ass. Do something useful."

Tommy nodded.

"You know, Captain, I've been tending bar a long time. I thought I'd heard all the secrets of life. But that's a new one, even for me."

Luke smiled crookedly. "I don't care what anybody says, Tommy. You're a good egg."

"But, Captain," mused Tommy, wiping a glass, his brow wrinkling as he thought about it. "You're a destroyer captain. You go out and fight with the Fleet. So how does that work? Are you doing something useful for the world?"

Luke grinned. "Yep. I make sure the bad guys don't blow up our capital ships by sticking my little destroyer in the way of the enemy, so it gets blown up instead. I call that useful."

Tommy continued to wipe the glass, frowning.

"But...there aren't any bad guys now, right? We beat the Singheko. We've got peace now, right?"

"Yeah. No more bad guys. I may have to find another job, Tommy. Not much call for destroyer captains these days."

As Tommy left to attend to other duties, Luke gazed blearily around the pub. The locals were out, enjoying the warmer weather of southern England in springtime. He waved at an acquaintance, who waved back at him.

I am so fucking bored.

Luke heaved a large sigh.

I want Bonnie.

His inner voice spoke up.

So? Go see her!

No. She's busy, sorting out the mess at Singheko.

But she's going to be relieved by Shigeto. Just go! She'll find time for you!

No. I'm trying to be a good husband. I'm giving her the space she needs to get her job done.

Yeah. Temporary Ambassador to Singheko. Who would have dreamed it?

Well. She's the best qualified. Nobody knows more about those bastards than her and Ollie.

Yeah. Ollie. I'm not happy about that situation.

Ah, you worry for nothing. Ollie's just a good friend. There's nothing there. Nothing between them. And Ollie is still grieving Helen. You know that.

Yes. I do know that, actually.

Hmm. Here's an idea. Shigeto's leaving for Singheko on the Asiana *to relieve Bonnie. Why don't you hitch a ride with him? Then you and Bonnie can go see Jim and Rita at Stalingrad! Jim has to be feeling pretty lonely right now. He's 1,275 lights from Earth. The only Human in the whole damn system. I bet he'd like to see you!*

Good idea.

Luke slammed his glass back on the bar, empty.

Damn good idea!

I think I'll do just that!

Surface of Venus
Sol System

Commander Rauti was in his go-anywhere caterpillar aspect - six feet long with 40 legs, his body a hardened, carapace-like shell that could withstand nearly any environment. He gazed around him with radio eyes and was pleased. His Goblin detachment had successfully completed the first phase of their surface base on Venus. They were off to a good start.

Had a normal Human been able to survive in the hellish atmosphere of Venus for any significant period of time, they would have seen two low mounds, crossing in their centers like the letter 'X'. Each side of the 'X' was two hundred and fifty yards long.

Beneath those mounds were the command and control

centers, living quarters for his crew of 200 Goblins, and storage areas for their gear. That structure would be their home for the next 150 rotations of the planet. 36,525 Earth days. 100 Earth years. Venus rotated quite slowly compared to Earth.

Gazing farther afield, Rauti contemplated the crop of microbots that extended as far as he could see. From horizon to horizon, the surface was covered with them. The microbots soaked up the carbon dioxide, converting it to oxygen and carbon nanotubes. Within a few more years, the self-replicating microbots would cover the entire planet.

Rauti looked off to the west at the base station for the space elevator. The small mountain there had five tunnels exiting its base, equally spaced around the mountain. Each tunnel mouth had a tether coming out of the tunnel and running along the ground for a half mile, anchored to the surface.

Lifting his eyes, Rauti looked at the top of the mountain. What had once been a mountain peak was now flat, chopped off to form the base station for the space elevator. Rising up out of the flat top of the mountain, the cables were combined to create the final tether. That was just a stub so far, ending a few dozen yards above the top of the base station.

Looking up, Rauti adjusted the wavelength of his radio eyes so he could see beyond the dense atmosphere. There, far above, he picked out the other end of the incomplete tether. It terminated at a dumbbell-like structure in geosynchronous orbit. Four asteroids were clustered around the dumbbell structure, feeding raw materials to the microbots building it.

It would take another fifty years to complete the space elevator. But that made no difference to Rauti. He had all the time in the world to complete it, because that was not the critical link in Rauti's terraforming design. The critical link was still higher, well beyond the terminus of the space elevator.

Adjusting his eyes again, changing to a wavelength that gave him more detail at extreme distances from the planet, Rauti looked with satisfaction at the beginnings of the Dyson shell. That was the structure that would someday block a significant portion of solar radiation from the planet, allowing him to cool it to a more reasonable temperature.

The shell so far was only twenty miles in diameter, a round disk making a dark dot on the sun. Beside the disk were many smaller dots. Those were asteroids brought in to provide raw materials for the Dyson shell construction. Most of them were rocky asteroids, selected for their high carbon or iron content. A few were ice balls, selected for water and trace elements.

It would take Rauti a full century to reduce the carbon dioxide out of the atmosphere, complete the Dyson structure screening Venus from the Sun, and bring the temperature down to a reasonable level.

But Rauti wasn't concerned. He had plenty of time.

Stalingrad System
Dyson Ring

Jim Carter was sitting in the easy chair in his apartment, reading on his tablet, when someone knocked at the door. Muttering under his breath, he got up and went to open it. A Goblin stood there - a large male android, one he didn't recognize.

He knew it was a Goblin for two reasons.

One - it was naked. All the androids at Stalingrad went around naked. They seemed to abhor clothing.

Two - he was the only Human in the entire Stalingrad solar system. So everyone else for a dozen light years was an android or some other kind of Goblin.

"Yes?" he asked.

"May I come in?"

"Of course, please," Jim responded. He stepped aside and let the android in. The android moved to the fireplace and turned, smiling at him. Jim, puzzled, stared at him in confusion.

"How can I help you?"

The android's smile got even bigger.

"Don't you recognize me?"

"No, I'm sorry. Should I know you?"

The android moved toward him. It got closer, moving into his personal space. Jim recoiled, backing away until the wall prevented him from moving any farther.

"What...?"

The big male android kept coming. It reached out both arms and put them around Jim's neck.

"What are you doing?" he exclaimed in shock.

The android winked at him.

"Hello there, big boy," it said.

CHAPTER THREE

Stalingrad System
Dyson Ring

"Don't ever, ever do that to me again!" Jim said, for the second time. "You scared the ever-loving crap out of me!"

Rita sat in Jim's easy chair, still laughing. Jim was too upset to sit. He paced back and forth across the living room of their apartment, wearing a path in the carpet.

"Oh, I wish you could have seen the look on your face," Rita said. "I thought you were gonna faint dead away!"

Jim paused in his pacing and shook his fist at her in mock anger. "One of these days, Rita. One of these days!"

Rita - still in her male android body - smiled. "Oh, this is fun. Wow - think about it. I can sneak up on you anytime, in any kind of body I want, and you'll never be the wiser!"

Jim glared at her. "Just keep it up, babe. Just keep it up and see where it gets you!"

Rita purred softly, in a seductive voice. "Why don't you come up and see me sometime..."

Jim, exasperated, shook his head again. "What would I have to do to get you to switch back to your normal body?"

"Um...cook dinner? For the next three nights in a row?"

"Done. Just please put yourself back to normal."

"Normal? What's normal, babe? I'm a Goblin now. Normal is whatever I want it to be..."

Jim growled. "You know what I mean. A female."

Rita grinned mischievously.

"You want tall or short? Blond or brunette? Maybe a ginger?"

Jim rolled his eyes. "How about the way you were when we woke up this morning?"

Cruiser EDF *Asiana*
Enroute to Singheko

"Thanks for the lift, Admiral."

Admiral Dewa Shigeto smiled back at Luke Powell from the head of the wardroom table. "Happy to do it, Captain! Sorry we had to double you up with Ensign Brady, but at least we squeezed you aboard!"

Luke smiled at the young Ensign at the other end of the table.

"No problem. Ensign Brady has been telling me all about his days at the Naval Academy."

The young ensign blushed at the attention from his seniors.

"Any of those stories you'd care to pass along?" asked Mark Rodgers, winking at Luke from across the table.

Luke grinned as Ensign Brady flushed an even deeper red.

"I'd better not," said Luke. "Roomies have to respect each other's confidence, you know."

Ensign Brady turned to his meal, hoping the arrow of attention would move in another direction. Mark stifled a laugh and mercifully changed the subject.

"So does Bonnie know you're coming along with us?"

Luke nodded. "Yes, I sent her an ansible message as we were launching."

At the head of the table, Admiral Shigeto's face turned a bit serious. "Captain Powell, you know we're thinking about revising the fraternization rules in the Fleet."

"Yes, sir. I've heard."

"If we decide to make the change, couples will no longer be allowed to serve on the same ship or under the same commander."

"Yes, sir."

"That would mean you and Admiral Page would have to be

in separate commands."

"Yes, sir. We're reconciled to that possibility."

"OK. Just thought I'd highlight that for you."

"Do you know when the decision will be final?"

"Most likely at the New Year. So you've the rest of this year before we'll have a final decision."

Across from Luke, Mark leaned back with a grin. "Enjoy it while you can, Captain!"

Luke nodded, musing.

Enjoy it while you can.

But that's assuming I even get a slot in the peacetime navy. Dragon *is still in the docks at Dekanna, shot to pieces. Bonnie is being replaced by Shigeto, so she won't have much influence on policy anymore.*

I may never get another ship, much less have to worry about being under Bonnie's command.

"...vacation?"

Luke realized Shigeto was still talking to him. He quickly tried to reconstruct the thread of conversation he had missed.

"Uh...yes, sir. Bonnie and I've decided to go to Stalingrad. Along with my daughter Tatiana, her husband Mikhail - Misha, as we call him - and their new baby, Marta. We're going to visit Rita Page and Jim Carter. At least, that's the plan so far."

"Well, any vacation is certainly well deserved," added Shigeto. "What Bonnie and her fleet accomplished at Dekanna was a flat-out miracle. And your role...well, I have to tell you, Captain. I'm not sure I would've had the balls to stick my shot-up destroyer in front of an enemy battlecruiser cube to protect my flagship. You deserve everything that's coming to you, sir."

Luke acknowledged the compliment with a dip of his head. "Well, actually, Admiral, to be honest - if I'd had more time to think about it, I probably wouldn't have done it!"

Shigeto laughed along with everyone at the table.

"I suspect that's a common theme, Captain. I wonder if any of us would put ourselves in that kind of harm's way if we stopped to think about it!"

Luke, embarrassed, attempted to change the conversation. He looked across the table at Mark.

"So where is your lovely wife this evening, General?"

Mark looked a bit sour. "Call me Mark, please. I haven't been an active General for nearly three years. And Jilly thinks the baby is running a slight fever, so she didn't want to leave her alone."

"Would you like the ship's doctor to take a look at her?" asked Shigeto.

"No, sir, I don't think that's necessary, at least not right now. It seems to be just a slight fever. Nothing serious."

"Well. Let me know if you change your mind. We'll get Dr. Warner to take a look."

"Thank you, sir."

"Mark, I understand you know Jim Carter quite well?"

Mark half-smiled. "Yes, sir. He's my brother-in-law."

Shigeto looked surprised. "Oh, really? I did not realize that. I knew you were taking care of his child for him, but I didn't realize..."

"Yes, sir. Jilly - Gillian, my wife - is Jim's sister."

"Ah. That explains it."

"But...to be honest...I knew Jim before. Or should I say...I chased him. Before I met Gillian, I mean."

"You chased him?" Shigeto spoke in puzzlement.

"Yes, sir. I was in charge of tracking him down three years ago when he was attempting to hide *Jade*."

"Amazing. And did you track him down?"

"Yes, sir. But I didn't keep him long. He escaped."

"Ah, yes. I remember the story now. He escaped custody and that led to the big battle at Dutch Harbor."

"Yes, sir."

"Were you there? At Dutch Harbor?"

"Yes, sir, sort of. I was not involved much in the actual fighting. I was up on top of the mountain most of the time."

"Except when you and Gillian were ejected out of an exploding C-37, right?" said Luke from across the table, grinning.

Mark grimaced. "Well, yeah. How'd you know about that?"

"Bonnie told me all about it."

Mark waved a hand. "Well, except for that one little detail, I didn't have much involvement."

"Oh?" Luke continued. "Bonnie said you drove up to *Jade* in a Stryker combat vehicle and pulled her, Jim and Rita out of the wreck about thirty seconds before the cruise missiles hit."

"Well, I guess it might have been thirty seconds," shrugged Mark. "It seemed like a lot less at the time!"

***

After dinner, Mark Rodgers returned to his cabin. Gillian was sitting on the couch crying. Surprised, Mark went to her, sat beside her, and put his arm around her.

"What's the matter, Jilly? What happened?"

"Nothing," sobbed Gillian. "Nothing happened. I just...I just know Rita is going to take her! We'll lose her!"

Mark looked at the two-year old sleeping in the bunk in the corner of the cabin. He rubbed Gillian's back, trying to soothe her.

"We don't know that, Jilly. Jim and Rita may take her away, or they may not. Don't get all upset before you know anything!"

Gillian tried to choke back her sobs, wiping at her eyes. She bowed her head and stared at her lap.

"No. I just know. I just know they'll take her."

"No, you don't," said Mark. "You're letting your imagination run wild. You know no such thing."

Gillian shook her head. "No. As soon as Rita gets acclimated to her new...state...or whatever you call it...she's going to want her daughter. I know it."

Mark pulled her closer, wrapping his arms around her. "Jilly. Calm down. First of all, there's absolutely no indication that Jim and Rita will take Imogen permanently. And second, we knew up front that we were doing this for Imogen. Not for ourselves. So whatever is best for that child, we have to do it."

"But...," Gillian sobbed, "...if they take her...if she goes off to the stars with them...we'll never see her again!"

Mark held his wife, holding her tight. He looked across the small cabin at the wall. Gillian had mounted a viewer there for watching vids and showing pictures. And she had loaded the viewer with pictures of Imogen, their foster daughter.

The daughter of Jim Carter and Jim's wife Rita.

Rita, who had been Fleet Admiral of the Earth Defense Force, fighting the Singheko in space.

Rita, whose body had been so damaged by poison that the Goblins had transformed her into an android to save her.

Rita, now a Goblin.

The Goblin who might take Imogen away from them.

She might take our sweet Imogen. Take her away to who knows where. We could lose her forever.

We'll just have to bear that.

***

27 lights away, Lieutenant Colonel Oliver "Ollie" Coston sat on the edge of his bunk in the Human embassy at Singheko, his head in his hands.

Helen.

His thought processes were muddled. He was drunk. And not just a little. Ollie was thoroughly, professionally drunk.

Helen. I miss you.

Heaving a sigh, Ollie lifted his head. He found he had a bit of trouble keeping it steady. He leaned forward and placed a hand under his chin, steadying his head enough to focus on the photoframe across from him on the desk.

Helen.

The photoframe showed an attractive female Marine lieutenant, in the prime of life. In the background was a rifle range. The woman held an M7 rifle across her body with one hand. In the other hand she held up a scoring sheet, with "249/250" in large black letters, circled. She smiled at the camera, clearly enjoying the moment. Over one corner of the photo frame was draped a Navy Cross.

Why'd I let you go on that mission? Why didn't I force you to stay with me? It's my fault. I could've said no.

There was a gentle knock on his door. Ollie stared at the door stupidly, not sure what to do. He was far too drunk to get up and answer the door. In fact, he was too drunk to even tell his personal AI to open the door. He gave it a try anyway.

"*Quantico*...open...open the..."

Before he could make another attempt, the door clicked.

Ah. Bonnie.

Ollie knew it was Bonnie, because she was the only person who could override his door control. The door swung in gently and his commanding officer, Admiral Bonnie Page, poked her head in cautiously around the edge of the door.

"Are you decent?" she called out.

Ollie tried to respond, but all that came out was a grunt. Bonnie peeked in farther, saw him sitting on the edge of his bunk in the darkness, and pushed into the room.

"Oh. That again," she said. Bonnie came on into the room and stood in front of him, shaking her head.

"I came to ask if everything is ready for Admiral Shigeto's arrival tomorrow."

Ollie attempted to nod, but his head wobbled too much. He had to grab his chin with his hand to steady up.

"S..ready, milady," he managed to get out. "Ever...thin... ready..."

"Good," said Bonnie. She stared at Ollie. "You're off duty, Colonel; and I know what you're going through. So I'm not going to rake you over the coals about this. But..."

Bonnie turned and looked at the picture of Helen Frost in the photoframe, then turned back to Ollie.

"...you need to get hold of yourself, Ollie. It's not your fault Helen died. She knew what she was doing. Her plan was a good one. You did the right thing to approve it. You did everything right, and she did everything right. But it just didn't work out. The enemy gets to play a card in these things too. You know that."

Bonnie squatted down and faced Ollie. He wasn't just her Security Officer - he was a friend. She reached out both arms and put her hands on his shoulders.

"Ollie. I know you loved her. I know it hurts. But get a grip on yourself. People die in war. You didn't kill her."

Ollie gazed at her dully. "Aye, milady," he stuttered.

Bonnie released his shoulders, stood up, and shook her head, knowing it wasn't going to be that easy.

"Shigeto's arriving tomorrow, Colonel. And a week later, we're leaving for Stalingrad. I need you on your 'A' game, Ollie. Get your shit together."

Ollie lifted his head, coming to a position of attention on the edge of his bunk as best he could, knowing there was no way he could get to his feet.

"Aye, milady," he said as crisply as possible.

Bonnie turned and moved to the door, pausing just before she exited. She turned and looked back at the forlorn man sitting on the bunk. Ollie was already staring at the photoframe again, oblivious to her departure. She sighed and went out, closing the door gently behind her.

CHAPTER FOUR

City of Mosalia
Singheko System

Next day, still slightly hung-over, Ollie stood several paces behind Bonnie as the shuttle from *Asiana* settled to the ground, a slight vapor of dissipating gas coming from the rear.

With a slight pop, the ramp on the side of the shuttle cracked open and started down. As it touched the ground, Admiral Dewa Shigeto's junior aides stepped out, turned, and formed an honor guard on both sides of the ramp.

Right behind them came Luke, who also stepped into place as part of the honor guard.

At the sight of her husband, Bonnie's heart leaped.

Luke. My love. God, I'm glad you're here!

The more senior members of Shigeto's staff stepped off the shuttle next and took their place in the honor guard formation.

Finally, Admiral Dewa Shigeto stepped off the shuttle. He immediately saw Bonnie with her own honor guard, waiting twenty yards in front of him. He gave her a huge smile and walked directly toward her.

They had agreed in advance there was no point in delaying the changeover. They would conduct it at the spaceport, right now.

Shigeto marched to her, stopping two yards in front of her, and saluted. Bonnie brought up her own salute and they stood, facing each other.

"Admiral Page, I relieve you," said Shigeto.

"Admiral Shigeto, I stand relieved," replied Bonnie in the age-old formality.

With smiles, they dropped their salutes and shook hands. Then the two of them turned and headed for their staff cars. Bonnie managed one more loving glance at her husband Luke, and a quick wink, as she slid into her car beside Shigeto. As Bonnie's personal bodyguard, Ollie slid into the front seat beside the driver. The rest of the aides - and Luke - found places in other vehicles. With a lurch, the procession started off toward the Human embassy in Mosalia - an embassy in existence for only two months.

In front and back were troop carriers, full of heavily armed Special Forces. Overhead, two squadrons of Merlin fighters loitered at 40,000 feet, ready for action. Every intersection was blocked off by another troop carrier full of Special Forces.

"I thought we had a peace treaty in place," mused Shigeto.

Bonnie laughed. "We do. But the Singheko hadn't lost a war in 700 years, you know. Then the upstart Humans come along. Next thing you know, they've lost the Battle of Dekanna and been forced to surrender. They're not too happy about that."

"Well, I didn't think they would be. But is there such danger to require this kind of protection?"

"Admiral, trust me - there is. There's a significant part of the Singheko population that would like nothing better than to cut our throats. You'd be wise to take the same precautions I do. Especially since I think they will likely test you as soon as I'm gone."

Shigeto smiled at her. "You're saying, they may not fear a peacetime admiral as much as the one that kicked their ass at Dekanna."

Bonnie shrugged. "I'm just sayin', Dewa. Take it any way you want. But if I were you, I'd keep my guard up."

Shigeto nodded. "OK. I got it. I'll follow your advice."

"Now," added Bonnie. "About agenda. You'll find a detail handover document in your office. But I can summarize what you need to know in thirty seconds. First of all, the Singheko want a decision about rebuilding their fleet. They're saying that since we now have a peace treaty, they should at least be allowed to repair their damaged ships. I've not made a decision on this; I left it for you. But you'll need to give them an answer pretty soon. They're about to pop a cork over it."

"Ah. And what is your advice on that?"

"I'd let them - within reason. I think they could build back to a moderate-sized Home Fleet, to protect their planet. But I'd limit them to that. Keep their total fleet size significantly less than they had at Dekanna. That way, we'll know we can always kick their ass if they come at us again."

"And they'll know it, too," smiled Shigeto.

"Too right."

"What else?"

"I put a stop to those head-chopping mass executions they do in the arena. They're really pissed about that. They claim it's their right as a sovereign nation to kill criminals and war prisoners any way they please. I told them you'd take the suspension under consideration."

"I might be OK with criminals, but prisoners of war? No way."

"Exactly. If you can convince them to limit it to criminals, duly convicted of a capital offense in a fair trial, then I guess maybe - just maybe - we could defer to their ancient customs. But for POWs? Absolutely not. We can't tolerate that, and I've already told Asagi that."

"Tell me about Asagi. How's he to work with?"

"He's OK. As their highest-ranking survivor of Dekanna, he sort of fell into the role, you know. He's still trying to get used to the fact he's the new Grand Admiral. And trying to form a civilian government. They had civilian government before, you know. Up to about a thousand years ago. But for the last millennium, the civilian government's been just a figurehead, a puppet of the military. Now Asagi is trying to shift power back to a true civilian government, and it's not easy. He's not only fighting his own people in the military, but even the civilian population is afraid of it."

"Are they going to make it?"

"Yes, I think so. But you're going to have your work cut out for you, Admiral Shigeto."

"I never expected otherwise, Admiral Page."

"So…we'll have meetings for the rest of this week, ensuring a good handover. Then I'm off to vacation."

"Ah, yes. That's what Luke said. And you're planning to go to the Stalingrad system?"

"Yes. A whole gaggle of us will be going. Jim's sister Gillian and her husband Mark, taking Jim and Rita's child Imogen. Luke and I of course. Also Luke's daughter Tatiana, her husband Misha, and their new baby Marta. And I'm bringing my flag aide Rachel Gibson and my Security Officer Ollie Coston. We're all going to drop in on Jim and Rita and see how they're doing. Sort of a reunion."

"Excellent. I wish I could give you the *Asiana* for your trip, but I need to keep her here."

"No problem. I've made arrangements to take a corvette."

"The infamous *Armidale*?"

"Exactly. The corvette that rescued a couple hundred shot-up pilots at Dekanna."

"Well, enjoy your vacation. It's well deserved, Admiral. You'll go down in the history books."

Bonnie grimaced. "You know that's not what it's about, Dewa."

Shigeto nodded slowly. "I know. It's about doing it."

"Yes. Because someone has to."

Stalingrad System
Dyson Ring

"I miss my body," complained Rita.

Jim looked at her across the apartment. He didn't quite know what to say.

"Well…you have your pick of bodies, I thought."

Rita shook her head, shaking off Jim's suggestion. "Yeah, but...I miss my old body. I liked it."

Jim had to smile at that. "I liked it too."

Rita gave him a wry frown. "Yeah, I noticed."

She turned and looked down at her current body - an android body that was close to her original Human form, copied from it by her Goblin mentor, Tika. She had the same slightly coppery skin, the same short black hair, the same flashing brown eyes.

"This one feels just a bit heavier," she said. "It just doesn't feel the same."

"Can't you have Tika make one a little closer to your liking?"

"Yeah, I asked her about it. But she said for me to try this one for a while longer. She said I'd grow into it."

Jim shook his head. "I just can't imagine, babe. I'm sorry."

"It's OK. I know this hasn't been easy for you, either."

"It's nothing for me, compared to what you're going through."

Rita turned and looked at herself in the mirror. For a change, she was wearing clothes. Since she had been at Stalingrad, she had adopted the Goblin habit of avoiding clothing unless absolutely necessary. But today they were meeting the corvette *Armidale*, arriving from Singheko with their daughter Imogen and all their friends from the Singheko War.

So today, Rita was dressed, wearing a striped dress shirt with a brown jacket and slacks. Jim had suggested she wear her Admiral's uniform, but Rita had demurred.

"We're in the Reserves now, babe. Not gonna wear that monkey suit unless I have to."

A chime sounded in their comm implants, letting them know *Armidale* was arriving at the dock in twenty minutes.

"We'd better go. I want to be there when they arrive," said Rita.

"Yep."

Together, the two of them departed their apartment and

walked to the dock. There, Rita's Goblin mentor Tika was waiting for them.

As always, Tika was naked. No amount of coaxing would convince her to put on clothes for this meeting.

Jim had finally given up and accepted it. He had sent a short message to *Armidale* to prepare Bonnie and the rest of their visitors for the quirks of the Goblins.

In the large flatscreen mounted on the side of the dock, Jim could see *Armidale* on final approach, coming up to the bump on the side of the Dyson Ring. The bump extended a docking tube, and the corvette inched up to the tube. With a slight clunk it latched on and was secured. After a few minutes of checks and confirmations, the inner hatch opened.

Jim's sister Gillian stepped out first, holding Imogen in her arms. Her husband Mark was right behind her. The two of them looked at Tika's nakedness in some shock; but they managed to suppress it, trying to accept the ways of their hosts.

Imogen looked around curiously at the strange environment. She was now a bit over two years old; not a baby anymore. She waved a hand at Tika with a smile. Tika waved back at her, and Imogen giggled.

Behind Gillian and Mark, Bonnie and Luke came through the hatch, followed closely by Luke's daughter Tatiana and her husband Misha, who was holding their baby Marta. Finally came Rachel Gibson, Ollie Coston, and the captain of the *Armidale*, Duncan Stewart.

"Welcome to Stalingrad!" called Jim, waving.

Battlecruiser *Victory* - Earth Orbit
Sol System

The alarm sounding in Captain Joshua Westerly's comm implant was loud and harsh. It was meant to be that way; there was a need for attention when Battle Stations was sounded.

After so many years in the military, Westerly snapped

awake instantly. He rolled out of bed and into his warsuit in seconds, stamping his feet into his boots. Grabbing his pressure helmet, he ran to the circular stairwell leading from his bedroom up to his day cabin. Reaching the top, he sped through the small cabin and out the door onto the bridge.

His XO, Commander Fabian Becker, had beaten him to the bridge and was leaning over the Tactical Officer, studying his screen.

"What is it?" Westerly called out.

Becker turned and looked at Westerly grimly.

"A fleet entry at the mass limit. It's an attack, I think."

"Who is it?"

"No idea. Not anyone we recognize."

Westerly stared at the holo. He could see the oncoming fleet now, a huge flock of specks on the holo, so many that they merged together into a single large mass of red.

"How many?"

Becker straightened, lifting his gaze to Westerly's with the face of a dead man.

"Three hundred ships."

CHAPTER FIVE

Stalingrad System
Dyson Ring

Bonnie was laughing and she couldn't seem to stop. She twisted in her chair, cackling until tears ran down her cheeks.

"...and then...and then...Jim said, 'But Rita - you have two sets of memories - mine and Bonnie's. You're the only person in history who has experienced being both a man and a woman. So which is better? Being a man? Or being a woman?"

"And?" asked Gillian eagerly, leaning forward.

"And I said to Jim, 'you don't need to ask that question - I already know the answer! And it ain't being a man!' And then... Rita looked at me and winked!"

Rita, Gillian, Bonnie, Tatiana, and Rachel cracked up laughing. Across from them Jim, Mark, Luke, Misha, Ollie, and Captain Stewart looked at each other with various expressions of dismay.

"I think we're outgunned here," said Ollie.

"Agreed," said Jim. "Discretion being the better part of valor, shall we retire to the drinking room?"

Rachel gave a look to Ollie, then switched her gaze to Jim.

"There's a drinking room?" she asked.

"There will be after we get there," said Jim.

"Ah. Well, I'm going with you," said Rachel. "I could use some serious drinking about now."

The group rose from the dining table, Jim raising his hands above his head to stretch.

"That was some meal, Tika," he said to the android seated at the head of the table.

There was a silence. Tika did not respond. She seemed to be gazing off into the distance.

Suddenly she snapped to her feet.

"Earth is under attack," said Tika.

***

The group stood, stunned. Then everybody began talking at once, asking questions.

Tika raised her hands. Everybody fell silent.

"We have received an ansible message from Singheko. Two hours ago, Earth reported they were under attack by a large fleet of unknown origin. Then all communications fell silent. All attempts to re-establish communications have failed."

"Attack?" asked Jim. "Who would attack Earth at this point? We have a peace treaty with everyone."

"We thought we had more time," Tika spoke, almost to herself. "We thought they would wait..."

"What are you talking about?" Jim asked. "Do you know who attacked us? Who?"

Without a word, Tika turned and strode to the door of the apartment. She opened the door and paused, turning briefly back to the astounded group standing by the table.

"The Stree. We thought they would give us more time."

Then Tika stepped through the door and was gone.

Rita and the rest looked at each other in amazement. Everybody was in shock. Rita finally managed to say what all of them were thinking.

"We have to get to Earth."

San Diego, California
Sol System

Zoe DeLong was no dummy. She had come up the hard way on the streets of Chicago, losing her mother at the age of ten and thereafter surviving in the midst of hunger, loneliness, drugs, and the omnipresent gang warfare of the streets. As soon as she graduated from high school, she escaped to the

Marine Corps. She spent her first tour as an enlisted grunt, fighting in the African Wars, coming out with the Silver Star for gallantry under fire.

War had changed Zoe. She had always been driven, determined to escape the mean streets. But after fighting as a grunt, she was a different person. She set her sights higher. Taking advantage of the G.I. Bill and student loans, she completed her engineering degree at Purdue in only three years. Then, against the advice of her friends and family, she joined the Navy as a pilot candidate. Two and a half years later, Zoe DeLong was a Marine F/A-48 pilot stationed off the coast of Africa, on the aging supercarrier USS *Doris Miller*, continuing the fight against the ever-growing threat of piracy and terrorism enveloping that continent.

Ironically, she was only one day from the end of her second tour on the *Doris* when the Stree nuked Earth. If it had occurred one day later, she would have been in San Diego - and would not have survived the attack that left a crater 340 yards deep where that city had been. And if she had not been in the air when the attack struck, she would have gone down with the *Doris*, as it returned to its home port of San Diego, and was caught in the backside of the blast that destroyed that city.

But Zoe had been Squadron Maintenance Officer for VMFA-323. A recalcitrant F/A-48 had been late coming out of an engine replacement. As the *Doris* approached her home port, all the other pilots of the carrier Wing departed, flying off the ship's aircraft to Naval land bases in southern California. But Zoe had elected to stay behind and fly off the last jet when it finished maintenance.

When the plane was finally ready, Zoe had taken off from the *Doris* to check it out and fly it back to shore. Needing to perform a supersonic dash to fully test the engines, she had turned out to sea for the test flight, instead of boring straight in toward San Diego.

She had flown for ten minutes, checking out the engine and the other systems of the aircraft, when the world seemed to come to an end. Something flashed sun-bright behind her, and before she could even turn to see what was happening, the plane slammed forward, nearly knocking her unconscious as her helmet slammed into the back of the ejection seat.

In a daze, she realized the plane was spinning down to the ocean below her. Fighting the controls, she got the crippled jet back to some semblance of normal flight. One engine was out, and the other was not happy. Working to save the plane, she was too busy to look behind her for many minutes. When at last she had secured the bad engine, gotten the plane back to an even keel and turned back toward San Diego, the mushroom cloud in front of her left no doubt in her mind what had happened.

She could see the *Doris* was gone - even from this distance, she could see the two upturned halves of the ship. It had been fifty miles closer to the blast than she - it was broken in two. She knew in her gut there could be no survivors.

Instinctively, she turned back to the west, away from the ship, putting the seat's armor plate between her and the radiation. Assessing her options, she glanced off to the northeast. Sure enough, she could see another mushroom cloud ascending into the sky over Los Angeles. Glancing south, she saw another large mushroom cloud over the Mexican coast well south of her.

That looks like Ensenada. No help there, she thought. *That means this is a full-scale attack of some kind. All the major cities will be gone. No chance of Miramar or LAX or anything like that.*

She glanced at her fuel. On one engine, she might make it three hundred miles. If she was lucky. If the wind was with her...

Well, not going to Mexico. Under these conditions, that'll be anarchy for sure. I'd rather take my chances in the States, even if all the cities are gone.

She pulled up her electronic map and did some quick calculations. She wasn't an expert on radiation, but she thought if she moved quickly, she could thread the needle between San Diego and Los Angeles, and get east of both before the fallout got too bad.

Then maybe I can get to the Sierra Nevada mountains and find someplace to put it down before I run out of fuel.

Threading the needle between the mushroom cloud over San Diego and the one over Los Angeles, Zoe flew until she was well east. She could see more mushroom clouds northeast toward Las Vegas, and northwest toward Edwards AFB and Bakersfield.

No help there.

She turned north, toward the Sierra Nevada, thinking she might place herself in the middle of all the mushroom clouds surrounding her - and get some shelter from the radiation in a deep mountain valley. An hour later, as she approached Kings Canyon National Park, the F/A-48 was running low on fuel. It was getting dark. She was running out of options.

She noticed a small cabin off to the side of a high mountain meadow, in an area roughly equidistant from the remnants of the ugly mushroom clouds. Running on fumes, she turned the damaged fighter toward the large meadow near the cabin, put the flaps down, and came in on the aching edge of a stall, the warning horn blaring in her ears. Just before impact, Zoe closed the throttle, shut off the fuel, and crossed herself. She had time for one quick prayer.

Help me out on this one, Lord.

Then there was a brutal impact as the jet slammed into the ground. The landing was brutal; fighters were not designed to land in rough mountain meadows. The jet slewed, spun around once, then lifted up on a wing as if it would go over. Finally, it settled back, upright, and slammed into a tree at the end of the meadow.

Banged, bruised, scraped up, Zoe got disentangled from the cockpit. As night fell, she managed to get her aching body out of the wreck and trudged over to the nearby cabin. No one was there; but she found a little food stored in the cupboard, and a water bag which she filled from a nearby stream.

The next morning, the radiation sickness came. Zoe lay in the cabin, barely able to move, expecting every day to die.

Stalingrad System
Dyson Ring

As Rachel entered the Council Chamber of the Goblin leadership followed by the rest of the Humans, her feeling of *deja vu* was overwhelming. It seemed like only a few days ago she had stood in this room, pleading for the lives of humanity. But that had been many months ago.

Yet it all came back to her in a rush. There were the nine benches for the judges. There were the conference tables, one on each side of the large room. There was the small dock, with a railing on three sides, where she had stood - and where she had argued that humanity was worth saving. Where, in exchange for the planet Venus, the Goblins had agreed to help humanity defend against the Singheko.

Tika directed them to one of the conference tables and had them sit facing the judge's benches. The group of Humans had just begun to settle into their chairs when the door at the back of the room opened and a Goblin walked in. The Goblin - female, and naked as usual - strode swiftly to the table and sat down directly across from the Humans. There was no preamble. She got to the point quickly.

"My name is Leader Tagi. I regret to inform you that your planet has been destroyed," the Goblin said. "The Stree have also attacked Singheko, Dekanna, Nidaria, Asdif and Ursa. All are destroyed."

The Humans sat in stunned silence. Rachel was the first to recover her voice. She spoke in shock and denial.

"No. Not destroyed. Attacked, maybe. But not destroyed."

Tagi shook her head.

"I'm sorry. I wish I could give you better news. But Earth has been nuked back to the stone age. I'd be greatly surprised if there are more than a few thousand people left alive on your planet."

"No," whispered Gillian. "No, it can't be!"

Gillian turned and fell against Mark's shoulder, sobbing. Rita reached out a hand and held onto Jim's arm.

Rachel sat frozen in shock.

Dan. He was at Dekanna. He was working on Dragon's *repairs.*

My Dan.

My Dan is gone.

"I am so sorry," said Tagi. "We thought we had more time."

Jim finally managed to speak. "What do you mean? You knew this was coming? You let this happen?"

The Goblin turned to him. "We know the Stree hate us with great passion. We knew they would try at some point to eliminate us. But we never thought they would attack our biological allies first. It is a grave mistake in our judgment."

"A grave mistake?" Jim yelled. He shot to his feet. "A grave mistake? You failed to warn us about this? You let them attack our planet?"

The Goblin nodded. "We are at fault in this, and we recognize it. But we cannot change it. We can only move forward from this day."

"Move forward?" Jim roared. "Move forward? How do we move forward?"

Rita stood now, beside Jim, and reached for him. She put her arms around his shoulders and pulled him into her. Slowly, with coaxing movements and gentle words, she got him to sit down again.

Everyone sat in stunned silence. After a few seconds, it was Mark who spoke next.

"We need to get back to Earth."

Tagi shook her head. "That would be a mistake. There is nothing there for you but death. A nuclear winter. Radiation. Dead cities. You will not live long if you set foot on that planet."

Mark stood up.

"I don't care. I'm going."

Gillian got up and stood beside him.

"I'm going too," she said.

Rita also stood and nodded at Gillian.

"I'll go with you. Let's go fetch Imogen." The two turned and left the room.

Mark Rodgers gave a long stare at the others. Then he followed the two women out of the room.

The rest of them - all except Rachel - rose and looked at each other. They turned and followed Mark toward the docking bay.

Rachel sat alone for half a minute.

Dan. My Dan.

Then, moving like a robot, she slowly rose to her feet and followed.

CHAPTER SIX

Stalingrad System
Dyson Swarm

The corvette *Armidale* boosted hard at 500g for the mass limit, pushing to get back to Earth. Jim, Rachel and Tika were too restless to stay in their cabins. As their speed built, the three sat on the bridge behind Captain Stewart, watching the various structures of the Dyson Swarm pass as they headed out-system.

Suddenly an alarm sounded. Captain Stewart looked at the holo and saw two large ships coming in from behind.

Two battlecruisers. Coming right at them. Two huge black battlecruisers.

Stewart reached up a hand to order Battle Stations, but before he could do so, Tika interjected.

"Don't worry, Captain Stewart. Those are our ships. Our Leaders have ordered them to escort us to Earth."

Rachel turned and glared at Tika. "When I was here last, you said you no longer had a fleet of warships. You said you didn't need them anymore."

"Maybe we lied," said Tika quietly.

Rachel's face showed a look of pure anger. "Maybe you lied? There's no maybe! You lied to me!"

Tika bowed her head and closed her eyes. "I was ordered to do it, Rachel. I'm sorry."

Rachel turned back to the holo, too angry to speak.

"So...how big is your fleet?" asked Jim. "Although I suppose you won't tell us that either."

Tika continued to look down at the deck. "I cannot give you the details you ask for. But I can tell you that we have been preparing to meet the Stree for two centuries. So it is a large fleet."

Jim was so angry, he sprang from his jump seat behind Captain Stewart. "So Paco died for nothing? All those pilots that died getting you to the *Tornado*? For nothing? Because you didn't want to commit warships to us?"

Tika looked up at Jim. "That's not true, Jim. We took the approach we thought would work best. And it did - think about it, Jim. Think it through. If we had sent a dozen battlecruisers, or even two dozen battlecruisers...how many more would have died before we defeated Zukra? On both sides, yours and ours? Thousands? Tens of thousands?"

Jim stared at Tika. The venom in his gaze was apparent. Without a word, he stalked off the bridge. Rachel, also shooting arrows at Tika with her eyes, got up from her jump seat and followed Jim.

Captain Stewart had turned in his chair and watched the exchange between the three of them. Now he also glared at Tika, anger evident in his face.

"I suggest, Tika, that you retire to your cabin and stay there for a while."

Tika nodded and rose, departing the bridge. Stewart turned back to the holo. As he watched, the gargantuan Goblin battlecruisers slotted into escorting positions surrounding the *Armidale*, leaving the corvette looking tiny and vulnerable in the middle of the formation.

Earth
Sol System

Twenty-five days later, seven Humans and two Goblins stood on the bridge of the *Armidale*, staring at the display in horror.

Below them, the Earth rotated silently, as it always had.

But it was no longer a beautiful blue and white planet. A new reality overwhelmed them, covering them like a black blanket.

The Humans on the bridge of the corvette could only stare. The horror was too great for them to speak or think. All they could do was stare, and hurt, and cry.

Rachel especially was devastated. Great, choking sobs racked her body. She sank to her knees on the bridge, unable to continue standing. Ollie, on her left, sank down with her and held her, barely able to hold back his own tears. Rita, on Rachel's right side, also sank to the floor, holding Rachel's hand, trying to comfort her in the midst of indescribable grief.

The dayside of the planet below them was a nearly uniform dark gray, with streaks of white and black shot through it, giving it a cancerous, mottled appearance. Where large cities had been, great fires still burned, leaving a hellish glow beneath the dirty cocoon of devastation. The planet they had known and loved had been transformed into something unrecognizable.

In a spontaneous group moment, everyone who was still standing also sank to their knees. Jim, Luke, Mark, and Misha knelt on the deck. Tika, behind them, followed suit, emulating the Humans in sympathy.

Rachel, tears streaming down her face, began to speak. Nobody else on the bridge spoke Gaelic; but all on the bridge recognized the rhythm of the Lord's Prayer. As Rachel continued reciting from her Irish heritage, her words mixed with Gillian's muted sobs.

Ár n-Athair Ár n-Athair atá ar neamh, Go naofar d'ainim, Go dtagfadh do ríocht, Go ndéantar do thoil ar an talamh mar a dhéantar ar neamh. Ár n-arán laethúil tabhair dúinn inniu, agus maith dúinn ár bhfiacha mar a mhaithimidne dár bhféichiúna féin. Ach ná lig sinn i gcathú, ach saor sinn ó olc.

As Rachel completed the prayer, silence covered the bridge. After a minute, Jim Carter rose to his feet. He looked over at

Captain Stewart.

"We have to decide what to do next."

Stewart nodded, and rose. "Let's move to my cabin. XO, you have the conn."

The group moved through the back hatch into Stewart's cabin. They crowded together around the small conference table.

For some reason - perhaps because he was on duty - Captain Stewart seemed to hold himself together. He began the discussion.

"We think they detonated around 3,000 nukes, most of them between 25 to 50 megatons," said Stewart.

"Why so many?" wondered Jim bitterly.

"Because they wanted to be sure to eliminate you as a threat," said Tika.

"But we were not a threat to them!" wailed Rachel. "Why attack us?"

"Their ultimate goal is to destroy us Goblins," said Tika. "Evidently they decided to first destroy our allies, to leave us isolated."

"But why you?" asked Rita. "What have the Goblins ever done to the Stree?"

"We exist," said Tika bitterly. "That is enough for them. They are a fanatical species, led by a fanatical cult. They hate and fear the concept of a sentient artificial intelligence. They have made war on us twice in the past. Both times, we fended them off. But they keep coming back. And this time, they are stronger than we have ever seen them before."

Rachel spoke bitterly. "And you couldn't tell us about them before? You couldn't give us a chance to prepare? A chance to survive?"

"We simply didn't realize the Stree were ready to come at us again. It's been more than two hundred years since they last attacked us. We thought we had plenty of time," Tika replied.

Mark Rodgers deflected the conversation, trying to avoid another round of anger and confrontation that would lead nowhere.

"What do the sensors tell us about the surface, Captain?" he interjected.

Stewart glanced at his tablet.

"Average surface temperature is already down by 16 degrees C, a bit more than 28 degrees F below normal. Our AI model predicts the global average temperature will bottom out at 18 degrees C below normal."

Stewart looked up. "That's 32.4 degrees F below normal. Enough to bring on a new ice age. That will kill almost all plant life on the planet, and most of the animal life. There may be a few plants that survive near the equator, but it's doubtful anything large will make it through."

"How about the oceans?" asked Rita.

"They'll be devastated too," said Stewart. "Some plants and marine animals will survive, but probably nothing near the surface. The ozone in the upper atmosphere is destroyed. So once the smoke and ash clouds start to thin out, that lack of ozone will allow UV radiation to flood the planet. Nothing will be able to live near the surface of the oceans. At least, nothing that we know of now."

"So no life on land, and little life in the oceans," said Mark bitterly.

Tika interjected. "There will be small patches of life that survive. It takes more than this to kill a planet completely. But I doubt there will be many Humans that make it through the bottleneck."

"How many?" asked Jim. "How many Humans will survive?"

Tika looked grim.

"As many as we can rescue before they die of cold and starvation."

Surface of Venus
Sol System

With a start, Commander Rauti awoke. His forty caterpillar

legs twitched uncontrollably as he lay on his back, trying to orient himself.

What happened? I was on an inspection tour of the mountain. Then this...

Slowly his senses started to re-sync. He realized where he was. He had been deep inside the mountain, reviewing the construction of the tunnels that would be used to anchor the space tether. Something catastrophic had happened, knocking him out. His self-repair process had kicked in.

Checking his basal time clock, he was shocked to realize four weeks had passed. Other sensors told him there was a high radiation level seeping in through the tunnel from outside. It came to him instantly as he put all the facts together.

The Stree. It has to be the Stree.

Moving slowly, he rotated his body to stand up on his legs. He looked around the tunnel. It had caved in, leaving only a small space where he had somehow survived. But he could see a glimpse of light through a hole in the pile of rock in front of him. That meant the blockage was thin. He could dig through it.

There were a dozen other caterpillar bodies lying around - the remnants of his staff. Most of them were crushed under the cave-in. All were dead.

The Stree. The fucking Stree, Rauti thought. *They destroyed my beautiful, beautiful project. I'm going to fucking kill them.*

Earth
Sol System

Over the next few days, the Humans at Earth put together a rescue effort. The *Armidale* took up an orbit over Central America. The Goblin battlecruisers that accompanied them established geosync orbits equidistant from them, allowing coverage of the entire planet. They scanned for anything that looked like a life sign. Shuttle after shuttle of Goblins went to the surface searching for survivors, concentrating their efforts on the areas between blast zones - places where life might have survived.

Initially, Jim and the rest of the Humans also went down by shuttle to various points where sensors indicated there might be life. With the travel time from Stalingrad, it was now nearly a month after the attack. Survivors were few and far between. But they worked steadily, trying not to give up hope.

Cocooned in their environmental suits, protected from the radiation and noxious chemicals of the atmosphere, the Humans assisted the Goblins. They found a few survivors in mountainous terrain, tucked away in caves or other enclaves that had protected them from the worst of the blast and radiation - places where water could be had from streams and lakes, where small creatures such as rabbits and mice could be had for food.

Those they found were brought back to the orbiting ships, decontaminated, fed, and placed into hastily constructed dormitories in the cargo holds of the battlecruisers.

But after a few days, Jim and Rita realized they needed to change the process, to provide a more Human touch for the rescued survivors.

"We're wasting our time going to the surface," Jim said as they convened in the galley of the *Armidale* on the fourth day. "The Goblins are ten times as effective as us in finding survivors. We need to let them take that part of the effort. But the stress of being rescued by Goblins is leaving some of the survivors too shell-shocked to communicate - especially if they are rescued by Goblins in non-Human aspects. The children are the worst - I saw some yesterday that were rescued by Goblins in their caterpillar aspects, and those poor kids were still shaking in fear a half-hour later. We should concentrate on welcoming the survivors on the ships, giving them a Human face to see when they come aboard."

Jim glanced at Rachel. She was withdrawn - almost catatonic. She had been that way since they left Stalingrad.

Rachel had lost the love of her life, Dan Gibson. He had been in charge of the shipyard at Dekanna, repairing the EDF ships damaged in the Singheko War. She was taking it harder than anyone else.

Jim knew she was on a long, downhill slide to despair. He needed to find a way to break her out of it, bring her back to a place where she wanted to live.

"Rachel, would you take charge of assigning us to the battlecruisers, please? We need a couple of us on each ship to meet the survivors as they come aboard from the shuttles."

Rachel looked at Jim sullenly. She gave one short nod, then her head went down again, staring at the table. Jim glanced at Rita, who smiled slightly. Rita was back in her normal aspect, the android body that looked remarkably like her old biological one.

Sometimes, when Rita was in her normal Human aspect, Jim forgot she was now a Goblin - although he had been abruptly reminded when they went to the surface. Before their first trip down to look for survivors, Rita had switched into the caterpillar-like Goblin aspect that could withstand nearly any environment.

The first time she did it, Jim had shuddered, turning his head away for a few moments while he got used to it.

Now I know how Alice in Wonderland felt, he had thought. *Next, I'll see the White Rabbit running by...*

But the strangeness had quickly passed. After the second trip to the surface, Jim and the rest of them adapted to Rita's ability to switch into different body aspects. It turned out to be quite handy - in her caterpillar aspect, she could lift tons of material, go nearly anyplace, and had senses that were ten times as sensitive as a normal Human. Rita had found dozens of survivors they would have missed with their Human senses alone.

Jim smiled across the table at his Goblin wife and continued.

"Once Rachel assigns you to a ship, work out your plan to

greet the survivors as they come out of decon. Welcome them, show them around, help them get settled into the cargo bay dorms. Try to put a Human face on things to minimize their shock."

Nods went around the table as everyone agreed. Jim saw Rachel raise her head slightly.

"Also, we need to start thinking about what to do next. The number of survivors diminishes every day. At some point, we'll stop finding people. We should agree on how long we search, and what we do when we no longer find survivors."

Tika spoke next. "Our AI models suggest that once we go for two weeks without finding a survivor, the chances of additional Humans being alive approaches zero."

"Two weeks sounds reasonable to me," said Jim. "How about the rest of you?"

"I'd like to add another week to that," said Mark. "We should give it every possible chance."

Jim looked around the table. Everyone seemed to be in agreement.

"It's agreed, then. When we find no survivors for three consecutive weeks, we declare the rescue effort terminated and move on."

"Move on to where?" wondered Rachel bitterly, the first time she had spoken all day. "Where can we go? Stalingrad? That's not even a planet! How will we live? Do we all become Goblins like..."

Rachel stopped suddenly, glancing at Rita in embarrassment.

"I'm sorry, Rita. I didn't mean that the way it came out..."

Rita winked at her, smiled. "No worries, Rachel. I understand."

Rachel looked back at Jim. "But...what's to become of us? Where will we go?"

"Our leadership has identified a planet in the Arm that is remarkably like Earth," spoke Tika. "It's eight hundred lights beyond Stalingrad. We think it will make a good home for

Humans for the half-century or so it will take before Earth is habitable again."

Kings Canyon National Park, California
Sol System

It took Zoe two weeks to realize she was going to live after all. All her hair had fallen out, and she had puked three to four times a day for two weeks. But finally the radiation sickness seemed to pass. She realized she might live. At least for a while. If she could find more food.

She started hunting, setting snares near the cabin for rabbits. She caught a few fish in the stream.

She was setting a snare nearby the cabin when she heard the whine of a shuttle passing over. It went by, turned, come back toward her. She had thought to run, hide from it - but the insignia on the side of it looked somehow familiar. She tried to remember where she had seen it before. Then it came to her. The insignia of the Earth Defense Force. The EDF. The fleet that was supposed to protect the Earth, but had clearly failed.

The shuttle landed in the meadow nearby, and the ramp lowered. Zoe walked toward it. And the strangest creature she had ever seen made its way down the ramp toward her. It was a huge jet-black caterpillar, six feet long, with at least twenty legs on each side. She froze, afraid to step forward or backwards, not knowing how to react. But before she could make a decision, a male Human stepped into view behind the caterpillar, waving at her.

"Hello!" he shouted. "How are you?"

CHAPTER SEVEN

Stalingrad System
Dyson Swarm

The *bong, bong, bong* of the General Alarm did not awaken Goblin Captain-Leader Bagi; for Bagi was not asleep. He had, however, powered down for a diagnostic and repair period, which - for a Goblin - was pretty much the same as sleep. And as he often did during these repair periods, he had accelerated his time sense by a factor of one thousand. Thus each hour in the real world went by for him in only 3.6 seconds. To his time sense, the universe was a movie being played one thousand times faster than normal.

But the General Alarm snapped him out of that state instantly. In fact, it snapped him back to one-half time; now the Universe went by at half speed, not only for him but for every Goblin on the cruiser *Blue Quark*.

From the bunk in his cabin where his normal android body lay at the moment, Bagi switched to his warbody on the bridge. The short, squat cube of his warbody had no need of a pressure suit or other protective gear. Welded to the deck, it would take a direct hit on that heavily armored cube to harm Bagi.

In a matter of seconds, Bagi ran through a series of internal displays that would have taken a Human a good five minutes to analyze. He had no need of a holotank; all he had to do was issue a mental command and the entire bridge became transparent, allowing him to look directly at the enemy. He magnified the image and took a good look.

Thirty-six Stree warships had entered the Stalingrad

system at the mass limit, 14.77 AU from the central star - and one-quarter AU from Bagi's current position as Commander of the Goblin Home Guard.

Bagi decided immediately this was not a full-on attack; the Stree force was too small. Thirty-six Stree ships would not have much of an impact on the Goblin defense. Even the sixteen ships of his cruiser squadron could fend them off if they were allowed to operate at full capability.

But he would not be able to do that; he must operate at only 70% of his normal capability - for now. The Leaders had stipulated the Goblin Navy's true capability must remain hidden until the full Stree invasion force appeared. It was an attempt to deceive the Stree. The Goblin leadership felt any slight advantage would help, once the true battle started.

"This is just a reconnaissance in force," Bagi called to his bridge crew over the internal comm link. "They'll probe us, test our weapons and maneuverability, then withdraw. Order the squadron to assume formation Delta-Four. Set all operating systems to run at 70%, including the missiles. Lock and load."

"Aye, sir," he heard his bridge crew call. "All systems set to 70% of normal capability. Locked and loaded. The ship is fully ready for battle."

Bagi knew that running at 70% of normal would give him a disadvantage fighting the Stree. But his battle sense fired anyway.

One deck below, Bagi's inert android body suddenly smiled, a transient echo of his feelings on the distant bridge.

"In range in forty-four minutes," called his Tac Officer. "All ships operating at 70% capacity. All ships ready for action."

Come on, you Stree bastards, Bagi thought. *I'd like to have a word with you.*

***

Stree Sub-Commodore Gellen watched the Goblin force come at his formation head-on. Eight thousand klicks wide, the Goblin squadron rushing to meet him consisted of two cubes, side by side. Each cube contained eight wedge-shaped cruisers bristling with point defense cannon and lasers. Each flat-black Goblin cruiser showed eight missile tubes in front, pointed straight at him. He knew there were other missile tubes in the rear of each cruiser, which could fire another six missiles to turn and come directly at him.

So Gellen knew that in less than one minute, 224 missiles would come out of that formation directly at his Stree ships.

"Well, they're not shy," he remarked to his XO.

"They are an abomination," interrupted the Guardian Officer, Sub-Prophet Miwod. "They are not even alive. They are garbage."

"Garbage that can kill us, Sub-Prophet," Gellen said mildly. "I would advise you to tighten your combat harness a bit. Things are about to get interesting."

"Bah. I do not fear these unholy machines," Miwod responded. But Gellen noticed Miwod reach down and pull up the straps on his combat harness to tighten it.

Gellen smiled. Guardian Officers were a necessary evil. In his book, the Fleet would be better off without the zealous monks who spouted religious dogma on the bridge of every Stree ship.

But to say that out loud...well, death would be swift and sure. He had once served under a captain who thoughtlessly uttered such a dangerous comment in the heat of battle. After the Guardian Officer forced the ship's crew to eject that captain into space as an object lesson, Gellen had been promoted to fill the empty spot. The lesson had been clear.

But I could certainly do without his inane comments that bear no relation to reality.

"Incoming! 224 missiles as expected! Point defense armed. Thirty seconds to impact!"

"Fire at will, Tac," Gellen spoke, quietly but firmly enough to be sure he was heard. He felt his cruiser buck as his own volley of fourteen missiles launched simultaneous with the rest of his squadron.

"Twenty seconds to impact! Point defense active!" called his Tac Officer.

Gellen leaned back in his chair, forcing his muscles to relax. It was all up to the Tac Officer and the point defense cannon now. There was no more strategy to consider. He watched, detached, almost like an outside observer, as the Goblin missiles came on. The chatter and vibration of the point defense cannon began, a sound so familiar to him.

For some strange reason, he realized that the sound settled him, put him in a kind of peace. It was the sound of his job, his work. The high point of his profession. The measure of his quality as a commander.

The point defense intensified, vibrating the entire ship. As a Goblin missile penetrated through the cannon fire and smashed into his cruiser, knocking him sideways against the combat harness holding him in place, a ghost of a smile touched Gellen's lips.

Stalingrad System
Dyson Swarm

"Incoming, 448 missiles, point defense activated," called Bagi's Tactical Officer.

It was redundant to make the call - Bagi could see the incoming missiles in his Augmented Reality - AR. But it was a time-honored tradition to make the calls anyway, in case the Captain's AR fluctuated or disappeared during battle.

As expected, Bagi thought. *Their ships have the same number of missile tubes as us, but they have twice as many ships. My reinforcements are still ten minutes away; I imagine this battle will be over before they get here.*

"Very good, Tac. Fend off as many as you can."

Bagi watched as one of his own missiles leaked through the enemy defense and smashed into a Stree cruiser, knocking it up and to one side. The rest of his first volley was swatted away by the Stree point defense, exploding harmlessly and filling the void with debris.

"Incoming, impact in five seconds."

Bagi knew his squadron's point defense could never swat away the number of enemy missiles coming at them. They would be hit, and hard. Just before the impact, a random thought went through Bagi's mind.

The cleanup crews will have their hands full tomorrow getting all this shrapnel rounded up. Glad I don't have that job.

Then the *Blue Quark* jolted as a terrific noise assaulted his hearing. His AR blinked, went out, returned, and stabilized.

"Damage report, please," called Bagi.

"Two missiles hit us in the bow, low but just above the belly armor. Three front missile tubes out of action."

Could have been worse.

"Fire at will, Tac. Give 'em hell."

"Aye, sir. Firing second volley."

Stalingrad System
Dyson Swarm

Ten minutes later, Gellen had all the information he wanted about the Goblin defenses. He had watched in satisfaction as his task force damaged four Goblin cruisers. Two of his cruisers had suffered moderate damage, including his own, but all of his ships could still fly and shoot.

The Goblin cruiser squadron had passed through his formation at speed, firing as they went through, and started turnover to come back at him. Gellen knew he could continue on into their system if he wished, attacking some of the nearby Dyson structures. And he very much wanted to do that.

But another five squadrons of Goblin cruisers, and two of battlecruisers, were moving to intercept him. The nearest Goblin cruiser squadron was only five minutes away now. If he got tangled up with them, he might be delayed until the other Goblin formations caught up to him. And that would be suicide.

"We've got the information we came for," he called to his bridge crew. "Let's get out of here. Vector X14 and put the boot to it."

"Aye, Skipper," called his XO, gesturing to the Nav officer.

"What? No!" yelled Miwod. The Guardian Officer spluttered in rage. "You leave now when we have missiles left to fire? We must expend all our ammunition! We cannot return to Stree with unfired missiles! It is cowardice!"

Gellen looked at the Guardian in amazement.

How can anyone who claims to be a Naval officer know so little about how to fight?

"Sub-Prophet Miwod, I am glad to stay here and expend all remaining missiles if that is your command. However, we will all be dead within twenty minutes if we do so. Please quickly give us the Last Rites so that we may die in peace."

Miwod looked at Gellen stupidly. The confusion on his face showed he was paralyzed in fear. He clearly failed to comprehend the situation. Gellen waited for another five seconds, but Miwod was still frozen, unable to process the information he had been given.

With a sigh, Gellen waved at the XO. "Take us out of here, XO. Vector X14 and quickly!"

Gellen felt a little residual Coriolis force as the cruiser nosed up, taking a line away from the ecliptic and out of the system. The carefully calculated escape vector would take them away from the onrushing Goblin ships and allow them to disengage and leave the system unharmed. Gellen felt the g-force come on, pushing him down into his seat as they accelerated beyond the ability of the compensators. As the perceived force approached 8g and continued to rise, he heard a groan from Guardian Officer Miwod.

Good. Maybe that will keep the idiot bastard's mouth shut...

Surface of Venus
Sol System

Outside the mountain, Rauti stared at the mess in front of him. The Stree had wiped out his installation on Venus. Undoubtedly, they had also destroyed the tether fixtures in orbit; and probably the barely-started Dyson shell as well.

Rauti was pissed.

The Stree will think we're all dead. Which is fine with me, because I'm going to build a little surprise for them. To hell with terraforming this planet. I'll turn every resource I have, every microbot, every tool, to one purpose. I've got the resources of a whole planet to use.

Rauti knew what he had in mind to do was a violation of the Goblin Commandments. But he was going to do it anyway.

The universe had changed. Rauti didn't think the Commandments made a difference anymore. And certainly not to him, stranded on Venus.

If the Stree attacked us here, that means they are also attacking Stalingrad. I have no communication with Stalingrad, but I'm sure their backs are to the wall. The Stree would never dare attack me here unless they were sure of defeating us. The survival of our species is on the line.

And there's also Clause Eighteen of the Goblin Commandments...

Rauti smiled.

Thou shalt not let the species die.

He thought through his plan. It would work, of that he was sure. He wasn't sure how long it would take, but he didn't care. If it took a month, or six months, or a year, he would take this fight back to the Stree.

CHAPTER EIGHT

Earth
Sol System

Five weeks later, the Humans at Earth gave up the rescue effort. They had found and rescued 21,146 Human survivors. Most of them were in bad shape; burned by thermal heat from the bombs, savaged by radiation, bandaged, broken, dying of thirst or starvation.

The Goblins had started a round-robin shuttle of survivors back to Stalingrad. Every few days, another battlecruiser departed for the Goblin home system, with makeshift dorms in the cargo hold packed to capacity with survivors. At the same time, an empty battlecruiser appeared to take its place.

But they had found no more Humans alive on the planet for three consecutive weeks. The rescue effort was over. They had also checked the Human settlements on Mars and the Moon, but the installations there had been wiped out as well. And on Venus, the Goblin projects were gone, the surface installation a vast crater a half-klick wide.

And the orbitals of Earth were filled with the debris of ships, all of them smashed and scorched and burnt. Every satellite had been destroyed, leaving millions of pieces of debris orbiting the desolate planet.

They found the remains of the EDF Home Fleet well out past the orbit of Mars, where they had met the enemy. The broken pieces were still coasting out-system on a vector to nowhere.

And in the center of the debris field, the fragments of the battlecruiser *Victory* were found, in a dozen pieces. Not a single missile was left in her armory - the *Victory* had fought to the bitter end.

They collected up the larger pieces of the destroyed battlecruiser and launched them into the Sun. The Human team stood on the *Armidale*'s bridge at attention, while Bonnie Page recited the names of their dead friends as the last fragments of the once-proud battlecruiser disappeared into the glare of the Sun's corona and was gone.

Then they left. There was nothing more for humanity in this solar system. There wouldn't be a habitable planet here for at least fifty years, maybe seventy-five or a hundred. Their AI model wasn't quite sure how long it would take.

They discussed stopping at Singheko on the way back to Stalingrad; but Tika assured them it was pointless. The Goblins had rescued a few thousand Singheko survivors there and taken them to Stalingrad; but the planet of their recent enemy was also destroyed, unlivable for many years.

And the EDF fleet that had been stationed at Singheko was the same as the one at Earth - fragments floating in the black.

Merkkessa - gone.

Asiana - gone.

Every ship of the EDF Alliance - gone.

And the same was true at Nidaria, and Dekanna, and Asdif, and Ursa. The Stree had been thorough. They had not taken any chances. They had wiped the slate clean of any species that might aid the Goblins.

The Humans on the *Armidale* gathered in the galley for the departure. In the wall viewer, they watched the Sun fade in the distance as they headed for the mass limit. In the last weeks, they had already passed through so many emotions; first shock and numbness, then depression and despair on the long trip back to Earth, giving way to dogged determination as they searched for survivors. Now most of them had worked their way out of that pit of raw emotion to a sort of semi-stable plateau - a plateau of resignation and acceptance.

"There she goes," said Jim as they sank out, the system

engines shutting down and the tDrive whining as it came to life. The Sun winked out and was gone.

"Next stop Stalingrad," said Mark.

"And then what?" asked Rachel. "Earth Two? Build log cabins in the wilderness, like the pioneers in the Old West? Scratch out a living from the dirt?"

Bonnie glanced across at Jim and Rita. Rachel wore her bitterness like a blanket now, never letting it go. It permeated her, had become part of her.

"If that's what it takes," Bonnie said at last. "But I think we can do more than that, if we put our minds to it."

"We can," said Jim. "We're military. We can go on. But I don't know about the rest of the survivors. I think they're too shell-shocked to do much except survive at this point."

"So we just dump them off on a new planet and wish them luck?" Rachel spoke sarcastically.

"No, we can do more than that," said Tika. "We rescued fertilized ovum from several thousand species of animals. We can populate the new planet with horses, cows, sheep, goats, more than a hundred animals that will be valuable to the colonists there. We loaded up the contents of the Svalbard Global Seed Vault from Norway. So we'll be able to plant almost any crop that people want. We have microbots that can build prefab housing for them. They'll have a decent life there, for the most part."

There was a short silence. Gillian was the next to speak. "But it won't be Earth," she said. "It won't be home."

"We'll make it home," said Luke. "We have to."

"But the Stree...," said Gillian. "They'll find us. They'll come back."

Jim shook his head. "They won't bother us. We're too weak to hurt them now. They're after the Goblins."

"Should we even go back to Stalingrad now?" asked Mark. "What if we arrive just as the Stree attack?"

"That's a chance we have to take," said Rita. "We have to stabilize the Human survivors, get them healthy, let them make their own decisions about what to do next."

"Their own decisions? What is there to decide?" asked Rachel. "They go to this new Earth or they die, right? What other choice do they have?"

Jim looked at Tika meaningfully. She nodded.

"There's one other option," said Jim.

Corvette *Armidale*
Returning to Stalingrad

"Another option?" asked Rachel. "What other option is there? Either they go to this new planet the Goblins have found, or they stay at Stalingrad. What else is there?"

Jim gave a second glance at Tika before he continued.

"Become a Goblin. Fight these bastards as an android. An AI."

There was a shocked silence in the galley as everybody tried to wrap their heads around Jim's words. Rachel was the first to come back at him.

"Bullshit," she said.

Tika took up the conversation.

"Not bullshit," she replied. "It can be done. Any Human can have their consciousness transferred into AI form."

Rachel glared at Tika as if she were the enemy.

"You want us to give up our bodies? Become machines like you? Losing Earth isn't enough for you?"

Jim spoke gently.

"Rachel. It's not Tika's idea. It's my idea."

Rachel turned her glare to Jim. "Why would you even think about that? What's the point of it? And why now when we're still grieving Earth?"

Jim continued to speak gently, trying to calm Rachel down.

"Force multiplication, Rachel. Think about it. As a biological being, I have only one body to give. If I fight them and they kill me, that's it. I'm done. But as an AI, I can be cloned into dozens of entities. Each one of those can fight them. If they destroy my ship, I can translate to another ship. It multiplies our Human force by at least a factor of ten, maybe a factor of one hundred."

There was a long, pregnant pause. Jim saw a visible shudder go through Gillian. She was the next to speak.

"It's unholy," she said. "Duplicating ourselves. It's blasphemy."

Jim nodded. "Each to his own opinion, Jilly. No one has to do anything against their own conscience."

Mark reached, placed an arm around Gillian's shoulders in support.

"I'm with my wife. That's something I'll never do."

"Understood, Mark. And I respect your opinion. But likewise, you should respect mine. I'd do it in a heartbeat, if it meant I could kill more of those Stree bastards."

"Me, too," said Ollie with venom in his voice. "Where do I sign up?"

Rita felt it was the appropriate time for her to jump in.

"As I'm the only person here who has ever done this before, I should probably tell you a few things."

"Please," said Jim, giving her the floor.

"It's very disorienting when you first wake up. It's almost like being in a waking dream for the first day or so. You have incredible energy, more energy than you've ever felt in your life. I can only compare it to when you were a child and you had boundless energy, when you could go all day without stopping. But at the same time, your body doesn't respond the way you expect it to. It's more powerful but also heavier. So it takes days to adjust, to get the hang of that part of it.

"And then your senses. They intentionally bring you out after the transfer with your senses dulled, so that they're a close match for your old Human senses. But they still feel incredibly powerful. Your vision is the best it's ever been. Your sense of taste and smell is the same. Your hearing is perfect.

"Combining all those things, it'll take you several days before you can do things normally without falling over or stumbling or stuttering when you try to talk. But after that...

"After that, you feel wonderful. It's a heady experience. You learn how to switch your consciousness to another aspect. You learn how to increase the sensitivity of your senses on your own, when you feel ready for it. You learn how to talk with radio instead of with voice.

"You feel like you've been re-born. I would never go back."

Gillian shuddered again. "This is blasphemy. I won't listen to this," she said as she rose.

"Before you go, Gillian, one thought," interjected Jim.

Gillian paused on her way to the door. "What?"

"You believe that God created this Universe. Have you ever considered - maybe He allows this as a natural progression to a higher form of living? That maybe this was His grand design all along? Would He even allow the Goblins to exist if He disapproved?"

Gillian stared at Jim strangely.

"We don't know yet if He will allow the Goblins to continue to exist, do we?"

With that, she departed through the hatch. Mark stood, grimaced at Jim, and followed his wife. In the aftermath of Gillian's sudden and somewhat surprising outburst, the rest of them sat and stared at each other.

"She's starting to sound like the Stree," muttered Tika.

Stree Prime
Battlecruiser *Great Prophet*

High Admiral Sojatta gazed at the plot as his six expeditionary fleets collected themselves back into a single, unified mass of warships orbiting the Stree home world. It had taken them eighty-five days to go and return - but they had accomplished the mission. They had eliminated the biological allies of the Goblins - the Humans, the Dariama, the Bagrami, the Taegu. All were dust now, dust blowing in the wind of their desiccated planets. As were the Singheko and the Nidarians - the Stree had not taken any chances.

Now there were no biologicals left to stand in his way. It was down to a one-on-one war, a simple fight of good versus evil. The good of the Grand Prophecy vs. the evil of the blasphemous and unholy Goblins.

And there was no doubt in Sojatta's mind how that war would end. Their victory was assured. The Universe fought for them. The Great Prophet had foreseen it and had given them the Word Ordained.

All Sojatta had to do now was implement the victory. He gazed at the holotank before him. Six expeditionary fleets had been sent to destroy the enemies of the Grand Prophecy: 300 warships each to the four major biological species, and 200 warships to the lesser ones of the Bagrami and the Taegu. 1,600 of his front-line warships.

Of those, 1,502 ships had returned. Sojatta was a bit shocked at the level of his losses; he had not expected the pitiful biologicals to fight so hard against their destruction.

But it was not a problem; his intelligence experts told him the Goblins had only 500 warships. He still vastly outnumbered them. It would be a quick war.

Sojatta turned away from the plot to his staff, standing around his conference table, and smiled.

"We have accomplished the first great objective of the war," he spoke. "We have eliminated the biologicals who might hinder us. Now we move to Phase Two - eliminating the Goblin Home Fleet and destroying their barbarous Dyson Swarm."

Sojatta moved to the head of the table and sat. He waved a hand at the Stree officers surrounding the table. "Sit, and let us plan our victory."

With a rustle of uniforms and the clink of medals, the members of his inner staff sat, adjusting in their chairs until they were comfortable. Sojatta waited until all were settled, then began again.

"The Goblins wait for us in their home system. We shall let them sweat while we repair and re-arm our ships. Admiral Hojoni - what is the estimate for readiness to depart?"

"Eight weeks, O Great High Admiral. There was more damage to our ships than anticipated."

Sojatta smiled. "Yes. The perverted biologicals fought harder than we expected. That makes our decision to eliminate them by surprise even wiser. If we had allowed them to prepare and join forces with the Goblins, our victory might have been delayed.

"But now...the time to victory will be shortened considerably. Eight weeks to repair and re-arm our fleet. Another four weeks to Stalingrad. And then we smash these Goblins.

"Admiral Deyeunna. Ensure that our maintenance crews are closely supervised. We must be ready to launch in eight weeks. There is no other acceptable outcome."

Admiral Deyeunna bowed his head in acceptance of the task. "Thus it shall be, O Great Chief Admiral."

"Thus it shall be," echoed Sojatta in the timeworn mantra of the Stree priesthood. "Then let us move on to the strategy for the destruction of the Goblin fleet twelve weeks from now. Please present your plan, Admiral Hojoni."

CHAPTER NINE

Stalingrad System
Dyson Ring

While Jim and his company had been at Earth rescuing survivors, the Goblins had re-configured a large area of their main Dyson Ring to become a long, narrow facsimile of Earth. In the middle of a longitudinal strip was an open park, covered in greenery, with hiking paths, playgrounds, even a couple of creeks feeding into small lakes. It also contained a large Amphitheater for community meetings. Several thousand feet above it, the ceiling was blue, an imitation of the blue sky of Earth. A long artificial Sun ran down the center of the ceiling, simulating the brightness of Earth's own star.

On the sides of the open area, Goblin microbots had assembled housing for the survivors. Six huge apartment blocks surrounded the park, providing space for all 21,146 Human survivors.

Jim, Rita, and the rest of the team stood on the roof of one of the apartment blocks, staring at the view below them in wonderment.

"How could they do this in only twelve weeks?" asked Gillian.

"Our microbots are extremely effective," said Tika. "If they can build a Dyson swarm in two centuries, building apartment blocks is child's play for them."

"But where did you get the greenery?" asked Rachel.

"We've always had plants from Earth," said Tika. "Remember, I told you before at Dekanna - we've been secretly visiting Earth for well over twenty thousand years. Through the years, we've collected millions of samples of plants and animals. This basic park was already in existence, used by our people for a leisure spot. All we had to do was build the apartment blocks around it."

"It reminds me of Central Park in New York," said Jim.

Rachel turned on him. "Something that doesn't exist anymore," she spoke angrily. She marched off toward the stairs.

The group watched her go, until Gillian spoke.

"We have to do something to help her."

"There's not much we can do," said Rita. "She's mourning Dan. She just has to get through her grief process somehow."

"Here comes the last group," Tika called.

Below them, a large group of Humans came out of a subway entrance in the center of the park. The Humans walked out onto the surface in amazement. They milled around in shock, staring at the apartment blocks, the greenery, the lake beside them, the artificial blue sky above them.

"I can't even imagine what's going through their minds," said Jim.

"Shock," said Luke. "Pure shock. After what they've been through...it has to be incredible."

"But with relief mixed in," said Bonnie. "They thought they were going to die, there on Earth. Huddling in caves or underground, a surface covered in ice and snow, no visible sun, little to no food, contaminated water. At the most, a few more weeks to live. They must have been making their peace with God when we came along."

"And then rescued by alien androids, packed into a battlecruiser cargo hold like sardines, brought to a strange system that looks like nothing ever seen by a Human before," added Rita.

"And then this," continued Jim. "Disembarking from their ship, a ride on a subway, climbing a flight of stairs and coming out in Central Park. It has to be mind-boggling for them."

Below them, they could see the group of survivors being led by several Goblins toward the apartment block where they would be housed. The Humans straggled along, faces turned left, right, up to the artificial sky and the artificial sun, children lagging behind to play with ducks on the pond, parents turning back to gather them up and move them on.

"It looks so normal now," said Bonnie. "It's too good to be true."

"Yes, and it *is* too good to be true," Tika spoke. "The Stree are still out there. We think they're holding off because they have to collect up their expeditions and repair any damage, re-arm, prepare for a massive attack on us. Or else they want to terrorize us - intimidate us. But they'll be coming soon - they'll not want to give us too much time to prepare. We need to get these people stabilized and then moved to the new planet as soon as possible."

"The ones that want to go," said Jim.

Tika looked at him. "Yes. The ones that want to go. The rest can stay and help us fight."

Stalingrad System
Dyson Ring

One day later, Jim, Rita and the rest decided it was time to formally present all options to the Human survivors. Although they had already announced the news about a new planet where people could be relocated, they had said nothing about other options.

Now they called for a mass meeting. Thousands of people showed up in the Amphitheater. They milled about, waiting for the meeting to start, wondering what was happening.

Jim, Rita, Bonnie, Luke, Rachel, and Ollie stood on a stage at the front of the assembly, waiting to start the meeting. Finally the appointed time came, and Jim stood to address the crowd. As he began speaking, his voice boomed out over speakers arranged around the Amphitheater.

"People of Earth. My name is Jim Carter. I am the moderator for today's meeting.

"As you have probably heard, the Goblins have found a planet eight hundred light years from here which is remarkably like Earth. For the purposes of this discussion, I'm going to call that planet Phoenix - because it will represent the re-birth of Humanity. You can always rename it when you get there, if you wish.

"Now - the atmosphere and climate of Phoenix are suitable; Humans can live there. It'll be primitive at first; you'll be living better than the pioneers of old, but not by much. It will be a challenge; but those who go will most likely survive. For those who decide to go there, the Goblins have agreed to begin transport starting Monday next."

A murmur ran through the crowd. Jim saw some people smiling, congratulating each other, happy. Others were more sullen, standing silently, glaring at Jim.

I guess you can't satisfy all of the people all of the time.

"You will also have to share this planet, at least temporarily, with other survivors. As you may know, the Goblins also rescued a small number of Dariama, Taegu, and Bagrami from their destroyed planets. At the moment, Phoenix is the only place these survivors can go. They will be placed on the opposite side of the planet from our Human colony. However, as soon as the Goblins can identify another planet that is suitable for them, they will be moved, so please understand this is a temporary solution."

"What about the Singheko and the Nidarians?" came a shout from the audience.

"The Goblins recognize that because of our recent war with the Singheko and the Nidarians, it wouldn't be a good idea for us to share a planet. So they've identified another planet, several hundred lights from Phoenix, which is suited to them. The Singheko and Nidarian survivors will be taken there."

A quiet fell over the audience as people contemplated what Jim had told them. Waiting a bit, he continued.

"This evening at seven PM here in the Amphitheater, there will be a meeting to begin planning for transport to the new planet. If you want to consider this option for your future, please plan to have a representative at the meeting tonight."

"Now...there are a couple of other options for you," Jim continued. "A group of us have decided to fight the Stree. We'll be staying here, working with the Goblins to take the fight to the enemy. Any of you who decide to join us will be welcomed. However, let me warn you; the odds are against us.

"The Goblins believe the Stree outnumber us considerably. It will be a fight like no other in history. The Goblins are masters of AI; the Stree have the numbers.

"If you join us in this fight, the first option will be to continue as a Human, fighting in spaceships or on the ground, as the need arises. You'll be subject to normal military discipline and training. You'll have to follow orders - and that includes the orders of a Goblin, if they are in your chain of command. Make no mistake about that aspect of the command structure. We will be a separate Human detachment, but we will be subject to orders of the Goblin leadership, just like any other unit. Anyone who can't accept that should get on the transport ships and go to Phoenix."

Another mutter ran through the crowd as people began to discuss the option. Jim gave them a few seconds to absorb his words, then dropped the last bombshell.

"There is one other option."

He waited as silence slowly settled over the crowd. When it was quiet, he continued.

"There is a way for a small number of Humans to fight the Stree with more effectiveness. A way to fight them with the greater effectiveness of a Goblin. It is possible to convert a Human into a Goblin."

For a few seconds, there was silence. Then there was an eruption of noise. People shouted, yelled at each other, yelled questions at Jim, a cacophony of voices that prevented any further communication. Jim waited patiently for the crowd to settle down, turning to glance at Rita, who was standing behind him with a wry smile.

Finally the crowd began to calm, although there were still pockets of loud argument in places. Jim held out his hands in a downward gesture, trying to get the group quiet enough for him to speak.

"Please calm down, everyone. Please listen. Please let me speak."

Eventually the crowd settled down enough for Jim to continue. He gazed across the crowd, trying to formulate the right words.

"I realize this is a difficult concept to wrap your head around. I understand that most of you will not consider it, and that's fine.

"But for those who want to fight the Stree, this is the most effective way to do it. For anyone who wants to get back our own at the bastards who killed our planet, give this at least a moment of consideration.

"Now, some of you may already be aware of this, but my wife - Rita Page, who is standing behind me right now - "

Jim gestured to Rita behind him. She had reluctantly consented to put on her full Admiral's uniform for the occasion, in hopes it would set the right tone. Now she stepped forward to give the crowd a better view.

"...my wife Rita has already undergone this transformation. She states it is completely painless. It required only a few days of training and adjustment to be fully functional in her new body. And her new abilities are incredible. She is three times stronger. She can see farther, hear better, can communicate with the Goblins in their native language. She can translate herself into a new body at will, even into a spaceship body if necessary. If her current body is damaged, she can switch to a new one and continue on her way.

"So - tomorrow at ten AM we'll have a separate meeting for those interested in either of these last two options - either fighting the Stree as Humans or fighting them as Goblins. It will be held here in the Amphitheater. Rita and I will answer all your questions then. I hope to see some of you there. And don't forget about the meeting tonight at 7 PM to talk about transport to Phoenix."

With that, Jim turned and ended the meeting. As the team left the stage, they heard loud conversations. Several arguments broke out behind them, loud voices shouting at each other.

"I hope they don't start fighting each other right here," said Bonnie.

"You know Humans," said Jim. "They can always find something to fight about."

"Have you thought about a government for Phoenix?" asked Tika. "You need some kind of structure in place when these people arrive. Otherwise, it'll be mass chaos."

"Yes," Jim agreed. "We've discussed it among ourselves. We have a proposal to make at the Phoenix meeting tonight."

CHAPTER TEN

Stalingrad System
Dyson Ring

That same evening, the seven PM meeting on the move to Phoenix was packed. Mark Rodgers stood on the small stage at the front of the room, assessing the crowd. Glancing back at Gillian standing directly behind him, he smiled.

"Are you sure you want to go through with this?" he asked.

Gillian nodded. "Absolutely."

"OK, then," Mark said. He turned back to the crowd.

"Folks, if I could have your attention, please," he called. The speakers on the side of the Amphitheater boomed out his voice. The crowd began to settle. Mark gave them a few seconds, then repeated his request. After another ten seconds, it was quiet enough for him to proceed.

"The purpose of this meeting is to inform you about the transport to Phoenix and what you can expect to find there when you arrive. My name is Mark Rodgers. I am a former General in the U.S. Army. I retired a little over three years ago after a thirty-year career in Army Intelligence. I was asked by Jim Carter to conduct this meeting. I will be assisted by my wife, Gillian Rodgers.

"Phoenix is a bit over eight hundred lights from us here at Stalingrad. The Goblins have agreed to allocate seven large transport ships to us for moving people and equipment to Phoenix. One of those ships has already been dispatched back to Earth to salvage some heavy equipment for us. Things like a couple of large turbines that can be used to generate electricity from rivers, a half-dozen wind turbines to get us started in wind energy, a couple of thousand solar panels, some construction equipment, that kind of thing. That ship will bring the items salvaged directly back to Phoenix and meet us there."

A hand raised in the front row of the audience. Mark paused and pointed.

"Yes? Oh, and please state your name for the record."

"Rick Moore. Why couldn't the Goblins make that equipment for us?" asked a young man, his tattered clothes almost falling off him. He looked like he had been through a lot; but he also looked like he was game for more.

Mark smiled. He made a note of the young man's name. The young man had asked a smart question, going straight to the point. There would be a place for tough, smart people on Phoenix.

"They could. They offered to do it for us. But we felt they should use their resources to prepare to battle the Stree. Also, although it may be a little harder on us to install the equipment and make it work, we'll understand the details of it. We'll know how it was put into operation and we'll be able to repair it when it breaks."

The young man nodded and settled back into his seat.

"Now. The other six Goblin ships will start shuttling passengers to Phoenix. One ship will depart every seven days. That will continue until everyone is transported to Phoenix that wishes to go there.

"Each ship can transport three thousand people. I'm not saying it will be comfortable, but it will be tolerable. Families will be kept together; we'll make special accommodations for pregnant women and mothers with small children. My wife Gillian will talk about that in a few minutes.

"The first ship will carry only young, healthy people who have no children, along with a team of Goblin volunteers to assist them. The Goblin volunteers will teach this first group how to manage the microbots that will perform the construction.

"That first group of three thousand people will use those microbots to establish housing, in the form of apartment blocks, for themselves and the next group to arrive. By that, I mean that first group will construct housing for a total of six thousand people. They'll also start building a water treatment plant. When the next ship arrives, the next group of three thousand will extend the process, getting trained on the microbots and using them to build housing for another three thousand people. This process will continue until everyone is transported and has food, water, and shelter."

Another hand went up in the audience. Mark pointed to a young woman in the third row. Her hair was a short fuzz, an indicator of recent recovery from radiation sickness. She wore a well-worn and somewhat blood-stained USMC flight suit. She stood to ask her question.

"Zoe DeLong. Who's going to be in charge of this operation?"

"An excellent question. Obviously, there has to be some kind of management or government in place to get all this done. We're going to talk about that in a few minutes, so if you'll hold off just a bit longer, we'll get to it after I finish talking about transport."

The young woman nodded, satisfied, and sat back down.

"Now. There are photosynthetic native plants on Phoenix which are remarkably like those of Earth. That's why it has an oxygen atmosphere. But otherwise, it's just a bare planet. There don't appear to be any native land animals. There may be some sea life, but we haven't determined that yet. There's nothing we've identified that could be used as a food crop. So this is going to be a real challenge. But we can do it - if we put our minds to it. The atmosphere and the climate work in our favor.

"Our biggest challenge after water and shelter is getting crops established for food, and pasture prepared for livestock. Before we can do that, we have to prepare the soil. The Goblins have been kind enough to send a crew ahead. That crew is already on Phoenix, putting down microbots to mulch thirty square miles of flat land to make it suitable for farming and pasture. The microbots will put down Earth biota, the nitrogen-fixing bacteria, and earthworms and such that we'll need to make Earth grass and crops work properly. And to anticipate your question, the Goblins have had Earth-based plants in this park for twenty thousand years, so they already had the biota they needed.

"I want to make something perfectly clear right now, before we go any farther. There will be no place on Phoenix for the lazy. If you are not willing to work - whether it be farming, or building shelter, or doing any of the other hundred things that have to be done - then you won't eat. That is a promise I make to you now. You will work, or you won't eat."

Mark paused for a moment, surveying the crowd. They were quiet, considering his words. He turned to Gillian and she came up to the front of the stage.

"My wife Gillian will now lead a presentation regarding the government of the new colony on Phoenix."

Gillian smiled at the crowd and began to speak.

"One last word on transport before I move to the government discussion. Beginning with the third transport, there will be accommodations for pregnant women and mothers with children under four years of age. I just wanted to throw that out there, so you don't worry too much about it. Once we're assured there's food, water, and shelter in place for you, we'll get you there as quickly and safely as possible.

"Now. About government. Without government in place, the strong simply take what they want, leaving the weak with little or nothing. Regrettably, that seems to be the way of the Human animal. I'm sure it would be the same on Phoenix if we left things to evolve on their own. Therefore, we're not going to do that. We're going to put a strong government in place from day one.

"The government will be made up of a council and a governor. The council will be made up of people who have the expertise and experience to lead the colony. They will develop the rules of operation for Phoenix. The governor, however, will have veto power over council decisions if they are not in the best interests of the colony."

Gillian paused and waited for her words to be absorbed by the crowd. Generally, she thought the concept had been well-received. For the most part, people were nodding approval. There were pockets of argument and some loud voices raised, but at least no fights broke out.

Far in the back, someone yelled out. "Who's going to be on the council?"

Gillian nodded an acknowledgment. "We're going to have an initial council of nine members. That initial group will elect a governor from among themselves. The governor who is elected will then appoint his replacement, so that we still have a council made up of nine members.

"You'll note there are six apartment blocks surrounding this park. Each apartment block will elect one council member. Nominations for these positions will be open for the next twenty-four hours. Each apartment block can nominate three persons. Three and only three persons, people. Please understand the rules. Immediately after this meeting, each apartment block will have a separate meeting to discuss and nominate candidates.

"However, each candidate nominated will have to be vetted by us - the people you see in front of you right now. The reason for that is simple - to prevent unqualified people from being elected, and to prevent cliques or gangs from controlling the process.

"Once the slate of candidates is approved, we'll vote on Saturday, three days from now. I know it's short notice, but these are dangerous times. We have to get things moving as quickly as possible if we are to survive."

"What about the other three members of the Council?" someone yelled from the crowd.

"The people you see before you on this stage invested a lot in your rescue; it was not easy finding you and bringing you here for a chance at a new life. We have no intention of letting the train jump the tracks now. Therefore, the last three members of the Council will be myself, my husband Mark Rodgers, and Admiral Tatiana Powell from Deriko.

"We aren't doing this for personal gain or glory. I'll tell you, this is the last thing I want to be doing right now. I would much prefer to sit back and let others take the lead. But the fact remains we have the background, experience, and training to do the job, and we have a moral and ethical responsibility to ensure that Phoenix starts off on the right foot. So we intend to do what is necessary to make it successful.

"This I promise you; as soon as things are stable on Phoenix, and a few natural leaders rise to the surface, I'll be the first to resign my position on the Council. I have other things to do with my life and I'm eager to get on with them. But until that day happens, I intend to do my duty to keep you safe. That's my promise to you."

Two separate rumbles moved through the crowd. One was a rumble of approval. The other was a rumble of discontent. Gillian stepped back to place herself beside Mark. They listened to the swell of conversation and looked at each other.

"Some like it, some don't," said Mark.

Gillian nodded. "The ones that don't like it are the eternal discontents. I wouldn't worry too much about them. They won't like anything unless they're in charge. And that's the very people you don't want to be in charge."

CHAPTER ELEVEN

Stalingrad System
Dyson Ring

Dino Cerutti smiled across the table at the two men opposite. One was Russian - Vladimir Sergeevich Turgenev. Turgenev had a lazy smile on his face and was leaning back comfortably in his chair, enjoying the confrontation in front of him.

The other man glared at Cerutti with great suspicion.

"Why should I form an alliance with you?" he spat in accented English, his brow furrowed in distrust.

"Ah, Kim Geun-shi, what a marvelous opportunity we have here!" exclaimed Cerutti. "Would you let this pass you by? The chance to own an entire planet? The chance to be the masters of every Human in existence?"

Kim continued to glare at Cerutti with suspicion - but he paused. Cerutti could see the wheels turning in his head.

His greed and lust will overcome his concerns, Cerutti thought. *As I knew it would...*

Slowly Kim relaxed back into his chair. A sullen expression replaced the hatred on his face.

"I will listen," he said.

"That is all I ask," Cerutti replied smoothly. Glancing at Turgenev, he continued his pitch.

"Now...they tell us the Goblins have found a planet for us. And our rescuers will shortly relocate us to that planet. If you've heard, there are only about 21,000 survivors left. If we play our cards right, we can take over the entire planet."

Turgenev grunted an objection. "But they said our rescuers will form a government."

Cerutti smiled. "Let them! That makes our task easier. They form a government and get things organized for us. Meanwhile, we lay our plans. When things are ready, we take over the government. That is the way of the strong!"

Cerutti looked over at Kim across the table from him. "Think of it, Kim Geun-shi! The best food, the best housing - all at our feet! A whole planet to rule!"

Cerutti could see Kim weakening.

"And the most beautiful women, Kim Geun-shi! Anytime you want!"

Cerutti saw Kim's reaction. The involuntary twitch of an eye revealed his inner weakness.

I've got him.

Turgenev glanced at Cerutti. "So - how will we do it? There are three of us - who will be top dog?"

Cerutti nodded. He knew he had won the day.

"We divide up the spoils. Kim Geun-shi was a gangster in Seoul. So he knows how to run the rackets. He can have the sin. The gambling, the numbers, the prostitution, the black market - all the things he already knows how to do."

Turgenev nodded suspiciously. "And me?"

Cerutti gazed at him. "You can have the government. We'll get you on the Council, then we'll get you elected Governor. After that, we'll dismantle the Council and you'll be in sole charge."

Turgenev, still suspicious, cocked his head at Cerutti.

"And you? What do you get?"

"I'll take the Security Team. That will allow me to protect you and Kim to ensure your success. And I'm not greedy - I can make enough from graft and bribes to satisfy myself."

Cerutti sat quietly for a minute as Turgenev and Kim thought through the proposal. He could see their lust for power slowly overcoming their suspicions.

Ah, such easy men to manipulate, Cerutti thought. *Once they have helped me take over the planet, they'll meet with a sudden accident. And then I will be governor. And I will own the world.*

King of Phoenix. I like the sound of that.

***

The next morning, a second meeting took place. The ten AM meeting to discuss fighting the Stree began in the Amphitheater, with Jim and the rest on the stage at the front of the crowd.

"Not much of a turnout," said Jim.

"Well, you can't really expect much, can you?" said Bonnie. "Think about what they've been through. Starving for weeks, huddling in caves and holes, barely surviving. Thinking they were as good as dead. Then plucked out of their holes by Goblin androids, taken to space, crammed into the cargo hold of a battlecruiser for three weeks, unloaded into empty apartment blocks. Told they have only two choices - life as pioneers on a virgin planet, or a desperate fight against a powerful enemy. I'd probably think twice about joining that fight."

"I guess so," said Jim. "How many do you think we have here?"

Bonnie scanned the crowd, estimating. "I'd say about two hundred."

"Looks like about 80 percent males," Rita interjected. "Evidently not a popular option among females."

Bonnie grunted. "Well, war never is. But I'll take two hundred. That's more than we had when we woke up this morning."

"Looks like everyone that's coming is here," said Jim. "I'll get started." He stepped to the front of the stage, with the others lined up behind him.

"Hello all," Jim began. "I assume by your presence here you have some interest in fighting the Stree. As I said yesterday, there are two ways you can fight. The first way is the traditional way - crew on starships, ground support personnel, logistics, intelligence, all the normal activities of the Navy. For those who elect that option, you should know that the Goblins will take the lead in this war. They will bear the brunt of the heavy fighting. We Humans will perform specialized roles - sort of Special Forces, if you will. And those missions may be dangerous. For example, we may work behind enemy lines, or perform targeted missions that require small, focused teams. I'm not going to sugar-coat it for you; people will die. But we *will* take the fight to the enemy, and I for one intend to get revenge on them for what they did to Earth.

"The second way you can fight is to become a Goblin yourself. My wife Rita has already undergone that process, so I'll let her speak to that option."

Jim stepped back, and Rita stepped forward. She gazed around the room. By all appearances, she was a normal human female, albeit a bit taller than most. Her flashing brown eyes reflected the lights. She was once again wearing her Admiral's uniform, and her black hair was cut short in a military style. She held her uniform cap under one arm as she spoke.

"My name is Rita Page. Some of you may know my story, but I'll recap it for you anyway.

"Until six months ago, I was an Admiral in the EDF - the Earth Defense Force. At that time, I was captured by the Singheko. Well, I knew too many secrets of our defense plans to allow myself to be tortured by them, so I was forced to take poison. Through a long chain of circumstances that I'll skip for now, I was freed by my husband, Jim, and returned to the EDF. Unfortunately, it was too late for my biological body to survive. The poison was slowly killing me. Just before my biological body died, my consciousness was scanned by the Goblins and placed into an android body. I was brought back here to Stalingrad. I completed four weeks of training to adjust to my new body, and then I was released to go live my life. A life I would not have - if not for the transfer process provided by the Goblins."

Rita paused, scanning the room. It was quiet; people were focused on what she had to say.

"I want to tell you just three things about my life as a

Goblin. First, I would do it again in a heartbeat. They saved my life. More than that, they gave me a chance to be with my daughter again. My daughter Imogen means the world to me, and thanks to the Goblins I have the chance to see her grow up.

"The second thing I'll tell you is that the process is painless. It's not nearly as scary as you might think. Yes, waking up the first time is strange. Your coordination is off. It's like your body is drunk, but your brain is not. It'll take you several days to get your coordination back. But once that is done, you'll be stronger, faster, and more coordinated than ever before. And you'll have marvelous abilities. You can switch from your primary android body to other types of bodies, such as a spaceship AI, or a hardened fighting android or something we call a caterpillar. You'll be able to think faster, hear better, see farther and in other wavelengths, communicate via radio or laser instead of just voice.

"But the last thing I'll tell you is that there's no going back. Once you are transferred into a Goblin aspect, you cannot go back to your biological body. You will be a Goblin for the rest of your existence. You will have a primary body that will be a close copy of your original body; as you can see, I still look pretty much as I did before. But there's no transferring back into your old biological body. You're a Goblin forever.

"Would I do it again? Yes - in a heartbeat. Knowing what I know now, would I do it again even if I wasn't dying? Yes, in a heartbeat. Because I intend to fight the Stree with every ounce of ability I have. I invite you to do the same - either with your original biological body, or with a Goblin body, but either way - let's fight them. Let's show them what a terrible mistake they made when they destroyed Earth.

"Thank you."

You could have heard a pin drop. Rita stepped back, and Jim stepped forward again. He gazed at the crowd.

"I wish we could give you more time to think about this and make up your mind. But unfortunately, we have little time before we'll be fighting the Stree. We can only give you until the date of your scheduled transport to Phoenix to decide.

"Everyone here has been assigned a transport date. Once that date arrives and you get on the transport ship to Phoenix, the window is closed. Before that date, you can still elect to join the new force. There is a sign-up booth at the back of the Amphitheater. Please take a form with you and make your decision. Thank you for your time."

Venus
Sol System

Rauti had relocated to the wreckage of the destroyed space elevator terminus, thousands of miles above the surface of Venus. It had not been easy; he first had to build a small rocket capable of getting him there. That had taken a week. Working in the hellish conditions of Venus without the support of a base was incredibly difficult, even for his hardened caterpillar body.

Microbots still covered the surface of Venus, diligently converting the carbon dioxide to oxygen and carbon nanotubes, oblivious to the fact there was no longer a system to transport the carbon. Using several billion of these microbots, Rauti re-purposed them to new tasks.

The dead bodies of his friends littered the floor of the caved-in tunnel where he sheltered. Using the microbots and materials from those bodies, he first built a new caterpillar body for himself, only three inches long, and switched into it.

Then he turned the microbots to the task of building a rocket. It didn't need to be large - there was only one of him, and he was now tiny. The final product was only ten feet in length and twelve inches in diameter. On the seventh day after waking in his protected tunnel, he had the microbots carry the rocket outside and lean it against a rock pointed up toward space. He crawled inside and launched. He didn't need software or a guidance system - Rauti guided the rocket himself. Two hours later, he docked at the destroyed space tether terminus, now just a collection of debris orbiting the planet.

But it was his debris, and he knew how to use it. Although their orbits had been highly perturbed, the four asteroids that were originally used as raw materials for building the terminus were still floating in reasonable proximity. It took Rauti another week to bring the closest asteroid back to its position beside the wrecked terminus, re-connect the piping, and start the flow of raw materials to his assembly location inside the debris field.

From that point, things got easier. He didn't need an airtight space; he didn't need food; he didn't need water. He got his energy from the Sun's radiation. Within two days, he was back in a large caterpillar body, and had completed the design of his first missile. The hard part was the tDrive to give it interstellar capability; tDrives were a very specialized thing to build. Under normal circumstances, an interstellar-capable tDrive had to be in a radiation containment vessel to protect any biological material nearby.

But this was a special case. There would be no biological material to protect. The missiles Rauti was building would fly directly from Venus to their target.

Rauti skipped the radiation containment.

CHAPTER TWELVE

Stalingrad System
Dyson Ring

"We need a strategy," said Jim. "We can't just go straight at these Stree bastards. We'd have no chance. We need a way of getting to their backside."

"I'm not seeing any backside," said Rita. "The Stree have the numbers and the initiative. The Goblins are on the defensive. The Stree have us on the ropes."

"There's always a backside," said Jim. "We just haven't found it yet."

"How do we find it?" asked Bonnie. "We know almost nothing about these assholes."

Jim looked seriously at the team assembled around the table.

"We go there. We scout them on the ground."

Everyone looked at him in a stunned silence."

"You're crazy," said Luke. Rachel, sitting at the far end of the table, lifted her head in interest.

"What do you mean?" Rachel asked.

"I mean exactly what I say," said Jim. "We get off our asses, go to the Stree home world, and scout them. Find a weakness we can exploit."

"And if there is no weakness?" asked Luke.

Jim stared at him. "There will be. Every society has one. And we'll find it."

Rita looked down the table at Tika, who was at the far end. "But if the Goblins haven't found any weakness so far, how can we expect to?"

"We've never actually gone to their home planet," said Tika. "We've only done scouting and remote sensing from the edge of their system."

"My Lord," exclaimed Bonnie. "You can't be serious! With your ability to translate into any form, you've never gone to their planet?"

Tika shook her head. "No, we haven't. Our leaders felt it was too risky and might precipitate another war."

"A bit late for that," growled Rita.

"So," said Jim. "What do you know about their society?"

"It's a religious theocracy," said Tika. "They are ruled by a caste of priests and monks. Anyone who questions the priesthood is killed. The priesthood funnels up to a supreme leader called the Great Prophet. The Great Prophet is infallible; his word is called the Word Ordained. The priesthood fear and hate AI with a deep-rooted passion. They allow dumb computing, but nothing that can approach sentience. As a result, their ships tend to be a bit clumsy and slow compared to ours. But it's clear they vastly outnumber us."

"By how much?" asked Jim.

"We think about three-to-one," said Tika. "It appears they've been building ships at some location we didn't know about. We've monitored their home system for years - and all these ships didn't come from there. We were as shocked at the number of ships as you were."

"So they have a secret base somewhere," said Jim.

"That appears to be the case," answered Tika. "The number of ships they used to attack the bio worlds is far greater than we expected."

"So. Who's up for infiltrating the Stree home world?" asked Jim.

There was a long silence. Finally, Rita smiled grimly. "You know as well as I do that only Goblins can do it. We'd have to take Stree form. So that means Tika and I."

"And me," said Rachel. "I've decided to become a Goblin."

The group looked at Rachel in amazement.

"You?" Bonnie blurted out before she could stop herself.

Rachel continued bitterly. "Dan's gone. Without him, I don't have much reason to continue living as a Human. So I've made up my mind. I'll convert to Goblin and go with you on this mission."

Rita spoke gently. "Have you really thought this through, Rachel? You know there's no going back. It's a one-way trip."

"I know," Rachel responded. "I've been thinking about it for days. I've made up my mind. I have nothing to live for without Dan, except my revenge on these Stree bastards. So I'm in."

Rachel turned to Tika. "How soon can we do the conversion?"

Tika glanced once at Rita, then back at Rachel. "It doesn't take long. We'll need to scan your Human body to get data for your android template. Then we build your new body. When your android body is complete, you'll transfer over to it and start your training."

"Then let's do it today," said Rachel. "The sooner the better. I assume we need to leave on this mission right away?"

Tika nodded slowly.

"It's 40 days to Stree, right? Can I complete my training enroute?"

Tika nodded again. "If necessary," she replied. "It's not ideal, but I think we can make it work."

"Then let's get it done, please," said Rachel. She stood up from the table. "I'm ready."

Tika stood. She gave a long look at Rita, silently asking for permission. Rita gave a slow nod. Tika turned and led the way out of the room, Rachel following.

Rita turned back to Jim and shook her head. "I didn't see that coming," she said. "Did you?"

"Sorta," said Jim. "I knew she was in a dark place. I suspected she might take that option as a way out."

Rita changed the subject.

"So," she said, addressing the group. "I've got an idea."

"About what?" asked Jim.

"About how to infiltrate the Stree."

"And?"

"We bootstrap our way into their command center."

"Bootstrap?" Ollie asked from the other side of the table, putting down a beer.

"Like a computer does. First it loads a single small program from a known place on the disk. Then that program loads a larger program. Then that loads an even larger program, until the whole computer is up and running."

"Oh, booting!" said Bonnie. She wrinkled her nose. "What does that mean in terms of the mission, though?"

Rita leaned forward to expound on her idea. "First, we take over a little station somewhere in their system, well out from Stree Prime - their home planet. That gives us a base of operations. We use that as a springboard to take over another installation on the surface of Stree Prime, but far away from their capital city. Now we have a base for ground operations on the planet. Then we use that to worm our way into their command headquarters. From there, we can gather all the intel we need and try to find a way to influence the coming battle. Maybe disrupt their communications, or plant a virus in their fleet."

There was a short silence as the group absorbed the idea and thought about it. Ollie knew he had to begin the discussion; he had long since figured out that Jim, Bonnie, and Rita had a philosophy of letting their juniors speak first, so as not to contaminate any first-blush ideas with the pressure of their senior officer opinions.

"It's just crazy enough that it might work," Ollie said.

Jim went next. "Crazy, yes. But...maybe."

Bonnie nodded last. "I don't see what else a small team like ours could do, so why not?"

"So," Rita continued. "It'll have to be Goblins for the insertion. So Tika and myself for that. And Rachel if she's ready in time."

"Yeah, you three for the ground part," said Jim. "I'll stand by out-system coordinating comms and support."

"And me," said Bonnie.

"We don't have much time," Rita added. "Goblin intel thinks the Stree fleet will leave for Stalingrad within a week to ten days. If we have any hope of getting there in time to change the outcome of this war, we have to get our ass in gear!"

"So let's get moving," said Bonnie. "Let's get the *Armidale* loaded up and get the hell out of here."

Rita nodded at the rest. "Agreed. The first transport of Human survivors to Phoenix departs Monday. We could launch on Tuesday if we can get approval from the Goblin leadership. We'll have to have some support from them - we can't do it alone."

Suddenly, Ollie rose to his feet. He looked around the group, a strange expression on his face.

"Guys, I've been sitting here thinking about it. I'm converting too. I...I just...I don't want to live as Human anymore without Helen. I hope you can all understand."

And with that, Ollie suddenly turned and marched away after Tika and Rachel, so quickly that the stunned group simply sat, unable to speak for a long moment.

Finally, Bonnie spoke.

"I think Rachel's decision tipped him over the edge, too."

Rita gave a slow nod of agreement. "Yeah. But I think it's more than what he just said. Have you guys noticed him making side-eyes at Rachel lately?"

"What?" Luke asked. "Rachel?"

"Yeah," Bonnie smiled at Rita. "I've noticed that. In spite of what he said, I think he's getting past Helen, and starting to fall for Rachel."

"No!" exclaimed Luke. "Ollie and Rachel?"

"Maybe," said Bonnie. "He may not know it yet himself. You know how men are. You have to drop a rock on them before they realize some things."

"Well, he could do worse," said Jim. "Rachel's cute."

Rita gave him a mock slap on the shoulder. "Cute?"

Jim rubbed his shoulder where Rita had hit him. "My dear, please remember that you are now a Goblin, but I'm still Human. That left a bruise, I think."

"Oh, sorry," Rita grimaced. "I forget sometimes. But don't change the subject. You think Rachel's cute?"

"No," mused Jim, "now that I think about it, she's actually gorgeous."

Rita slapped Jim's shoulder again. "You're digging your hole deeper, bud."

Jim rubbed his shoulder once more and grinned back at his wife.

"And that's what I get for telling the truth!"

***

Hours later, Jim and Luke were sitting in Jim's apartment, each clutching a cold beer, when the door chime rang. Jim got up to let in Tika. As Tika plopped down on the couch in front of them, Jim had to suppress a laugh as he saw Luke turn half-sideways in his chair so he wouldn't be looking directly at her. Jim had gotten used to it; but having serious conversations with a completely naked female android was still new to Luke.

"I have bad news, good news and good news," Tika began. "Which do you want to hear first?"

Jim grimaced. "Always the bad news first."

"Our leadership has disapproved the use of the 200-odd Humans who agreed to fight with us while remaining in their biological state. They are afraid the Humans might have an unconscious bias to side with other biologicals against Goblins, either now or in the future. Those Humans will have to continue on to Phoenix as originally planned."

"Crap," Luke interjected. "Those people are going to be really disappointed."

"Yes, exactly," Tika agreed. "But now for some good news. There were thirty-seven Humans that agreed to convert to Goblins. Our leadership has accepted those few into our ranks. And in fact, they have a special mission in mind for them."

"What mission?" asked Jim.

"I don't know, it's classified," Tika said. "But they are giving them a ship - an old cruiser called the *Darkstar* - and sending them on a special mission somewhere. That's all I know."

"Well, at least that group will have a chance to do something useful," said Jim. "What about the rest of us? What about our proposal?"

"Your request for a mission to infiltrate the Stree High Command has been approved by our Leaders," said Tika. "However, they honestly think you're delusional to believe you can sneak into the Stree system, make it all the way to Stree Prime, and get into their Naval Headquarters without getting caught. On the other hand, they have nothing to lose. And there's always that one-in-a-billion chance you'll succeed."

Jim grunted. "C'mon, Tika. At least give us one-in-a-million."

"Fine," grinned Tika. "One-in-a-million. Feel better?"

"Much," grinned Jim back at her. "Can we leave on Tuesday as we proposed?"

"Yes. That works perfectly. Transport One will depart for Phoenix with the first batch of colonists on Monday. We can leave the next day."

"You're coming with us?"

Tika grinned even wider.

"I wouldn't miss it for the world. I can't think of anything better than to take this fight right to those Stree bastards on their own home world. We may not win the war, but I'll bet we get to kill some Stree!"

Jim was now so excited he sprang to his feet, pacing around the room. "So who'll be in charge? You?"

Shaking her head, Tika responded. "No. Our leadership wants this to be a Human mission, not a Goblin one. Rita will be in overall command. Our Leadership considers her the ranking survivor of the Human EDF at this point. Bonnie will be second-in-command. Of course, Captain Stewart will have operational command of the *Armidale*."

"What else?" asked Jim.

"They'll give us one Goblin Intel team for support. Other than that, you Humans are on your own."

"That's fine. I like it that way. That gives us a chance to get our own back for their attack on Earth."

"Exactly. But of course, there's another reason the Leadership prefer this to be a mostly Human mission."

"And what's that?"

"They don't think Stalingrad can hold against the Stree. After the war, there may be no Goblins left to carry on the species. Their thinking is that maybe any Humans that survive your mission can at least carry on the memory of who we were."

Grimly, Jim looked at Luke, then back at Tika.

"So you're saying, we're a remnant tossed to the wind, in hopes we may survive when all else is lost."

"Exactly," said Tika. This time, she wasn't smiling.

***

"Did you hear?" Rita asked Jim, cuddling with him in their apartment. Both were hot and sweaty. They had been proving once again that all the bodily functions of Rita's android body worked properly.

"Hear what?" Jim asked, playing with her hair. "I've been too busy to hear anything."

"Luke's not going with us on the mission. He's going to Phoenix with Tatiana."

Jim pulled his face back from Rita to look at her clearly.

"What? You're kidding!"

"No. He told Bonnie he thinks his place is with his daughter and grandchild now. He said he's fought his wars; now he wants to take care of Tatiana and baby Marta."

"And what did Bonnie say to that?"

"She's disappointed, of course. But she agreed with him. She told him to go, and she'll catch up to him at Phoenix after the war."

They were both silent. Both were thinking the same thing.

If Bonnie survives the war...

"And because of that, Bonnie has decided to stay in Human form," Rita added.

"What?"

"Yeah. She doesn't want to convert. She said if Luke is going to Phoenix as a Human, then she's going to stay Human as well."

"But Rachel and Ollie are converting?"

"Already did. Last night. They've already started training with Tika."

"Both of them took it really hard, losing their lovers like that."

"Well. We all took it hard. We all lost people."

"But those two lost everything. Family, friends, and their lovers. More than anyone else."

"Yeah," Rita agreed.

"So when's Luke leaving?" Jim wondered.

"Monday. On the first ship. With Mark and Gillian."

"So let's have a little celebration for them all, what do you say?"

"Like what?"

"Maybe a picnic? Tomorrow? In the park?"

"That sounds good."

After a short silence, Rita spoke again.

"I need to tell you something."

"What?"

"I've decided to send Imogen with Gillian."

"Well. I knew you would."

"No. I mean permanently."

"Oh."

"I thought we had put war behind us; but looks like it seeks us out no matter what we do."

"Yeah. I've noticed."

"It's not fair to Imogen or to Gillian to keep this up in the air. So if you agree..."

"Yeah. I agree. War is no place for a child, and it looks like we can't escape from it. That seems to be our destiny. So - yeah."

CHAPTER THIRTEEN

Stalingrad System
Dyson Ring

"I hereby call the first meeting of the Phoenix Council to order," said Mark, gazing around the table. Somehow a gavel had been found, and he tapped it gently.

He sat at the head of the table. Beside him sat his wife, Gillian. At the far end of the table, opposite Mark, was a Goblin android.

Between them sat seven people - the new Council members of the government of Phoenix. One of them was Rick Moore - the young man who asked Mark the first question during the meeting in the amphitheater. Another of them was Zoe DeLong - the female Marine pilot Mark had noticed during the meeting, the one who had asked the second question. Mark had gone out of his way to research them, investigate their backgrounds, and had liked what he found. He had then lobbied their respective apartment blocks to have them nominated for the Council, and each of them had won election.

Gillian had chided him for interfering in the nomination process, but Mark had gone ahead with it anyway. He had been in the Army too long to leave things to chance when he found good leadership, and he was sure he had found it.

"Has everyone introduced themselves?"

Nods and acknowledgments went around the table.

"Good. Then let's get started. We have a lot to do. Let me begin by introducing Beto, our Goblin friend at the end of the table. The Goblins have been kind enough to provide us with a team of advisers. That team of Goblin advisers will travel with us to Phoenix and help us get established there. Beto will be the leader of the team and serve as a non-voting adviser to this Council. He is a biologist and botanist. A good combination to help us."

Beto inclined his head slightly. The Humans around the table returned the nod, greeting him.

"Our next order of business is to elect a governor. Do we have any nominations?"

"Yourself," Zoe said quickly, beating everyone else to the punch. "You have the most experience in both administration and military affairs. It only makes sense."

Rick Moore happened to be gazing across the table at this moment. He saw a sour look flash across the face of the man in front of him - Turgenev - then just as quickly dissipate, the man's face returning to the semi-permanent smile he had worn since they sat down.

Turgenev, thought Rick. *He didn't like that.*

"Second," Rick said quickly before anyone else could jump in.

"Ah," said Mark. "I thank you. Do we have any other nominations?"

At the far end of the table, one of the new council members, a Korean named Jeo Deok Won, raised a hand.

"I nominate Mr. Turgenev. He operated a large food distribution company in Russia. He also served as an officer in the Russian military. I believe he would be best qualified to serve as governor."

"I second," spoke up a Chinese woman, Choi Ri. Rick noticed a quick glance between her and Turgenev.

Ah, thought Rick. *Something doesn't smell right here.*

"Do we have other nominations?" asked Mark. Everyone looked around, but no one spoke.

"Then, since I'm now a nominee, I'll hand the gavel over to Mr. Moore to chair the discussion of qualifications and conduct the vote," said Mark. He winked at Rick as he passed him the gavel.

Stalingrad System
Dyson Ring

"What a beautiful day!"

Tatiana held baby Marta and smiled at the sky. She spun in a circle, winking at Misha as she spun by him.

Luke and Misha had no choice but to laugh at the comment.

"Every day here is a beautiful day," Luke chuckled.

"Well, yeah, but still…it's beautiful!"

High above them, the artificial sun of Central Park stretched from one end of the Human section to the other. The long, fat tube a quarter mile above them was just far enough away to provide a warm, sun-like glow of heat on their skin.

"To me, though, it gets monotonous," said Jim, sitting on the grass on a bright checkered tablecloth. In front of him, a near-empty picnic basket stood, the contents pretty much demolished by the group. Nearby, Imogen ran through the grass, Rita and Gillian chasing after her. In a playground across the small creek from them, children played, laughing and calling out to each other.

"Monotonous?" asked Bonnie, just finishing up a remarkably realistic chicken drumstick provided by the Goblins.

"Yeah," Jim replied. "Every day's a perfect day. Not too hot, not too cold. Twelve hours of light, twelve hours of darkness. The food's an almost perfect imitation of Earth food. The water is pure. The apartment blocks are clean, and everything works. There's nothing broken or out of place."

"So far, you're describing Utopia," Mark said with a smile.

"No. It's not," said Jim. "It's a trap. It's a trap that sucks people in, makes them think they have nothing to worry about, that everything will be just fine."

"And we know better," Luke agreed. "Phoenix is out there waiting for us. A primitive planet that'll take everything we have to survive. And beyond that, the Stree. Preparing their attack."

"I have a question," said Mark. "Why won't the Goblins let some of us stay here? It's a perfect environment. Obviously providing for us doesn't stretch their resources much. They could let the women and children stay here, for example, until the men have a viable colony established on Phoenix. Then the women and children could follow."

Jim's smile disappeared. Digging at the grass with a stick, he frowned, sighed, and shook his head.

"The Goblins have serious doubts they can survive this war," he said. "And they know the Stree will destroy this Ring if they get a chance. The Goblins don't want to be responsible for thousands of Humans dying if it comes to that."

"Ah. Yeah, I can see that," Mark mused, thinking it through. "So I guess we'll be safer on Phoenix, even if the conditions are primitive."

"What's this I hear about you appointing Luke to the Council?" asked Jim, winking at Tatiana as she returned to the group and sat across from him, bouncing baby Marta on her lap.

"Well, you know I was elected Governor," Mark said.

"Yep, I heard that. And I heard it was quite a close call."

"Yeah. I won by one vote. Turgenev and his buddies put together quite an effective coalition, and in a damn short time, too. Not sure how they did that. If it weren't for Rick Moore and Zoe DeLong, Turgenev would be governor now."

"But you won. So it's all good."

"Yeah, I won. Barely. But anyway, well, you know the Governor gets to appoint his replacement. I think Luke is perfect for the job. So I tapped him to replace me."

Winking at Tatiana and Luke, Jim looked back at Mark.

"Well, I think you screwed up. Anybody crazy enough to stick their destroyer in front of a full battlecruiser cube has no business claiming sanity."

Luke frowned at Jim.

"I seem to remember a Merlin fighter off my port beam about that time. One I believe had your name painted below the cockpit."

"Touché," grinned Jim. "Two of a kind - and both crazy!"

"You got that right," Mark said, laughing at them both.

Jim looked past them toward a trio approaching.

"Oh, my Lord," he said. "Look who's coming!"

They all turned to see.

"Oh, gosh!" blurted Tatiana. "It's Rachel and Ollie!"

Sure enough, Tika, Rachel and Ollie approached the group. Rachel and Ollie were walking a bit strangely, somewhat jerkily. Both had their head down and seemed to be concentrating on placing their feet properly.

"Oh, I know that feeling," Rita said. Jim turned to see Rita behind him, holding Imogen and staring at Rachel. "The first couple of days, you feel like you're learning to walk all over again," she added.

As the three approached, everyone stood to greet them. The two came up to the group and stopped, Tika stepping to one side to allow Rachel and Ollie to be greeted first.

Bonnie stepped forward quickly and gathered Rachel in her arms, giving her a huge bear hug, while Jim jumped up, moved to Ollie, and grabbed him around the shoulders, shaking his hand.

Bonnie stepped back, reached up and smoothed Rachel's hair where the wind had blown it askew, and then leaned forward and gave her a kiss on the cheek.

"Welcome back, hon. We're so glad to see you. How do you feel?"

"Basically, great!" said Rachel. "Just as Rita described. I have tons of energy; I feel like I could run a thousand miles. My senses are incredible. But my coordination is off. This body is so much more powerful than my old one. But Tika says I'll be fine after a few more days."

Rita handed Imogen to Jim and stepped over to Ollie, kissed his cheek, then moved to Rachel. She embraced Rachel and also kissed her cheek.

"It gets better, guys. It took me a while before it became second nature to me. I don't even notice it now. It just feels normal."

Ollie nodded hopefully. "Good. That's encouraging. Because right now I feel like a two-year old."

One by one, the rest of the group greeted the two, hugging them and making them welcome. After a while, the two newly converted Goblins sat down at the tablecloth with the rest of them.

"I'm sorry, there's not much food left," said Mark.

"No worries," Ollie replied. "We don't have to eat anymore; only if we want to appear Human to strangers."

Rita nodded in agreement. "Another benefit of being a Goblin."

"Hmm. I'm not sure that's a benefit," said Mark, finishing off one last piece of chicken. "This is a pretty good drumstick."

"Oh, don't get me wrong," said Rita. "We can eat if we want to, and the experience is exactly like before we converted. It's just that if we don't want to, or we have no food, we can mentally flip a switch in our brains and the hunger goes away."

"Handy for missions," said Jim.

"Exactly," said Rita.

Jim couldn't help but notice an involuntary shudder go through Gillian. He decided he'd better change the subject. He looked across at Mark.

"So...the first transport ship leaves tomorrow afternoon. And the entire Council is going?"

Mark nodded. "Yeah. I see no reason to leave any of the Council members here. The Goblins can handle this end of things."

Jim smiled at Gillian. "Well, Sis, you keep Mark under control out there. Don't let power go to his head!"

Gillian chuckled. "It already has. He told me this morning I'm to be in charge of Housing Administration. Without even asking me first!"

"And what did you say?" asked Jim, knowing his sister.

"Fat chance! I've got better things to do - I have to take care of Imogen!"

Jim cast a glance at Rita. He saw the shadow pass across her face briefly, then disappear.

"Too right," Jim said. "She's a handful!"

In his lap, Imogen squealed and squirmed at the mention of her name.

"So. You leave on the first transport tomorrow," Rita said to Luke. "So this is goodbye, for a while."

"Yeah, I guess," Luke replied. He looked around at the group. "I'll miss you guys."

There was a long silence as everyone contemplated the future. They were going their separate ways - some to try and survive on a primitive planet, others to war.

Rita glanced at Bonnie. She knew Bonnie was taking Luke's decision to go to Phoenix hard. She saw Bonnie put her head down, pulling at a blade of grass on the ground. Rita spoke again.

"Luke - Mark and Gillian are going to have their hands full getting the colony organized. Please help them all you can."

"I will," Luke said. "Misha and Tatiana and I will be there for them. We'll make it work."

"And help Gillian with Imogen for me. Please."

Luke nodded solemnly. "I will, Rita. I promise."

CHAPTER FOURTEEN

Stalingrad System
Dyson Ring

"Bonnie's crying," Rita told Jim.

Jim looked across the landing bay where the crew of the first transport to Phoenix was loading. He could see Bonnie, wrapped in Luke's arms, both of them clearly distraught at the thought of being separated. He didn't need Rita's enhanced vision to see the tears streaming down Bonnie's face.

"Well," Jim said, and stopped. He couldn't think of anything else to say.

"I'm going to go be with her," said Rita, and she moved, stepping out to go across the landing bay toward Bonnie.

Jim stayed in place. He knew to leave them be. That was no place for a man who had once been Bonnie's lover.

Former lover now, Jim thought. *But still fresh enough that Rita has spurts of jealousy from time to time. Better to stay out of this.*

Jim continued his work of guiding the last of the Human passengers thorough the rear loading tube of the transport ship. Anyone could have done the job; but Jim wanted to be here, wanted to take a personal hand in seeing off the first group of survivors to their new home on Phoenix.

It was important to him; after all, these were the people who would re-populate humanity. He wanted to say hello to them as they passed by, help them on board, wish them well.

Smiling, he held out an arm, directing a confused young couple toward the boarding tube. With a start, he realized the end of the line was approaching. The loading of Transport One was nearly complete. Another dozen people went by him, and suddenly it was done.

Jim stood back as Goblin crewmen began closing the hatch. With a thud, it slid down and latched, sealing the boarding tube. Another sound reverberated, and Jim knew the hatch on the ship side had also closed.

Three thousand people. Almost the entire day to get the ship loaded. But done.

Turning, Jim walked toward the front loading tube, which was reserved for crew. Now only Tatiana Powell and her husband Misha, with their baby Marta, remained outside the front boarding tube.

And Bonnie and Luke, with Rita hovering nearby. Still wrapped in a long embrace, Bonnie and Luke finally pulled apart as Jim approached. Jim stood back, not wishing to intrude. He watched as Luke reached up and brushed away the tears from Bonnie's face.

"Be safe out there, hon," he heard Luke say. Luke leaned forward for one last kiss, then turned to face Tatiana and Misha.

Misha glanced at Luke, read something in his face, and turned to enter the boarding tube first. Tatiana held Marta and followed close behind Misha, turning at the last second to wave and smile at Bonnie. Then she disappeared down the boarding tube.

That left Luke standing in the entrance of the boarding tube. He turned back to Bonnie with a forced smile.

"See ya later, babe," he said. Then he was gone, disappearing down the boarding tube toward the ship.

Rita quickly stepped forward and put her arms around Bonnie's shoulders. Bonnie slumped into Rita, putting her head down to hide her tears. Jim stayed well out of it. There was no place for him in that embrace.

"Jim!" he heard from behind, and turned to see his sister Gillian approaching with Mark. Gillian was pushing Imogen in a stroller - a sight so normal it caught Jim by surprise.

1,275 lights from Earth, on a Dyson Ring populated by Goblins, preparing to leave for a virgin planet, and here comes my sister pushing my child in a stroller like it's a Sunday walk in the park.

"Hi, Sis," said Jim. "Where in heck did you get a stroller?"

"Tika. I explained what it was, and she had them 3D print one for me. What do you think?"

"I think you're a genius," said Jim.

"Well, that goes without saying," Mark interjected, smiling at his wife.

Jim reached down and took Imogen from the stroller, cuddling her in his arms as he heard Rita and Bonnie come up beside him. Bonnie, still wiping tears from her eyes, stepped forward and hugged Gillian, then shook hands with Mark.

"I'll say my goodbyes now, guys. Have a safe trip. Make a home for us. We need a place to come back to, after the war. We're counting on you."

Mark nodded. "We'll do it. Just make sure you come back to us."

Sniffling, Bonnie nodded. She turned to Jim and leaned forward, kissing Imogen on the cheek. "And take care of this little munchkin," she added.

Then Bonnie turned suddenly and walked away, head down, still wiping her eyes. Mark watched her go.

"She's taking this hard," he said.

"She is," said Rita. "She's lost a lot in the last few years."

Rita gave a subtle sideways glance at Jim.

Including you, my husband. Maybe the greatest loss of all for her.

Then she continued. "She didn't expect Luke to go to Phoenix with Tatiana. She expected him to stay with her. So she's still in a bit of a state."

"I think I was surprised, too," Mark responded. "I understand his motivation, but I really didn't think he would leave the Fleet like that."

"There is no Fleet anymore," Jim said somewhat bitterly.

"Ah, yes. I tend to forget that," Mark spoke.

Stepping forward, Rita reached out her arms for Imogen. Before releasing the child to Rita, Jim kissed her on both cheeks, making her giggle. As Rita took her, Jim gave a slight head tilt to Mark, then stepped away toward the boarding tube. Mark followed him, puzzled. When they were a dozen yards away from the women, Jim paused.

"I heard some scuttlebutt I thought you should know about."

Mark nodded, uncertain.

"Zoe DeLong pulled me aside as she was going on board. She said she heard from a friend of a friend that one of the council members is a ringer. Evidently a former Russian mafia guy."

"Turgenev," breathed Mark. "That son of a bitch."

"Exactly. Watch your back. He's almost certainly not working alone."

"Roger that. I can't believe we have to deal with this while we're trying to survive on a new planet."

"Evil is universal, Mark. You know that. Develop a network of people you can trust to help you keep an eye on him and his pals. They'll be trying to put a shiv in your back from the get-go."

"I think I'll put Luke in charge of the Security Team. He's a good one."

"That he is. Anyway, good luck. You're going to need it."

Mark nodded. He looked across at Gillian and Rita. They were walking toward him slowly, conversing. Rita was holding Imogen. Reaching the boarding tube, they stopped for their final goodbyes.

Jim saw tears in Rita's eyes. He knew letting go of Imogen was hard for her. But behind her, four Goblin crew were standing impatiently, ready to close the hatch.

Rita kissed Imogen, once, twice, again, then reluctantly let Gillian take her. Jim leaned in, kissed his daughter one last time, and then Gillian put her in the stroller. Mark gave Jim one last thumbs-up, and the three were in the boarding tube and gone. The hatch came down and sealed the tube.

Jim moved to hold Rita as the tears streamed down her face.

"Oh, Jim. Are we doing the right thing? Should we just go to Phoenix and let someone else fight this war?"

Jim smiled. "You know we'd never be happy sitting on Phoenix while others fought this war. And besides - if we don't fight and win, the Stree will be coming for our daughter. We can't let that happen."

Rita leaned into him, forgetting for a moment her new, heavier body. It was all Jim could do not to lurch to one side. But he managed, putting an arm around her shoulders as the tears came down her face.

"We'll see her again soon, babe. We just have to kill a few Stree first."

Stalingrad System
Dyson Ring

Next morning, Rita and Tika went onboard *Armidale* for final cargo loading before their mission departure to Stree. Standing in the cargo bay, Rita looked at Tika with some concern.

"Do you think this is a good idea?"

Tika thought about it for a while before she answered. She was staring at eleven containers packed in the cargo hold of the *Armidale*. Two were small, roughly the size of a fat suitcase. Eight were larger and looked like coffins. The last was even larger, like an oversize coffin for a giant.

"Yeah. I think it is," she mused. "And what other choice do we have?"

"Well, yeah," said Rita. "But I'd rather think we have some chance of success than think of this as a suicide mission."

"Absolutely," agreed Tika. "I wouldn't be going if I thought we had no chance."

"No chance of what?" asked Bonnie, coming through the hatch.

Tika grinned at her. "No chance of kicking Stree ass."

"Ah, gotcha. Well, I think our chances of kicking Stree ass are excellent," replied Bonnie. "Are those the blanks?" she asked, pointing to the eight coffins.

Rita nodded. "Yep. Dormant Stree bodies."

Bonnie paused before Tika, hands on hips. "Can I see one? I've only seen holos so far."

Tika shook her head. "No, not now. The containers are sealed until we need them. It might cause a glitch if we open one prematurely."

"Eight of them?"

"Yep. Rita, Rachel and I, plus the Intel crew that are coming with us," said Tika.

Bonnie walked to the smaller suitcase-sized objects and stared at them.

"And this is what you use to zombie somebody into Goblin form?"

Rita frowned at her, but with a twinkle in her eye. "Yeah. And you're next."

Bonnie shook her head. "I don't think so, babe. Since Luke is staying Human, I am too. Besides, I've decided I like me just the way I am. And what's that big coffin? Is that the bodybuilder?"

"Yep. It allows us to assemble an android body from the scan of a bio. So when I zombie you into Goblin form, I've got someplace to put you," laughed Rita.

"Hmm," said Bonnie, staring at the coffin-shaped device. "So is that what *Jade* used to make you in the first place?"

"Of course not," replied Rita. "I was originally cloned from Human DNA. *Jade* grew me into adult form as a pure bio. That was Singheko tech, not Goblin tech."

"What an adventure you've had," Bonnie said.

Rita shook her head. "Adventure is not the word I'd use, babe."

Behind them came a voice. "As much as I hate to interrupt your nostalgic moments, we have a lot of work to do. We have to perform final prep on the scanners and the bodybuilder."

Bonnie, Rita and Tika turned. Two rather large Goblins

stood at the cargo hatch.

"Ladies, let me introduce Commander Hajo and Lieutenant Luda," said Tika. "Commander Hajo will command the Goblin Intel team for our Stree mission. In addition to being an intelligence expert, he's also a master pilot and guru of all things logistical. And Lieutenant Luda is our expert on the bio scanner and the bodybuilder. If we have to zombie any Stree, he's the one that can do it."

"Pleased to meet you," Bonnie said. Rita nodded in agreement. "We'll get out of your way and let you get to work!"

Hajo smiled. Rita couldn't help but notice he seemed to be smiling mostly at Tika.

Ah ha, thought Rita. *I think Tika has a secret admirer. Or not so secret...*

"Thank you," Hajo spoke. "We should have all cargo loaded and be ready to depart in about an hour. I suggest you ensure you have all your personal gear on board and stowed in your cabins. It's a long way back from Stree Prime if you forget something."

Bonnie and Rita laughed. "Too right. We'll get to it!"

Stalingrad System
Dyson Ring

The old Goblin cruiser had been in mothballs for at least fifty years. The Goblins had converted the ship's AI to one copied from the *Armidale*, and modified the controls to better suit a Human crew. They had verified the engines and systems were operational. Then they handed over the keys.

The small Human crew - recently converted to Goblins - were still unsteady on their feet, still trying to fully assimilate their new state of existence. But their impatience had gotten the better of them. They had finally convinced their trainers to let them go aboard the old cruiser and check out their newly assigned ship.

Surveying the bridge, Commander Ying Woh shook his

head.

"This is a piece of junk," he said to Captain Gilbert Ostend. "I'm surprised it evens hold pressure, considering Goblins don't actually need pressure to survive in their ships."

Ostend couldn't resist a wry smile. "Don't forget, Commander Woh. We don't need pressure anymore either."

Woh shook his head. "Dammit, I keep forgetting that. You know, it isn't just the physical conversion that's so upsetting. It's the mental one as well. I keep thinking like a biological creature."

Ostend nodded. "We're all going through that. I keep finding myself wondering when we're gonna have chow, then I remember that eating is optional now. It's a really disconcerting feeling."

Woh looked around the bridge at the crew diligently checking and re-checking consoles, bringing up systems, checking weapons, and trying to get the engines started. He heaved a long sigh.

"We've got a lot to do to clean up this old tub."

"Well, yeah. But we can't expect them to give us a front-line warship."

"Yeah, but still…this old tin can? If this were the old EDF, I'd refuse this thing and send it back to the yard for refit."

Ostend had to laugh at that. "The 'old' EDF? That's funny. After all, the EDF was only created three years ago. So it can hardly be called 'old', you know."

"Well, you know what I mean."

"Yeah," mused Ostend, gazing off into the distance with a thousand-yard stare. "I know. Back in the old days. When the EDF still existed."

"Yeah. Any more details on our mission?" asked Woh.

Ostend shrugged. "Only a bit. Tagi told me we won't be fighting the Stree directly. They have something else in mind. Something more covert, she said."

"That's disappointing. I was really hoping to punch some holes in some Stree ships."

"Well, doesn't matter. As long as we have something useful to do."

Woh nodded and began walking around the bridge, looking over the shoulder of the crew, trying to make sense of the Goblin consoles. Ostend remained standing at the back of the bridge, shaking his head.

"I'm glad I converted to a Goblin," he muttered under his breath. "In this old wreck, I think I'm gonna need nine lives."

CHAPTER FIFTEEN

Stree Prime
Stree Flagship

High Admiral Sojatta sat in his command chair on the main bridge of the flagship SGH *Prophecy*.

Loosely translated, the Stree characters SGH stood for *Stree God's Hand*. And that was exactly how Sojatta felt today.

God's Hand. The Hand of Righteousness. The Universe is with us. We will crush the apostate Goblins. We will grind them into powder. When we are through, the Universe will not even have a record they ever existed.

"The Fleet is ready, O High Admiral," said Sojatta's Flag Lieutenant.

Sojatta inclined his head in a short nod. "We await the Word," he replied, looking at Guardian Prophet Zutirra sitting beside him.

Zutirra smiled, reveling in his recent promotion. He was now the senior Prophet in the Fleet. Sojatta couldn't make a move without his blessing.

At last. I have achieved my dream. And after we destroy the Goblins...I may fall into the line of succession for the role of Great Prophet.

"Destroy the Goblins," intoned Zutirra. "It is the Word Ordained."

"It is the Word Ordained," repeated Sojatta. He motioned to his Flag Lieutenant. "Let us depart."

Slowly, but with ever increasing velocity, the Stree Fleet began to move out-system toward the mass limit. Ten separate groups made up the armada. Each group contained 150 warships - battlecruisers, cruisers, and destroyers. A total of 1,500 ships, moving in coordination, accelerated toward the mass limit where they would sink out and speed toward Stalingrad.

Enroute to Stree Prime
Corvette EDF *Armidale*

The *Armidale* was six days out from Stalingrad when the news came. Rita, Jim, Bonnie, Ollie, and Rachel were having coffee in the galley. Captain Stewart stepped in, his face dark. He paused before them, looking grim.

"What?" Jim asked before anyone else could react.

"The Stree have launched," Stewart said.

Rita closed her eyes, grimacing.

"I hoped we'd have more time," she said. She opened her eyes, staring at Bonnie. "That gives us only six days at Stree Prime before their fleet attacks Stalingrad. That's not much time to accomplish anything."

"Well. We'll have to do what we can with the time we have available," said Bonnie.

After a short silence, Jim spoke up. "We need to accelerate our plan a bit."

"I don't see how," Rita said. "We're already pushing it to the limit."

"Then we have to push some more," said Jim. "Our only hope of changing the outcome of the war is to infiltrate Stree command headquarters before the Stree fleet arrives at Stalingrad. So when we arrive at Stree Prime, we'll have exactly six days to get that done."

"Maybe more," said Bonnie. "They may hover outside the Stalingrad system for a few days, getting themselves organized. Like the Singheko did at Dekanna."

"But they won't wait for long," Rita interjected. "They know they've got the Goblins vastly outnumbered. They have no reason to delay."

"Still. We may have six days when we arrive. Or we may have eight. Or even ten. We just don't know," Bonnie replied.

"But we have to assume worst case," said Jim. "So we have to go into this with the assumption we'll have six days from our arrival at Stree Prime to find some kind of leverage to blunt the Stree attack."

Phoenix System
800 Lights from Stalingrad

The newly established colony on Phoenix lay in a long, broad horseshoe of a valley. Fifty miles in width and seventy miles long, the huge valley had a medium-size river to the east, running past the colony to the sea a dozen miles south of them. There was a flat, clear area in the middle of the valley perfect for building, outside of which blue-green alien trees climbed the foothills to the mountains on all three sides.

At the moment, ten shuttles were parked in a neat pattern in the center of the clear area. The shuttles had ferried the Humans from Transport One to the surface of the virgin planet, along with four million pounds of bots and materials. On both sides of the landing area were hundreds of large tents, their canvas already turning brown after five days on the surface.

On the east side of the camp, several hundred Humans were wrestling a water tank into position. Beside the water tank were two small buildings. At the top of each of the small square buildings, the roof seemed to be moving as if alive, as microbots finished construction of the water treatment plant.

A long, straight line ran east from the water treatment plant toward the river, where the colony would take in drinking water. A thousand Humans labored along that line, digging the ditch that would contain the water pipe. Some things microbots just couldn't do as well as Humans.

On each of the four corners of the central flat area were four large apartment blocks, just completed by the microbots. Each apartment block could provide housing for 1,500 Humans. A steady stream of people moved from the tents to the newly completed apartment blocks, dragging their meager belongs as they relocated from their temporary shelters to their new permanent homes.

In a large tent near the shuttle landing area, Mark Rodgers sat at a makeshift desk, glaring at his tablet.

"Dammit!" he cursed, staring at something on the display. He punched the tablet with his finger as if that would solve his problem.

"What?" asked Rick Moore, sitting near him at another makeshift desk.

"The damn net went down again. Why can't we keep that thing up and running?"

Rick grinned at Mark. "Because we're pioneers on a primitive planet?"

Mark grimaced. "You don't have to remind me every time something goes wrong."

Rick, smiling, reached for a walkie-talkie on his desk and punched the button.

"Luke? The net went down again. Can you check it out?"

A burst of static nearly obscured a reply, but Rick barely made out Luke's acknowledgment.

"Luke's on it, Mark. He'll get it sorted."

"Thanks, Rick," said Mark. He stood up from his desk and stretched. "Since I can't work, I'll go walk around the camp."

"Sure thing, Guv," said Rick.

"And don't call me Guv," Mark spat, as he walked out the front of the tent. Behind him, Rick grinned even wider. Needling his new boss had become his third favorite activity - after working to save Humanity, and sleeping with Zoe DeLong. He and Zoe had fallen together on the sixteen-day trip out from Stalingrad. They made no secret about their relationship - and neither did any of the other hundreds of couples who had fallen together in this stressful time.

Outside, Mark walked north, toward the inland side of the colony - a colony they had named "Landing". It wasn't all that original, but the colonists had voted, and that was the name that had stuck. So Landing it was.

In the far distance, a rugged elevation rose, the apex of the natural horseshoe of mountains that enclosed the colony. The horseshoe of mountains formed a natural protective barrier for Landing, sheltering it from the somewhat harsher environment on the other side of the mountains.

On both sides of him - east and west - the open space of Landing gave way to alien blue forest. On the west side, within two miles the open area turned into jungle, one that got thicker and thicker for two dozen miles, until it thinned out as it began to rise toward the distant mountains forming the western side of the horseshoe.

On the east side of the colony, within three miles the open space ended and another blue forest began. This one was also thick, but despite its thickness it never turned into jungle. The land stayed flat for another fifteen miles, then began to rise gently. Twenty-five miles away, the gently rising land turned into more rugged foothills and rose rapidly toward the eastern side of the mountain horseshoe.

On the far east side of the open space, he saw the men erecting the water tank. Beside them, the water treatment plant was nearly complete, only the roof still showing movement by microbots.

Turning to the west, Mark saw apartment Block Five being assembled close at hand. They had completed the first four apartment blocks ahead of schedule and decided to go ahead with the next batch - Blocks Five through Eight.

Mark paused for a moment to watch. Sure enough, if you were very still and watched carefully, you could actually see the height of the walls increasing millimeter by millimeter as the microbots worked.

"Hey, boss," said a voice. Mark turned to see Luke Powell coming up to him, walkie-talkie in one hand. "We got the net sorted. You should be back online now."

"Good. Thanks, Luke." As Luke stopped beside him, they both turned to face the opposite direction, south. South was the ocean - it could not be seen from the colony, but it was there, just twelve miles away. The long, narrow area stretching before them, with the shuttles parked in it, would be set aside as a greensward.

"People are already calling this one Central Park too," said Luke. "I guess that was inevitable."

Mark nodded absent-mindedly. "A little touch of home, at least for the Americans. Any news from the scouting teams?"

"So far, nothing bad. Still no sign of any animal life. That matches up with what the Goblins told us. We've re-tested the vegetation and it doesn't appear to be harmful in any way to Earth-based life - but at the same time, it's not edible for us. We could actually eat it without harm, but we'd gain no nutrition from it. So again, that matches up with the Goblins' initial report to us. So far so good."

"We need a crop planted, and quick," said Mark.

"Yes, sir. Working on it. In fact, the last two shuttle runs brought down seed and root stock." Luke pointed to the east, toward a distant field that had several hundred people working in it. "Turgenev's people are prepping the first fields now. He said they'll start planting some of the fast-growing crops tomorrow. With any luck at all, we'll have our first emergency food crop ready in 45 days, and a second, larger one in about three months."

Mark shot a sideways look at Luke. He had already briefed Luke about Turgenev. "Keep your eye on him. I know something's up with him. He's got allies somewhere, but I don't know where yet. But at some point, they'll try to put a knife in our backs. Be ready for it."

Luke nodded. "Wilco, Boss. We'll watch him like a hawk."

39 AU from Stree Prime
Corvette EDF *Armidale*

"Do you think this will work?" asked Rita.

"I have no idea," said Jim. "Tika says it will. But we won't know until you're on the ground."

Rita gave a half-smile.

"Or not," she said.

Jim grimaced. It was the best he could do under the circumstances.

"OK. Let's do it. I'll see you when I see you," Rita said.

And with that, she lay back into the padded contours of the bunk where her android body would remain, inert, for the duration of this first mission.

Her eyes closed. Jim had been holding her hand. He felt one last squeeze. Then she moved her hand to her breast, laid it down there, and went limp.

And with that, Rita wasn't in that body anymore. Now it was just an empty shell, waiting her return.

If she returns.

Jim knew where she was now. The love of his life was now resident in a tiny caterpillar three inches long, housed in a carrier rocket only three feet in length. A rocket that was mounted to a hardpoint on the side of the *Armidale*, along with two other rockets containing Rachel and Tika.

The love of his life was about to be launched into Stree space.

Jim knew he wouldn't be able to see anything else from Rita's cabin. He walked back to the bridge. He took a jump seat behind Captain Stewart and watched the rest of the operation on the large screen at the front.

Staring at the three tiny rockets mounted on the outside hull of the corvette, Jim started to worry. Beads of sweat formed on his brow. The magnitude of the risk for Rita and her two companions had finally fully registered in his mind.

Thinking about it beforehand had been one thing; watching the actual event was like a punch in the gut.

This was it. His wife was going to be dropped onto an enemy

base.

With a whine, the tDrive engaged and the screen went blank for less than one second - to be exact, 696 milliseconds.

And the *Armidale* surfaced in the Stree system, 15 AU from the central star. They were directly behind a large gas giant, one with dozens of thick rings. To Jim, it looked remarkably like Saturn in the Sol System. But it was far indeed from Saturn. 3,275 light years, to be exact.

With a clunk that could be felt through the hull, the three tiny rockets were released from the corvette, along with a much larger item - an item disguised to look like just another big space rock.

Jim had only an instant to watch as the three tiny rockets floated in space, free of all attachment to the corvette, alongside the much larger fake asteroid. Then with a whine, the tDrive engaged again and they were gone, back out to their hiding place in the outer system.

The *Armidale* was once again back in the outer Kuiper Belt, 3.75 billion miles from the little moon called Tosong that orbited the ringed planet. Back at Tosong, it was now all up to Rita, Tika and Rachel.

Far from the love of his life, Jim felt the sweat start on his brow. He hated the feeling of being out of control, of not being able to protect Rita. Even though Rita was now a Goblin - more than capable of taking care of herself - it was a feeling he could never overcome.

CHAPTER SIXTEEN

Stree System
Moon Tosong - Listening Station #14

Rita had practiced being resident in the tiny caterpillar infiltration device a half-dozen times. She thought she had it down pat. But this was the real thing. It was different from the practice sessions.

A mistake now meant her life.

Per the mission schedule, she waited thirty minutes in radio silence after the *Armidale* departed back to the outer system. She scanned the environment with passive sensors, noting her two companions floating nearby. Slightly farther away, the much larger support package also floated silently.

There were millions of rocks and moons making up the rings of the Saturn-like planet. The *Armidale* had placed them several hundred thousand miles from the nearest ring; precisely in the path of a moon that would soon be coming around the planet in its orbit. The location was plausible for a few stray rocks that might have escaped the nearby ring through some gravitational perturbation.

Finally the required thirty minutes of radio silence expired without event, and Rita called to her companions on low-power RF.

<Tika? Rachel? You OK?>

<I'm good> replied Tika.

<Present and accounted for> said Rachel.

<Uh. That's a relief> Rita called. <OK. Let's work the plan>

<Sending the support package> Tika said.

Rita watched on her sensors as the support package fired a tiny ion rocket to boost away, out of the path of the moon that would soon be coming around the arc of the planet. The support package would move to a safe place several thousand klicks away, where it would wait until called.

<Done. Trajectory looks nominal> called Tika.

<Outstanding. OK, let's make our position adjustments>

And with that, the three fired their own tiny rockets to adjust their orbits slightly. When they were happy with their positions, they powered down and waited.

And waited some more. They had a five hour wait before the largest moon of the gas giant caught up to them.

Rita inserted a wait loop in her timing clock and went to sleep for four hours. When she awoke, her passive sensors showed the large moon directly behind them, coming up on their position. It would just miss plowing into them - but it would pass close enough to capture them in its gravity. The three of them would be sucked into a rapidly decaying trajectory, sending them crashing to the surface of the moon.

They were back on radio silence now. Rita longed to talk to her companions, ask if they were alright. But she didn't dare.

Because on the near side of the rapidly approaching moon was a Stree observation post. It was one of many in the Stree system, always watching for Goblins - the entities the Stree hated and feared above all else.

And three Goblins were about to pay them a visit.

Phoenix System

"It's a minor setback," Cerutti said. "Not to worry."

"Minor setback?" Kim spat, angry. "You said you would take over the Security Team! But Rodgers gave that to Powell instead! And Bob Hardy is second in command! Now what?"

Cerutti leaned back and shook his head at Kim, smiling.

"So impatient! Kim, how did you become successful in the streets of Seoul if you are so impatient?"

"There I just pulled out my knife and the people did what I said," Kim replied angrily.

"Ah. Yes, of course. But this is not Seoul, and pulling out a knife on Luke Powell is only going to get you gutted like a fish. I hope you understand that."

Kim glared at Cerutti. Before he could respond again, Turgenev interrupted. "But at least you got in the Security Force," he said to Cerutti.

"Yes. I'm third in command. And soon enough, Hardy will meet with an unexpected accident. And then I'll be second in command. And after that...well, let's just say a new colony is a dangerous place."

Kim interrupted. "No! That takes too long! We must take over before the people get organized! While they are still on one foot from everything that has happened!"

"I agree," said Turgenev. "I suggest we make our move immediately. As soon as possible. Otherwise, more transport ships will arrive. We must seize power now!"

Cerutti looked troubled. "I don't know. I think that might be moving too fast. I'd rather play it slow, stick with our original plan. Work our way into position, rather than take over by brute force."

"Bullshit," said Kim. "These people are so shell-shocked, they're like cattle. There's no point in waiting; we take over now."

Cerutti saw Turgenev looking at him appraisingly. Suddenly a cold feeling ran down Cerutti's spine. He knew that look. He had seen it before.

That was the look that meant, *agree or die*. Turgenev and Kim had already decided. Either he would go along, or he would have a sudden accident.

"I agree," he said, his mouth dry. "We'll start the takeover as soon as possible."

Stree System
Moon Tosong - Listening Station #14

A few minutes after the moon caught up to them, Rita and her two companions were descending rapidly toward the surface. To any casual observer, it would appear that a few small rocks had come off the nearby ring of the gas giant, gotten caught in the moon's gravity well, and were about to smash into the surface. A common, everyday occurrence. One that should raise no eyebrows on the Stree observation station, even if they somehow managed to detect it.

But Rita's hope was that the Stree observers were focused on bigger things. If they were anything like Humans, they'd be looking for a Goblin fleet...not a few space rocks.

Soon enough, the ground was coming up fast. Rita watched the distant Stree outpost carefully. The second it went below the horizon - and thus no longer able to see her on radar - she decelerated madly, trying to break her velocity before she smashed to bits on the hard rocks below. She had only a few seconds to save herself; if her rocket sputtered at all, she was done.

But it didn't glitch. It fired exactly as planned until she came to a gentle hover ten yards off the surface of a huge boulder. Sliding sideways to a flat spot, she put down on the surface of the moon.

Automatically, the carrier rocket split in two, leaving her free to crawl out. In her tiny caterpillar aspect, she quickly moved a dozen yards away from the rocket and stopped to take stock.

Twenty yards away she could see Tika's carrier, lying on the surface in one piece. Even as she watched, it also split, and Tika crawled out.

But there was no sign of Rachel. Using a low power radio pulse, one that couldn't be heard for more than a few hundred yards, she called for her.

<Rachel? Are you OK?>

There was a short silence. Then:

<Yes, dammit. I landed in a methane pool. I'm trying to

work my way out of it>

Rita looked around and saw a small methane pool nearby. Even as she watched, the tiny caterpillar that was Rachel broke the surface and crawled out of the pool. It made its way toward Rita as they regrouped.

<I have this instinctive need to shake myself> said Rachel, as the methane dripped off her.

Rita chuckled. She knew exactly what Rita meant. Something that only a Human who had lived around dogs could understand.

<We'd better get moving> Rita said. "Thataway, ho!>

And with that, she set out for the distant Stree station, now just over the horizon from them. In their three-inch caterpillar aspects, it would be a long walk.

Hours later, the trio reached the perimeter of the Stree station. There was a large central building, with a tall tower going straight up for 500 feet. Rita knew that was the primary sensing station, containing radar, lidar and laser detection equipment, as well as any number of passive sensors and comm arrays. There was another, identical tower on the far side of the moon, operated remotely, to give the Stree 24x7 sensing capability.

From the main building, three covered tunnels splayed out in three separate directions. Each ran a short distance and terminated in a round, bubble shaped dome.

Hajo's Goblin intelligence team had stated one of these outlying domes contained living quarters for the crew. Another one contained storage space. And the last one contained the life support systems.

Per plan, they were now directly opposite the life support dome.

<They'll have proximity alarms> said Tika.

<Roger that. Time to start digging> Rita replied. The three separated by several feet from each other. Then their caterpillar aspects dug down, burrowing into the regolith. Although not tightly packed, it was slow going. It took them

another 90 minutes to advance twenty yards underground, past the Stree perimeter.

When Rita surfaced, she found herself just outside the life support dome, right at the point where the dome intersected with the tunnel leading back to the control room. Tika was already there, waiting for her. A few minutes later, Rachel surfaced from the regolith.

Now they separated. While Rita and Rachel moved to the life support dome, Tika headed for the main building.

Slowly and carefully, Rita and Rachel moved up to the dome wall. There, they once again dug down into the regolith. Reaching a point one foot under the floor of the dome, they dug forward three feet and then angled upward until they reached the sealed floor of the dome.

They knew that if these structures were anything like most Human or Goblin space structures, the weakest point would be underneath. Since the regolith supported the building, only a thin, airtight shield of composite sandwich was necessary to form the floor of the structure.

Here's hoping we're right, thought Rita.

Boring into the bottom of the structure from underneath, Rita worked for a half-hour trying to make a small hole in the floor of the dome. At one point, she decided it wasn't going to work. She was just about to call to the others to abandon the attempt when suddenly, there was a slight, high-pitched hissing sound as pressure escaped through the hole, and she knew she had made it.

<I'm through> she called to Rachel on low power RF.

<Fantastic!> said Rachel.

Rita continued to work, enlarging the hole until it was big enough for her to pass through. When it was, she wiggled her way up through it and was in the life support dome.

Quickly she looked around, assessing. They had chosen their timing to arrive in the middle of the night - midnight, Stree time - and it seemed to have panned out. The room was pitch-black. No one was about.

Rita heard a slight crunch and Rachel's caterpillar head poked up out of the floor nearby. Crumbs of composite fell off her as she wiggled her way out of the hole she had made.

<Nobody about?> Rachel asked.

<No. I don't sense anyone> replied Rita.

The two of them scanned the room in infrared and radar. It was clearly life support. Machinery stood everywhere. Most things Rita could identify - a small nuclear reactor, oxygen generators, carbon dioxide scrubbers, rack after rack of emergency oxygen tanks.

Now the next phase of the plan began.

<Rachel. Alarm systems> called Rita.

<On it> answered Rachel. She immediately moved to an electronics panel and began assessing it.

<Tika. How's it going?>

<I'm in the main building, moving to the communications closet. Everything is as we expected - a skeleton crew is on duty, and most of them are half-asleep. I could drive a truck through here before they'd notice anything>

<Roger that. We're standing by>

Having issued her reminder commands, Rita moved to the oxygen system. Her job was to disable the oxygen supply to the other buildings. If Rachel did her job correctly, no alarms would sound. By removing the oxygen from the station, the entire crew of the station would fall unconscious. Tika would disable the comm systems beforehand, ensuring that no warning could go out, even if one of the Stree realized what was happening at the last minute and tried to call home.

<In position> called Tika. <Ready>

Rita turned her focus to Rachel.

<How's it going, Rachel?>

<Still checking to make sure I got all of them> said Rachel.

<Take your time, Rach. We can't afford a mistake now>

<Roger that>

Rachel checked her alarm systems one last time, then called to Rita.

<Ready. All alarms disabled>

<Tika?>

<Ready. All communications blocked>

<OK, then. Here we go>

Rita turned off the oxygen system. She opened the emergency vent system in each building to space.

The Stree in the station had three minutes to live.

CHAPTER SEVENTEEN

Stree System
Moon Tosong - Listening Station #14

Someone was pounding on the door of the life support module. The sound was diminishing, though. It got weaker and weaker, changing from a pounding to a scrabbling sound.

Finally it went away.

Rita looked over at Rachel.

<Someone figured it out> Rita said.

<But too late> replied Rachel.

<Tika? Any activity?>

<None. They're all dead> called Tika. <I'm looking for the door controls>

<Roger>

<Oh, here they are. I found them, I think. Let me see...>

With a clunk, the hatch of the life support dome clicked open.

<Got them figured out. You're cleared through>

Rita and Rachel scurried to the hatch, slipped through the crack, and exited out to the tunnel leading to the main structure.

The body of a dead Stree was lying on the floor. His hands were bloody where he had scraped at the door in one last-ditch attempt to survive. To Rita and Rachel in their tiny caterpillar bodies, he looked twenty feet long. Rita couldn't help but think of the old fairy tale of Jack and the Beanstalk.

Ignoring him, they ran at maximum speed toward the main control room. Arriving there, they found a room that seemed as big as a football pitch to them in their tiny aspects. Huge chairs and consoles seemed to reach to the sky. Stree bodies lay everywhere. Tika was nowhere to be seen.

<Tika? Where are you?>

<Up here on the comm console>

They looked up. Peeking over the top of a counter top was Tika's head, looking tiny compared to the size of the console.

<Come on up, the weather's fine!> Tika said.

Rita and Rachel made their way to a nearby chair, climbed up the legs, up the armrests, and jumped to the console where Tika waited.

<We ready to call in the support package?>

<Roger. I re-connected the dish, re-enabled the comm console, and pointed the dish back toward our package. We're ready to transmit>

<And you're sure the power levels are just high enough to reach our package?>

<Yep. I checked, double checked and triple checked. Power is set to the absolute minimum required to signal the package>

<OK. Let's bring it in>

Tika turned to the console and leaned on a button. With a click, it depressed. Twenty thousand klicks away, their support package received the signal. It turned, oriented itself toward the distant moon, and fired its thrusters.

A short while later, the support package had chased down the moon in its orbit and made a soft landing just beside the Stree station. Rita, Tika and Rachel were waiting for it. They moved quickly to the lander and with a sigh of relief, switched back into full-size caterpillar aspects stored inside the lander.

<God, am I glad to get out of that tiny thing!> exclaimed Rachel.

<Myself> echoed Rita.

<OK. Let's get the oxygen system back in operation, double-check all life support, and call in the guys!>

Phoenix System

800 Lights from Stalingrad

Luke was exhausted. It had been a long day. He had spent most of it settling minor disputes between people.

It seemed that in spite of all their planning and organization, they had overlooked one important aspect of government - a judiciary.

The Council members - and Mark as Governor - were strong on executive action. They could plan, organize, and issue orders with no problem. But they had not foreseen the number of disputes that would arise between people and groups.

Carving out a new colony on a raw planet was causing extreme stress among the settlers. Fights were becoming a daily occurrence. People were organizing into cliques, bands, even gangs. Luke's security team had their hands full. Just to maintain the peace, he was recruiting new members every day to add to his police force.

And Luke had somehow become a *de facto* judge. Dispute after dispute was brought to his desk to be settled. He'd been forced to set up his courtroom in another tent, to prevent disruption to Mark and the other Council members as shouting groups of settlers were brought in front of him, each group proclaiming the rightness of their side of things at the top of their lungs.

Today he had spent his entire day settling such disputes. People fighting over everything imaginable. Couples fighting over the things couples have fought over for ten thousand years. Disagreements over where people should live. People who refused to work. People attacking those who refused to work, instead of referring them to Security. Fistfights over women. Two knife attacks, as settlers found ways to turn necessary tools into weapons.

And of course, the age-old crimes that hung like millstones around the necks of humanity. Today Luke had also conducted criminal trials for two robberies and a rape. He did it because there was no one else to do it. Everyone else on the Council was busy trying to keep the colony alive, handling food, water, and shelter. Luke had somehow, and against his will, become the Supreme Court of the colony.

As he wrapped up the last case of the day, he felt the burden of his role weighing heavy on his shoulders. This last case had been the rape of a young girl. The perpetrator had been caught red-handed. The evidence was overwhelming. Luke had quickly declared the man guilty.

But then it came time for sentencing. The girl's family howled for the man to be put to death - to be hung from one of the tall blue trees down by the river as an example to all. It took every one of Luke's newly appointed court bailiffs to hold back the crowd while the prisoner was hustled out of the court and into the jail - a jail they had not expected to need so soon, one hastily constructed just within the last week.

Now Luke was faced with a dilemma. He had always opposed the death penalty. Throughout his life, he had never understood how two wrongs were somehow supposed to add up to justice.

Yet the small colony had no prison. There were no resources to house and feed prisoners for any length of time. It was something they had simply not thought of in their planning process. Keeping prisoners would tie up valuable resources needed for their survival.

Wrestling with the problem, Luke stepped out of the tent to see his daughter Tatiana coming toward him. He waved at her, and she turned and came over to him.

"Hi, Pop," she called. "How goes the new job?"

Luke gave her a face. "It sucks. Actually, I'd like to talk to you about it if you have time."

"Sure," she said. "Let's grab dinner at the commissary and you can tell me all about it."

They made their way to the cafeteria, grabbing pseudo-plastic trays and wending their way through a long line to get their food. The food trays, like everything else made locally in the colony so far, was some kind of carbon compound - it was the easiest thing for the microbots to generate directly from the soil and the atmosphere.

Sitting down at a table, Luke looked at his daughter as they began eating.

"How's my granddaughter?" he asked.

"She's fine, happy as a clam," said Tatiana. "She doesn't know we're in a dire situation - every day is an adventure for her."

"Yeah. Nice to be a child if you have to go through this. I hear Misha and some of the other dads have got a day-care thing going."

"Yeah. There's quite a few single parents with small children who have to work away from home. Doc Winston, for example. She's our most experienced doctor. She set up the hospital in Block Five, and she's supervising the setup of small clinics in some of the other apartment blocks. But she also has two small children. There's dozens of other people in similar situations. So Misha and some of the other people got together and organized a day-care system. Now every apartment block has a day-care. Misha goes around from one to another all day long, checking on things, working out bugs, ensuring that the workers are doing a good job. Marta tags along with him and she just loves it. She thinks she's the one in charge. She goes running into every day-care ahead of Misha and starts giving the staff the third degree."

Luke grinned. "That's my granddaughter, alright."

Tatiana pursed her lips.

"So. What did you want to talk to me about?"

"Well," Luke began, then paused. "It's a bit of a tough issue."

"Spit it out, Dad," Tatiana said. "Don't stand on ceremony."

"Well. We have a convicted rapist in the jail right now. He raped a little girl. The family wants the death penalty. They're howling for blood. Tomorrow morning I have to pronounce sentence. If I don't sentence him to death, there's gonna be trouble."

Tatiana looked at her father across the table. She was well

aware of his feelings toward the death penalty.

"You don't want to kill him, do you?" she asked.

"I think it sets a bad precedent. If I sentence this first one to death, the floodgates are opened. Soon enough, people will demand the death penalty for more and more crimes. It's a slippery slope. Like in the Old West, when they killed people for stealing a horse, or in the Middle East when they stoned women to death for adultery. I don't want our new society to end up like that."

"But?"

"But we have no facilities to keep a prisoner. I have no intention of wasting our precious resources to build a prison and staff it to keep criminals. We simply don't have that luxury."

"So what do you propose?"

"I don't know. That's why I wanted to talk to you. I thought maybe you might have some idea."

"Actually, I do. Something you may not have thought of yet."

"What?"

"Have you ever talked to Tika about the Goblin approach to capital crimes?"

"No. The subject never came up, I guess. I didn't even realize the Goblins had criminals."

"Not many. Their incidence of crime is about one ten-thousandth of what Humans experience. But still, they have a few. And some of them are what we might call capital crimes."

"So what do they do with them?"

"They sentence them to become a ship AI. They get loaded into a starship brain and aren't allowed to return to android form and re-join society for one thousand years."

"Wow. That's a long time."

"Well, yeah. But not if you're an AI."

"So. Do you think the Goblins would do that for us?

"Sure. Send him back to Stalingrad on the next return transport. Have the Goblins convert him to an AI. He can drive a starship for them for the next thousand years. Then we'll see how he feels about attacking little girls."

"Assuming Humans are still around in a thousand years."

"Yeah. There is that."

39 AU from Stree Prime
Corvette EDF *Armidale*

Two hours after Tika transmitted the signal, it arrived at the *Armidale*, 25 AU farther out in the system. Jim had been trying to get some sleep, but it was nearly impossible. He would drop off, then suddenly wake in a sweat, convinced that Rita had been captured and killed.

When the call from Captain Stewart came over his comm, he almost collapsed in relief.

"We have the recall signal, Commander."

Jim heaved a sigh of relief. "On my way, Captain," he answered. He threw himself into his warsuit and rushed to the bridge, settling into the jump seat behind Captain Stewart.

"Any problems?"

"No, they transmitted the coded pulse for A-OK. Looks like they pulled it off. We're just about ready to go in."

Jim nodded. In the holotank, he could see their position, 25 AU opposite the ringed gas giant that was their target.

"All systems ready for translation, Skipper," called the XO.

"Good. Let's do it," Stewart said.

The tDrive engaged with its typical whine, and a second later, they were nestled up against the backside of the gas giant, just outside the ring system. Approaching in the near distance was the large moon Tosong, with the Stree space station clearly visible on the surface facing them.

"Comm from the Stree station, Captain."

"Read it, please."

'Welcome and please put down directly beside the main building to the west. We'll rejoin you on board.'

"Very good, XO. Lieutenant Hodges, put us down right there

in that little flat spot to the west."

"Aye, Skipper." Hodges deftly settled the *Armidale* down on her landing jacks in a small flat area beside the Stree station. As the *Armidale* came to a halt on the surface, Jim jumped from his seat and practically ran to Rita's cabin. As he entered, the status lights on the walls changed from red to yellow, and he heard the status change announced over his comm.

"Set Condition Yellow. Set Condition Yellow. That is all."

At the same time, Rita's android body opened her eyes in her bunk and smiled. She winked at Jim.

"Hello there, big boy," she said. "Why don't you come up and see me sometime...?"

"Welcome back, babe," Jim breathed.

Phoenix System
800 Lights from Stalingrad

Luke's second-in-command on the Security team was Bob Hardy. Hardy had been keeping a close eye on Turgenev - to the best of his ability. But there were many tasks for him to perform, and many crises for him to deal with. He couldn't be everywhere at once. Thus he had missed the secret meetings that occurred between Turgenev, Cerutti and Kim.

That turned out to be a fatal mistake.

It was well after midnight, and Hardy was just about to go to bed. But the call came in over the radio - a riot in Apartment Block Four. Despite their dire situation on a new planet, despite their priorities of generating enough food and water to survive, people still found ways to fight. When the call came in over the walkie-talkie, Hardy rushed to the apartment block to assess the situation and assist his meager security team.

It was an ambush. As he ran into the lobby of the apartment block, Hardy was hit with a stun gun. Falling to the floor, he saw his own assistant on the Security team - Cerutti - leering over him. Cerutti's hand contained a large knife. With a twisted smile, Cerutti slammed the knife down into him, over and over, until the universe no longer existed for Bob Hardy.

Stree System
Moon Tosong - Listening Station #14

Huddling in *Armidale*'s galley for debriefing, Rita, Tika and Rachel sat across from the senior Goblin Intelligence officer, Commander Hajo. Beside them, Jim, Ollie, Bonnie, and Captain Stewart listened as they finished up their description of the mission.

"It went pretty much as we hoped," Rita recounted. "One of them managed to figure out what was going on and even got to the hatch of the life support module, but he wasn't able to get in. After that, everything went per plan."

"Good," Hajo said. "OK. Next steps are underway. My Goblin Intelligence team has set up shop in the station. They're going through the comm logs. We have five hours until the next routine check-in. By then, we should have the system figured out well enough to send in the next report without causing suspicion."

"So. We have a foothold in their system now," said Stewart.

"Right," Hajo agreed. "This will be our base of operations from here on in. We're ready for Phase Two."

Rachel bowed her head and scratched her forehead - a gesture that Jim recognized as a reflex action from her Human life, as androids didn't itch. He had seen it before, and he knew it meant she was thinking hard.

"I'm not totally sold on this next step," she said. "I've been thinking about it, and it seems to me we're moving too fast. The original plan was to next take a small outpost somewhere on the backside of Stree Prime. Now you're telling me you have a better plan. Are you sure about this?"

Jim, sitting across from her, glanced at Hajo, and then spoke before Hajo could reply.

"I've gone over this with Hajo, and I think his new approach is a much better plan. I think we were lucky to pull this station caper off the first time. I wouldn't want to try it again. There's such a thing as pushing your luck. Let's go with Hajo's modification."

Rachel looked askance at Jim, but she acquiesced. "OK, Mr. Marine. You're the expert," she said rather sarcastically.

Jim gave her a fake glare. "Keep it up, sister, and I'll put you over my knee."

Rachel laughed. "You couldn't even lift me up, buster."

Jim rose and walked around the table to Rachel, accepting the challenge. With a huge grin, Rachel rose, ready for the test. Jim grabbed her around the waist and attempted to lift her. He was initially unsuccessful; he paused, looked at her in puzzlement, then tried again. With a grunt, he lifted her off the deck by a few inches. Putting her back down, he shook his head in wonder.

"How much do you weigh now?"

"81 kilos. Right at 180 pounds."

"Damn. You've grown, little girl."

Ollie laughed at Jim's expression. "She's a tad bit heavier than she was before," he said.

"I would say," Jim remarked, returning to his seat. The interlude had lightened the mood all around the table as Hajo continued.

"OK. Phase Two. We're going to skip right over the part about capturing an outpost and go straight to infiltrating Central Command. My intelligence team has identified our best target. One Sub-Captain Elvenen, to be precise.

"Elvenen has just received orders to transfer from a little mountain listening post on the backside of Stree Prime to Command Headquarters at Komihu, their capital city. He's taking his adjutant and aide with him. They're to report day after tomorrow, Stree time."

Hajo looked across the table at Rita, Tika and Rachel. "That gives us just enough time to map out the details, get you three to their base, and do the exchange. He's the perfect patsy; he's an Intelligence officer, he's single with no apparent family entanglements, he's being transferred from a remote, isolated base back to Headquarters, and he's a communications specialist. What's even better, he's being promoted to full Captain upon his arrival at Headquarters. It's damn near perfect."

"But do we have to switch into male officers?" asked Rachel. "That scares the hell out of me!"

Hajo nodded. "Sorry. But it's a male-dominated hierarchy. There are no female officers in the Stree military. There are a few in the enlisted ranks, but that wouldn't help us."

Rachel hunched her shoulders in a near-shudder. "I'm not happy about this," she said.

Rita reached across and patted her hand. "Relax, Rachel. I've been there before. It's not that bad."

Jim grinned across the table at them. "You'll get used to it quick enough, Rachel. Just remember not to get kicked in the crotch."

Jim and Ollie snickered as Rachel blushed. Hajo looked puzzled, but finally smiled and continued the briefing.

"You'll depart early tomorrow. The cargo is already loaded onboard the shuttle. Lieutenant Luda will be the bodybuilder technician. I'll be your pilot. We'll time it to arrive at 1600 tomorrow afternoon Stree time, an hour before they quit for the day. With any luck, most of the staff will depart early and we'll have the place to ourselves."

"Except for Captain Elvenen," said Rita.

"Right. We've arranged a fake meeting - we set up an appointment for him at 1600 hours tomorrow to receive a classified briefing on his new posting at Headquarters. That should hold him in his office until we arrive. No way he would skip that kind of meeting."

"We hope," said Rachel.

"Yes. Exactly."

CHAPTER EIGHTEEN

Phoenix System
800 Lights from Stalingrad

Luke Powell sat at his desk in the Headquarters tent, head in hand. Bob Hardy had been a good friend. Luke was devastated by his murder. Beside him, Dino Cerutti sat quietly as Luke processed the situation.

"Still no idea who did it?" Luke asked.

"No, sir," Cerutti replied. "There were no witnesses. The security cameras in the lobby had been disabled. So far, we have nothing to go on. I've got my team canvassing the residents of the apartment block, but so far nothing."

Luke sighed. "Keep at it, Dino. We have to get to the bottom of this. This was a planned attack - not an accident."

"Yes, sir. I'll keep my team on it until we figure it out."

Luke turned his head toward Cerutti, hesitating. Then he came to some kind of decision.

"I'd better bring you into something, Dino," he said. "Turgenev. He's ex-Russian mafia. Hardy had been assigned to watch him, watch his contacts. We suspect he's hooked up with some of the Koreans in Block Two. We don't have any hard evidence yet, though. I need you to take over that surveillance. We need to find out what he's up to, and soon."

Cerutti nodded emphatically. "You got it, boss. I'll get on it. We'll figure it out."

"Thanks, Dino," Luke responded. "I'll see you later."

With a final nod, Cerutti rose and left, leaving Luke alone in grief. As he departed the Headquarters tent, Mark Rodgers came in, carrying two small bags. He handed one to Luke.

"Breakfast," he said. "I assume you've been up all night?"

Luke nodded sadly. "Yeah. Thanks, boss."

"Any leads?"

"No," Luke said. "Not a clue. But it has to be Turgenev. Who else could it be?"

"Any evidence? Anything we can pin on him?"

"No. It was a very professional hit."

"So what's next?"

"Dino's on it. He'll handle the investigation and take over the surveillance of Turgenev."

"Hmm… Do you trust him?"

Luke looked up at his boss.

"What do you mean?"

"Dino. He's from New York City, right?"

"Yeah, I think so…"

"Well. Just saying. New York was a rough town. And Dino has some pretty rough edges. He's pretty smooth with us, but I've heard some talk. He's got a different face when he's out in the ville. Pretty coarse with the people. Shoving people around."

"Really? I haven't heard that."

"Just saying. Keep an eye on him in that regard."

"I will," said Luke.

Mark sat at his desk, opened the bag containing his breakfast, and started eating. Luke joined him, and they two sat quietly for a bit, thinking. The front tent flap opened and Zoe DeLong entered, followed closely by Rick Moore. They greeted Mark and Luke and moved to their desks.

"Any word from Bonnie?" Mark asked Luke.

"Nothing for a couple of days," Luke replied. "Last ansible message stated they were on schedule and on plan. That's all she said."

"Fingers crossed," Zoe said with a smile.

Luke acknowledged her comment with a smile. "Yep, absolutely."

"Zoe," Mark said, turning to her. "I guess you heard about Bob Hardy last night."

"Yes, I did. I'm so sorry," Zoe said, glancing over at Luke. "Any progress on the investigation?"

"Nothing so far," Luke said. "But we should tighten up security for the Council members. I don't think this is an isolated incident."

Mark jumped in.

"He means this could be the first step in a coup. Let's plan accordingly," said Mark.

"A coup?" asked Rick. "You've got to be kidding, right? Who would try something like that while we're fighting for our very survival here?"

Mark looked grim. "That's exactly when they would try, Rick. When things are at their most precarious."

"Let's double the security team for the Council," said Luke to Zoe.

"OK," Zoe responded. "If you say so."

"I think it wise," said Luke. "I'll assign another six people to you."

Mark picked up the conversation, turning his attention to Zoe.

"Now...moving on. How's Transport Four going?"

"It arrived from Stalingrad at four AM this morning, and we started shuttles at five. We've gotten thirty loads down so far, running all ten original shuttles plus the four new ones Transport Two brought us. We're focusing on passengers first, getting them down and settled into Blocks Thirteen through Sixteen. We'll bring the cargo down last - there's nothing on the cargo manifest we need urgently."

"And Transport Three?"

"Departed back to Stalingrad yesterday. Transport Five is enroute. Everything is on schedule at the moment."

"Excellent. What's our total population now?"

"With Transport Four, we'll have 12,000 people on the ground by the end of this week."

"Wow. It's getting a little scary, huh? Rick, what's the farming status?"

"So far, we've got 1,500 acres of grass for cattle planted across the river to the east. It's coming up well, things look good over there. The grass seems to like the planet. On the crop side, we've got 3,000 acres planted in vegetables, and another 3,000 being planted in wheat right now. Turgenev may be a son of a bitch, but he knows how to motivate people. He's getting the job done."

Mark grunted. "But...that's not nearly enough for the full population, right?"

"Right," replied Rick. "We'll need another 8,000 acres of grass across the river for livestock, and another 8,000 acres of farmland on the east side. So we're not even half-way yet."

"Do we have enough food to make it?"

"Barely, if the rest of the Goblin transports get here on time. Assuming they all arrive before the Stree attack, and all the food is on board, and we don't lose any bringing it down from orbit, and we don't lose any in the warehouses, and we don't lose any crops, and the in-vitro cattle grow on schedule, and the cattle can eat the transplanted grass, and Turgenev can keep people motivated..."

"I get the idea," Mark grunted. "Just keep on top of things, Rick. Our lives are on the line here."

"I know, Guv."

"And don't call me Guv," Mark sighed.

Stree Prime
Stree Shuttle 868

The Stree shuttle the team had liberated from the Tosong listening station was not large. It had just enough room for a flight crew of two, and either fourteen people in the back or 80,000 pounds of cargo. It was lightly loaded at the moment - with Hajo and Rachel in the cockpit, 2,000 pounds of crates and equipment in the back, and Rita, Ollie, Tika, Luda, and

Liwa sitting in fold-out jump seats beside the cargo.

If everything went as planned, they had all they needed.

If everything goes right, thought Rachel. *So many things can go wrong.*

On approach to Stree Prime, they were challenged by Approach Control.

"Now we find out if the entry codes are still valid," said Rachel in the cockpit. She leaned forward and triggered the transponder. Seconds went by with no response.

"Oh, crap," she said.

Then: "Shuttle 868 cleared for approach. Have a good day," came over the radio.

Rachel nodded in relief to Hajo, who continued their approach to Stree Prime. Their target was on the opposite side of the planet from the Stree capital city of Komihu. Nestled in a mountain range that stretched for 4,000 miles across the backside of the planet, it was a backwater area where they were reasonably certain they could pull off the next phase of their mission.

Entering the atmosphere, the shuttle buffeted a bit before it settled down to stable atmospheric flying. Soon they were over the curve of the planet, hidden from the capital city. In another half-hour, they were on approach to the small spaceport that was their destination.

The spaceport was mostly deserted. Most of the crew who worked at this small facility would already be gone, headed out for the day. There were a couple of small shuttles parked on the apron, and that was it. There wasn't a Stree in sight anywhere.

Gently, Hajo hovered the shuttle and moved it to a parking spot, put it down on the skids, and shut off the engines.

"Showtime," Tika said in the back. Unbuckling, Tika, Luda and Rita walked to the back of the shuttle. Rachel came out of the cockpit and stood, staring, as the three prepared to leave.

The seven of them had switched to the spare Stree bodies they had brought from Stalingrad. The bodies were humanoid, short and squat. A small thatch of hair at the very top of their heads splayed in all directions, unmanaged as was the custom. Their faces were rounder than a Human's, but otherwise quite similar. Compared to a Human's, their nose was angular, almost square.

Upon first seeing a hologram of a Stree, Rita had remarked that they looked like short, fat Buddhist monks.

"In fact," she had added, gazing at the hologram, "they remind me of that Great Buddha statue at Kamakura, Japan."

Now Rachel stared at the three Goblins preparing to depart the shuttle in their Stree bodies, and realized that Rita had been correct about the Stree looking like little fat Buddhas.

"All you guys need are yellow robes, a tambourine and a drum," she said.

Tika and Luda looked puzzled. Rita laughed. "Never mind. Inside joke," she said.

Tika grinned, a strange sight in her Stree body. She was wearing the uniform of a Stree Navy commander, while Rita and Luda were dressed as Stree Navy lieutenants. Rita and Luda carried large cases.

Tika gave Rachel one final wink.

"If all goes well, you'll hear from us soon," she said.

The three opened the exit hatch and stepped out toward the nearby Naval communications complex and listening station.

"Looks like we guessed right," said Rita. "This place is nearly deserted."

"Right. Here we go, then," said Tika as they approached the building. She gave one final smile to Rita.

"Now we find out if our bodies and speech pass the test," she said.

"Right."

Entering the building, they approached the security desk. A short, squat Stree male stood behind the counter, watching them approach.

"Good afternoon," he said. "Can I help you?"

"Commander Pamasa to see Sub-Captain Elvenen," spoke Tika. "We have an appointment."

Phoenix System
800 Lights from Stalingrad

"OK, you got rid of Hardy. Why didn't you take out Luke Powell at the same time?" asked Turgenev. "You're dithering around like an old woman!"

Cerutti glared at the Russian. "I do things my own way. Don't rush me. Rushing is how mistakes are made."

"Bullshit," said Turgenev. "We've got the upper hand here. Powell put you in charge of the investigation! They don't suspect a thing! Just kill him and let's get on with it!"

Cerutti shook his head. "You're overconfident, Turgenev. There are still things that could go wrong. Remember - the Council has tremendous support with the people, at least so far. If we don't do this carefully, we'll end up hanging from one of those alien trees down by the river."

Turgenev shook his head. "You're an old woman, Cerutti. Why don't you let me take over that part of it? I can have Powell dead and buried before the next transport ship arrives!"

"No. I'll take care of it. This week. He'll have an accident this week. Just stay off my back, let me do things my own way," Cerutti argued.

Even though they were in a secure location, Cerutti instinctively looked around to see if anyone was listening. It was just before midnight. They were standing in one of the small tents that housed farming implements. Two of Cerutti's men and two of Turgenev's men were standing guard outside. There was no danger of eavesdropping. But Cerutti was still nervous.

With a disgusted wave of his hand, Turgenev turned and left. Cerutti stepped out of the tent and watched as Turgenev disappeared into the night toward his apartment block.

Maybe Luke Powell is not the only one, thought Cerutti. *I think another accident may happen very soon.*

***

Zoe had been watching Cerutti all evening. Instincts

developed over a lifetime of living in the slums of Chicago, and fighting in the hills of Africa, had told her something wasn't right about Cerutti. Without Luke's knowledge, she had tailed him all afternoon, and even as the dusk turned to darkness. As the hours wore on, she stuck with him. She knew he would slip up sooner or later.

And finally he did. She watched as he left for the east side of the colony, two guards in tow. She followed from a discreet distance as he went on a roundabout circuit through the camp, clearly checking to see if he was being followed. And she watched as he finally entered a small tent where she knew farming tools were kept.

Ten minutes later, Turgenev showed up and joined him. She didn't try to get close enough to hear their conversation; she didn't have to. There was only one thing they could be discussing.

Fifteen minutes later, Zoe watched as Turgenev came out of the tent. He waved to his two guards and they fell in behind him as he departed.

And then Dino Cerutti came out of the tent and stood, silent, watching the Russian stalk away. Zoe watched Cerutti wave at his guards and start back toward the west side of Landing toward his quarters.

Zoe didn't follow; she knew all she needed at this point.

Cerutti's dirty. And he's in with Turgenev.

Luke's going to be extremely interested in this.

Then she heard a rustle behind her. She had just enough time to turn her head and see a dark form.

A tremendous blow hit her in the head, and everything went dark.

CHAPTER NINETEEN

Stree Prime
Stree Listening Station #144

Rita sat in Sub-Captain Elvenen's office chair, smiling at him as he lay on the floor beside her, trussed up like a pig ready for slaughter. Luda sat on his chest, holding him in place. His grunts through his gag had finally died away as he glared at Rita with utter hatred in his eyes. Beside him, Tika stood, holding one of the large cases they had brought into the building. On the floor in front of the desk, Elvenen's adjutant and aide lay unconscious.

Rita looked at Tika.

"Have at him, guys," she said. Tika knelt down, opened the case, and took out a metallic helmet covered in microcircuits. Elvenen jerked violently as Luda reached up and grabbed his head, holding it in place. Tika pushed the helmet over his head, winking at him as she did so. She pushed a button on the side of the helmet, and Elvenen went limp.

Luda moved to the open case beside Tika and checked some dials inside. "Connection is good, scan is starting."

Rita stood and walked over to the window. It was a severe clear day - the blue of the sky was remarkably like Earth, and Rita felt a tremendous pang of homesickness for her native planet. Looking out at the distant mountains, she decided they reminded her of the Sierra Nevada mountains of California. With some surprise, she realized she had never seen the Sierra Nevada - it was one of Bonnie's memories that was coming to the fore. Even after all these years, she was still sometimes surprised by the phenomenon of remembering things she had never personally experienced - wayward memories from Jim or Bonnie, loaded into her brain when she was cloned.

The thought of Jim and Bonnie brought another pang of nostalgia and loneliness. For several seconds, she allowed her mind to go to a place she rarely permitted - she let Bonnie's memories take control. In those few seconds, she became Bonnie. It was easy to do. All of Bonnie's knowledge, memories and emotions were still there in her brain. All she had to do was relax and let them come to the fore, and she was Bonnie. It was a strange, but somewhat liberating feeling.

As Bonnie, she remembered the day when she had fallen in love with Jim - the wonderful days and nights they had together before Rita was created. And she felt, deep in her gut, what Bonnie had lost when Rita had taken Jim away from her.

A tear rolled out of her eye. She kept her head averted from the others as she dabbed it away. Quickly she returned to her own true self, to Rita, and pushed Bonnie's memories and emotions back into the recesses of her mind. She re-focused on the distant mountains, trying to stabilize her emotions.

"God, it's beautiful out there," said Rita. "How can a species with a planet this beautiful make war on everyone else?"

"One has nothing to do with the other," said Luda. "The planet may be beautiful, but the people are ugly. Warped. Perverted."

Rita nodded. "True."

A beep came from the helmet. Luda checked his dials and smiled up at Rita. "Scan complete. Are you ready for transfer?"

"Ready," said Rita. She returned to the chair and leaned back. As she closed her eyes, Luda transferred a copy of Elvenen's consciousness into a read-only spot in Rita's extended memory. After a few seconds, Rita opened her eyes again.

"Got the installation command codes side-loaded," she said. "But God, what a pervert! I'm going to take great pleasure in whacking this asshole's scan as soon as I get the chance!"

Stree Prime
Stree Listening Station #144

Grunting, Stree Private Taclayo pushed the long, heavy crate out of the shuttle cargo bay onto the forklift. When he had it positioned safely, he wiped his brow and looked over at Corporal Cetnexi in the driver's seat of the forklift.

"What the hell are we doing?" he asked.

"I have no fucking idea," Cetnexi said. "Sub-Captain Elvenen sent an order for us to fetch these crates to the storage area, so we fetch the crates to the storage area."

Taclayo nodded. "Yeah, OK. It all pays the same, right?"

"You got it," replied Cetnexi. Reversing the forklift expertly, he turned and headed for the back of the building, with Taclayo walking behind. Reaching the rear, Taclayo opened the large door into the storage area and stepped aside as Cetnexi carefully drove the forklift inside. Cetnexi lowered the big crate to the floor, backed the forklift off to one side, and shut it down.

"Done," he said. "That's the last one. I'm outta here."

"I'm with you," said Taclayo. "Let's get changed and into town before Elvenen finds something else for us to do."

As the two Stree left, closing the outside door behind them, Luda stepped out of the shadows in the corner of the storage area. He moved to the large crate and started unpacking it. Fifteen minutes later, he had removed all the framing and packing materials around the bodybuilder. With a silent radio signal to Rita, he waited for the next step.

Phoenix System
800 Lights from Stalingrad

Rick Moore knew something was wrong. Zoe had told him she had something to do, but she would return by 1 or 2 AM at the latest.

So when 2 AM came and went, he knew she was in trouble.

He called her on her portable radio, but there was no answer. He got up, dressed, and went out, roaming around the camp looking for her. There was no sign of her. Periodically, he called on the radio, but no response was forthcoming.

By 3 AM, he was becoming seriously concerned. He didn't know what she had planned to do - she had not confided in him - but he knew Zoe. He knew it had to be something to do with Turgenev. He knew Mark Rodgers and Luke Powell were both suspicious of the Russian. And Bob Hardy had just been killed by persons unknown. He had overheard Mark and Luke discussing it, and Turgenev's name had been mentioned. He was sure Zoe had overheard the same conversation as she came into the headquarters tent.

And Rick knew how her mind worked. Although she had other duties, she saw herself as the prime protector of the Governor and the Council. If she thought something was a threat to them, she would be all over it.

So it had to be Turgenev. In some form, she was investigating him. Rick was sure of it.

But where? Where would she be?

Running back to the headquarters tent, Rick entered and ran to a locker. Unlocking it, he took out a drone and checked the battery. It was fully charged. Grabbing a controller, he ran outside toward the east side of the colony. He jogged across the wide expanse of green that had been named Central Park, until he came to the shuttle landing zone. Several shuttles were parked, silent in the night, dew gathering on their exposed surfaces. Rick moved into position behind one and paused, looking across the park. On the other side, between the park and the open fields, was a large tent - Turgenev's headquarters for management of fields and pastures. As he expected, the tent was dark.

Rick had been thinking it through. If Turgenev was dirty, then somewhere he had to have a secret headquarters. A place where he could plot and scheme without fear of interruption. Logically, it would be to the east, because all his key activities were on the east side of the colony. That was where the fields were being planted. That was where the river was for irrigation.

Somewhere out here, Turgenev had Zoe. He was sure of it. And Rick had to find her.

Stree Prime
Stree Listening Station #144

"Hallway is clear," said Tika, looking down the hallway from Elvenen's office toward the rear storage area. "The building's locked up, everybody's gone home for the day."

"Awesome," said Rita. "Let's get this done." Reaching down to the inert body of Sub-Captain Elvenen on the floor, she lifted it effortlessly and slung it over her shoulder. With Tika ahead of her running point, she left the office and quickly moved to the storage area. Luda held the lid open as Rita dumped Elvenen's body into the bodybuilder. Quickly and efficiently, Luda and Ollie stripped the clothing off the unconscious Stree and closed the lid of the bodybuilder. Luda pushed a button, and a slight hum started as it began scanning Elvenen's body.

"How long until we have a new body?" asked Rita.

"Two hours," Luda responded. "Thirty minutes to scan the old one, one and a half hours to build the new one." Luda looked over at Tika and grinned. "Is it too late for me to change my mind? I've always wanted to be a Captain."

Tika laughed. "No, sorry, Luda. This one goes to Rita. I get the adjutant and Rachel gets the aide."

Rita smiled. "Sorry, Luda."

"We'd better get the other two out of the office and down here to the storage area," Tika said. "Then get the extra materials loaded in the bodybuilder. It'll finish scanning soon and it can't start building a new body without some additional materials."

Rita nodded and they headed back to Elvenen's office. As they walked, a thought occurred to Tika.

"What if one of these three had an appointment for later tonight? Wouldn't somebody get worried or raise an alarm?"

Rita shook her head. "We're good. Elvenen didn't have anything when I checked his sideload scan. Luda checked the scans of the other two, and they don't have any pending appointments either. All of them are scheduled to be at Command Headquarters in Komihu tomorrow morning for their new assignment, so it appears they've already cut their ties here. That's the good news."

"What's the bad news?" wondered Tika.

"I'm having second thoughts about this plan. We're going to walk right into the lion's den. So many things can go wrong. The slightest mistake on our part and we're caught."

Tika nodded in agreement. "Well, yeah. I know. But that's war, isn't it? Everything's a risk. We could get caught. But we could also be with the Goblin fleet at Stalingrad and get blown to hell there. Or be shot down as we approach the capital because we have the wrong codes. Or lose an engine and crash into the mountains on the way out of here. There are no guarantees in life, you know."

"I know. But I hope this works."

"Well, if you wake up back on the *Armidale* in your old body, you'll know it didn't work."

Rita laughed. "Yeah. Restored from backup. That'll suck, because I won't know why the mission failed."

Phoenix System
800 Lights from Stalingrad

Zoe came back to her senses slowly. Her head hurt as badly as it had ever hurt in her entire life. Her wrists hurt like the devil, too. She realized her hands were tied behind her, tightly, the ropes cutting into her skin. She was up against something hard and rough, hurting her back. There was a blindfold over her eyes.

Someone moved in front of her, and the blindfold came off.

She looked up to see Turgenev in front of her, a wicked smile on his face. Behind him she could see forest, the alien blue forest that surrounded the colony in all directions. She realized she was tied to a tree, someplace well away from the colony. Around her she could see several tents and the equipment of a small camp.

"Welcome back, DeLong," he said. "I trust you are feeling somewhat better?"

"Fuck you, Turgenev," she managed to get out. She realized her ribs were bruised - evidently they had smacked her around a bit while she was unconscious. There was more blood drying on her cheek where it had dripped down from her scalp.

"Ah, dear Zoe, how wrong you are. It will be the other way around. One of us will be fucked, but it won't be me, my dear."

Then, casually, he reached up and hit her in the face. It was not the hardest hit he could have given her, but it was hard enough to knock her head to one side and break her lip.

"Now. How much have you told the others? Luke Powell and Mark Rodgers? What do they know?"

Zoe spat blood from her broken lip. "They know it all, you slimy bastard," Zoe said.

"I doubt that," Turgenev smiled. "In fact, what you just said leads me to believe they don't know anything at all. Because it would be impossible for them to know everything, and the mere fact you say that tells me you are lying."

And Turgenev hit her again, this time with his left hand, breaking her lip on the other side. A fresh gout of blood streamed down her chin, dripping down on her thigh as she stood tied against the rough surface of the tree.

"Now," said Turgenev. "That was for lying to me. I will ask you again. And this time, the consequences of lying will be much more severe. This time, if you lie to me, I simply walk away. Which leaves you to my guards. To do with as they will."

Turgenev leaned forward, leering into Zoe's face. "And they will do you up right, DeLong. Of that I can assure you. Now - for the last time...how much have you told the others?"

CHAPTER TWENTY

Phoenix System
800 Lights from Stalingrad

The radio woke Luke at dawn. Half asleep, he grumbled and cursed at the radio as the voice of Rick Moore - heavily mixed with static - pulled him out of sleep.

"What?!" he yelled at the radio.

<Zoe's gone missing, Luke. I've been looking for her all night. I can't find her anywhere>

Luke came suddenly awake. He sat up in bed. Something - some instinct, some built-in circuit designed for trouble - fired in his brain.

Turgenev.

He knew it instantly, as certainly as he knew his own name.

Turgenev has her.

"Where are you?" he called.

<I'm headed for Headquarters right now. I'll be there in five minutes>

"Wait for me there. On my way."

Luke slammed out of bed and into his clothes, thinking all the while.

He'll have her someplace we can't find her easily. So not in the colony - he'll know that anywhere in the colony, we might stumble across her in a search.

She'll be outside the colony area.

But where? North, south, east, west? Where would he hide her?

Luke finished dressing and ran to the Headquarters tent. Rick was there waiting for him, agitated and pacing, cursing under his breath. Luke entered and went directly to his desk, motioning Rick to the chair in front of him.

"First of all, calm down, Rick. We can't help her if we're too excited to think straight."

Rick nodded and went to the chair. He sat, fidgeting, playing with his portable radio.

"Tell me what you know so far."

"Well, she didn't come home last night. She said she had something to do. She said she'd be home no later than 2 AM. When she didn't come home, I started looking for her."

"Where have you looked so far?"

"The office here, the hospital, the mess hall, the entire area around here. Then I flew a drone over Central Park with infrared. Nothing. Then I went to Turgenev's headquarters across the Park and broke in, searched that place. Then I flew the drone out over the east side forest as far as I could take it. But I found nothing.

"Good. So we're both thinking the same thing, at least."

"Yeah. Turgenev. It has to be," Rick agreed. "She must have caught on to something and went to investigate it."

"And got caught," Luke added. "He has her, for sure. I can feel it in my bones."

Rick nodded. "So what do we do?"

"We find her," affirmed Luke. "I'm certain she won't be in the camp anywhere. He's too smart for that. There's 12,000 people in this camp now. Too much chance of someone stumbling across her. She'll be out in the wild someplace."

"Oh, God, Luke...you think? He'd put her out in the forest?"

"Yeah, but not alone. She'll have guards with her. My bet is he's already set up a remote camp somewhere out in that damn blue forest. Getting ready for his coup. It's the only explanation that fits all the facts."

"You can't be serious."

"I am. I think he's preparing to take over the colony. Zoe must have found out something about it, so he took her. That's where she'll be, Rick. Somewhere out in the forest, a good distance from the camp."

"How will we find her? There's hundreds of square miles of alien forest out there."

"We'll find her," Luke said grimly. "OK. First things first. I want you to go get Mark, Gillian, and Tatiana out of bed and get them over here as quickly as possible. Keep it quiet and try not to get anyone else involved. Tell them it's an emergency, but don't give them any details yet - someone might overhear. Tell them to hurry. Don't make a big fuss and don't get a lot of people involved. Got it?"

"Got it."

"Then go."

Rick got up and darted out of the office. Luke sat for a second, gathering his thoughts. Then he made a rare call on his internal comm - the internal comm that had been built into his brain when he commanded the EDF destroyer *Dragon*. A comm that could only communicate with EDF ships or with other EDF officers.

Or with Goblins.

<Beto. Are you available?>

<I am available, Captain Powell>

<I need your help, Beto>

Stree Prime - Stree Listening Station #14
Stree System

It had taken most of the night to use the bodybuilder to convert the bodies of the three Stree officers to androids. Rachel had intellectually understood how the process worked and had accepted it. But once in the reality of it, she shuddered, became nauseous, and ran to the toilet.

That her android Stree body could throw up had come as quite a surprise to her. *There's such a thing as too much realism*, she thought, wiping her mouth as she returned to the storage area where Hajo, Luda, Ollie, and Liwa were converting the bodies.

The bodybuilder had two modes. One mode created an entirely new android body from scratch, using new raw materials poured into hoppers mounted on the side, and the measurements scanned from an old body. That was how her original android body had been constructed; Tika had scanned her consciousness and used raw materials to build an entirely new body for her, based on the scan of her old one.

But that wouldn't work here on Stree Prime; they had insufficient raw materials to create three new bodies from scratch, and no time to go find such materials. So they had no choice but to use the other mode of the bodybuilder.

That second mode converted the dead bodies of the Stree directly into raw materials. Luda then added only what was needed to make up the difference - in this case, mostly metals and silicon they had brought with them on the shuttle. It was an efficient way to create new android bodies; but to Rachel, it was hard to think about the process that was occurring inside the bodybuilder. Thankfully, the device had an opaque cover, so she didn't have to see the process in detail.

But just thinking about it had been enough to send her puking to the toilet, once again surprised by the accuracy of the android bodies made by the Goblins.

And the timing had been close. They had worked all night, preparing the android bodies, switching themselves over to the new ones of Elvenen and his aide and adjutant, storing their original blank ones back in the travel coffins, researching the information obtained from the three dead Stree, and preparing for the journey to Stree Naval Headquarters. It was now morning; the military shuttle was coming at 6 AM to transfer Rita, Tika, and Rachel - in the Stree bodies of Elvenen, his adjutant and his aide - to Komihu, the capital city.

Rita, Tika and Rachel rushed to help the others reload the bodybuilder and other cargo back on their shuttle. As dawn broke, they just managed to get Hajo launched with their shuttle toward the safe house near Komihu, and trot across the field to the passenger terminal with their luggage.

They arrived at the terminal just as the military shuttle came in to land. And the shuttle pilot was impatient; he had a lot of stops to make and didn't want to waste any time. He sat on the tarmac, engines idling, and dropped the rear ramp, waving at them to get aboard.

Trotting around to the rear of the shuttle, Rita walked up the ramp to find it packed with cargo and with Stree, officers and enlisted. Evidently a lot of them were enroute to the capital city today. A long row of cargo pallets occupied the center of the shuttle, with rows of flip-out jump seats down both sides.

There were only two seats available; she prepared to take one, but the loadmaster, wearing a headset, waved her forward. Over the sound of the idling engines, the Stree sergeant pointed to the cockpit. "There's a jump seat available in the cockpit, Sub-Captain. I suggest you take that one."

Rita nodded, turned to look at Tika and Rachel, and pointed to the two empty seats along the cabin wall. The loadmaster took her bag and shoved it into an overhead compartment. Then he led her to the front and into the cockpit. Stepping in, she found the jumpseat behind the pilots and took it. For the moment, busy with takeoff checklists, the pilots ignored her. She strapped in and waited.

This is the first test. If I can't fool these two, then we have no chance at all.

The shuttle engines spooled up. It lifted, translated to the left to clear the terminal building, and began to accelerate into the bright blue sky. When they had reached cruising altitude, the pilot put the shuttle on autopilot, leaned back, said something on the radio, and scratched himself. Then he turned to look at the Sub-Captain sitting behind him in the jump seat.

"Good morning, Sub-Captain Elvenen. Welcome aboard. We'll have you in Komihu in about an hour. Can I get you something to drink?"

"No, thanks, Lieutenant," Rita replied, quickly reading the

rank of the officer's collar pips. "I'm fine."

The pilot nodded and turned back to his duties. Rita, gazing out the window, saw a beautiful mountain range on her left, stretching from horizon to horizon. The peaks reached high, a few of them more than 15,000 feet. Once again, she was struck with the beauty of the Stree home world - and the contrast of that beauty with the horror of the Stree genocide that had killed her own planet, and was attempting to kill every Goblin in the universe.

Strange, she thought. *You'd think a species surrounded by so much beauty wouldn't think of killing others. But that's not true. Even in our own world, it wasn't true. The Huns, the Nazis, the Khmer Rouge, the Rwandan genocide...the list goes on and on. All of them living in a beautiful world, but bent on killing those who were different.*

"...promotion, Sub-Captain," she heard from the pilot.

Rita realized she had missed something over the noise of the engines. The pilot was looking at her expectantly.

"I'm sorry, what was that?" she asked.

"Congratulations on your upcoming promotion, sir. I understand you'll be in the Signals Section?"

Rita started to reply; but some instinct of her military experience gave her pause. She didn't know if Stree security measures were as stringent as those of the EDF she had served; but it they were, this was a question she should not answer.

"I'm sorry, Lieutenant. I can't comment on my assignment. But thank you anyway."

The pilot gave her a nod of approval and turned back to his flying. A bead of sweat formed on Rita's brow and ran slowly down her forehead. Unobtrusively, she wiped it away.

So far so good.

Moon Tosong - Listening Station #144
Stree System

Sitting beside Captain Stewart in the control room of

the Stree station they had commandeered, Jim leaned back, contemplating their next steps.

Beside him, Captain Stewart gazed absent-mindedly at the large, oversize holotank in the center of the room. "What's the latest from Rita on the ground?"

"She reported the bodies have been converted and they've made their transfers. They've cleaned up and should be on the shuttle to Komihu by now."

"And Hajo?"

"His team found a small farm on the outskirts of Komihu to use as a safe house. He left with the shuttle at dawn to go there and hide it in the barn. He'll unload the equipment into a rented van and stand by for Rita's next move."

"Cross your fingers," said Stewart. "How about news from Phoenix?"

"Contact!" yelled the Tactical Officer. "Five shuttles, coming hard. Classify as combat shuttles, thirty to forty personnel apiece, coming fast over the horizon! ETA two minutes!"

Stewart looked at Jim, shock written over his face. Both of them realized there was no possibility of getting to the *Armidale* and away from the moon in time.

"They found us. Somehow, they found us."

"Oh, crap," Jim said. "We are so screwed..."

CHAPTER TWENTY-ONE

Phoenix System
800 Lights from Stalingrad

Mark entered the Headquarters tent unhappy. It was early for him, and he had objected to getting out of bed and coming to the office at dawn. But Rick had insisted, which put Mark in a foul mood. As he entered the office, he glared at Luke.

"What the fuck is so important that you have to get me out of bed at this ungodly hour?"

"Zoe's missing. We think Turgenev has her."

Tatiana and Gillian had entered the tent behind Mark. Now the three of them stood stock-still, shock on their faces.

"What?" came their universal response.

Rick Moore came into the tent behind them as Luke began explaining. As Luke and Rick described the events of the morning, the other three slowly sank into their chairs, their faces showing their dismay.

When Luke and Rick had recapped the situation, Tatiana was the first to speak.

"If Turgenev really has Zoe, he'll hold her hostage. He'll expect us to find out, and he'll know we'll have no choice but to take action against him. So he'll use her as leverage."

"Yep," agreed Luke. "But first things first. I think we have three main priorities.

"One - we have to get Gillian, Imogen, Misha, Marta and Tatiana to a safe place. Turgenev will make them his primary targets to leverage the rest of us to do his will. We've got to get them out of here.

"Two - we have to locate Zoe. Until we know where she is, there's not much we can do to help her.

"And three - we have to assume this incident will push Turgenev and his gang to move faster. So we need to prepare for a coup attempt as early as today. It's quite possible they're already in motion. We need to assume the worst."

"You can't be serious," Gillian said. "We're fighting for our very survival here. Who would be crazy enough to endanger the entire colony just to take over power?"

Luke grimaced. "Believe me, Gillian, they'll do it. These are people who are totally ruthless. Completely, 100% self-centered. They won't hesitate to kill. That's the first thing you need to understand. This is no joke. This is life and death. Especially for us, because we're members of the Council. They'll strike at us first."

"So what do we do?" Gillian asked, her voice shaking.

"The first thing we do is hide you, Imogen, Misha, Marta and Tatiana. We can't allow them to take any more hostages. Transport Five is coming into the system right now - it'll be in stable orbit in twenty minutes. Rick's going to take you to get Imogen, Misha and Marta and get you on a shuttle. Beto has agreed to fly you up to the transport. When you get there, halt all shuttle flights down to the surface until we've got this situation under control."

Gillian looked at Mark, who nodded at her.

"Luke's right, Jilly. We have to get you out of here - before anything worse happens. You need to go."

Gillian nodded, tears beginning to stream down her cheeks.

"But what about you? Mark, I can't leave you!"

Mark rose and went to his wife, put his arms around her, and kissed her cheek.

"I'm the Governor, Jilly. I can't leave now. And this is a job for those of us who've been trained by the military. I'll be fine. You just go along with Rick now. He'll take you and the kids to the shuttle."

Rick rose and went to the exit, waiting. Tatiana rose, but stood stock-still, staring at Luke.

"I'd like to stay, Pop," she said. "I'm military too. Misha can take care of Marta."

Luke shook his head.

"Tatiana, you're our backup plan. If we fail, you'll have to take things forward. Please. Go with Rick and let him take you to the shuttle."

Tatiana stared at her father for a few seconds, then gave a curt nod. Gillian, still crying, kissed Mark one last time. Then Gillian and Tatiana followed Rick as he led them out of the tent.

Stree Prime
Komihu - Capital City

The Stree military shuttle let down slowly to the tarmac at the Komihu Naval Base, translated slightly into a parking spot, and shut down. The door in the rear of the cockpit opened, and the loadmaster stood there, standing aside for Rita to leave the cockpit. She unbuckled from the jump seat, stood up, and stepped out of the cockpit to stand in the rear compartment as the back ramp starting whining down.

Rita - in the Stree body of Sub-Captain Elvenen - had already determined she was the senior officer on board. But what she didn't know was Stree naval protocol.

Does the senior officer get off first? Or last as in the EDF?

She scanned the consciousness of Elvenen in her extended memory, but for some reason that item of information was not there. She didn't know why - it was missing in his scan.

Something's wrong. Everything should be there. Did we get a bad scan?

She realized that if the senior officer got off last - as she hoped - then the junior officers on the shuttle would jump up and grab their bags quickly, to get off and make way for their seniors.

She decided to wait and see what the other people on the shuttle did. If she were wrong - if the senior officer was supposed to get off first - then she expected that nobody would move quickly, and some would turn to look at her. In that case, she would grab her bags, and start for the exit.

As the engines started winding down, the Stree on the shuttle jumped up and started reaching for their luggage. With a sigh of relief, Rita realized she had guessed correctly. She glanced over at Tika, in the male body of her adjutant, who smiled back at her. The three of them waited until the other passengers had departed the craft. Then Rachel and Tika preceded Rita down the ramp and out of the shuttle.

Walking into the terminal, Rita saw a sergeant holding a sign with her name on it. Within a few minutes, they were in a staff car, heading for the center of Komihu.

Rita tried not to look around goggle-eyed; she supposed that all three of the Stree officers they were impersonating had been to the capital before. But it was hard not to look; the city was huge, and made up of great edifices of white marble, red brick, granite, and every other building stone possible. It was clear the Stree built for permanency; there was almost no wooden construction visible on the drive from the shuttleport. The streets were wide, clean, and well-maintained.

Rita knew the Stree made extensive use of slave labor. She wondered if that was why the streets were so clean.

And how can they claim to be religious while using slave labor to build their cities?

But...the Romans also claimed to be religious. As did the Christian nations who conquered Africa and the Americas, killing and enslaving millions.

Perhaps I've got it backwards - maybe religion enables evil. Once you've convinced yourself that your religion has the right to consume all others, you can justify anything.

"We're here, Sub-Captain," said their driver. He pulled over into a small parking area in front of a large building. "I'll deliver your bags to the BOQ and have them put in your rooms, sirs."

Sirs. Rita was still getting use to the fact she was impersonating a male Stree. It was not the easiest thing she had ever done.

Per the protocol they had now figured out, Rachel got out first and held the door, then Tika got out next. Rita came last. Rachel closed the door of the staff car and waved the driver on. With a slight whine, the car departed.

The three of them turned and stared at the building in front of them with some trepidation. It was an imposing red brick building, with a central hall of five stories, and large wings of offices on each side.

It was also the Command HQ of the Stree Navy.

There was a large plaza between the sidewalk and the building entrance, with a square reflecting pool in the middle of it. A row of trees on each side of the reflecting pool were bright green, growing beautifully in the spring weather of Stree Prime. Squat Stree officers and personnel of every rank bustled in and out of the building, moving the business of war to and fro.

Turning, Rita stared across the wide boulevard to the other side of the street. There was the Great Cathedral of the Stree. That was where Great Prophet Videlli and his staff worked.

They were less than two hundred yards from the enemy's true power.

This had better work, or we're totally screwed...

Rita turned and glanced at Tika and Rachel, standing slightly behind her.

"Let's dance," she said, and winked. Then she turned and walked toward the building entrance. She walked proudly, as befit a Stree officer who had been transferred to Headquarters and was about to be promoted to Captain. It was a straw in Elvenen's cap, and she knew it.

Best to act the part.

Approaching the front entrance, she pushed through the

revolving doors and saw a security area, with security badge readers on the right and a long desk full of security personnel on the left. Marching directly to the security desk, Rita presented her ID badge and spoke arrogantly.

"Sub-Captain Elvenen reporting for duty, along with my adjutant Commander Pamasa and my aide, Sub-Commander Olvia."

The sergeant behind the desk took her badge, examined it, looked up at Elvenen, then looked at Tika and Rachel standing behind her. He waved them forward, and they stepped up and presented their badges as well.

Trying to maintain their calm, the three of them watched as the sergeant took the ID badges, sat down at a screen, and started typing. He typed slowly, one finger at a time, in the arcane language of the Stree that required two to three keystrokes for each letter. It seemed to take forever.

Rita, trying to keep things loose in this most tense situation, turned and winked at Tika. Then she realized that might look a bit strange - just for a second, she had forgotten they were both Stree males right now.

The sergeant's search seemed to go on forever, as he stumbled around on the keyboard pulling up their records. Rita realized she was sweating. She couldn't help but have a quirky thought about it.

Am I sweating? Or is Elvenen sweating?

She looked at Tika. Tika appeared to be as cool as ice. No sweat showed on her face, and no tension appeared evident in her body language.

Maybe I should have let Tika be Elvenen.

Looking back at Rachel, Rita saw more of the same. No sweat on her brow, no apparent concern. The perfect picture of a relaxed, somewhat bored aide.

"Here you go," she heard from the sergeant. She turned back to see him presenting all three badges to her. She took them and nodded.

"Through the security gates and take the elevator to the

fourth floor," he said. "Your section will be at the far end of the hall, overlooking the front of the building."

"Thank you," Rita replied. She turned, handed Tika and Rita their badges, and marched to the security gate, Tika and Rita following right behind her.

Laying her badge on the reader, she waited with bated breath. There was a ping, and the light on the top turned green. She walked through and headed for the elevators.

It worked! It actually worked! I can't fucking believe it worked!

Phoenix System
800 Lights from Stalingrad

"Now what?" asked Mark. He stared at Luke across the office. "We've sent our loved ones to a safe place. What next?"

"Now we find Zoe," replied Luke. "I've contacted Beto. When he gets to the transport, he'll have the captain use their sensor suite to help us. They'll scan the forest around the camp. We should know in a matter of minutes if Turgenev has a hidden camp out there somewhere."

"OK. And then what?"

"I've got Cerutti putting together a rescue team. I told him to get our best people assembled and hand out weapons, get ready for a fight. He's on it."

"How many people?"

"I told him to get at least fifty, more if possible. We have no way of knowing how many Turgenev has. But I find it hard to believe he could have more than about fifty. Even if he was able to stoke a lot of discontent, most people are reasonably satisfied with the way things have been going. And most people have enough common sense to know we can't survive fighting among ourselves."

"I hope fifty's enough," Mark grunted. "If Turgenev has more than that, we're in trouble."

"If he has more than that, we're not going to stop him. At least for the short term, we'll have to give him the government.

I suppose we can try to assemble another coup at some point in the future, restore a democratic government."

Mark shook his head grimly. "If he wins this one, it won't be us doing that in the future. We'll be dead. He'll never leave us alive to cause trouble."

"Yeah. I know," said Luke. "How did we let this get so far? We should have taken action against Turgenev as soon as we realized he was a threat to us."

"That's the downside of a fair and democratic government," smiled Mark. "Democracy insists on proof of a threat before taking action. Dictatorships don't wait that long - as soon as they have a suspicion, they kill the threat, even if innocents are killed with the guilty. It's always a trade-off."

Luke nodded sourly. "Yep. I guess."

"So," Mark continued. "Split milk at this point. Let's move on."

Dino Cerutti rushed into the tent, carrying an M-7 assault weapon. "We're ready, Luke," he called. "I've got a dozen people guarding the Council members. And fifty standing by to go rescue Zoe. Any word on the remote sensing?"

"Not yet. But any minute now."

"Good," said Cerutti. "The guys are excited. This is the first chance we've had to use the militia on a real mission. They can't wait!"

CHAPTER TWENTY-TWO

Stree Prime
Komihu - Capital City

"Welcome to your new job, Elvenen! What with the war and all, we're short-handed. We've been looking forward to your arrival!"

Rita - in the body of Sub-Captain Elvenen - nodded and reached into her storage of Elvenen's consciousness to respond appropriately. "Thank you, Admiral. I exist only to serve the Prophet."

She was standing before the desk of Admiral Riato, head of Fleet Intelligence for the Stree Navy. She had wiped the sweat off her forehead in the elevator; but it was threatening to come back. She could feel the heat on her forehead.

One false move here...and we're all toast.

"So. The first order of business is to make your promotion official."

Admiral Riato stood, stepped around his desk, and moved up to Rita, holding something in his hand. Rita rose to attention. Now Riato was so close, she could smell him. He smiled at her, his eyeteeth showing. His breath spread across her, a pungent, earthy smell that made her want to retch. But she didn't dare move a muscle.

He handed her two brass collar insignia. "Congratulations, Captain! And well-deserved. You've done an exemplary job of operating the listening station at Jower. I'm glad to have you on my staff!"

"Thank you, sir. All is done to serve the Prophet!"

"Yes, exactly. Well, Elvenen, again, welcome aboard. My aide Awasifu will show you to your offices. And I'll see you in staff meeting Thursday at 10 AM."

Rita nodded, turned smartly, and departed the Admiral's inner office, Tika and Rachel falling in behind her. In the outer office, a Commander awaited them, his nametag reading "Awasifu".

"Greetings, Captain Elvenen. I'll show you to your office suite," the aide said. Rita nodded and followed the aide as he left the Admiral's suite and marched down the hallway.

It was a huge building, and the aide led them at least three hundred feet to a corner, then another three hundred feet to a door. He opened the door and stepped through.

Inside, a large room contained a dozen desks. Each desk was occupied by an officer or enlisted Stree, all of whom snapped to attention as they entered.

"As you were," Rita called. The staff relaxed to a loose parade rest. Rita walked around the room, letting each of her new staff members introduce themselves. Then Awasifu led her into her new office. It was spacious, with a large desk having three chairs in front of it. To one side was a large couch, with a coffee table before it. On the other wall was a viewer, currently showing a display of the Stree system and dozens of icons representing Stree ships moving in and out of the system.

"Your office, Captain," said Awasifu. "Your aide is next door to your left, and your adjutant next door to your right. I suggest you get things started by meeting your Number Three, Sub-Commander Fawa. He is the most knowledgeable about everything in your department."

"Thank you, Awasifu. It is appreciated. All praise to the Prophet."

"All praise to the Prophet," Awasifu responded, and left the office. Outside, Rita could see a Stree hovering respectfully, obviously waiting to enter her office. She waved him in.

"Sub-Commander Fawa reporting, Captain. I am the Signals Intelligence head. I'm responsible for day-to-day operations of the Signals Branch."

"Very good," Rita responded. "I assume you're responsible for my daily briefing as well?"

"Yes, sir."

"Good."

Rita sank back into her chair and waved Tika and Rachel to the couch on the side of the room. As they sat, she looked at Fawa.

"You can start now. Bring us up to date."

"Aye, Captain. Well. As I'm sure you know, the Fleet departed thirty-six days ago for the attack on the Goblins. They will arrive at Stalingrad in four more days. So far, nothing but routine message traffic back and forth. No major issues, all ships are performing nominally."

"Good," said Rita. She glanced over at Tika and Rachel, the irony of the situation not escaping them.

"Also, we have three new cruisers arriving tomorrow from Gomorrah, to reinforce the Home Guard fleet."

"Ah. Good." Rita tried to resist frowning in puzzlement. Clearly Fawa thought she should know what Gomorrah was. But she didn't. Elvenen's consciousness didn't have that knowledge. She was beginning to realize the scan of Elvenen's consciousness was flawed. Something had gone wrong. It was missing critical information. There was a defect in the scanner.

"And finally, we captured a Human ship last night. A spy ship. They had taken over the listening station on Tosong."

Phoenix System
800 Lights from Stalingrad

Mark, Luke, Rick and Cerutti had been waiting impatiently in the Headquarters tent for nearly a half-hour before news came. But when it came, Luke leaped to his feet.

"Beto found the camp!" he yelled as the information came in over his internal comm. "Five miles northeast!"

Cerutti jumped to his feet. "Outstanding! I'll go get the troops ready!" He rushed out of the tent, Rick right behind him.

Luke got to his feet, staring at Mark.

"You should stay here, Mark," Luke said. "We need a central point of contact. Also in case something goes wrong, you're gonna be it."

Leaping to his feet, Mark disagreed.

"Bullshit. I'm the Governor. I'm going!"

"Mark," said Luke quietly. "What if all of us are killed? Including you? Who'll protect Gillian and Imogen?"

Mark hesitated, the thought clearly impacting him.

"Stay. Be our rock, Mark. We need one right now."

With a slow nod, Mark sat back down. Luke smiled grimly and left the tent, carrying his radio and a pistol on his hip. He followed Rick Moore and Dino Cerutti as they headed northeast across Central Park toward the distant spot marked by the Goblin sensors.

Within fifteen minutes, they were in dense forest, the morning sun now mostly hidden from them by the canopy overhead. Although it was dimly lit, it was still hot. Luke found himself sweating buckets as they marched on. But they made good time, and within two hours they were approaching Turgenev's camp.

Cerutti had sent scouts ahead of them. The scouts reported back by radio that the camp had been located. As they came closer, Luke saw the first tents through the trees.

"Let's spread out and envelop them," Luke ordered. "No shooting unless they shoot first."

Cerutti nodded and issued the orders. His troops began to spread out into a half-moon formation, enclosing the camp on three sides. Luke continued to move forward, now only a few yards from the edge of the camp. Nothing moved.

Stepping into the clearing with Cerutti slightly behind him, Luke saw Turgenev come out of one of the tents. Behind

Turgenev, a guard pushed Zoe DeLong roughly with the barrel of a rifle. Her hands were tied behind her and there was a gag in her mouth. She shook her head violently at Luke, trying to tell him something.

Puzzled by her actions, Luke glared at Turgenev.

"You're surrounded, Turgenev. You have no chance. Give it up."

Turgenev smiled a lazy smile at Luke, then waved his hand at the troops standing in a large circle around them.

"Perhaps you'd better look again, Mr. Powell. I'm not the one that's surrounded."

Stunned, Luke saw that every one of the militia members around him had their rifles pointed straight at him. Suddenly he felt the push of Cerutti's rifle barrel in his back. As he looked once more at Zoe desperately trying to signal him with her eyes, all the pieces fell into place.

***

Turgenev and Cerutti marched Luke, Rick, and Zoe back to the colony. By the time they returned, Turgenev's troops had captured Mark Rodgers and secured the Headquarters area. Escorted to the newly built jail, they were installed in cells next to each other.

As Cerutti's guards departed, Luke looked at Mark through the bars.

"Well, here's another nice mess you've gotten me into," Luke quipped. It was an expression he had picked up from Bonnie, which she had picked up from Jim Carter as part of his Marine heritage.

Mark smiled grimly. "Outfoxed and outplayed," he said. "You have to give Turgenev credit. He took a small incident and turned it into a win."

"I'm so sorry," said Zoe from the next cell. "This is all my fault. If I hadn't been caught following Cerutti, this would have never happened."

"Oh, it would have happened," said Mark. "Just later, and in a different way. In a sense, you did us a favor. At least this way, we were able to get Gillian and Tatiana and the children to safety. I think that's the only reason they haven't killed us yet; they want to use us as leverage to get them back to the surface."

"Yup," Rick said, sitting on his bunk. "If that happens, they'll have no more need of us."

"Will they come back down?" asked Zoe.

"Not likely," said Rick.

"Quiet, guys," Luke interjected. "I'm sure they've got the place bugged."

"Shit," Rick said. "I didn't think about that."

"Just remember everything you say is going straight to Turgenev," Luke admonished.

Stree Prime
Komihu - Capital City

"What?" Rita exclaimed before she could stop herself. "Humans?"

Fawa nodded, a large grin on his face.

"Aye, Captain. Eight Humans and a dozen Goblins. We captured them alive, including their ship, a small corvette. Clearly they were trying to infiltrate our system."

Rita tried to maintain her composure. It wouldn't do to appear too shocked by the news.

"But...I thought all the Humans were dead. We...we killed their planet!"

Fawa shrugged. "Obviously some survived, probably on Stalingrad. Now they're working with the Goblins. But they'll be dead soon enough, I'm sure. The Great Prophet will see to that."

Rachel, sitting on the couch to one side, saw the distress on Rita's face and interjected a question to distract Fawa.

"Where are these spies now? Here on Komihu?"

"Obviously not the Goblins, Sub-Commander. Those abominations were launched directly into the star as soon as they were captured. But I believe the Humans were brought here. Although of course, their location is a secret. That doesn't fall under Signals."

"Ah. Of course," Rachel replied. "Need to know."

"Yes, exactly, Sub-Commander."

"Very well," said Rita, having recovered her composure. "Anything else?"

"Nothing important, Captain. The listening station at Tosong is being restored. It should be back in operation by this time tomorrow."

"Well, thank you, Sub-Commander Fawa, for an excellent briefing. I believe I'll consult with my Chief of Staff now, and then we'll go to the BOQ and get settled. Since there is a staff meeting at ten AM Thursday, please be prepared to give us a full update tomorrow morning at eight AM. That will be all."

Fawa bowed, turned, and departed, closing the door behind him. Rita stared at Tika and Rachel in disbelief.

<We'd better use radio voice> Tika said before anyone could speak. <I'm sure this office is bugged. These Stree don't trust anyone>

Rita nodded. <Yeah, you're probably right> Rita bowed her head, still in shock. <I can't believe they captured Jim and the *Armidale* team>

<What are we gonna do?> Rachel asked.

Rita looked up at the two of them.

<We continue the mission. We just add a new sub-project to it>

<Which is?> Tika asked.

<Find Jim and the rest of them and save their lives> Rita answered.

CHAPTER TWENTY-THREE

Stree Prime
Stree Naval Headquarters

Unlike the day before, Fawa's Tuesday morning briefing was conducted in Rita's conference room, next to her office suite. Rita sat at the head of the table, with Tika and Rachel next to her. Fawa stood at the other end of the room before a large display, conducting the briefing. For thirty minutes, Fawa went over reports from every significant signals location both in-system and in the distant Fleet, ensuring that Rita was up to date on everything. He closed by noting that the Stree Fleet was now only three days away from their assault on Stalingrad.

But he did not mention the *Armidale* or the status of her crew.

It became obvious the briefing was drawing to a close. Rita spoke silently to Tika and Rachel via her radio link.

<Should I ask him about the *Armidale*? Would that be suspicious?>

<I think it's a bad idea> Tika replied. <It's outside the area of our duties. Too suspicious>

<Agreed> said Rachel.

<OK> Rita acquiesced. <But we have to find out where they are keeping the *Armidale* prisoners and what Videlli's plans are for them>

<Not now, though> said Tika.

With a slight flourish of his tablet, Fawa completed his briefing and stood, silent, waiting for any comment from Rita. Trying to appear realistic in her role, Rita asked several questions about their operations and their daily responsibilities. But there was nothing exceedingly difficult about her role, she soon realized. Her unit had responsibility for ensuring messages flowed smoothly across the Fleet. Messages received from distant stations were routed and filed. It was a simple process with a professional staff.

"Not a bad operation," Rita noted as she, Tika and Rachel returned to her office, closing the door behind them. "Fawa runs a tight ship."

"Yes, he takes his job seriously," said Rachel. "A career officer."

<Switch to radio> Rita transmitted. Tika and Rachel nodded as they sat on the couch. Rita sat in the large chair across from them.

<I think we've made a mistake> began Rita. <There's nothing we can do here in Signals to hurt the Stree fleet. They're operating pretty much autonomously. Like a fire-and-forget missile. If we sent a fake recall order, they'd just ignore it>

Rachel nodded. <You're right. This is a waste of time>

<So what do we do next?> asked Tika. <We're here. We spent all this time getting into their HQ. There must be something we can do to make use of our position here in Komihu>

<There is> Rita said. <But you're not gonna like it>

<Oh, oh> Rachel said. <I hope you're not thinking what I think you're thinking>

Rita grinned widely. <We're gonna cross the street>

Tika looked at her in horror. <The Cathedral? Are you crazy?
>

Rita shook her head, still smiling. <We're going to join the priesthood>

Phoenix System

800 Lights from Stalingrad

In orbit 22,000 miles above the Human colony, Tatiana, Gillian, and Misha sat with Beto, the Goblin assigned as a non-voting adviser to the Council. They listened in shock as Beto finished telling them about Turgenev's coup and his full takeover of the colony.

"And he's declared himself Governor?"

"Yes," replied Beto. "Turgenev is now Governor. He declared the Council disbanded. His militia has taken over every apartment block and put his goons in charge. They're recruiting more members for their gang. And anyone who objects too loudly has a sudden accident."

Tatiana looked at Misha.

"We can't let this stand, Misha. We have to fight them."

"I know, milaya. But how?"

Tatiana closed her eyes momentarily, a habit of hers when thinking hard. Opening her eyes again, she spoke to the group.

"If we can take an entire planet from the Singheko, we can certainly take a small colony from this Russian prick."

Looking at Beto, she asked the obvious question.

"Will the Goblins help us in this?"

Beto shook his head.

"We cannot take sides in such an altercation between Humans. You will have to work this out yourselves."

"But," Tatiana wondered, "will you at least provide us with transport to the surface?"

"That much we can do," Beto said. "I will order the transport captain to follow your wishes in that regard."

"Good," said Tatiana. She looked at Misha. "OK. Let's call a meeting of the colonists and tell them what's going on."

Calling a meeting was not that simple, however. Transport Five was - well, a transport. There was no area with enough space to assemble a large group of the colonists for a meeting.

But they were saved by the foresight of Jim Carter and Mark Rodgers. Weeks ago, before the first transport ship had left Stalingrad, Jim had insisted they organize the colonists into a militia. After all, he said - they had no way of knowing what they would find on Phoenix. No way of knowing what challenges they would face on a new and virgin planet. No way of knowing if dangerous animals had been missed in the initial surveys. No way of knowing if the Stree would attack them shortly after their arrival. In the end, Mark had told Jim to go ahead and do it.

And of course, Jim Carter was a former Marine. There was never any doubt in his mind as to how the militia should be organized. As a result of Jim's forward thinking, the colonists were already divided into squads, platoons, companies, and battalions, based on the rapid maneuver model of the Marine Corps. They had loaded into the ship that way; mad silliness to some, but to others a reassuring form of much-needed order.

Now Jim's planning paid off. Tatiana didn't have to assemble thousands of colonists in a central location. All she had to do was make a call over the PA system. Within two hours, she was in the cafeteria of Transport Five, standing in front of a small group of people. Before her sat twelve company commanders. They represented the 1,658 members of the militia organized on the transport before their departure from Stalingrad.

Uncertain what was happening, concerned because off-loading of colonists to the surface hadn't started yet, the group stared in puzzlement at the tall, imposing woman standing before them. As Tatiana waited for everyone to arrive, an undercurrent of voices rumbled across the people seated before her. In a mixture of uncertainty, irritation and anger, the people muttered among themselves, impatient to understand what was happening.

Tatiana Powell could be a deceiving figure. Her half-Ukrainian, half-English features gave her a somewhat exotic, Slavic appearance. Her tall, muscular body left one with the impression of an athlete, perhaps a former gymnast or wrestler. The last thing any stranger would suspect was that she was a warrior.

But appearances can be deceiving, and those who knew Tatiana's history knew what she was: most recently, an Admiral in the now-defunct EDF - and before that, the general of guerrilla forces fighting the Singheko on Deriko.

Sent to the Singheko as a slave by the Ukrainians, she had started with a small cadre of only a few hundred women from her slave ship. From that nucleus, she had put together a resistance movement and fought the Singheko at Deriko, growing her army until she had 80,000 soldiers under her command. Then she had marched halfway around the planet, freeing upwards of 300,000 slaves from four species, killing or capturing every Singheko she could find. After a few months of fighting her, the seven-foot-tall, leonine-like Singheko had given her a nickname - 'Walking Death'.

Now, as the last of the colonists arrived, Tatiana turned, pushed one of the cafeteria tables into position in front of them, and lightly jumped on it, turning to face the group.

"Hello everyone," she called. "I'm going to use English today because I believe the majority of you understand it, or have a translation earpiece." She pointed to her ears. "If everyone who understands me will raise their hand, please."

Scanning the crowd, Tatiana saw that everyone had their hand up.

"Good, thank you," she continued. "If anyone has difficulty understanding me during this presentation, just raise your hand and I'll repeat myself.

"Now - the bad news. A group of thugs - a gang, if you will - has taken over Phoenix. They've imprisoned the legal government and set up their own dictatorship. They're running wild on the surface - killing people, raping women, collecting slaves - all the things you'd imagine from a gang of thugs. We've managed to get some intel back from people on the ground. I'm sending the details to your tablets right now." Tatiana nodded at Gillian, who triggered the transmission. Her audience looked down, examining the photos and vids. Several of them shuddered and looked away.

"So here's the important thing: do you want a democracy on Phoenix? Do you want to protect our individual freedoms? Or do you want a dictatorship run by a group of thugs?

"To help you decide, let me give you the picture of your future with each. First let's talk about a democracy. We all know there is no perfect system, right? And democracies have their own set of problems. There will be inequities. There will be conflict. The inevitable, never-ending battle between the rich, trying to claw more and more of the society's wealth for themselves, and the poor, trying to retain some of it for their own families. The inevitable distrust between races, leading to race conflict. The inevitable battles between ignorant cliques trying to force stupid, selfish decisions on the society, and the wiser heads trying to hold them back.

"Now let me contrast that with the dictatorship that is forming below us on the surface. An oligarchy of thugs and sadists. Holding your sons and daughters under their thumb for the rest of their lives. Your sons working in the fields as slave labor. Your daughters relegated to assault, rape, and slavery at the whim of their lords. Those who voice the slightest dissent killed; their bodies disappearing, never to be seen again."

Tatiana stopped speaking for a moment. She gazed around the group as they sat in shocked silence, trying to come to grips with her words.

"I'm not going to make this decision for you. I cannot. I can only tell you what is happening, and what the future will bring. You and your people must decide what to do next. There are only two choices. Go back to your quarters, accept your fate, and prepare to be enslaved. Or go back to your quarters, mobilize your people, and prepare to fight.

"Time is short. We must act quickly if we are to have any hope of stopping this coup before it gets too firmly established. If we move quickly and decisively, we can do it. If we hesitate, move too slowly, fail to attack them as aggressively as possible, we will *not* be able to dislodge them.

"Therefore, we will make a final decision at 1800 hours tonight. That gives you six hours to go back to your people, discuss the situation with them, and make a decision. I wish I could give you more time, but I can't. If we are to win the battle, we must attack immediately. And make no mistake about it - this will be a battle. People will die. This is not a game, nor an adventure. This is survival.

"So. Go back to your people. Tell them the situation. And ask them the question. Democracy or dictatorship. Fight or roll over. An imperfect system of democracy - or a perfectly imperfect system of slavery."

Tatiana fell silent. She looked at the individuals seated before her. These were people who had shown leadership during the trying times of the evacuation from Earth, and the confusing days on Stalingrad getting things organized. These were survivors; strong, robust people who instinctively knew what had to be done and stepped forward to do it. Slowly, with almost no conversation, they got up from their seats and headed to the door to take the word to the people.

Stree Prime
Great Cathedral of the Stree

Even for a Stree, Head Jailer Cotrapi was fat. So fat, he looked square - a big, fat, Stree with arms like a tree trunk, a huge Buddha-like belly sticking out, and a great fat head stuck on his shoulders leaving no discernible neck at all.

And Cotrapi was in a bad mood. Things had been going along swimmingly for him recently - living his pleasurable, run-of-the-mill life holding his run-of-the-mill Stree prisoners until their short trials and quick executions. On Stree Prime, it didn't take much to be sent to the special dungeon in the deepest part of the Cathedral basement.

There were hundreds of religious offenses that could get you killed. Even accidentally meeting the Great Prophet's eyes was sufficient cause if you were not a priest.

But having eight Human prisoners suddenly appear in his prison had terribly upset Cotrapi's carefully organized routine. Now, staring at Jim Carter and the other Humans in the cell, he was pissed. He had already tortured two of the Humans to death; but the ape-like creatures had told him nothing that he didn't already know.

And Prophet Tarilli was putting a lot of pressure on him to get answers.

Keying a translation device worn around his neck, Cotrapi spoke to the prisoners.

"Humans. You seem to be a frail species. How many more of you must I kill, until you tell me your mission?"

In the cell, the six remaining Humans looked at him sullenly, barely understanding the broken English coming out of the device. None bothered to rise from their rock-hard bunks. Cotrapi tried to watch all of them at once, to pick up on any sign of weakness he could exploit in his torture sessions; but none of them flinched.

Cotrapi sighed. "Very well. You have chosen your fate. I will take another of you tomorrow."

Once again, Cotrapi watched carefully. None of the six Humans in the cell showed any reaction to his words. In disgust, Cotrapi turned and marched away, his two aides at his heels.

Watching him go, Jim Carter lifted his head slightly to look across the cell at Captain Stewart. They all assumed the cell was bugged, so were being careful with their words.

"Really glad I didn't convert to Goblin before this trip," Jim said with a slight smile.

Stewart nodded. "Yeah. They sure are paranoid about Goblins. A one-way trip straight into the star. They wouldn't even bring them to their planet as prisoners."

"Why not?" asked Brady, Stewart's XO.

"Afraid they'll take over their computers and get into their systems," Jim grunted. "They're terrified of Goblins."

"But clearly not terrified of us Humans," Stewart

interjected.

"Yeah," Jim nodded glumly. "Not sure if that's bad or good, the way things are going. Maybe being launched into the star would have been better."

Great Cathedral of the Stree

Tika moved carefully. She knew the danger she faced. The slightest mistake, the smallest miss-step, and she would be discovered as a Goblin. And as events with the *Armidale* had proven, the Stree were deathly afraid of Goblins, and wasted no time disposing of them.

She had entered the Cathedral late in the evening, a half-hour before the huge edifice closed its doors for the day. At the entrance, she had studied a map mounted on the wall, recording it in her memory. Then she walked toward the front of the basilica, using her infrared vision and radar to locate all the cameras, motion detectors and other sensors in the huge hall.

Moving to the front of the basilica, Tika joined several other Stree before the altar. Kneeling, she pretended to pray.

<There's a door in the far-right corner. According to the map, there's a restroom behind that door> she transmitted. <But there's a priest standing beside the door on watch>

In her pocket, the two one-inch-long caterpillar aspects that contained Rita and Rachel responded.

<Just tell him you need to use the restroom>

Tika prayed for ten minutes, until only herself and a couple of others remained. Rising to her feet, she genuflected per the Stree ritual, turned, and made her way toward the door on the far right. Tika, although still in the body of the male Stree officer Pamasa, had changed to civilian clothing. As she approached, the priest moved to a position of alertness and challenged her.

"The exit is the other way, sir," he said.

"I need to use the restroom urgently," Tika said. "Is there one nearby?"

The priest paused, then nodded grudgingly. "Through this door to your right."

Tika nodded and passed through the door. The priest came in behind her and moved to the door of the restroom. He leaned forward, opened it for her, and took a position outside the door to wait for her.

<He's going to stand guard outside the door> Tika transmitted.

<No problem> replied Rita from her pocket. <He'll leave when you do. Any cameras or motion sensors in here?>

Tika moved to a stall and pretended to do her business, scanning the room as she did.

<I don't see anything. It looks clear>

<OK. Turn us loose>

Casually, Tika took the two caterpillars out of her pocket and laid them gently on the floor behind the toilet. Then she turned, went to the lavatory, washed her hands, and left the restroom, ensuring she turned out the lights as she departed. As she nodded a silent thanks to the priest and left through the door to the main basilica, she sent one last message to the two behind her.

<Good luck, folks>

In the darkened restroom, two tiny caterpillars waited behind the toilet, motionless.

CHAPTER TWENTY-FOUR

Phoenix System
800 Lights from Stalingrad

"They've voted," said Gillian. She sat in the cafeteria of Transport Five with Tatiana, Misha, Beto, and Taito, the Goblin captain of the transport. "The result was as we expected. The colonists voted to fight. The commanders are organizing right now, getting things ready. They say they can be ready to drop by tomorrow noon."

"Weapons?" asked Tatiana.

"About seven hundred rifles and pistols. The rest are making swords, knives, clubs, whatever they can put together."

"Seven hundred," Tatiana mused. "What's our estimate of the firearms on the surface?"

"According to our records, there were eight hundred twenty firearms on the surface as of the last transport. But of course, they have 3D printers down there. We have to assume they're making more as fast as the printers can churn them out. So our best estimate right now is about nine hundred to nine hundred fifty working firearms available to them on the surface when we drop."

Beto stared across the table at Tatiana.

"You are vastly outnumbered and outgunned," he said.

Tatiana winked at him.

"I've been outnumbered and outgunned in very battle I've fought," she grinned. "If I let that stop me, I'd still be a slave on

Deriko."

A slight grin creased the face of Captain Taito as he looked at Beto.

"According to Beto here, I'm not supposed to help you in anything except transport," Taito smiled. "However, it just so happens I have a dozen 3D printers onboard that are not too busy right now. If for some strange reason they went berserk and began printing rifles, I'm afraid it might take us hours to track down and correct the problem."

Tatiana smiled at the captain. "Technology's a bitch, ain't it?" She turned to Misha and Gillian. "When can we launch?"

Misha stepped into the conversation.

"We have four shuttles. Each shuttle can carry eighty troops with their weapons and loadout. According to the battalion commanders, they've got 1,597 people ready to go. So we need a total of twenty shuttle trips to get all the troops and equipment to the surface. That's five trips per shuttle.

"We'll have to land at least twenty miles from the colony to be over the horizon from them and out of sight, and so they don't hear the shuttles come in. So we'll have a long march into Landing. But if we push hard, we can be there by dawn Wednesday."

Tatiana thought for a moment, then shook her head.

"No. I don't want to rush this. They have to know that we escaped to the transport, and they have to suspect we'll put together an assault. I want to give them more time to get complacent, and us more time to organize. We'll target getting everyone on the ground by Thursday night instead."

Tatiana leaned back, gazing around the group.

"We'll split our forces into two battalions. Battalion East and Battalion West. Misha, you'll take Battalion East. You'll insert twenty miles from Landing, to the northeast, right where the forest gives way to the foothills. I'll take Battalion West. We'll insert twenty miles to the southwest. Captain Taito has agreed to use remote sensing to find us decent landing zones.

"Each battalion will march half-way to the colony the first night, then hunker down and dig in, hide from them all day Friday. Friday night, we'll march the rest of the way to Landing. Then we'll assault Saturday morning at dawn. That way, our troops will be reasonably fresh, and theirs may be drunk or hungover from Friday night partying."

Gillian pursed her lips.

"Why not early Sunday morning? Wouldn't they be more drunk or hungover after Saturday night partying?"

"Yes," smiled Tatiana. "Which is exactly why Turgenev would be expecting us then."

"Ah," nodded Gillian.

"What else?" asked Tatiana.

"Well...the attack plan you described. Are you sure about splitting our forces like that?" asked Misha.

Tatiana nodded in certainty.

"Absolutely. As Beto says, we'll be out-numbered and out-gunned. Deception is the only way we can win this battle."

Misha shrugged, but remained silent. Tatiana reached out and playfully touched his cheek.

"You know how much I need your input. Tell me what you're thinking."

"I'm thinking that these are thugs and gangsters. They have no military experience. We just assault them directly at dawn and they'll fold up like a pack of cards."

Tatiana smiled at her husband.

"And how much military experience do our troops have?"

There was a short silence as Misha digested her words. Then he continued his objection.

"But...we'll still have the element of surprise. So we'll still have the advantage."

"No, we won't," said Tatiana. "They'll almost certainly detect your battalion coming in from the east."

Misha shook his head in disagreement. "But we'll be careful. We'll land twenty miles away. We'll move in slowly through the forest. With any luck at all, they'll never know we're there."

Tatiana looked at Misha in amusement.

"Misha, milaya. I don't depend on luck to win my battles. I thought you had learned that by now. They will definitely detect you coming in from the east."

"But how?" Misha continued to argue.

"Because I intend to make sure of it," Tatiana told him.

Stree Prime
Great Cathedral of the Stree

At one AM, Rita and Rachel came to life in their tiny caterpillar bodies. They moved slowly from behind the toilet and across the floor to the door of the restroom. Carefully, they moved under the large crack at the bottom of the door and assessed their position.

To their left was the door back to the basilica. To their right was a short hallway that ended in another door. Scanning, they found a camera in the top right corner of the hallway.

<I think we're outside the field of view of that camera> Rachel transmitted. <It's set for the height of a Stree - it's pointed a bit too high for us>

<As we hoped> Rita said. <Let's go>

Scuttling down the hallway at a speed that defied any biological insect, the one-inch-long Goblin caterpillars moved quickly to the next door and peeked under it.

<A cross hallway> said Rita. <To the right looks like it leads outside the building. Let's go left and try to work our way back into the main offices>

<Watch out for the camera and motion detectors up there> Rachel said. <Up to your left>

<Ah. I see them> Rita responded. <If we stay pressed right up against the left baseboard, I think we'll be alright>

<Yup, agree. Here we go>

And with that, they launched off into their reconnaissance of the building.

Stalingrad System

"You sure about this?" asked Woh.

Ostend shrugged. "That's our mission. The last words I heard from Mark Rodgers and Tatiana Powell were for us to follow the orders of Goblin leadership. If we don't follow these orders...well, then, what? Do we just go off on our own?"

Woh was pissed. He shook his head. "This sucks. I want to go kill some Stree."

Ostend waved his hands in the air helplessly. "As do I. I thought we were signing up to fight. But...Tagi gave me my orders. And either we follow them as we agreed to do when we signed up, or we go rogue."

Woh heaved a deep sigh. "No. I've never disobeyed a lawful order in my life. I don't think I'll start now."

"Then let's get to it."

The two rose from their seats in Captain Ostend's day cabin and stepped through the hatch onto the bridge of the *Darkstar*. Their ship was ready; their crew was ready. It was time for them to go.

Ostend sat in the Captain's chair, and Woh moved to his XO position. When they were settled, Woh glanced at his Captain. Osten nodded and pointed toward the front of the ship.

"Out there," he grinned.

Woh smiled in return. "Out there," he answered, and turned to his bridge crew. "Take us out of the system, Helm. We've got a long way to go."

Far away, just outside the Stalingrad system, the Stree approached. In another twenty-four hours, the Stree fleet of 1,500 ships would be surfacing at the mass limit, ready for their attack on the Goblin defenders.

But the *Darkstar* would not be here. The cruiser began to move, increasing speed rapidly. Thirty minutes later, the ship was 4.9 million miles away from the Dyson Ring, moving at 19,743,452 mph. Its vector pointed directly toward the core of the Milky Way galaxy.

Phoenix System
Battalion West

Corporal James Warren MacIntosh had the shakes. Bad. Really bad. It was all he could do to keep it from the others. He gripped the rifle as hard as he could, trying to hide his trembling hands.

It had seemed so simple when they voted. As they left Stalingrad, all the young able-bodied colonists had been organized into a militia. They were assigned to companies and platoons. From there, each platoon had elected a platoon leader, and been divided up into squads and fire teams. Mac had no prior military experience - but he had taken Junior ROTC in high school. So he was assigned a squad - twelve soldiers, plus himself. And given the rank of Corporal. At the time, it had seemed like a great game.

And when the company commander had called them together the other day and told them what was happening on the surface of Phoenix, like most of his company, Mac had voted to take back their government by an assault on Turgenev's forces below.

But it was different now. He was sitting on a shuttle with 79 other people. They were packed in like sardines, holding their rifles between their knees, with packs of ammo around their waist, combat packs at their feet.

It was getting a bit too real.

Mac had been enamored of the military his entire life. One of his earliest memories was playing with toy soldiers as a child. Growing up, he read everything he could get his hands on about the military. Caesar. Grant. Churchill. Schwarzkopf. As soon as he could, he joined J-ROTC in high school. By junior year, he was already communicating with his local senator to get an appointment to West Point. As a senior, he was added to the list of candidates by his local congressman and felt his acceptance to West Point was assured.

Then the Stree came. He had been on a camping trip in the Cascades, far from the big cities, when the bombs came. The next few weeks were a blur - fighting for his life, trying to find food and water. Radiation sickness, day after day, puking his guts out, until he wanted to die, but couldn't quite do it. Then recovering, and walking, always walking, looking for any other living Human. And finding none. Until he was rescued by the Goblins.

But this was different. This was really, really different from his imagined first trial by fire.

First of all, this was a transport ship, not a warship. It wasn't designed to launch combat shuttles. They had to load through a normal cargo deck, shuffling along in single file, cramming themselves into jump seats along the sides of the shuttle while their platoon commander and platoon gunnery sergeant yelled at them, trying to bring some order to the chaos of inexperienced militia. Most of them had been on a shuttle only once in their entire life - when they were picked up from Earth, half-dead.

And after they were loaded, the platoon leaders roamed up and down the aisle, giving them last-minute instruction as the shuttle powered up and the engines began to whine. Then there were bumps and clanks as the shuttle translated from parking to the rotating launch bobbin and was locked on. A big lurch, and he felt the rotation as the launch bobbin turned. And suddenly he could see space outside the windows, and then another clunk, and they were floating free outside the transport.

In nothingness. There was no ground. Nothing to stand on. Just the Black, and stars.

His guts came up and he was puking. His platoon sergeant, Briggs, was yelling at him, and others, for he was not alone. Up and down the length of the shuttle, people were bringing up their breakfast.

Finally there was nothing left to bring up. He continued with the dry heaves for a bit longer, but finally, he managed to damp it down. Wiping his mouth, he raised his head and looked around. Others were in a similar state; but somehow, they were getting it together.

The shuttle's engines fired, and they were off, performing a retrograde burn to drop out of orbit and land. Mac felt some relief now; at least they were moving. Moving was better than just floating around in the Black.

Mac shivered. His hands had stopped trembling while he puked. Now they started again.

This is it, he thought. *In a half-hour, I'll be on the ground. In enemy territory, more or less. Anything could happen.*

Beside him, his friend Olivia nudged him.

"You scared?" she asked.

Mac nodded. He didn't see any use in lying about it. He had just thrown up his guts in front of the entire platoon. Along with two dozen others.

"Me, too," Olivia said. "I'm scared shitless."

Mac managed a smile at that.

Not like I imagined it at all, he thought.

Stree Prime
Great Cathedral of the Stree

By two AM, Rita and Rachel had completed their reconnaissance of the Cathedral. They were ready for the next step in their plan.

They had determined the Cathedral proper contained the office suites and apartments of the high-ranking members of the Stree hierarchy - Great Prophet Videlli, Prophet Tarilli, and others. Those areas they avoided.

Behind the Cathedral proper they had discovered an administration building, separated from the main Cathedral by a small yard. At the extreme rear of that administration building was a parking lot. And a loading dock at the rear of the building was precisely what they needed.

<That's the only place we can bring in our materials> Rita

pointed out. <We have to control that loading dock>

They had also located the Security Control Room in the center of the administration building, three hallways from the rear. Inside that room were security screens covering an entire wall. Two Stree security guards sat at a counter in front of the screens, watching the monitors, checking alarms - and drinking the Stree equivalent of coffee to stay awake.

And next door to the Security Room was the main computer closet, containing a half-dozen racks of dumb computers controlling the entire complex - including the security systems and video feeds.

<If we control those computers, we control it all> said Rachel.

<Agree. You know what we have to do>

<Yeah. But we need to hurry. It's getting late> said Rachel.

<Agree. Let's do it. Go big or go home>

Quickly, Rita transmitted the details of the setup to Tika, waiting three blocks down the street in a cargo van with the rest of the crew. Then Rita and Rachel moved to the computer closet next door to the Security Office. Peeking under the door in their tiny caterpillar bodies, they ensured the room was empty. Crawling under the door, they ran hard across the room until they were behind the row of computer racks.

<You take the left; I'll take the right> called Rita. Each of them began climbing up the racks, pausing at each computer long enough to quickly take a reading on the inputs and outputs of the computer.

<Found them> called Rachel. <I've got three computers in a stack over here, all controlling the security systems and feeding video to the monitors in the next room>

<Right. On my way. Contact Luda and get him started> Rita called.

Rachel acknowledged as Rita made her way back down the rack of computers she had climbed, across the floor, and up the rack where Rachel waited. Arriving at Rachel's position, she noted that Rachel had inserted a probe into a spare data port on a computer and was feeding data to Luda via radio. In two minutes, Luda reported he had access to the computer and began feeding data back across the radio link to Rachel, who injected it into the data port.

<Luda has a good link> Rachel called. <He's working on taking control of the network>

<How long?> asked Rita.

<He says five more minutes and he'll have it all>

<OK> responded Rita. <But time's getting short. It'll be daylight in another four hours. We need to move faster>

<Roger. He knows>

Rita sat impatiently as Luda worked on obtaining full access to the Cathedral's computer systems. Five minutes and ten seconds later, she heard Luda speaking on her radio band.

<I have full control> he called. <All the cameras for the parking lot, the rear dock and the rear hallways have been looped. We'll be invisible to them now unless they physically get off their ass and walk around. We're moving into the parking lot with the van>

<Roger. We'll meet you at the loading dock> Rita replied.

Rachel and Rita left the room without being observed, scurried down the darkened hallways, and set up guard positions at each end of the rear hallway.

<Oiling the door guides> she heard Luda call. In another minute, the large door of the loading dock creaked upward slowly, squeaking slightly, oil dripping from the guides. Behind the door stood Luda, Ollie, and Tika in their full Stree aspects, their arms loaded with equipment.

As Rita and Rachel switched from their tiny caterpillar bodies to their full-size Stree bodies lying passive in the back of the van, the other three departed into the building with their loads.

Activating their Stree bodies, Rita and Rachel jumped up and began unloading the bodybuilder from the van. Placing the heavy crate on a cart, they pushed it down the rear hallway, around the corner and up to the next hallway. Turning into that hallway, they went mid-way down the hall and through a door.

Inside was a large storage area, filled with miscellaneous crates, unused furniture, and boxes of paper. There was so much material in the room that the back wall couldn't be seen. Luda and Ollie were busy re-arranging a spot to hide the bodybuilder behind the stack of materials.

<I can't believe priests are so messy> Ollie spoke over the radio link.

<Just be thankful they are> Luda responded. While Rita and Rachel joined in to help them, Hajo left to move the van out of the parking lot and secure the rear entrance.

Step One was complete. They were in.

CHAPTER TWENTY-FIVE

Stree Prime
Great Cathedral of the Stree

By 2:45 AM, Rita, Rachel, Hajo, Liwa and Ollie had cleared a space behind the assorted materials in the storage room and completed unpacking the bodybuilder there. Only by threading through a narrow gap in the stacks of boxes could it be accessed.

In an empty office on one side of the storage area, Luda had cleared space and unpacked the remainder of his equipment. He sat now behind the desk, monitoring the network and the Security Room, ensuring no alarms had been given.

Rita stood at the front of the room, checking the placement of the bodybuilder.

"I can't see it from here," she reported. "We're good on placement."

"OK. Next step," said Tika. "Are you sure you want Ollie and Liwa in the security guards? I still think you should go for someone higher up. Maybe the Manager of Security?"

"No. Security guards are practically invisible. They can go anywhere. Nobody questions them. I think that's best."

Tika shrugged. "OK. You got it. Shift change should be at eight AM. We'll go fetch them now and get them converted before things get busy around here."

"OK. Good luck. I'm going back to the office to cover our tracks there. See you this evening."

Tika winked at her. "Good luck!"

With a wave, Rita poked her head out of the storage area, confirmed no one was about, and quickly exited the rear of the building. She knew she had to cover the impending disappearance of herself and her two subordinates from the Signals Branch. Within a half hour, she was back in her office in Naval Headquarters across the street, finalizing her plan.

At 3:15 AM, she received a quick transmission from Tika on her radio band.

<We've got the Security Guards on ice. The first one's in the bodybuilder. He'll finish up about 5:15 AM. Ollie will take him and cover the Security Room until we get the second one finished. Then Liwa will take the second one. We should finish just before shift change>

<Roger. Good work. Keep me posted> Rita responded. <I've issued the orders for our trip. I'll be leaving around nine>

By 8 AM, Rita had put all the pieces in place to cover the impending absence of Captain Elvenen, his adjutant Commander Pamasa, and his aide, Sub-Commander Olvia.

As Rita completed her last bit of planning, Commander Fawa came into the office, hung his coat on the rack, and smiled at her.

"Good morning, sir," he called. "How are you this morning?"

"Excellent, Commander Fawa. However, I have a favor to ask. I need you to run the office for today. I've decided to make a quick inspection trip to our station at Red Mountain. I want to check out their operational procedures and equipment. I've scheduled a shuttle for ten AM, so I'll be leaving shortly. I'm taking Pamasa and Olvia with me, so you'll be in charge until we return."

Fawa looked confused. "But sir…you've only been here two days. Isn't it a bit early to take an inspection trip?"

"No time like the present, Fawa, to let people know I'll be watching over their shoulders. Helps to keep them on their toes."

"Aye, sir. If you say so. Shall I go with you, sir? I feel

responsible for the operation of the remote stations...I should go."

"No, Fawa. I need you here. You keep things running smoothly while I'm gone."

"As you say, sir."

Rita rose, took her tunic and hat off the rack, grabbed a bag she had prepared, and nodded at Fawa.

"I'll be back tonight, Fawa. See you tomorrow."

"Aye, sir." Fawa answered.

As Rita departed her office suite, she couldn't help but smile. Little did Fawa know that he would not see his Captain again.

It would be a tragic and unexpected accident.

Stree Fleet
Approaching Stalingrad

Sojatta was in the middle of his weekly briefing on the readiness status of the fleet when his Flag Aide rushed into the cabin with great excitement.

"We have an initial picture of the enemy fleet's disposition, Admiral!" cried Lieutenant Jassi.

Sojatta glared at the young officer. As Jassi shrank back, realizing he had interrupted a meeting, Sojatta took mercy on him. He grunted and pointed to an empty chair at the conference table.

"Sit, enthusiastic young Lieutenant, and let us hear your news."

Jassi ducked his head in shame and slunk to the empty chair.

"Show us," said Sojatta.

Jassi clicked a remote pointer. A tactical holotank popped into view. Suspended over the conference table, nearly five feet wide, the holo showed the Stalingrad system in great detail.

"Uh...here...sir," Jassi began, still somewhat nonplussed. "...here you can see the Goblin abominations have divided their meager fleet into four Wings, plus what looks like some kind of reserve force. Although they are still at anchor by their main Dyson ring, we noticed they put scouts out to the left and right of the direct line to our fleet. Based on that scouting, we believe they may be thinking of something like a pincer movement, trying to catch us in between two of those Wings."

Sojatta smiled.

"It is exactly as I have foreseen," he said. "They will bring out two of their Wings, one to each side of us. That is what I would do if I were as outnumbered as they are."

"So how will you counter that?" asked Zutirra.

Sojatta's smile grew even broader. "I do not need to counter it, Guardian Officer Zutirra. It is a futile gesture on their part. They have only 550 ships against our 1,500. We will plow right through them like a hot poker. Nothing they can do will be able to stop us. There is one, and only one, strategy to follow. We drive for the Dyson Ring, we destroy their Fleet on the way, and when we arrive, we destroy the Dyson Ring and all the other artificial structures in that system. We leave nothing behind but the memory of these abominations."

Zutirra smiled in joy at the thought. "Even so, Admiral. That is exactly what we shall do."

Phoenix System
Battalion West

With a large thump, the shuttle from Transport Five landed in a small clearing twenty-five miles southwest of the colony. As soon as it was firmly on the ground, Mac's platoon sergeant started yelling.

"Check your gear! Make sure you have everything! Unbuckle! Stand up!"

As Mac got to his feet, the back ramp started down with a whine.

"Face the rear!" yelled Briggs as the ramp touched the ground. "Ready - move!" he yelled. Mac led his squad out, shuffling off the shuttle and down the ramp. It was about five in the afternoon, local time. As Mac walked down the ramp, the brightness overwhelmed his eyes, and he had to squint. He saw it was not a large clearing; no more than a hundred yards wide.

Only four shuttles could land at a time, and they were right up against each other. Briggs was yelling, but so were three other platoon sergeants from other shuttles, and most of the company commanders, so he couldn't really hear what anyone was saying. But he could see his platoon leader and some others, moving off toward the alien blue jungle to the east. He waved to his squad to follow.

As they approached the edge of the clearing, he turned for one last look behind him. The four shuttles sat in the clearing, idling, close together. Four lines of troops were streaming out of the shuttles, each line moving to a convergence point behind him and following his company into the jungle. Olivia's squad was behind his, and she smiled at him and winked. Mac smiled back. Just as he arrived at the jungle edge, the first empty shuttle powered up and departed, running low, over the treetops toward the southwest, away from the colony.

Then he was in the blue jungle. Except for their color, the blue-green trees looked no different than ones on Earth. In seconds, they were in near darkness under a thick canopy. He could barely see the sky.

And then they marched. They marched, and for hours more they marched, until his feet were blistered, and his arms hung down like dead sausages and the sweat turned his clothes rank and salty. And it got dark, and he could hardly make out the person in front of him, and still they marched, a long line of people moving through a dark, nearly invisible jungle.

Occasionally someone lost contact with the person in front of them in the darkness, and stopped abruptly, and the whole line of people had to stop behind them, until a squad leader or a platoon sergeant came back and sorted it out, got them moving again.

He passed the company NCO, Gunny Sparks, standing beside the trail watching people pass by, assessing their condition. He realized the Gunny was wearing a VR helmet, and could see in the dark, and track his people. He was glad of that; it meant if he got his squad totally lost, Gunny could still find him. At least they wouldn't die out here in the jungle.

Once an hour, they took a rest break, falling down wherever they happened to be, sipping water from their canteens, exhausted.

There was not much undergrowth. That, at least, was a blessing. He realized that if there had been thick undergrowth, they would be moving at a snails' pace. But there wasn't, and he thought they must be making good time. But there was no way to know. Nobody was telling them anything. It was just march, and rest once per hour, and then march some more.

He realized his hands weren't trembling anymore.

Stree Prime
Great Cathedral of the Stree

At ten AM, a military shuttle departed the spaceport, remotely controlled by Hajo. Two hundred miles later, as the shuttle passed over the ocean on its flight path, both engines suddenly and unexpectedly stopped. A last mayday call went out, and the shuttle arced over and began a long, one-way trip to the bottom of the ocean, at a spot where it was much too deep to ever be recovered. It was a tragic accident. Captain Elvenen, Commander Pamasa, and Sub-Commander Olvia were lost forever.

Back at the Cathedral, both third shift Security guards had been taken over by Ollie and Liwa. Hours later, as their shift started at midnight, the two entered the Security Room, said goodbye to the departing guards, and settled into their seats to play their parts.

An hour later, at one AM, Rita came in through the back door and went directly to the storage room. As she entered, Tika was sitting behind the desk in the empty office, surrounded by boxes and spare gear.

"Hajo and Rachel are back to the safe house," Rita reported as she sat down in a spare chair in front of the desk. "And we won't have to worry about Elvenen anymore."

"Good," Tika said. "Are we ready for the next step?"

"Yes, I think so. Can you think of any loose ends we haven't covered yet?"

"Only one," Tika said. "You haven't told us who you're going to take over next."

"I haven't actually decided for sure," Rita said. "But I want to go well up the chain, to one of the senior priests. I think that's the only way we'll have the clout to accomplish anything. I'm thinking maybe the archbishop. He's number eight in the hierarchy. That should be high enough to give us the clout we need to get Jim out of prison, but low enough not to attract too much attention if we make a mistake in protocol or culture."

"Pretty ambitious," said Tika. "And how are you going to get to him? It's not like you can walk right into his quarters and ask him to come to the storage room so you can convert him to a Goblin."

Rita nodded. "True. But there has to be some way to get to him. We got this far. All we have to do is get one step farther."

Suddenly, the door to the room slammed open. A Stree monk stood in the opening, glaring across the room at them. He was dressed in a long white sleeping robe. His hand rose, and his fingers pointed straight at them.

"Who are you?" he called out. "What are you doing here?"

Before Rita could react, Luda, from behind the crates on the other side of the room, fired a stunner at the Stree intruder. The monk dropped like a rock in the middle of the doorway. Rita reacted quickly, rushed to him, dragged his body farther into the room, closed the door behind him, and then listened at the door to see if anyone came to investigate.

But nobody came, so she looked around at the figure on the floor. Luda and Tika were standing over him, Luda still holding the stunner.

"Sorry, boss," said Luda. "I reacted without thinking. I hope that's OK."

"That's fine," Rita said. "If you hadn't reacted when you did, he would have called for help and we'd be done. Good work."

"Who is he?" asked Luda.

Tika looked up at them with a concerned expression on her face.

"Tarilli. Great Prophet Videlli's Chief of Staff."

CHAPTER TWENTY-SIX

Stree Prime
Great Cathedral of the Stree

"Oh, this is not good," said Tika. "This is definitely not good. This is Tarilli. Number Two in the whole Stree hierarchy, next to Great Prophet Videlli. This is like taking out the Crown Prince of England. This guy will be missed in a matter of hours, if not minutes. We're in big trouble."

Rita perused the body lying on the floor, thinking. "Not necessarily. You forget, it's after 1 AM. I don't know why he was walking the halls at this unearthly hour, but he was alone. So it's quite possible nobody knows or even cares where he is right now. I suspect we've got a few hours before he'll be missed."

Rita looked at Luda. "Get him in the scanner, get him scanned, and get him in the bodybuilder for Tika to take over."

Tika looked at Rita in horror. "You can't be serious! This is Videlli's Chief of Staff! One tiny mistake and Videlli will be on to us instantly! And we already know the scanner is having problems - dropouts! It's certain I'll be missing some kind of key information that will give me away!"

Rita shrugged. "I don't see that we have a choice, Tika. We can't let him go, and if we keep him, he'll be missed within hours. Taking him over is our only real option. And after all - we wanted someone with influence. Well, we got that, for sure."

The two looked at each other, Tika's disagreement plain to

see. Rita could see she was going to balk, so Rita smiled at her, trying to defuse the situation.

"Tika. I know I'm going on instinct now. This wasn't part of the plan, and I know how uncomfortable it makes you to go off plan. But we have to look at this as an opportunity, not a setback. Please work with me on this. I have a feeling about it. I think this will work."

Tika rolled her eyes but nodded. "I don't like it. I think it's a mistake. But we agreed that you're in charge of the mission, so I'll do it. Just remember, though - if I wake up back in my body at Stalingrad with no memory of this mission, I'm going to kick your ass."

Rita smiled at her. "Roger that."

A half-hour later, Rita sat in the spare office, tapping a pencil on the desk, trying to think. For all her confidence in front of Tika, she was having serious doubts about the path she had chosen.

But...too late to turn back now. I wonder just how much clout Tarilli has. Will he be able to order Jim and the others freed from detention? If Videlli gets suspicious, it's all over. Maybe we shouldn't go down that path.

But...on the other hand...if Tarilli knows where Jim and the others are being kept...then at least we know where to go to break them out.

"You're not going to believe this," Tika said from the doorway. She had a smile on her face a mile wide.

"What?" asked Rita, puzzled.

"While we're waiting for the body to be rebuilt, I side-loaded Tarilli's scan to my temporary memory. Guess why he was here at 1 AM?"

Rita shook her head. "I give up. Why?"

"He's a dopehead. A drug addict. He keeps his stash in here." Tika pulled a bag out from behind her back and held it up for Rita's inspection. "There's enough junk in here to kill a herd of horses."

"Oh my Lord," exclaimed Rita. "A druggie? Tarilli?"

"Yep. That's why he was here alone, and that's why nobody will be looking for him."

"Wow. Did we get lucky or what?"

"You got that right. So..."

"So?"

"So...maybe you know what you're doing after all, boss."

Rita laughed. "Why, thank you, Tika. How are we doing on the bodybuilder?"

"It's going to be close, but I think we can make it. His android body should be ready by four AM. I can get myself transferred into it by five. According to the scan, his first task of the day is to wake Videlli at six. That gives me an hour to get back to Tarilli's room, change clothes and get to Videlli's chambers in time."

"This could be even better than I had hoped for, then. If he's a druggie, there have to be some symptoms of that. Surely Videlli has noticed and is aware of it, and just doesn't care. Maybe that will help to cover some of the initial clumsiness from this new body."

"Let's hope so. And also, I'm moving from a male Stree body to another male Stree body. I've had several days to acclimatize to the one I'm in now; hopefully Tarilli's won't be much different. That may help some."

"OK. Well. So, first of all, good luck."

"Thanks. And second?"

"Did his scan show where Jim and the rest are?"

"No. I wasn't able to find it in my initial pass through his sideload scan. I'll look again once I get transferred into his body."

"OK. And also try to find out if there's any way to recall the Stree fleet."

"I'll try, but we both know there's not much chance of that."

"Yeah, I know. I think I've pretty much given up on that happening. But keep your ears open."

"Roger. So what will you do in the meantime while I'm out winning the war?"

"I think we're going to hunker down until you get yourself organized as Tarilli. I don't want to go back to the safe house - it's too dangerous to move back and forth. And you may need me. So I'm just going to sit here in this dusty-ass storage room with Luda, until you've got Tarilli sorted out."

Phoenix System
Battalion West

For nine hours, Mac, Olivia and the rest of Battalion West had marched. It had started a light rain around midnight. Even though it was fairly warm, with the rain and the perspiration on their skin, they were freezing. It was now two AM. Then, abruptly, the line stopped moving. Mac bumped into the man in front of him before he realized something had changed. At first, he wasn't sure what was happening. Then the word came down the line - they had arrived at their bivouac.

Slowly, over the next hour, they got organized into a camp. It was slow going in the dark. No lights were allowed. They were still in the jungle, although they had reached a place where the trees thinned a bit.

As the line slowly shuffled forward, Mac turned back to Olivia.

"Where do you think we are?" he whispered to her. The lieutenant had passed the word - no talking. But Mac figured whispering was OK.

Olivia moved in closer to him so they could hear each other.

"I think we were making about 2 miles per hour," she said. "So if we landed twenty-five miles from Landing, we're about seven miles from it now."

Mac nodded. "Yeah, that's what I thought too."

"So what's next, you think?"

"The word I heard before we launched is we rest here all day tomorrow, out of sight. No fires, no cooking, no noise. That's what Lt. Raines said."

"Thank God. I don't think I could walk another hundred

yards."

The line shuffled forward, and suddenly they found Lt. Raines standing in front of them. He pointed to one side.

"Your squad over there, MacIntosh. Olivia, yours too."

Mac nodded and turned to the side, finding a bare spot near several trees. The members of the two squads settled in, running ropes between the trees, laying their shelter halves over the ropes, forming simple tents. Crawling inside, they fell to the ground in exhaustion.

Mac realized that Olivia had crawled in beside him. They were cold and wet, and somehow, without a word passing between them, they moved together to share the warmth of their bodies. Holding Olivia, her body heat easing the ache of his muscles and the shivering of his body, Mac passed out almost instantly.

Stree Prime
Great Cathedral of the Stree

Just before 6 AM, Prophet Tarilli waited outside the door of Great Prophet Videlli's chambers, accompanied by four sub-priests. Inside Tarilli's body, Tika's mind wrestled with the precarious situation she found herself in.

Tika had found that Tarilli's side-loaded scan gave her sufficient information to know the basics of his daily routine. She knew what to do at this point in time; per the morning ritual, she had gathered up her staff and made her way to Videlli's chambers. She knew the protocol to awaken Videlli and prepare him for the day. She knew the layout of the Cathedral, the daily routine for both herself and Videlli, even the pass codes for all the computers and security systems.

But she could hardly walk. This body was sufficiently different from the previous Stree male she had inhabited to cause her significant coordination problems.

And worse, she could hardly talk. An unfortunate side-effect of the scan transferred from Tarilli's original brain had been his drug addiction. He had not been able to get his drugs before they stunned him and scanned him. Tika's copy of Tarilli's brain scan was undergoing severe withdrawal symptoms. Each time she accessed it in her spare memory, it nearly knocked her to her knees.

Unable to delay any longer, she keyed in the pass code to the door and walked into the chambers of the Great High Prophet of the Stree Theocracy, hoping for the best.

Phoenix System
Battalion East

Eight miles northeast of Landing, Misha's Battalion East was waking up after their first night on the planet. They had landed their shuttles the afternoon before, twenty miles from Landing, in the foothills of the Eastern Mountains. Like Battalion West, they had marched at night. But they had marched slower. They were still twelve miles from Landing, well to the northeast.

Now, at dawn, Misha put down his communicator and sighed. He had just finished making his morning report to Tatiana. She was satisfied with their progress and told him not to worry.

But he worried, nonetheless. He understood Tatiana's plan. He got it. But he was not with her. He was here, and she was nineteen miles away, on the other side of Landing. Not being with her made him nervous.

And he kept thinking about their child, Marta. Marta was still on the transport, in orbit above them, in the care of Gillian.

What if neither Tatiana nor I make it back? What if both of us are killed tomorrow?

The thought wouldn't leave his mind. In the Singheko War, Misha had fought beside Tatiana on Deriko, battle after battle, with never a second thought. But that was different. That was before he had a child to consider.

What if Marta's an orphan? Will Gillian be able to take care of her? And what if we lose tomorrow? For sure, Turgenev will kill Gillian. Will he kill Marta too, even though she's a child?

Misha hung his head, unable to stop thinking about it. He knew it was pointless, and worse, it was stupid to dwell on it. But his mind just wouldn't stop thinking about it.

He needed something to distract him.

He crawled out of his tiny tent and looked around. They had picked a night camp surrounded by tall trees, with some understory of smaller trees beneath it. With only two layers, it wasn't a true triple-canopy jungle. He could have found a better spot, a camp with thicker canopy above, where he would have been better protected from drones. But intentionally, he did not.

It was ironic, Misha thought. Tatiana's plan called for his force to be discovered today, hopefully this morning. It grated on him, but he was doing his best to accomplish her plan.

His XO, Major Brett Jones, came up to him and saluted. Misha returned the salute, trying not to grin. It had been a long time since anybody saluted him. They were just a militia, but Tatiana had drummed it into them. Maintain military discipline - and military honors - at all times. So they did it. She was the boss.

"Scouts report an enemy squad about a half-mile west of us. They appear to have found us. They're just sitting, hidden in a gully, watching us."

"Very good, Major Jones. We'll keep up the pretense of trying to hide. Pass the word to maintain silence. No talking, no clinking of weapons. Everyone just stay quiet and very still."

"Aye, aye, sir," said Jones. He saluted, turned smartly, and departed.

Misha smiled. Some people just took to the military like a fish to water. Brett Jones was one of those. It was like Brett had waited his whole life to be where he was today.

"Drone!" came a call. Misha turned, looked up at the treetops and sky above. Sure enough, in the distance through a small break in the canopy, he could see the distant outline of a small drone, working its way toward the east. He knew the drone operator had seen them - the operator was trying to pretend otherwise, but Misha knew they were well in range of the drone's camera.

Playing the game of deception, he dived under the nearest tree, along with everyone else in the camp. 800 troops - his full battalion - huddled silently on the ground, waiting to see what would happen. The drone continued on, fading off into the distance toward the mountains. As soon as it was out of sight, Misha jumped to his feet and gestured to his XO.

"Get us moving toward the northwest. Pronto!"

Brett acknowledged and ran toward the nearby operations tent they had set up last night. Within thirty minutes, the entire battalion was on the march, heading to the northwest. It was an indirect line toward Landing, angling away from the enemy scouts that were between them and the river. It also moved them to the path already scouted by the passing drone. Still playing the game, Misha was attempting to convince the enemy they were trying to outfox the drone by moving to where it had been, rather than where it was going.

I hope Turgenev's people are smart. Just smart enough to out-think themselves.

Stree Prime
Great Cathedral of the Stree

Somehow, Tika stumbled through the process of awakening Great Prophet Videlli. She delegated all the important tasks to her junior staff and stood respectfully - and silently - in the background as they went about their duties.

The Great Prophet was a short, fat Stree, shorter and fatter than the average. He was obviously well fed. He awoke grumpy, and chastised both her and her staff continuously from the time of his awakening until he was bathed and dressed for the day in his elaborate set of vestments, with his bejeweled necklace around his neck.

After Videlli was dressed and had departed to his office suite, Tarilli/Tika was released to return to her own office. There she endured a seemingly endless queue of interruptions and requests by her staff members, which prevented her from launching into her greatest priority - finding out where Jim and the other Human prisoners were located. That information appeared to be missing from Tarilli's scan. It was becoming more and more apparent that their scanner was damaged - each scan seemed to have more dropouts than the previous one.

She was forced to maintain her deception of being the number two person in the Stree hierarchy all day. She pretended to process emails, had dozens of conversations about all manner of mundane things, and skipped lunch by claiming she was ill. She checked in with Rita by radio band several times during the day, to ensure all was well. And somehow, she got through without making any major mistakes that would draw attention to herself.

By late afternoon, she checked her calendar and realized it was possible to leave early - she had no important tasks left for this day. She begged off from her staff and retired to her quarters, where she immediately called Rita on the radio band.

<I'm back in my quarters. Today was hell. I was hanging on tenterhooks all day; certain they'd find me out>

<You did great, Tika. I'm so proud of you. No one could have done a better job>

<Any fallout from the disappearance of Elvenen and his staff?>

<The Navy has a tremendous search operation going on, but there's no chance they'll find the shuttle. It's 12,000 feet under the ocean. Elvenen is gone for good>

<OK. I'm still struggling with this asshole's drug addiction. Do you want to come over?>

<Maybe. I'm not sure. Where is it?>

<Actually, not that far from you. The rear part of the Cathedral, right in front of the Administration building. You

could literally walk out the front door of the Administration building, walk in the back door of the Cathedral, turn right, and you'd be there. At least it would give you a better feel for the lay of the land. And I put in the codes today to bump up your access. You're listed as a Security Consultant reporting directly to me. You can go anywhere in the Cathedral now - except into Videlli's private quarters, of course>

<Tell you what. I'll come over at midnight. I think that would be safer>

<OK. I'll pretend to sleep until then>

<See ya>

CHAPTER TWENTY-SEVEN

Phoenix System
Battalion West

Mac woke up. Something didn't feel right. He lay still, trying to figure it out.

He realized his pants were down around his knees. His middle was pressed up against Olivia's half-naked body. And her pants were also down around her knees.

His front was toasty, exceptionally comfortable. But his naked ass was freezing.

Slowly, it came back to him. The long, exhausting march from the LZ. Arriving at their bivouac. Stretching the shelter halves between the trees. Crawling in, both of them cold and wet, huddling together for warmth in the crude tent. And then suddenly, Olivia reaching for his pants, unbuttoning, pulling them down, both of them mad with desire, him pulling her clothes apart, ignorant to the world except for their need to be alive, to be with someone before they died.

He reached down and pulled up his pants, trying not to wake Olivia. But before he could finish, she reached out, grabbed his gentleman equipment, and held on. Without opening her eyes, she mumbled.

"One more round?"

"My ass is freezing, babe. And I can hear people moving around. I don't think so."

"Killjoy," she said, opening her eyes. She let go of him. He finished pulling up his pants and zipped up.

"I'm going to see what's going on. Be back in a minute."

Crawling out of the tent, Mac stood up and looked around. It was barely the crack of dawn. Dim light filtered through the triple-canopy jungle. It was nearly impossible to see the sky, with only the occasional slice of light showing through. Their officers had definitely picked a good, well-hidden location.

Mac saw his platoon leader, Lt. Raines, sitting on a rock a few dozen yards away. He walked over and squatted down by him, gazing around at the camp.

"So the plan today is we just sit tight, right, sir?" Mac said.

Tom nodded. "That's the plan. Rest, relax, clean our gear, stay out of sight. Get ready for a night march tonight."

"And no fires?"

"No fires. No cooking. No loud voices, no noise. Just sit and wait."

Mac smiled. He couldn't help it. He nodded at the Lieutenant and stood, walked back to his tent. Crawling inside, he lay down beside Olivia and pulled her to him.

"Change of plans, babe. Round Two is definitely on!"

Stalingrad System

"Enemy in sight, Admiral," called Lieutenant Jassi. "They are arrayed as you predicted. One Wing is deployed forward and to the left, and another forward and to the right. Two Wings hold the center. They'll attempt to catch us in a pincer move with the two forward Wings, reduce our numbers before we smash into the two Wings in the center."

"A good plan, actually the best plan they could assemble with the forces they have," mused Sojatta. "But it won't be enough. Those Assault Wings to the sides will hurt us, but they won't stop us."

Zutirra, sitting beside Sojatta in the Guardian Officer's chair, showed his teeth in a fierce smile of hatred. "Excellent, Admiral. We smash them now! We wipe these abominations out of the Universe!"

Sojatta looked at Zutirra with some displeasure. "Zutirra, we will smash their homeland, that is certain. But we will not wipe them from the Universe. Even though we chase down stragglers for a thousand years, we will never be able to find them all. Surely you recognize that."

Zutirra snarled in anger. "Still, we will try! We will do our utmost!"

"Yes," Sojatta said mildly, gazing at the holotank as they accelerated into the Stalingrad system, "we will do our utmost."

Sojatta turned to Jassi. "What are the final numbers, Jassi?"

"It appears they are still showing at 550 ships, sir. Four Wings of 125 ships each, plus that small force of 50 ships backed up to the Dyson Ring, which we assume is their reserve force."

"That reserve force will not do them much good," said Sojatta. "I can see even from here that those are tired, second-rate ships. They'll be lucky to get off one volley when we smash into them."

Jassi smiled. "Aye, sir."

Sojatta waved at the holo.

"Proceed with Battle Plan Alpha as briefed, Jassi. Straight at them. No deviations, no strategy, just brute force. Plow through them and kill them."

Jassi smiled again. "Aye, aye, sir."

Stalingrad System

Captain-Leader Bagi stared at the Stree fleet arrayed before him in disbelief.

1,500 ships. 3-to-1 odds.

Bagi's squadron of sixteen Goblin cruisers looked down the missile tubes of forty-eight Stree cruisers. And to his left and right, other cruiser squadrons faced comparable odds, as did the battlecruiser squadrons behind him.

Bagi knew his role in this first battle. When the Stree entered the system, Bagi's Assault Wing One moved quickly to a position well off to one side of the oncoming Stree. Assault Wing Two positioned to the opposite side of the enemy line of advance. The two Assault Wings were to decimate the incoming Stree, disrupt their formations, force them to turn and engage. Meanwhile, Assault Wings Three and Four would remain positioned in the center, in front of the Stree, waiting for them.

At the 10 AU point, Bagi's Wing turned in toward the enemy and boosted directly at them. The first dance in the choreography of death was starting.

But Bagi could see it wasn't going to be enough. The mass of Stree in front of them covered the sky, blanking out stars as they passed. Enemy cruiser and battlecruiser cubes stretched across their front, a mass of ships that boggled the mind.

Bagi had already accepted that he would not survive this battle. That was a given.

The bigger question was whether or not his backup copy in the Dyson Ring would survive. If the Stree defeated the Goblin fleet, they would certainly destroy the Ring, and every other object in the Dyson swarm that made up the Goblin homeland.

And that would be the end of Bagi and all the Goblins who died in this battle. There would be no backup copies after that. No resurrection into a new body to continue the fight.

This might be it, Bagi thought somewhat disinterestedly. *We'll see. But I'll take some Stree with me.*

"Battle Stations," he called as they approached the mass of enemy ships in front of them. Around him, the *bong-bong-bong* of the General Alarm started up. The condition lights switched from yellow to red. The ceiling of the bridge vibrated a bit as the heavy bodies of Goblins on the deck above ran to their battle stations.

"Time to missile range?"

"Fifteen minutes, sir," called his Tactical Officer. "All divisions report ready for action. Fighters going out now."

Bagi nodded absent-mindedly as he watched the holo. Thousands of Goblin fighters departed their carriers and battlecruisers and leaped forward toward the Stree fleet. At the same time, three times as many Stree fighters poured out of their ships, rushing toward the Goblin fighters in a cloud, a solid mass of death. In a matter of seconds, the two sets of fighters merged, surrounding the Stree fleet like a cloud of insects, a swirling mass in the holo that twisted and turned, with the streaks of lasers and missiles adding to the morass of dots in the holo - until it seemed some kind of artwork designed to confuse and puzzle the brain. Then hundreds, then thousands of those dots turned into bright explosions, glowing dots of fire in the holo that drifted out of the battle zone on long tracers leading nowhere.

And Bagi knew every one of those long tracers was a death. Either the permanent death of a Stree - or the death of a Goblin.

A temporary death - if the Goblins won this battle and protected the Dyson Ring where all backup copies were stored.

But if they lost...a death that would be permanent.

That has to suck, Bagi thought. *Dying and as you die, you don't know if you'll come back or not.*

A smile touched his mental lips.

That makes us just like Humans, I guess.

"Missile range in two minutes, sir," called the Tactical Officer.

"Thank you, Tac," Bagi responded. He was in his warbody - the large, armored cube on the bridge, welded to the floor. In this aspect, he had a full, 360-degree view of the battlefield. He had access to every control and station on the bridge with a simple thought. In theory, he could react twice as fast as a Stree commander.

Too bad missiles don't know theory, Bagi thought as the range closed. *The laws of physics apply to Stree and Goblin alike. Regardless of our processing speed, we're still subject to inertia. Our missiles can't maneuver any faster than the Stree.*

And then, suddenly, they were in range and it was no longer

time to think, it was time to fight. Bagi's squadron fired all 256 of their missiles at the vast array of Stree warships in front of them. Then his crew turned to point defense. The initial rain of Stree missiles that came at them was mind-boggling. In seconds, Bagi's squadron was facing 672 missiles, each one of them maneuvering wildly to evade his point defense.

As the cloud of Stree missiles came in range and his point defense cannon and railguns began to vibrate the ship, Bagi had time for one last thought.

We aren't going to survive this.

Stree Prime
Great Cathedral of the Stree

At midnight, Rita took a deep breath, cracked open the door to the hallway, and peeked out. It was clear. She glanced back at Luda watching from the back of the room, gave him a thumbs-up, and stepped out into the hallway.

She was back in one of the spare Stree bodies and wearing a Stree Naval uniform. Around her neck was an ID badge, with the identity of a captain in Stree Naval Intelligence. She strode confidently down the hallway, hoping she wouldn't meet anyone at this late hour.

At the end of the hallway, she rounded the corner and walked down the long outer hallway toward the front of the Administration building. As she approached the middle of the hallway, two Stree came around the opposite corner toward her. One was dressed in the long flowing robes of the priesthood. The jeweled pendant around his neck marked him as a high-ranking official. Her internal AI quickly processed his appearance, and his identity popped up in her internal display.

Prophet Gitweo. Third in the hierarchy of the Stree Theocracy. Head of the Secret Police.

Quickly Rita slammed herself against the wall, bowed as low as she possibly could without falling forward, and waited for them to pass. It was the accepted protocol for meeting someone of Gitweo's rank. As the two approached, her AI gave a quiet internal ping and the identity of the second Stree popped up on her internal display.

Cotrapi. Videlli's Head Jailer.

Rita maintained her position of obeisance, waiting for them to pass. They did and she straightened and continued down the hallway. As they moved farther away, her enhanced hearing heard several words of their muttered conversation.

"...three dead. Five left. I'll start on the next one tomorrow..."

Rita stopped, frozen in her tracks. The voice had come from Cotrapi.

He has to be talking about Jim and the rest. Oh my Lord, he's already killed three of them.

Rita started moving again. She had a mission to accomplish. She knew she couldn't let personal feelings prevent that. But in spite of herself, she stumbled as Cotrapi's words hit her hard.

Oh Lord, please, not Jim. Not Jim.

Forcing herself to keep moving, she came to the end of the hall. Stepping through the doorway to her right, Rita was outside, in the cold night air. She walked briskly across a small quadrangle to the Cathedral proper. On the right side of the huge building was another door. Raising her ID badge to the reader, she heard a click and the light turned green.

So far so good.

Opening the door, she entered and turned right. Following the directions Tika had provided, she walked past three doors and knocked gently on the fourth. The door opened and there stood Tarilli, wearing some kind of off-white sleeping robe. Even knowing that it was Tika inside the android body, it took a leap of faith for Rita to face the second-most dangerous Stree on the planet without flinching.

"In, quick!" the figure of Tarilli hissed. Rita stepped through the door, and Tika closed it behind her. Rita found herself in a private suite. Tika waved her to a couch beside a coffee table. Rita sat, Tika taking the opposite seat. They stared at each other for a moment.

<Do you think this room is bugged?> Rita asked in her radio voice.

"No. According to Tarilli's scan, it's one of the few places in the Cathedral that's not bugged."

"Good. How ya doin'?"

Tika shrugged. "I've been better. This asshole is going through withdrawal right now. There's enough residual discomfort from his scan to make it a real pain in the ass."

"Sorry. But otherwise?"

"Otherwise, I got through the day. I don't think I made any major mistakes. I kept telling the staff I was ill and to take care of things on their own. They seemed to accept it as normal. It makes me wonder if he does that a lot, when he's screwed up on drugs."

"Probably. Wow, I still can't believe it. The Stree Number Two - a druggie."

"Videlli has to know. I don't think there's any way he could not pick up on it."

"Well, it's not without precedent. Hitler - sorry, that was a crazy bastard back in the last century on Earth - he was a druggie too."

"I know who Hitler was. I studied Earth history on the trip from Stalingrad to Dekanna when I first met Rachel."

"Oh, sorry. Right."

"Anyway - what now?"

Rita paused, thinking. "Well - the battle at Stalingrad has begun, according to Hajo's latest intel. We're out of time. So we have two things we have to do. The first is to try and find some way to recall the Stree fleet."

"OK. And two?"

"Find Jim and the rest and see if there's any feasible way to rescue them."

"They're in the basement. I finally found it in Tarilli's scan."

Rita nodded. "Good. But we don't have much time at all. I overheard Gitweo and Cotrapi in the hallway on my way over.

They've already killed three of them and will take another tomorrow."

"So. What do you want to do next?"

Suddenly there was a gentle knock on the door. They were both caught off-guard by the sound. Before either could react, the knob of the door started to turn.

Acting instinctively, Rita dived behind the couch in one smooth motion. A second or two after she hit the carpeted floor on the other side of the couch, she heard the hinges of the door squeak as someone opened it and stepped into the room. There was a short silence. Then Tika uttered words that froze the blood in Rita's veins.

"Great Prophet Videlli!"

Turning her head slightly, Rita could see through a small crack between the couch and the end table. There, indeed, was Videlli - Highest of the High, Prime Leader of the Stree Nation, Great Prophet of the Stree Destiny. He had none of his usual vestments, wearing only a simple shift of white, but it was clearly him.

What the hell does Videlli want with Tarilli at midnight?

The supreme leader of the Stree moved slowly toward the figure of Tarilli, a smile creasing his lips. Tika, inside Tarilli's body, stood in shock. Videlli reached out his arms and put them on Tarilli's shoulders.

And leaned forward and kissed him.

CHAPTER TWENTY-EIGHT

Stree Prime
Great Cathedral of the Stree

In Tarilli's room, Rita watched in shock as Great Prophet Videlli kissed Tarilli/Tika.

<What the fuck?> she heard Tika on the radio band.

Rita grinned hugely as she realized what was happening.

<Exactly> she replied over radio. <It appears you took over the body of Videlli's lover!>

<What?> Tika practically yelled over the radio band as Videlli continued to press himself on Tarilli's body. <What are we gonna do?>

<I don't know about you, but I'm going to watch and laugh! > Rita said.

<Think of something!> Tika yelled over the radio net as Videlli began pushing Tika toward the nearby bed, his intentions clear. <You're the mission commander! Get me out of this!>

<Tika, I think you're gonna have to take one for the team!>

<Rita! I'm going to kill you for this!>

<Tika, listen. Keep him occupied for five minutes! I've got an idea!>

<Five minutes? Five minutes? You want me to put up with this for five minutes?>

<Trust me. Just give me five minutes!>

Rita quickly switched to Luda's channel.

<Luda! Emergency! Bring the scanner to Tarilli's room as fast as you possibly can! When you get here, wait outside the door, and ping me. Hurry, Luda!>

<Roger. On my way!>

Rita watched as Tika, now prone on the bed with Videlli on top of her, made a valiant attempt to buy time.

"Oh, Great Prophet," Tika said. "Can you give me just a minute to go to the restroom?"

Videlli grunted but lifted himself up off Tika's body onto one fat elbow. "Can't it wait?" he asked.

"Oh Great Prophet, it cannot wait! I'm sorry, I'll be right back!"

With that, Videlli grunted once again and allowed Tika to escape from beneath him. He turned over to his back, lay back on the bed, crossed his arms behind his head, and stared up at the ceiling. Tika dived off the bed and hurried to the restroom, closing the door behind her.

<Now what?> Tika asked in her radio voice.

<In exactly three minutes, I want you to come out of that restroom. Be sure to turn off the room lights. Then go back to Videlli and keep him occupied for another sixty seconds>

<Sixty seconds is a long time with a fat Stree on top of you!>

<I don't care. Get it done, soldier>

Tika didn't respond, but Rita could imagine her internal sigh. All was quiet for three minutes. Then Tika came out of the bathroom, turned off the room lights, went to the bed, and lay down beside Videlli. Videlli rose on his elbows, stared down at the figure of his lover beside him, and smiled. He leaned down and kissed Tika again, long and hard.

<Oh, fucking crap> Rita heard over the radio.

<I'm here!> called Luda from outside the door.

Carefully, Rita rose from behind the couch. In the darkened room, she moved slowly from behind the couch and across the room until she was beside the bed. Videlli was too occupied to notice her. She leaned forward and with an iron grip, grabbed Videlli around the throat suddenly and hard, jerking his neck backward so forcefully he had no chance to get out a shout before his air was cut off. She held him in an iron grip until he stopped struggling and his body went limp.

<Luda! Come in quick!> she called.

As the door opened and Luda entered the room carrying the scanner, Tika looked at Rita in astonishment.

"You can't be serious," Tika said out loud.

Phoenix System
Battalion West

Mac and Olivia slept through most of the day, rousing only twice. The first time, he and Olivia came out of the tent and sat on a tree bole to eat a late breakfast. Before launch from the transport, each had been given a half-dozen compact meals to carry in their packs, meals provided by the Goblins. They were similar to military field rations Mac had encountered in J-ROTC - something called an MRE. But, he decided, quite a bit tastier. Evidently the Goblins were better than Humans at putting such meals together.

Mac and Olivia got up once again in the early afternoon, eating another ration. After their meal, they walked down to a nearby creek to re-fill their canteens. As they stooped at the water, Mac noticed a tall woman sitting on a nearby rock. She looked somewhat familiar to him, although he couldn't place her. She smiled at him.

"Don't forget to drop your water purification tablets in there," she said.

"Right," Mac nodded. He glanced at Olivia to see if she recognized the woman, but she made no sign of it. Turning back to the stranger, he noted she seemed a bit older than most in the battalion. Probably pushing thirty, he decided. Not old, but older. Her features were somewhat Slavic, with high cheekbones. She was beautiful, he realized. Totally beautiful. Athletic, too, he decided. Her muscles looked as hard as a rock.

Putting the tablets into his canteen, he stood, hung it on his belt, and waited for Olivia to finish. Looking at the woman, he smiled back at her.

"How was the chow?" the woman asked.

"It was good, really good," said Mac. "Better than I expected."

"Good," she replied. "Where are you from?"

"Washington State," Mac said. "In the U.S."

"Nice. I've heard that's a beautiful state."

"Was," said Mac. "Was a beautiful state. Not now. Not anymore."

"Yeah, sorry. I forget sometime."

Mac nodded. "So do I. Sometimes."

The woman tilted her head at him, her smile drooping into a frown.

"It's easy to forget, isn't it? It seems like we could just get on the ship, fly back to Earth, and find it as we knew it, green and beautiful and full of life."

"Yeah," responded Mac. He gazed away wistfully at the trees and rocks surrounding them. "But...we'll make a new home. Here. We'll make this place blue and beautiful and full of life."

The woman looked at him with something like awe in her face.

"We will," she said. "As long as there are people like you, we'll make it. Somehow."

Mac nodded, smiled, and walked back toward his tent, Olivia beside him. Heads down, they were silent as they walked. The conversation with the strange woman had made them pensive, made them think. The challenge in front of them was becoming more real. Not only did they have to win the coming battle - but they also had to win this planet. Survive. Make it a home.

Olivia reached out and took his hand as they walked back to their tent. They crawled in. Holding on to each other, they went back to sleep.

Great Cathedral of the Stree

"He wants what?" Cotrapi asked in amazement. "Videlli himself?"

"Yes," came Tarilli's voice over the phone. "Bring the Human prisoner called Jim Carter to Videlli's audience chamber immediately. Right now."

"But..." Cotrapi hesitated. To question Great Prophet Videlli was death. And Tarilli - well, that was death too. Just maybe a bit slower.

"It will be done, Master. I'll have him there in ten minutes."

"Fine," said Tarilli, and the phone went dead.

Cotrapi shuddered. He had taken a Human prisoner to the torture chamber yesterday; and that one was now dead.

But luckily, it had not been the one called Jim Carter. He shuddered again to think what could have happened if he had killed the very one Videlli wanted this morning.

Not good. Not good at all. I ducked a bullet on that one.

"Aswar," Cotrapi roared at his second-in-command. "Get four guards and get the Human prisoner called Jim Carter out of his cell. Bring him to me. Quickly!"

"Aye, sir," called Aswar, jumping up from his desk and rushing out of the room. Cotrapi stood up, brushed the crumbs of his lunch off his tunic, and reached for his helmet. The helmet was his badge of office. If he was going to be in front of Great Prophet Videlli, the helmet definitely needed to be firmly on his head.

Checking himself in the mirror, he flicked another few crumbs off his clothing and decided it was as good as it was going to get.

Why in hell does the Great Prophet want to see a prisoner now?

Outside, he heard a commotion and then Aswar stuck his head in the door of the office.

"Ready, sir," he called.

Cotrapi nodded and followed Aswar out of the office. Outside in the hallway, the prisoner Jim Carter hung limply between the four guards. He had been beaten recently - just on general principle - and was weak from hunger and deprivation.

Shit! I hope he doesn't die on me before we get to Videlli's chambers!

"Follow me," Cotrapi growled, heading toward Videlli's audience chamber. "And try to keep him upright!"

Stalingrad System
Dyson Swarm

The flood of Stree missiles had barreled through First Assault Wing like a herd of rhino, leaving a junkyard of shattered Goblin ships behind them. The *Blue Quark* was shot to hell. She had lost one engine and could only generate 75% of normal thrust. Every missile tube was out of action, as was her entire array of point defense cannon. There wasn't a single compartment that wasn't shot through and through with shrapnel and railgun rounds, leaving great gaping holes in the hull of the ship.

Captain Bagi still lived, though. As did some of his crew. After the first assault pass, the *Blue Quark* had streaked through the Stree fleet and out into the Black, her damaged engine unable to decelerate and turn with the rest of his formation. Bagi ended up almost 1 AU behind the rest of his Wing before he got the ship fully turned around and headed back toward the battle.

In front of him, four large formations of warships could be seen. First came the Stree as they rushed directly toward their target - the Dyson Ring circling the star at 0.5 AU. Their intentions were clear. They were going to destroy the Goblin homeland and every Goblin in it.

The survivors of Goblin Assault Wing Three, with their greater accel of 500g, had moved out to one side of the Stree fleet, turned, and were boring in for a second engagement.

Assault Wing Four performed a mirror-image maneuver, putting them on the other side of the Stree fleet. Now they also pivoted to come in from that side. As in the original engagement in the outer system, the two Wings would catch the Stree in another pincer movement, attacking from two sides and then passing through them at high speed.

At the same time, Assault Wings Three and Four waited in front of the Stree. As the remnants of the other two Wings re-grouped and attacked from the sides, the battle would be joined, putting the Stree between three separate groups of Goblin ships.

Bagi did a quick count. There were 521 Stree ships left out of the original 1,500. The rest of them were burning, shattered hulks in the outer system. The first engagement had done its job, inflicting 65% losses on the Stree fleet upon their initial entry into the system.

But the Goblin fleet was also decimated. 206 Goblin ships had been lost in the outer system. Not counting the reserve of 50 older ships waiting in front of the Dyson Ring, only 244 Goblin ships remained to fend off the 521 Stree ships still intact and battle-ready.

The outcome was inevitable, and Bagi knew it. And worse, he knew he could not catch up to the Stree fleet before the next phase of the battle. His damaged engines, operating at only 75% of normal thrust, simply would not get him there in time. He would be an involuntary observer of the next pass.

Nevertheless, he pushed the throttle of the remaining three engines up until the entire ship shook like a leaf in the wind, the engines whining in protest. The vibration threatened to tear off more damaged pieces of the warship as it grudgingly began to accelerate back into the system toward the Dyson Ring.

I will not be there in time for the next pass. But I will be there for the final battle at the Ring. And that will be enough.

Great Cathedral of the Stree

Jim was thoroughly confused. One minute he had been sleeping in the dingy, filthy cell at the bottom of the Cathedral dungeon. Then four guards had suddenly appeared, jerked him out of his bunk, yanked him out of the cell, bound his hands, and dragged him roughly up two flights of stairs and down a hallway.

Then the head jailer Cotrapi joined them and took off at a fast pace, the four guards half-dragging Jim along behind, his legs and feet so weak he could barely move them in concert with the yanks and tugs.

He was dragged up another two flights of stairs to a well-lit hallway. Halfway down the hallway, large double doors led into an ornate room. Jim was pulled forward to a spot before an empty throne and thrown to the floor in a heap. He tried to lift his head to look around, but instantly a rifle butt slammed into his ribs, and another one into the back of his head, drawing blood. A harsh command was yelled. He didn't understand the command, but he got the meaning.

Keep your head down.

Now he slumped on his knees before the empty throne, hands bound tightly behind him. Blood dripped down the side of his face where the rifle butt had hit him. His ribs felt like someone had stuck a knife in them.

Suddenly another monk came into the room. Jim had seen him before - standing in front of his cell, glaring at the Humans, talking to Cotrapi. He had heard Cotrapi call him Tarilli.

One of the guards slammed a foot into the small of Jim's back, forcing him to lie on the floor. Then Cotrapi and the other guards all fell to the floor, prostrating themselves, eyes and forehead to the floor. Only the monk Tarilli remained alert, watching Jim carefully, sinking to a kneeling position to one side of the throne.

Out of the corner of his eye, Jim saw a door behind the throne open. The figure of Great Prophet Videlli appeared. He wore long, flowing robes of scarlet, trimmed with gold. Bejeweled necklaces and pendants covered the front of his robe. On his head was a high mitered crown, bespectacled with jewels and gold. His fat fingers were covered in golden rings.

Videlli moved slowly to the throne, an entourage of four priests following him on both sides. He took his place on the throne and settled in, making himself comfortable.

Videlli looked down at the tableau before him. He glanced at Tarilli and said something in Stree.

Lying with his forehead pushed against the floor, Jim realized he wouldn't live long. He was at the mercy of the Stree leader - who had vowed to kill every sentient AI in the galaxy and any biological creature who aided them.

I just hope they make it quick.

"You may look up, blasphemer," said a voice. "You are already condemned to death in any case."

Jim slowly raised his head to look at the Great Prophet. Videlli glared at him.

"By all rights, I should have you executed here and now, Human," Videlli said in Stree, words in English coming from a translator hung around his neck. "But it's interesting to me how you Humans have come so far in only three years, from monkeys cavorting on the surface of your planet to space warriors fighting us as if we were equals."

Videlli leaned forward, staring into Jim's eyes.

"We are not equals, Human. You are still but a monkey cavorting in the universe, with delusions of grandeur."

Videlli leaned back, adjusting his robe, and brushing away some lint. He smiled at Jim.

"Still, I would learn more about this. Perhaps your rapid rise from the jungle to space can be instructive to me. I think I will amuse myself with you before sentence is executed."

Videlli snapped his fingers. Beside Jim, Tarilli lifted his head slightly.

"Yes, O Great Prophet?"

"Have this monkey taken to my study. I would question it at my convenience."

"Yes, O Great Prophet. It will be done."

Videlli rose from the throne and turned to depart. The

four priests beside his path to the rear of the room prostrated themselves on the floor until he was gone. Then they rose and followed him dutifully through the door.

Now Jim was seized roughly and jerked to his feet. His guards hustled him out a side door of the throne room and down a long hallway. Cotrapi followed, clearly nervous. At the end of the hallway, the guards jerked Jim roughly through a door and into another corridor. Halfway down, they pushed him up two flights of stairs to the third floor, down a hallway, and through an ornate door on the right side of the corridor.

Jim found himself in a large study. On three sides, bookshelves lined the wall. On the fourth side was a large desk, with three chairs aligned in front of it.

The guards dragged Jim to the center chair, directly in front of the desk, and pushed him down into it. They tied his hands roughly to the arms of the chair. A noose was placed around his neck and ran down the back of the chair to a ring in the floor, ensuring he could not move. Then the guards departed, leaving him alone with Tarilli and Cotrapi. Tarilli looked at Cotrapi and waved him out of the room as well.

There was silence in the room. Jim looked around. Behind the desk was a large viewscreen. On the screen, Jim could see a prison cell. It was rough-cut stone, with a high window that let in a bit of light. There was just enough light to see Bonnie sitting on a crude bunk, her head lowered to stare at the floor.

"Bonnie!" Jim called involuntarily as he saw her.

"She cannot hear you," Tarilli said quietly in English. "You waste your breath."

To one side, a door opened. Great Prophet Videlli walked in, moved to the desk, and sat down. He had shed his outer robes and crown. Now he was dressed in a simple white robe trimmed in gold. He stared at Jim for a moment, then looked at Tarilli.

"Remove his restraints," he said in perfect English.

Tarilli nodded and moved to Jim's side. He removed the noose around Jim's neck, then the wrist bindings. Jim rubbed his wrists, massaging away the pain, and looked at Videlli, puzzled.

"Stand up, Human," said Videlli.

Jim stood, his mind a whirl of possibilities.

Maybe I can escape. Maybe I can kill Videlli.

But none of those things help Bonnie and the others. Maybe I'd better see where this is going.

Videlli stood up and walked around his desk, moving to a position directly in front of Jim. He stared at Jim with a twinkle in his eyes. There was a faint smile on his lips.

"Hello there, big boy. Why don't you come up and see me sometime?"

CHAPTER TWENTY-NINE

Stree Prime
Great Cathedral of the Stree

"Rita?" Jim was too astounded to say more. That was the only word he could get out.,

"You bet your ass, big boy," rasped Videlli, his guttural Stree voice totally out of place with the spoken words. "Welcome to Wonderland."

Hearing a giggle behind him, Jim turned to look. The monk Tarilli had one hand over his mouth, trying to hold back his laughter.

"Tika?" Jim asked, as the other shoe dropped.

"The one and only," said Tarilli. "I wish you could see the look on your face!"

With a whoosh, Jim sat down heavily in the chair behind him. His legs wouldn't support him anymore. Rita/Videlli leaned forward and patted his cheek.

"I'm sorry, hon. But I had to keep up the charade. I couldn't let on with witnesses around."

Jim shook his head, unable to speak for a moment.

"But what now?" he asked, looking up at Rita. "We're trapped in Videlli's study. How do we get out of here?"

"You forget," said Rita. "I *am* Videlli. I am the Supreme Prophet of the Stree. My word is the Word Ordained."

Jim nodded, still befuddled by the turn of events.

"But...to what end? What's your plan?" he wondered.

"Ah, yeah. There's the rub." Rita looked at Tika. "What *is* my plan?"

"Obviously, we have to make one last final effort to stop the attack at Stalingrad," said Tika.

"Well, yeah," said Rita. "But how to do that without raising suspicion? If I just declare the war over, they'll know something's not right. That would be totally out of character for Videlli."

Jim thought hard, musing on their predicament.

"We have to present a bigger threat to them than the Goblins. That's the only way they'll stop their crusade."

"What bigger threat?"

"It has to be huge. Something that will totally divert their attention."

Even as he spoke, the door opened and a strange Stree stepped in. Jim froze, sure they had been caught. But the Stree simply smiled at Jim, nodded at Tika, and spoke directly to Rita.

"Actually, we may already have that," the Stree said in English.

"Luda? What are you doing here?" asked Rita. "What are you talking about?"

Stree Prime
Great Cathedral of the Stree

"Luda? What do you mean?" asked Rita. "You have something that will help?"

Luda nodded. "I just received an ansible communication a few minutes ago."

"And?" asked Rita impatiently.

"It was from Commander Rauti."

Everyone in the room except Luda looked puzzled. Tika thought for a second, then breathed out her realization. "Rauti. The commander at Venus."

"Yes," said Luda. "Except he's not on Venus anymore. He

sent a warning on our coded command channel."

"What? What warning?" Tika was losing her patience. "Spit it out, Luda!"

"He warned all Goblins to get far away from Stree Prime. He's going to destroy the planet."

There was a shocked silence that lasted a good five seconds before Rita jumped in.

"How is he going to destroy the planet?"

"He built three big-ass pusher missiles with tDrives and flew them all the way here from Venus. He picked up asteroids out in the Kuiper belt and attached one to each missile. He's flying them into the system to smash them into the planet at thirty percent of light speed."

"Fuck," breathed Jim. "That'll do it, alright."

Tika exploded. "That's genocide! Against the Commandments! We don't make war that way!"

Luda shrugged. "Rauti's pissed. They destroyed his people on Venus and his entire project. He's not worried about the Commandments right now."

Rita focused on a more compelling issue. "When?"

"The first one will hit at midnight tonight. Then one every six hours after that until there's nothing left alive on Stree Prime."

Rita did a rapid calculation in her head.

"So based on that timing, he's already launched them."

"Yes. They're in flight, on their way into the inner system. Undoubtedly the Stree will detect them soon."

"We have to stop him," cried Tika. "We can't let him violate the Commandments like that! We've lived by those rules for 20,000 years! It would be the end of everything that we believe in!"

"And no biologicals would ever trust you again," said Jim. "You'll be the pariahs of the Galaxy. Every other species will turn their hand against you."

"It would be the end of the Goblins," Rita said. "We have to stop him."

"But..." Jim mused, "...maybe we can use this to help ourselves at the same time. Granted we have to stop him, but can we also use this as leverage against the Stree? Make them recall their Fleet?"

"It's all we've got," Rita agreed. "Let's try it. Luda - can you re-establish communications with Rauti? Will he listen to you?"

"I don't know, milady," Luda said. "I think he's not in his right mind."

"Try," urged Rita. "Try to convince him to follow our plan. Explain to him that recalling the Stree Fleet saves more Goblin lives than destroying Stree Prime."

"I'll try," said Luda.

Rita nodded. "Good. Hurry, Luda."

With a slight bow, Luda turned and departed the suite back to his makeshift equipment room.

With a "whoosh", Rita sat down heavily on the easy chair in Videlli's study, splayed out her fat Stree legs, stared at Jim and shook her head.

"We're in deep trouble, my love," she said.

Jim nodded in agreement.

"Either we stop Rauti, and lose the war, or we fail to stop Rauti, and the entire galaxy turns against us for genocide. We're damned if we do and damned if we don't."

"Unless the Stree believe Rauti is serious and recall their fleet," Rita replied.

Jim looked grim. "I don't think they'll recall the fleet. They've gone too far. But wait...you've got Videlli in there with you, right? Side-loaded in your temp storage? Can't you just look in there and see what he would do in this case?"

"Not really. I can read his memories and knowledge from the scan. I can pick up a hint of his emotions; but I can't really predict what he would do in this situation. There's too many variables."

"What does that hint of emotion look like right now?"

"Rage. Anger. I don't know if that would change later or not, but at the moment, I suspect he'd let Rauti destroy the planet before he'd give in."

"That's what I was afraid of."

"So. We have no choice that I can see. We send the Stree a message that Rauti will destroy their planet unless they recall their fleet immediately."

"Yeah. But at the same time, we work to stop Rauti. We can't let him actually do this."

"Agreed. And of course, we have one more little project to accomplish as quickly as possible."

"Yep," Jim agreed. "Get Bonnie and the rest of them out of that dungeon and off this planet."

Great Cathedral of the Stree

"What do you think?" Gitweo asked his aide Caisel. "Is this message credible?"

"I'm afraid so," Caisel responded. "The abominations put enough detail in it to make sure we could check it out. We confirmed that Rauti was the commander at Venus. We checked the sector they gave us; Doppler shows three objects approaching under steady acceleration. The size and shape of the objects match what they told us. The first one will be at 30% light speed in a matter of hours. It'll impact at midnight. And they're moving plenty fast enough to destroy the planet."

Gitweo shuddered involuntarily. "So. We recall the fleet, or they destroy our planet."

"Yes, Master. That's about the size of it."

Gitweo looked to one side, out the window of his office on the top floor of the Administration building behind the Cathedral.

"We need to take this directly to Videlli right now. Come with me."

The two left Gitweo's office and trotted down the hallway, slammed their way down the stairs and ran across to the Cathedral. They hurried up the stairs to the third floor.

Arriving at Great Prophet Videlli's suite, Gitweo knocked firmly.

"Enter!" someone called. Gitweo recognized the voice of Tarilli - Videlli's Chief of Staff.

And lover, Gitweo thought bitterly. *The asshole who gets everything - because he gives Videlli exactly what Videlli wants. I can't wait 'til the day I can shoot that bastard.*

Opening the door to the suite, Gitweo entered. He found Videlli sitting at his desk. On the couch across the room sat Tarilli. Gitweo moved to stand in front of Videlli's desk, knelt and prostrated himself, Caisel behind him doing the same.

Videlli grunted and waved a hand, instructing them to rise.

"What?" he spoke abruptly.

"Oh Great Prophet, we have dire news," said Gitweo. "The Goblin abominations threaten our very existence. They have accelerated a series of asteroids to smash into our planet. If we cannot stop them, they will destroy all life on Stree Prime. They demand we recall our fleet from Stalingrad immediately."

Videlli leaned forward, closing one eye in apparent deep thought for a few seconds.

"Can we stop these asteroids?"

"It is unlikely, sir. Our fastest ships can only make 25% of light speed inside the mass limit. The abominations know that quite well, Master. They have carefully calculated a speed of approach that forestalls any realistic chance of interception."

"Can we shoot missiles at them?"

"We can, Master. But at that velocity, it would be unlikely our missiles could hit their targets. And even if they did, it's unlikely we could damage an asteroid enough to destroy it or deflect it away from the planet. And we would have to hit not one, but three of them. We would have to be perfect three times. They've been very clever about this."

Videlli leaned back, appearing to think. He looked over at Tarilli, then back at Gitweo.

"What is your recommendation, then?"

"O Great One, I recommend we issue the recall order. But I

think Guardian Prophet Zutirra will not allow Admiral Sojatta to obey such an order. Therefore, I advise we evacuate all key personnel as quickly as possible from the planet. It is inevitable that the planet is destroyed."

Videlli perused Gitweo carefully. "You are certain that Guardian Prophet Zutirra will not obey the recall order?"

"I am certain, Master. He is a zealous guardian of the Stree Destiny. Especially since we have the abominations on the ropes at this moment, driving them back toward their last bastion of defense. He will assume the order is a ruse or a mistake. He will ignore it."

Videlli sighed, looking strangely at Tarilli. "Very well. Issue the order anyway. Give Zutirra all the facts. Tell him this order comes directly from me."

Gitweo turned and looked at Caisel, gesturing for him to go take care of the recall. Caisel nodded, bowed deeply to Videlli, and quickly left the room. Gitweo turned back to Videlli.

"Now, Great Prophet, we must get you off this planet immediately. The first asteroid will impact at midnight. We have little time."

Videlli nodded in understanding. "Very well. But where will we go?"

"Aslar, Master. That is our most civilized colony planet. The climate is benign, the infrastructure most advanced."

"That is acceptable. I'll be ready to go in a half-hour."

"Very good, Master. I'll be back in a half-hour to escort you to the shuttle port."

Gitweo bowed low and began to turn away.

"Oh, Gitweo!" Videlli called.

Turning back, Gitweo waited.

"I'm not through with those Human prisoners yet. Put them on their own ship under guard and have them travel with us. I want to question them more when we arrive at Aslar."

Gitweo looked puzzled. "But Master...there will be thousands of Humans available to us on that new planet they are settling. The one called Phoenix. We can take ample prisoners there."

Videlli nodded. "Yes, I know. But these are the ones who came here to infiltrate us. I suspect they know more than those poor bastards on Phoenix. We'll hang on to them for now. Put Cotrapi on their ship with a few of his guards. He can continue questioning them enroute."

Gitweo bowed again.

"It will be done, O Great One."

Great Cathedral of the Stree

Something is not right about this, thought Gitweo as he returned to his office. *There is no reason to take the Human prisoners. Leave them here to die.*

Shaking it off, Gitweo set aside his curiosity and settled into making preparations to evacuate Videlli and his immediate hierarchy from the planet. He knew better than to attempt to take a large number of staff. The word would get out and cause a panic. It might be such a panic as to prevent him getting to the spaceport and off the planet.

And it was at that moment that the thought struck him. He gasped as it materialized full-blown in his brain. A thought that frightened him to his very core - and yet exhilarated him beyond belief.

If something happens to Videlli during the evacuation...there won't be anybody left to investigate. I'll never have a better chance at him. And Tarilli too. Both of them. If something happens to them on the shuttle...

I'll become the Great Prophet.

Gitweo let the thought roll around in his mind for a few minutes. It was a daring, audacious plan. But could he pull it off?

Maybe. If he kept the number of people involved small, and finessed Videlli and Tarilli carefully.

How to do it?

Gitweo sat immobile for a full five minutes as he ran

scenarios through his mind. And at the end of that time, a subtle smile ran across his face.

It will work. I can do this. They'll never suspect a thing until it's too late.

"Caisel! Come here! We have work to do!"

Great Cathedral of the Stree

<So, Luda. No joy with Rauti?>

<No. I tried for twenty minutes. He will not accept our wishes to stand down. He is no longer sane, I think. The experience of being nuked by the Stree, losing all his team, surviving alone on Venus, and building the missiles seems to have locked him into a path from which he cannot turn."

Rita turned to Tika.

"Any ideas, Tika?"

"Not really," Tika replied. "I can also try to talk to him, if you like."

"Please. We have to try every possible avenue to get him to turn aside and spare Stree Prime."

"Luda - can you patch me through to him with the equipment you have here?"

"Yes, here you go. You are connected>

<Commander Rauti. This is Tika. Can you hear me, Rauti?>

There was no response.

<Rauti. Do you remember when we were children? We played together. You always told me you wanted to be an engineer, building great structures. That was your dream. I remember it well>

<*Is that you, Tika?*>

<Yes, Rauti. It's me>

<*If that is you, Tika, then tell me. Tell me what we did to the teacher when we were learning to fly shuttles*>

<We swapped bodies. You went as me, and I went as you. It drove him crazy, didn't it?>

<*Ah, yes. It did drive him crazy. How are you, Tika?*>

<Good, Rauti. I'm good. Except that I will soon be a member of a species guilty of genocide. Which will destroy all Goblins everywhere. Every species we meet across the Galaxy will turn their face away from us. We'll be hounded from one end of the Galaxy to the other, outcasts and pariahs>

<*You are clever, Tika. But not clever enough. There will be no Goblins left to become outcasts. I am well aware of what is happening at Stalingrad. The Stree will defeat us. Our fleet will be destroyed. The Dyson Swarm will be destroyed. The biologicals have finally obtained their dream. Goblins will be no more*>

<Rauti, some of that is true. But not all of it. There are many Goblins alive still. A half-dozen here with me, and likely many more who will survive the battle at Stalingrad. We will survive, and we will regrow our species. But if you destroy Stree Prime, then we will never have a homeland again. The biologicals will never allow us a place to lay our heads. It's not the Stree who will perform the final destruction of the Goblin species, Rauti. It's you>

Tika waited for a response, but there was none. A long silence later, she spoke again.

<Rauti? Do you understand? You are the one who will destroy the Goblins. Not the Stree. The name that will go down in history as the killer of the Goblins will be...Commander Rauti>

<*Goodbye, Tika. I hope you are able to survive*>

<He has broken the connection> Luda reported.

Tika smashed her fist on the desk in frustration. <Any change in his course?>

<No. He is still on course for arrival at midnight. There is no change>

CHAPTER THIRTY

Stree Prime
Spaceport

By the time the cavalcade of ground cars arrived at the Komihu Naval Spaceport, it was already afternoon. There were a dozen of them, a parade of vehicles that caught the attention of many as they pulled into the VIP area on the west side of the field. Security guards piled out of the first three vehicles and formed a protective cordon. Two priestly bodyguards exited the fourth vehicle, moved to a nearby shuttlecraft and inspected it, then returned outside and stood beside the ramp at attention.

Gitweo and Caisel left the same vehicle and moved to open the doors of the armored car behind them. Tarilli and Videlli got out of the rear of the armored car. They moved to the shuttle, Gitweo and Caisel staying protectively close to them.

Stepping up in the VIP shuttle, Videlli moved to a luxurious leather seat and sat down as Tarilli came in behind him and sat across from him. Gitweo and Caisel entered the shuttle. Both bowed low to Videlli.

"Everything has been done as you ordered, Master. We will be on board the battlecruiser *Resolute* in thirty minutes. Warrior Priest Cotrapi and his guards are loading the Human prisoners on the captured corvette. They will follow us to Aslar."

"And the cargo?"

"The cargo has been loaded as you specified, Great Prophet. Nine large crates. And of course, there are servants on board to address your needs."

"Excellent, Gitweo. I can always depend on you."

"Then by your leave, Master, we'll go to ensure that all is in order for our departure."

"Very good, Gitweo. See you on board the *Resolute*," Videlli responded.

Gitweo and Caisel backed out of the shuttle, bowing low as they did so. Two warrior priest bodyguards entered the shuttle and closed the hatch behind them, then retired to the rear compartment with the servants.

Moving toward their own shuttle, Gitweo looked back one last time at the VIP craft containing Great Prophet Videlli.

"Everything is in order?" he asked Caisel.

"Yes, Master. Their shuttle will explode as it approaches the battlecruiser. There will be plenty of witnesses to confirm their deaths."

"And you're sure you can trust Cotrapi?"

"Yes, Master. He is the most trust-worthy operative I have. The job will be done right."

Gitweo smiled.

All is prepared. All is ready. In an hour, I'll be the Great Prophet of the Stree. My time has come.

Boarding his shuttle, Gitweo settled into his seat, Caisel behind him. The engines started spooling up. Out the window, he could see the Human corvette also preparing for departure.

Gitweo smiled. As soon as Videlli was dead, he would order the *Resolute* to destroy that Human ship as well. The last thing he needed right now was Human prisoners. Nothing but a pain in the ass.

With a slight lurch, his shuttle lifted off. On the displays mounted on the wall, and the small holotank at the front of the cabin, he saw the other shuttles following as they took up a vector for space. The Human ship brought up the rear, piloted by Cotrapi and his hand-picked guards. In a few minutes, the sky began to darken as they approached space.

Only minutes now. When we approach the battlecruiser,

Cotrapi will set off the bomb. And that will be the end of Videlli and Tarilli.

Phoenix System
Battalion East

Misha and his battalion made good time, moving to the northeast in the thinning forest. As soon as they were five miles from their previous camp, they stopped and set up a new bivouac. They were a bit closer to the river now, almost there, but still in the forest. In front of them, toward the river, the forest thinned out a bit because of some rocky humps and hillocks the trees didn't like.

Misha had to smile. He couldn't have planned it better. When they departed tonight for their final march to Landing, they'd have to pass right through that thin spot. As they crossed the river, they would be in full view of Turgenev's infrared drones, which he was sure would be out in force.

Well, Tat, you wanted us to be obvious without being completely obvious. I think this should meet your requirements.

He grabbed his radio and reported in to Tatiana. Misha had never had a problem working for his wife. He had, early on, recognized her genius for guerrilla warfare. He knew his own talents were more pedestrian, not on the same level as hers. Thus, in this present circumstance, even though he disagreed with her plan - because it rankled him to give himself away unnecessarily - he went along with it. She was the commander. She was the talent.

And in more ways than one, thought Misha. *She's the talent, alright. In battle and in bed.*

Remembering their last night together, Misha grinned, a huge grin that was still in place when Brett Jones stepped into his tent, catching him off guard. He tried to wipe the grin off his face as Jones snapped to attention in front of him.

"Colonel, all troops present and accounted for, all troops ordered to their tents to rest."

"Outstanding, Major. Thank you. Please issue an officer's call and let's make sure everybody is on the same page."

"Aye, aye sir. Officer's call on the way."

Misha saluted Jones and watched him go. Within ten minutes, his officers had assembled in his tent. He let them get settled, then he went over the plan one last time.

"We'll kick off at midnight per plan. We leave everything here except our weapons and ammunition, plus one ration per trooper. We've got seven miles left to go. With that light load, we should be able to march at three miles per hour, even with these untrained troops. That puts us one mile from Landing at 0200. We'll rest there for 15 minutes, as quietly as possible, and launch our attack at 0215 hours. You company commanders and platoon leaders, it's up to you to ensure every unit stays on schedule. No stragglers, nobody getting lost, no noise. Everyone precisely on the Line of Departure, locked and loaded and ready to fight at 0215. Any questions on schedule?"

Misha had three company commanders and nine platoon leaders in front of him. All nodded their understanding.

"Excellent. Next - objectives. Our last intel from the ground was that Turgenev has taken over two apartment blocks for his militia - Blocks One and Two. Those are the two center apartment blocks, opposite the shuttle parking area, Block One on the west side and Block Two on the east side.

"As briefed, Bravo Company will attack directly into the rear of Block Two, take the building and set up firing positions on the roof. Alpha Company will swing around Block Two on the north side and dig in even with the building. Charlie Company will push around to the south and also dig in along a line with the building. As hard and fast as possible, folks. Make no mistake about it - they will know we are coming. They will be ready, and they will be dangerous. Our best chance is to hit them so hard and so fast that even with their forewarning, they can't hold against us. Any questions on the assault plan?"

Misha saw a hand go up.

"Yes?"

"Sir, what do we do if Battalion West is late coming in from the west side?"

Misha smiled.

"They won't be, son. I know the person leading them personally. They'll make schedule or die trying."

There were no more questions. Misha smiled at his officers.

"OK, then. Everybody go get some rest. See you this evening."

After the meeting, Misha forced himself to lie down and try to rest. It was impossible to sleep; they would be in battle in a bit more than twelve hours. But he tried, dozing off for a few minutes, a fitful state of almost-sleep that left him more tired than when he started. By 1800 hours, he gave up and sat, pulled out his maps, and started studying them again, looking for anything he had missed, anything he could use as an advantage in the coming battle. But there was nothing new there; his job was a simple one, straightforward.

March to Landing, attack Turgenev from the east, pin him in place. Let Tatiana come in from the west and catch him in a crossfire.

Misha sighed.

It won't be that simple. It never is.

Stree Prime
Entering Orbit

Cotrapi and his guards had lashed Bonnie, Stewart, and the other Human prisoners to the floor of *Armidale*'s cargo bay, sitting them on the cold surface with their hands tied behind their backs. Then Cotrapi had gestured to two of his guards, who left for the bridge to make ready for flight. Cotrapi and the two remaining guards moved to the front of the cargo bay and sat in the jump seats there, their stun guns hanging loosely, ignoring the Humans for the moment.

In a few minutes, Bonnie heard the *Armidale*'s engines start to spool up. She turned to Stewart. He noticed tears in her eyes as she spoke in a low voice.

"So I guess Jim is dead. He didn't return from Cotrapi's last torture session."

Stewart gave a slight nod, watching Cotrapi to see if he was listening. The Stree jailer seemed to be ignoring them.

"I'm sorry, Bonnie. I know you and Jim were close."

Bonnie hung her head, her tears leaking out and falling on the cold floor of the cargo bay. She couldn't speak.

"If it's any comfort to you, I don't think he talked," continued Stewart. "If he had told them anything, they wouldn't need us anymore, and we wouldn't be going along on this little expedition. We'd already be at the bottom of a ditch somewhere."

"Cold comfort," sniffled Bonnie.

Stewart turned away, giving her some privacy. The *Armidale*'s engines surged, and the ship gave a slight lurch as it came unstuck from the surface. He heard the landing legs retract with a whine and then the engines decrease in volume slightly. He knew they were off the ground and headed for space.

Bonnie looked around the cargo area, knowing it was probably the last time she would see it. She was certain that upon arrival at their destination, they would be thrown into another deep hole, then tortured until all were dead. She had no hopes of any other future.

Suddenly Bonnie realized Cotrapi was standing directly in front of her. She was amazed that the huge fat Stree could move so quietly. Cotrapi gazed down at her, a strange smile on his lips.

"Would you like to see something amazing, Humans?" he spoke.

Both Bonnie and Stewart lifted their heads in puzzlement. Suddenly Bonnie felt one of the Stree guards behind her, loosening her restraints. Then she was free. The guard moved to Stewart and began removing his restraints as well.

"Come with me," said Cotrapi, moving toward the hatch at

the front of the cargo bay. Stewart looked at Bonnie, shrugged, and got to his feet. Bonnie stood up beside him, rubbing her wrists where the restraints had bit into them. Silently, they followed Cotrapi as he went through the hatch and climbed a short ladder to the next deck. Moving down the corridor, he led them to the bridge. Entering, he gestured with a flourish toward the jump seats behind the captain's console.

"Sit, Humans. Be comfortable. I have something interesting to show you."

***

Bonnie and Stewart were still in a state of shock at the events of the last few minutes. They stared in wonderment at Cotrapi as he gestured to the holotank at the front of the bridge. In the holo, they could see three shuttles in front of the *Armidale*. The corvette, being in the rear, gave them a perfect view of the formation as they progressed toward a Stree battlecruiser in orbit around the planet.

"Do you see the shuttlecraft at the head of the formation?" asked Cotrapi.

Bonnie, completely puzzled, nodded at Cotrapi. "Yes, we see it."

"Keep your eyes on it. That shuttle is about to have an unexpected and disastrous engine failure."

"What?"

Cotrapi smiled enigmatically. "It seems that someone doesn't want Great Prophet Videlli and Prophet Tarilli to reach their destination."

And with that, even as they turned to stare at the holo, the leading shuttlecraft exploded into a thousand pieces. The fire of its destruction left a great red-orange ball of flame in front of them. The following shuttles swerved to avoid the debris field, as did the *Armidale*.

Bonnie gasped. Then she turned, glared at Cotrapi.

"Why? Why would you show us this? Why should we care that Videlli is dead?"

"Oh, I'm sorry," said Cotrapi. "Did I say that Videlli is dead?"

Bonnie hesitated. "Well…yes. You said…"

"No," corrected Cotrapi. "I said only that someone wanted him dead."

Bonnie shook her head in frustration. "Didn't his shuttle just blow up?"

"No," grinned Cotrapi. "That was Gitweo's shuttle. Videlli is safe and sound on the one behind it."

***

Cotrapi ushered Bonnie and Stewart into the captain's ready room off the side of the bridge. He sat them down at the conference table and took a chair opposite them, still with an enigmatic smile plastered on his fat face. He sat in silence for many seconds, until finally in exasperation Bonnie spoke first.

"What do you want from us?" she spat, losing her temper. "Why did you bring us here?"

Cotrapi tilted his head to one side. "Pardon me for stringing this out, but I'm having so much fun."

Bonnie hung her head in frustration. She was too angry to respond.

But Stewart began to get it. His eyes opened wide, and he pulled his head back in total shock.

"You're not Cotrapi," he blurted out.

Lifting her head, Bonnie looked at the oversize Stree sitting at the head of the table. She stared at him closely. He was grinning, a stupid kind of grin totally out of place on the big Stree head.

A stupid kind of grin that Bonnie could swear she had seen before.

A stupid kind of grin…

"Oh my God," she breathed. "It can't be…"

"Oh, but it can," said Cotrapi. "Did you miss me?"

CHAPTER THIRTY-ONE

Stalingrad System
Dyson Swarm

If Bagi's warbody could cry, there would have been tears leaking out of the metal cube welded to the bridge of the *Blue Quark*. As he raced in toward the inner system trying to rejoin his Wing, he watched in silent agony.

Far ahead of him, three Goblin formations attacked into the Stree Fleet. A silent chaos of battle followed. Thousands of missiles streaked as the flash of pulse cannon lit the Black like some kind of deranged light show. Then the slow-motion explosion of shattered ships and debris expanded in all directions. Stree and Goblin wrecks littered the battlefield indiscriminately - so many smashed-up ships it would have been suicide for him to attempt to fly through the mess. He was forced to vector up, arcing over the debris field on his race to the inner system.

And then it was over. The once well-organized and fiercely proud Goblin Assault Wings were smashed in every direction. The enemy, in spite of horrific losses, came on undeterred, with more than 200 ships remaining.

To Bagi's horror, he realized the Goblin Fleet had only 97 ships still capable of maneuver - and most of those were heavily damaged. Now in front of the Stree stood only the Reserve Wing - the oldest, slowest ships of the Goblin fleet. A pitiful reserve force that would be swatted away by the Stree without breaking stride.

The damaged remnants of the Goblin Fleet turned, and boosted hard, trying to get back to their Reserve Wing for a last stand in front of the black Dyson Ring that was their home.

And Bagi would be there in time for that fight. Even with his reduced accel, he would have just enough boost to pass over the top of the Stree fleet, decel back down, and join with the rest of the survivors directly in front of the Dyson Ring.

Where they would die.

Phoenix System
Battalion West

Olivia and Mac were rousted out of their tent at 8 PM with the rest of the battalion. Lieutenant Raines told them to leave everything behind except their weapons, ammunition, and one day's rations, and prepare to march. By 9 PM, they were ready.

Then they sat, on rocks or tree boles or just on the ground, performing the timeless ritual of an army - hurry up and wait. Nothing happened until nearly 10 PM, when finally the word came down.

Check weapons - prepare to march.

Olivia and Mac checked their rifles, ensured they were clean, loaded, and secured. They put on their packs, slung their rifles, and got into line with the rest of their platoon. Ahead, Mac could see Lt. Raines and SSgt. Briggs, standing, waiting. Farther out, Mac saw his company commander and Gunny Sparks, also waiting, impatient, stamping at the ground in the cold and damp. Beyond them, nearly out of sight in the dim jungle, he saw the tail end of Alpha Company.

Mac looked at his watch, thinking.

9:57 PM. We've got about seven miles to go. If we make 2 miles an hour in this thick-ass jungle, we'll get to our Line of Departure about 1:00 to 1:30 AM. From there, we'll have 1 mile - or maybe a bit less - to go. If we start our assault at 2:30 AM - which is my guess - we'll be fighting right after that.

Mac looked over at Olivia. It was hard to see her in the darkness, but he thought she looked stressed.

She's thinking the same thing I am. If things go south, we could be dead by 3 AM.

I hope this Tatiana whoever knows what she's doing...

"MacIntosh!" called a voice. Mac looked up to see Lt. Raines walking toward him. He snapped to attention.

"Yes, sir?"

Raines stopped in front of him. "Mac, two squads for a special mission. Yours and Olivia's. You're in command. Assemble your squads and report to the front of the column, to General Powell, stat!"

Mac gulped. "Aye, sir!" he nodded. As Raines departed, Mac turned to his squad. They were standing around him, all ears.

"You heard the man. Grab your gear. Make sure you've got everything. Then let's go find this General Powell."

As he picked up his weapon and pack, Mac glanced at Olivia. Even in the darkness, she looked scared. He gave her a smile, even though he didn't feel it inside.

"It'll be fine," he whispered. "Not to worry."

Olivia gave a weak nod. Together, they started the long walk up to the front of the battalion. They passed through their own company - Bravo - and then walked past Alpha Company. Finally, they came to Headquarters Company. That consisted of a small group of officers and men at the front of the formation, sitting on rocks and tree stumps like the rest of them.

Mac looked around for the General Powell he was supposed to report to but didn't see anyone that fit the bill. To one side, though, he noticed the tall woman he had met down by the river, so he walked over to her.

"Excuse me, mum, but do you know where I can find General Powell?"

Tatiana Powell smiled at the young man. "That would be me, Corporal. And you're Mac?"

"Aye, mum."

Two other officers moved in to stand close beside Tatiana. Olivia moved up from behind Mac to listen.

"OK, you guys sit down here in a circle and let me brief you, OK?" said Tatiana.

Mac and Olivia waved their squads down in a tight circle. As they sat down, Tatiana stood in the center in the darkness.

"Is everybody here familiar with the layout of Landing?"

Looking around, Mac spoke up for them. "Aye, mum. We've all been briefed on it."

"Good. We believe the leaders of the original democratic government are being held in the new jail. It's roughly fifty yards due west of Block One, maybe thirty yards south of the Headquarters Tent. Everybody with me so far?"

Mac looked around, ensured that everybody was on board, and answered for the group. "Aye, mum."

"Your job is to infiltrate to the jail right after the main assault starts, and free those prisoners."

Tatiana stopped speaking, letting the impact of her words be absorbed by the group. When everyone had stopped looking around and seemed to be ready for more, she continued.

"As much as I'd like to personally lead you - especially since that's my father and my best friends locked up in there - I won't be able to do that. I have to stay with the main assault force. So..."

Tatiana looked directly at Mac. "I'm counting on you, Corporal. When we're approaching the Line of Departure, I'll detach you and send you on ahead. You'll work your way around and set yourself up west of the old tent camp that's still standing out there. There should be nobody left in the tent camp, but you never know. There could be people in there for various reasons - I'm sure you can guess. So you'll have to be careful setting up.

"Once you're in position, you'll hear the first assault start from the east side of the camp. That'll be Battalion East coming in from behind Block Two. At that point, do nothing.

Remain in position. Don't let yourself be drawn off by that. Understood?"

"Aye, mum. Hold position when Battalion East starts their assault."

"Excellent. The next thing you'll hear is our assault start about fifteen minutes later. We'll be coming in from due west, which will be slightly south of you. As soon as you hear our assault begin, drive at maximum speed for the jail. You should be there in less than five minutes.

"Once you're past the tent camp, you should see two larger tents. The first one is the cafeteria, the second one is the Headquarters tent. The jail is a new building just south of the Headquarters tent. I expect it to be heavily guarded. That's why I'm giving you two squads. That should be enough to do the job. Get in there, free the prisoners, and keep them safe until we arrive. Any questions?"

Mac looked around at his two squads. They looked scared but determined.

"No, mum," answered Mac. He stood up. "We'll get it done."

Tatiana smiled. "Thank you, Mac. Stay with us until I cut you loose. See you there."

Mac nodded. Tatiana rose, stretched, turned in the darkness, and waved at two squads standing at the edge of the group - her scouting squads.

"Let's roll," she said.

The two scouting squads disappeared into the night like ghosts. Moving slower, Tatiana and her staff started walking east. As the last of HQ company pulled out on the trail, Mac fell into line behind them. He heard his two squads moving out and turned, looking to make sure they were all in place. Behind them, he saw Alpha Company begin to move.

Seven miles to go, thought Mac.

Approaching Stree Battlecruiser SGH *Resolute*

On Videlli's shuttle, one of the Stree warrior-monk

bodyguards came out of the back compartment to check on Videlli and Tarilli. He bowed low before them.

"Is there anything needed, O Great Prophet?" he asked.

"Yes, Parti," replied Rita/Videlli. "As soon as we are on board the *Resolute*, I want to get the hell out of here. No telling how far the splashback will reach when that first asteroid hits."

"It will be done, O Great Prophet," the bodyguard responded verbally. He bowed deeply and returned to his seat in the rear compartment.

But on their radio link, an entirely different conversation was occurring.

<I take it there's no change in Rauti's approach?> Rita asked.

<None> responded Hajo, posing as the warrior-monk. <The first asteroid will strike at midnight>

<Is there anything else we can do?>

<The Stree Home Fleet will attack the asteroids soon; but the chances they can stop them are almost zero. At 30% light speed, there's no missile in existence which can target them successfully. And no warship which can chase them down - except of course the *Armidale*, because it has Goblin drives>

<I hate this. I hate this so much> Rita said. <Yes, they destroyed my planet. But two wrongs don't make a right, as we say on Earth>

<As you *once* said on Earth…> Tika interjected unhelpfully. "Remember these bastards killed your planet."

<But still…> Rita said. <All those innocent lives. I can't bear it>

<Not innocent lives> growled Tika. <They destroyed six cultures. Billions upon billions of sentient creatures. Earth. Singheko. Dekanna. Nidaria. Ursa. Asdif. And now they are nearly complete with the destruction of Stalingrad, the homeland of my people. They are far from innocent>

There was a short silence. Rita heard the shuttle engines change pitch as it began to maneuver to dock with the battlecruiser.

<Still. The children. The children are innocent>

<The sins of the fathers> spat Tika. <From your own Earth religions. The children must pay for the sins of their fathers>

With a clunk, the shuttle came to rest on the outside of the battlecruiser and latched to a docking bobbin. The platform began to rotate, carrying them inside the ship. Rita looked across at Tika.

<But you know, and I know, that it isn't right, Tika. Regardless of what the Stree did, we have no right to kill their children>

Tika looked at Rita, her face impassive.

<And yet now that we cannot stop it, I have to tell you - part of me is glad. Glad that the Stree will live no more>

Corvette *Armidale*

"How? How in the world did you pull it off?" Bonnie asked.

"Rita's in Videlli," replied Jim Carter, currently in the body of Cotrapi. "Tika's in Tarilli, his Chief of Staff. When we realized how much trouble we were in, we realized this was the only way out. I bit the bullet and went for the conversion. We grabbed Cotrapi and converted him in the bodybuilder. Then Luda scanned me and put me into Cotrapi."

"Fuck," breathed Bonnie. "That had to be scary, with no time to prepare for it!"

Jim grimaced. "Too right. I didn't have much time to think about it. I've never been so scared in all my life. In fact, I made Luda put me out before the scan. I couldn't bring myself to think about what would happen to my body after. I knew we'd have to leave it behind."

"Well," said Stewart, unable to think of anything else to say. "Well, well..."

Bonnie smiled for the first time since she was captured. "I would come over there and kiss you, but you're just too damn ugly."

Jim winked at her. "I'm told I'm quite attractive to a Stree."

"But..." Stewart stammered. "What now? What's next?"

Jim leaned forward. "The two pilots up front are Rachel and Ollie. The other guards are Luda and Liwa. They're releasing Brady and Hodges right now and explaining the situation to them."

"You're fucking kidding me!" Bonnie screamed in delight. "All of you?"

"Yep," Jim smiled. "It's our ship again."

"But not for long," said Stewart, glancing at the holo repeater. "We'll be aboard the Stree battlecruiser in about ten minutes. At that point, we become prisoners again."

"No. Rita - I mean Videlli - will tell the battlecruiser captain to keep us on ice for the moment. She'll tell him she doesn't want to contaminate members of his crew with exposure to Humans, so she'll order him to keep us on the *Armidale* for the trip to Aslar. We'll fly in formation with the battlecruiser. As far as they're concerned, I'm still keeping you prisoner here for the duration of the trip."

"How will she explain the explosion of the other shuttle?" asked Bonnie.

"The truth. Gitweo was plotting to kill Videlli and Tarilli, so Videlli killed him first."

"So that leaves us with just one problem, then," Bonnie spoke thoughtfully. "How will Rita and Tika - and Hajo - escape from the battlecruiser?"

"Well, I wish we only had that one problem. But we have a couple of bigger ones than that."

SGH *Resolute*

At its max accel of 305g, the Stree battlecruiser SGH *Resolute* boosted hard to escape the impending destruction of Stree Prime. The Human corvette *Armidale* followed close behind, still maintaining the pretense that the Humans onboard were prisoners of Cotrapi. In 20 minutes, the two ships were 1.5 million miles from the planet, moving at 8.2 million miles per hour and still accelerating.

Far in front of them, coming directly toward the planet, Rauti's three doomsday impactors sped on, the hammers of God. The first one had just reached its maximum velocity of 30% light - 55,885 miles per second. It was 21 AU from the planet - 1.95 billion miles. What seemed like a lot wasn't, not really. It would cover that immense distance and impact the planet in nine and a half hours.

Many hours behind it, the next impactor had reached 28% light, and the third one followed at a similar interval, already at 26% light. They would impact the planet after the first asteroid, at intervals of six and twelve hours. Rauti had planned carefully. The end result would be an even distribution of destruction around the entire planet as it rotated. Few, if any, Stree would remain alive on their doomed home world.

The Stree Home Fleet made one last valiant attempt to stop the impactors. Splitting into two groups, one group positioned themselves 20 AU from Stree Prime. As the first impactor approached from outsystem, they accelerated for all they were worth. Through heroic efforts, they reached 25% of light speed as the impactor sped through their fleet. Thousands of missiles and railgun rounds were then launched at it.

But the velocity differential was still 5% of light speed. In the time the Stree missiles moved one mile, the asteroid moved 9,314 miles. It was like shooting a spitwad at a speeding rifle bullet. Upwards of ten thousand missiles and railgun rounds were fired at the asteroid; three managed to actually strike it. Out of those three, not one caused sufficient damage to move the impactor off its course. It was a futile gesture in an impossible task.

The second group of Stree ships were slightly closer in, at 18 AU. As the impactor approached, hundreds of small Stree ships attempted to smash themselves into the fast-moving asteroid in kamikaze attacks. Only two out of hundreds were able to actually hit it, giving their lives in the hopes of deflecting it from the planet.

But the net result was the same as the earlier attempts had been. They moved the asteroid by inches - not nearly enough to save Stree Prime.

It was hopeless.

CHAPTER THIRTY-TWO

Stree Prime
Corvette *Armidale*

The crew of the *Armidale* had gathered on the bridge, watching the desperate attempts of the Stree to save their planet - and watching them fail. It was too much for Bonnie.

"We have to do something!" she called. "We can't just sit here and watch this happen!"

Luda looked bitterly at Bonnie.

"Why not? The Stree killed Earth. And five other cultures. Even now, they're destroying our homeland at Stalingrad. I'm thrilled to sit here and watch them die!"

"It's wrong, Luda! We can't trade evil for evil! That's not what a truly intelligent species does! We have to think of something!"

"There's nothing we can do, Bonnie," mused Jim. "The Stree have tried everything. They can't deflect them with missiles. They've tried the kamikaze approach. There's just no way to push them aside."

"Actually, there might be," interjected Stewart.

"What?" exclaimed the group. "How?"

Stewart looked solemn.

"Stree ships can only reach 25% of light speed inside a solar system. That's why Rauti chose 30% of light speed to push his asteroids. He knows they can't catch them."

Jim began to get it.

"But the *Armidale* has Goblin drives. It can reach 50% of light speed inside a system."

"Yes," nodded Stewart. "In this solar system, there is only one ship that can catch up to one of those impactors. This one - the *Armidale*. But - the laws of physics are working against us. We could only potentially catch the last impactor. It's too late for the first two. We'll never be able to catch them before they hit the planet."

"But we could catch up to the last one?" asked Bonnie. "And that might save several thousands on the planet, right?"

"Yes. If we start right now, and boost like hell," Stewart answered.

"But we run the risk of smashing the *Armidale*," Rachel said.

"That too," agreed Stewart. "There's a good chance we'll smash up our ship."

There was a short silence as everyone around the table considered the options. Finally Stewart broke the silence, looking at Bonnie.

"Bonnie. Even if the EDF doesn't exist anymore, you're the senior EDF officer. You call it."

Bonnie gazed around the bridge at the others. "For something like this, I won't make the decision alone. I need a vote."

Luda immediately spoke up. "No way. I won't lift a finger to help these murderous bastards."

Jim glanced at Luda, then back at Bonnie. "We have to try," he said. "I hate to go against you, Luda. But we're either a moral species, or we're not. There's no half-way."

Commander Brady raised a hand. "As much as I hate to say it, I have to agree with Jim."

Ollie, next, spoke simply. "We have to try."

Liwa shook her head in negation. Bonnie looked at Lieutenant Hodges, the only other Human survivor of *Armidale*'s original crew. Hodges shook his head.

"No, milady, with respect," he spoke. "They attacked Earth with the intention of destroying it. I vote no."

And beside him, Rachel also shook her head.

"They killed my Dan. I will never help them."

Bonnie looked over at Stewart. "Looks like you're the deciding vote, Captain Stewart. And that's fitting since this is your ship. What'll it be?"

Stewart made a face, grimacing as if in pain. "We'll try it. But say a prayer for my poor ship, please. I'm not sure she's going to survive."

And with that, Stewart turned and focused his attention on his bridge.

"We're short-handed, folks. We'll need some help here. Rachel, please take Tactical. Jim, please take Comms," called Stewart.

Nodding, Rachel moved to the Tactical console as Jim moved to the Comm console. Bonnie and Ollie remained in their jump seats at the back of the bridge. Behind them, the remaining team of Luda and Liwa stood silently beside the jump seats as Captain Stewart issued orders.

"You're sure there's no way to catch the first or second one?" asked Bonnie.

Stewart shook his head. "I'm sure," he replied. "We'll be damn lucky to catch up to the third one."

Settling into his Captain's console, Stewart addressed Jim.

"Jim, since you're in Cotrapi's body, you'll need to contact the *Resolute*. Inform them we're going to make one last ditch attempt to divert the asteroids. Commander Brady, set a course to intercept the last one and boost hard."

"Aye, Skipper," answered Jim and Brady simultaneously.

An uncontrollable smile crossed Rachel's face as she sat at the Tactical Officer console. Regardless of circumstances, even in this strange Stree body, it felt good to be in the seat of a warship once more. At the Comms console, Jim made a broadcast to the battlecruiser.

"Cotrapi to Resolute. *We're going to make one last-ditch attempt to divert the third asteroid. We can't do anything about the first two, but we'll try for the last one."*

Without waiting for a response, the *Armidale* swung away from the battlecruiser, striking out on a vector toward the last of the three asteroids. They would first have to accelerate out-system like a bat out of hell, then decelerate, turn, and accelerate back toward Stree Prime for one final, desperate attempt to catch the last of the three impactors and deflect it from the planet. It would take everything the little corvette had to perform the maneuver and catch up to the target.

Jim could only imagine what was going through the minds of Rita and Tika on the battlecruiser. Would Rita attempt to override their decision? Would she call them off and order them to return to their course?

Accelerating at 500g, the *Armidale* headed toward its destiny.

Phoenix System
Landing City

At 0125 Mac saw the first lights of Landing City through the jungle. He sank to a knee and waved his team down.

"Wait one," he whispered back down the line. Then, tapping Olivia on the shoulder, he waved her forward with himself. Quietly, moving as slowly and carefully as possible, the two of them inched forward until they were able to see through the trees.

In front of him, he could see the colony. He had come in slightly farther to the north than he wanted - he was about two hundred yards north of the old tent city. That put him about six hundred yards north of the jail. He surveyed the area, looking for guards, lights, anything that would tell him the layout of the place.

Pointing to a dark spot a few hundred yards southeast of them, he whispered into Olivia's ear.

"See that dark spot? There's a little gully there. When they built the tent city, they couldn't put tents there. We'll slide into that gully and move up as close to the tents as possible. That's where we'll wait."

Olivia nodded. They moved quietly back to their team and whispered the plan to the rest of them. Then the entire team faded back into the jungle for a quarter mile, turned to the south, and headed for the new entry point opposite the gully.

By 0145 they had made their position change and were at the edge of the jungle, directly opposite the gully. Crawling on their bellies, they moved out of the jungle and into the shallow ditch. There was water in the bottom of it. They ignored it and carefully, avoiding any splashing, made their way closer to the colony, until they were only fifty yards from the edge of the old tent city. There they bellied up to the edge of the ravine, heads just under the top edge, and waited.

Mac glanced at his watch. It was 0158 hours. Battalion East was scheduled to assault at 0215, followed by Battalion West at 0230.

Phoenix System
Turgenev Headquarters

Turgenev almost laughed out loud. He managed to suppress it, though. He didn't want his officers to think he was losing his mind.

But…it was funny. This bitch Tatiana thought she could outsmart him. The smile on his face got even wider as he thought about it.

The classic pincer move. Sending in a diversionary force from the East, then the main force sneaks in from the West. And she thought that would fool me.

As if.

Turgenev gazed around in the darkness. He had set up his troops in three compact groups. To the far north, in the forest just beyond the boundary of Central Park, his Northern Force lay well hidden. And far to the south, on the very periphery of Landing, lay the other half of his militia - his Southern Force.

In the center of Central Park a smaller force waited, the bait for his trap, which he called Center Force on his maps.

When Misha's Battalion East assaulted into Landing, they would be drawn directly toward Center Force. The Center Force would hold them, occupy them, make a terrific noise of battle. That would suck them in, ensure they committed to attacking into the center of the camp.

And then Tatiana Powell would show up. Her Battalion West would attack, their intent to catch his militia in a crossfire.

And someone would be caught in a crossfire. But it wouldn't be Turgenev. As soon as Tatiana Powell had committed her Battalion West to a fight against Center Force, his Southern Force would attack her flank. Simultaneously, his Northern Force would attack Misha's troops from the north.

Both of Powell's battalions would be caught between his more powerful formations. He would roll them up like a carpet.

The insanity of that bitch. I spent ten years as an officer in the Russian army. And she thinks she can out-fox me?

What a joke.

"Five minutes, General," called his aide. Turgenev grunted an assent.

"Pass the word. Northern and Southern Forces to remain absolutely quiet, absolutely still until they get the word to attack. No mistakes."

"Yes, sir," said his Chief of Staff.

Turgenev waited patiently, watching the minutes tick down on his watch. When his watch reached 0215, he stood up. In the far distance, well to the east of Central Park, he heard the first firing begin, sporadically at first, then increasing in volume.

He smiled.

Here they come. I'll let them waltz into the camp with little resistance. They'll think they've got it made. They'll report to Tatiana on the radio that they've caught us completely by surprise. When they come up against Center Force, we'll slow them down, hold them there.

Everything will be exactly as she expects. She'll come rushing in with her Battalion West, and that...

...that will be the beginning of the end for Tatiana Powell.

Stree Prime
Corvette *Armidale*

In the jump seats behind Captain Stewart, Ollie leaned over to Bonnie and whispered:

"Shouldn't we overboost to make sure we can intercept it in time?"

Glancing at a repeater console in front of her, Bonnie shook her head. "Another 8g would only make a difference of twelve minutes in the intercept time. That's not enough to make the discomfort worth it."

"Oh," Ollie said, understanding.

Bonnie smiled. "C'mon, Ollie. Us warship types have to have *some* special skills over you infantry types! Otherwise, there's no point to us!"

Ollie managed a tight smile. Bonnie could see he was stressed. She thought she knew why. She spoke quietly.

"Ollie. Don't try to fight it. You know as well as I do that you're falling in love with Rachel."

Ollie bowed his head, looking down at the deck. His head moved slightly, an acknowledgment of Bonnie's statement.

"I know. I guess I just don't want to accept it."

Bonnie reached out a hand and put it on Ollie's shoulder.

"You're not betraying Helen, Ollie. She'd be the first person to tell you to move on - to live your life. She'd be thrilled and happy about it."

Although it was hard to tell, Bonnie thought she could detect a tear in Ollie's eye. He tried to hide his face, bowing his head deeper toward the deck and raising one hand to cover his eyes.

"You great big grunt," Bonnie whispered, tears forming in

her own eyes. "I know you really loved Helen. But now it's time to really love Rachel. She needs you, and you need her."

With a huge sigh, Ollie lifted his head and wiped his eyes. He smiled at Bonnie and gave another nod.

"I know, Bonnie. I know."

Captain Stewart's voice rumbled from in front of them.

"XO, what's the flight profile?"

Bonnie looked up as Brady turned at his console to answer Stewart.

"Max standard accel for 4.9 hours, turnover and max standard decel for 4.9 hours, then max standard accel back toward Stree Prime for 5.5 hours to catch up to the last impactor. Total time to intercept 15.3 hours."

"Where will we make intercept?"

Brady looked grim. "One-half AU. Seventy-five million klicks from Stree Prime."

"Is that enough distance to deflect its path?"

"Barely, sir. If we're lucky. We'll only have fourteen minutes to try. Less whatever time you want to get clear of the impact zone."

"I don't want to be anywhere near that planet after the first two impactors have already hit it. It'll be a mess. How long to get clear of the planet at that velocity?"

"I'd want at least six minutes. That should put us...let's see...300 k-klicks clear."

"Alright, that gives us eight minutes to try and deflect the impactor. Then we get the hell out of Dodge. Plan accordingly."

"Aye, sir. Eight minutes to deflect the impactor, then get clear."

Stewart turned to look at the group behind him. He was still streaked with grime and dust from his days in the Stree dungeon. The lines on his face were cut deep from the strain, and especially the last few hours.

"Folks, you heard Brady. I have to tell you; this is a desperate attempt that is probably doomed to failure. But I've made the decision we're going to try. Anyone who wants to leave now can take our shuttle and head for the *Resolute*. There's still time to make a rendezvous with them if you hurry."

Bonnie was the first to respond.

"Not me. I'll see it through."

Beside her, Ollie spoke in agreement. "Me as well."

Stewart looked at the two Goblins standing beside them.

"Luda, how about you two? Last chance..."

Luda shook his head.

"No, Captain. I've come this far. I'll see it through."

Liwa stood fast, in silent agreement with Luda.

"Then you might as well go to your cabins and rest," Stewart said. "I'll call you when the first impactor is thirty minutes out from the planet."

Stewart smiled - a grimace more than a smile - and turned back to his work.

Phoenix System
Battalion East

On the east side of Landing, Major Jones reported to Misha, out of breath from running.

"We've begun the assault, Colonel. Resistance is light. We're moving forward at a good pace. We'll be fully engaged at the edge of Central Park on schedule at 0230 when General Powell assaults from the west. Everything is looking good."

Sourly, Misha looked at Major Jones. "Major, in war, everything is never looking good. If you think it is, you don't fully understand the situation."

Uncertainly, Jones nodded.

"I assure you, we did not catch them by surprise. If it looks that way, then Turgenev has some ploy going on. We need to think about what that would be."

Jones gulped and nodded again.

"So think about it, Major. Get your scouts out farther. Work them harder. Find out what that rat-bastard is up to."

"Aye, sir." Jones snapped to, saluted, and left at a run.

Misha sighed. Fighting the Singheko on Deriko for six months had taught him a lot. He knew what was happening right now was too easy. There was a surprise out there somewhere. But unless Major Jones could find it, he had to continue with the plan as outlined by Tatiana.

Advancing toward the colony through the forest, his leading elements continued to meet light resistance until they reached the edge of the clearway that was Central Park. They assaulted out of the forest into the rear of Block Two, and captured that building with little effort.

But from there his light troops found themselves up against a determined, well-concealed force dug in around the shuttle parking area. Turgenev's militia was using foxholes and trenches to protect themselves, and hiding behind the shuttles. Misha's troops had nothing in front of them but a clear space. It was suicide to assault directly across that open space, and his troops knew it. His advance ground to a halt.

At 0230, holding position as he had been ordered, he heard firing start up from the other side of the colony, roughly two miles away from his leading elements.

Here she comes, thought Misha. *I hope she knows what she's doing.*

Stalingrad System

In the end, Bagi made it back to the Dyson Ring just in time to make the final stand with the rest of the survivors. He had hardly gotten turned around and re-joined with the Reserve Wing when the enemy was upon them. As the Reserve Wing charged at the Stree, he boosted as hard as the damaged *Blue Quark* could manage, the ship shaking and vibrating in protest as his crew slammed the throttles home.

Even so, he fell behind, his damaged engines preventing him from maintaining formation. In a matter of minutes, the rest of the Goblin ships were a quarter-million miles ahead of him as they drove into the Stree formation. Bagi could only nurse his ship along behind, knowing he would arrive at the tail-end of this last battle.

Outnumbered by more than 2-to-1, the old, slow ships of the Reserve Wing were torn to pieces. Bagi could only wince as ship after ship of his formation disappeared from the holo. As he approached the battle at last, the count of Goblin ships on the holo fell steadily, first to 60, then to 50, then 40. As the Wing completed its pass through the Stree, Bagi was shocked to see only 32 combat-functional ships remained of the once-proud Goblin fleet.

Plus one beat-up cruiser coming late to the party, Bagi thought.

Selecting a target, Bagi suddenly switched to max decel. He had been traveling at 0.8 million miles per hour. Now, under max decel, each second his speed decreased by another 12,065 feet per second. The Stree battlecruiser he had picked out for his attention was coming at him a bit under 1 million miles per hour. The rage of missiles and railguns swarming at him increased, a storm of destruction that should have ended him and his crippled cruiser in a matter of seconds. But his sudden decel had caught the Stree off-guard. They had expected him to accelerate through their fleet, getting out of the zone of death as quickly as he could. He had done exactly the opposite; approaching slower than his fellows, and then actually decelerating instead of accelerating.

By the time the crew of the Stree battlecruiser understood what was happening, it was too late. Out of missiles, shot to pieces, no longer able to defend herself, the *Blue Quark* bore in on the battlecruiser with a precision only a Goblin crew could achieve. In the last few seconds, as the ponderous battlecruiser attempted to twist away, Stree missiles managed to penetrate the bridge of the *Blue Quark* at last. No warbody cube in existence could have withstood the storm of explosive that tore into the *Blue Quark* at the end. Bagi and his crew died instantly. But for the Stree battlecruiser, it was a hollow victory. As Admiral Sojatta looked on in calm acceptance, as Guardian Officer Zutirra screamed in fear and panic, the *Blue*

Quark hit the *SGH Prophecy* amidships. The two ships impacted at a combined velocity of just over 1.5 million miles per hour. Nothing but a highly refined cloud of hot plasma remained behind.

CHAPTER THIRTY-THREE

Stree Prime
Corvette *Armidale*

Called to the bridge again by Captain Stewart, Jim, Bonnie, Ollie, and the rest assembled to watch the first asteroid impact. Arrayed behind Captain Stewart, a gray cloud hung over their moods - a fatalistic feeling they couldn't shake off. Commander Brady began counting down the seconds to impact.

And then time was up. The leading impactor moved so fast that the last few seconds were incomprehensible. One moment it was approaching the planet. The next moment, the near side of the planet was turning itself inside out, ejecting gouts of molten lava into space, slugs of the planet's guts that looked like fiery blood. A ring of fire expanded from the impact point, rising, burning everything in its path. Following the ring of fire was a circular cloud, ash-gray and growing rapidly as it began to cover the near hemisphere of Stree Prime.

"The beginning of the end for the Stree," said Bonnie. "The next one will hit in six hours, one-third of the way around the planet. And the next one six hours after that if we don't stop it. Rauti is making sure he kills them all."

"They have colony worlds," Jim responded. "They'll recover."

"But not us, I fear," said Luda. "Now we are the outlaws of the Galaxy."

Ollie turned to him. "I guess I don't understand. The Stree also committed genocide. They destroyed six planets. Rauti only destroyed one. Why would you be singled out?"

"Because we are not biological," said Liwa. "We are the only known race of sentient AI creatures in the Galaxy. Because of that, we have always been feared by the bios. They have made war on us times beyond counting, seeking to eradicate us from the Galaxy. This will be their perfect excuse to finish the job."

"But that's not fair!" exclaimed Bonnie. "The Stree started the war! The Stree killed billions as well! Why is your response any different?"

"It's the unwritten rule of the Galaxy," Liwa said bitterly. "Bios can kill bios all day long, and that's just war. But Goblins - it's not the same. We'll be hunted down like dogs." Turning, Liwa stomped off the bridge. Luda glanced at Bonnie, then followed.

"I guess I just don't understand," Ollie complained, looking at Jim. "It makes no sense to me."

Gazing at the blazing planet in the holo, Jim spoke quietly.

"It's the age-old curse of being different. The one that is most different is the one the braying mob comes after with their pitchforks and torches."

Bonnie was quiet for a moment.

"So you think Liwa is right. The bios will come after the Goblins."

Jim nodded sadly. "Yes. They'll try to wipe us out for good this time."

And it was only in that moment that Bonnie remembered.

Jim was now a Goblin.

Phoenix System
Landing City

For Mac, everything happened right on time. At 0215, he heard rifles open up to the east, past the big open space called Central Park. He lifted his head ever so slightly and peered over the top of the gully. In the distance, about a mile away, he saw rifle flashes, more and more each second.

Then Turgenev's forces opened up from trenches and foxholes in the center of the open space, amongst the shuttles. Within three minutes a full-scale battle was taking place.

Mac hunkered back down and waited, watching his watch. And almost exactly at 0230, a new round of firing started, south of him. Tatiana's Battalion West was assaulting into the colony from the jungle there.

"Time to go," he whispered to Olivia. He waved at his squad, and they advanced over the top of the ravine and moved into Landing. Working their way through the abandoned tents, they moved quietly but quickly toward the Headquarters tent and the new jail just south of it. Twice they came across colonists. The first time, they saw the couple first, and Mac waved his team to one side, taking another path to avoid them.

The second time, a couple stepped out of a tent right in front of them, half-naked, trying madly to get into their clothes. They saw Mac's team, screamed, and ran like hell.

Mac ignored them; there wasn't much he could do. He had to grin a little, though.

In the throes of passion, then suddenly gunfire in the distance, then soldiers coming at you. That would put a damper on your evening.

Three minutes later, Mac settled his team into a position just north of the jail, hidden behind the Headquarters tent, and peeked around the corner.

He monitored the area by the jail for a minute, until he was sure he had found all the guards. There were ten of them by his count; eight standing in fixed positions at the four corners of the jail, and two roaming around. He saw only two rifles, so he guessed the rest of them had pistols.

Moving back into concealment behind the Headquarters tent, Mac briefed his team.

"Olivia, take your squad around to the left and assault into the jail area from that side. Take out the four fixed guard positions, then secure a perimeter on the north and east sides."

"Aye, got it," said Olivia. She appeared calm, almost relaxed. With some surprise, Mac realized that both of them had settled down considerably as the action got closer.

It's the anticipation that's so nerve-wracking, he realized. *Not the actual action.*

"My squad will assault the guards on the west and south sides and secure our perimeter there. Then I'll take my Fire Team One into the jail to secure the prisoners. Everyone else will stay outside and watch our backs. Any questions?"

Heads shook in the negative. Mac grinned.

"Then let's do this, folks."

Mac turned and led his squad to the edge of the Headquarters tent. They paused until Olivia was in position. When he got her "Ready" signal over his comm, he counted down.

"Three-two-one-go!" he called over the comm, and charged forward around the tent.

The battle to the east and south was in full swing now. There was a cacophony of gunfire from those directions. So much gunfire, the guards were mesmerized by it. The last thing on their minds was Mac and his team coming in from the north.

Mac shot three of the four fixed guards before they even knew they were under attack. The last one, and the roaming guard on his side of the jail, had just enough time to see them coming. The two guards managed to get their rifles up, at least, and one of them even got off a burst before he died.

Then Mac's team killed them. His squad quickly checked the bodies to ensure they were dead, then set up a perimeter. When Mac was sure they were secure, he rushed to the main door, his fire team behind him.

Peeking in, Mac saw three guards inside, all of them facing the door, rifles raised, ready to fight. Behind them, at the window in the rear of the jail, he saw Olivia's face poke up slowly into view. She assessed the situation, and then waved

Mac out of the way.

Pulling back, Mac crouched down beside the wall of the jail, waving his fire team down. Suddenly a burst of rifle fire exploded from behind the jail. A voice came over his comm.

"Clear," called Olivia. "You can go inside."

Mac rose, peeked in the door again. There were three bodies lying on the floor, and Olivia was grinning through the rear window. He nodded at her, focused on the door, and blew the lock off with his rifle. Pulling the door open, he gingerly stepped inside.

There was a hallway leading to the back of the jail. While his fire team checked the bodies, Mac stepped over them and moved cautiously down the hallway. The first two rooms were offices. Both were empty. Next came cells, three on each side. In the first cell, a tall, thin man with graying hair stood at the front, holding on to the bars. He looked haggard and had cuts and bruises all over his face.

"About time you got here!" he grinned at Mac.

Stree Prime
Battlecruiser SGH *Resolute*

From the Admiral's cabin of the Stree battlecruiser, Rita and her team watched the impact of the second asteroid. Even though Tika and Hajo were ambivalent about it, and in one sense glad the Stree were dying, there was still a grim mood pervading the room. Everyone knew the Goblins would be blamed for this genocide. And everyone knew the consequences would be dire for them.

As Rauti had so carefully planned, the planet had turned one-third of the way around in its rotation, giving the asteroid a fresh target. Rauti was ensuring that his destruction was complete.

Hajo continued to call Rauti up to the last second, but it was useless. Rauti refused to answer.

<He's gone round the bend> Hajo acknowledged a few

minutes before the second impact. <There's no reasoning with him>

<Which will be the perfect excuse for bios to wipe out Goblins in the future> Tika noted bitterly. <They'll point to Rauti as an example of what can happen when a Goblin goes nuts>

The results of the second impact were similar to the first. The seconds counted down, and suddenly it was over. A long streamer of plasma and molten lava exploded into space, a great gout of planetary guts centered over an ever-expanding ring of fire. The ring of fire soon overlapped the still-raging circle of destruction from the first impactor. All of them knew no living thing could survive in the area encompassed by those two raging circles of death.

Rita had cleared the room of any *Resolute* crew not part of her secret inner circle. Now she closed her eyes and bowed her head, saying a silent prayer for the billions of Stree killed with the impact of the first two asteroids. Finishing her prayer, she raised her head and stared at Hajo.

"Are you still talking to Rauti?" she asked.

"Yes. Of course, his first two instances are dead. They rode their impactors down to the surface. But his third instance is still onboard the last pusher missile. I'm trying to get him to respond, but he refuses to acknowledge my calls."

Rita sighed. "Keep trying. Keep trying to impress upon him - his revenge is already complete. He's killed more than two-thirds of the Stree populace. He's destroyed their home. It'll be something like a century or more before anyone can live safely on Stree Prime again. Try to convince him it's not necessary to kill them all."

"I will keep trying."

Rita turned to Tika and shook her head.

"It's all up to the *Armidale* now. If they can't stop the last impactor, there won't be a Stree left alive on the planet."

Tika's response showed her bitterness.

"If the *Armidale* fails, then it's the fate of the Stree to die. So be it."

"I know how angry you are, Tika," responded Rita. "But there's a greater morality here. The end does not justify the means. We do not take our revenge on the Stree by killing their children. We must try to save a remnant. Just as we saved a remnant of humanity from Earth. Just as we saved a remnant of the Singheko - our recent enemies. Just as there will be Goblins who survive this holocaust, to start the species anew. We cannot descend into madness, simply because the Stree did."

Tika replied bitterly.

"I do not care," she spat. "I will be happy if every Stree in the universe dies."

"That won't happen, Tika," Rita answered. "Even if the third impactor hits and there are no survivors on Stree Prime, there are other Stree colony worlds out there. And the survivors of the Stree fleet at Stalingrad. And this battlecruiser, which probably has a crew of hundreds, if not more than a thousand. A remnant of the Stree will go on, just as remnants of Humans and Goblins and all the others will go on. And I see a bleak future ahead if all these survivors do for the next few hundred years is try to kill each other. Is that what you want?"

"Fine with me," snarled Tika. "I'll gladly spend several lifetimes trying to hunt down every Stree I can find."

Once again, Rita shook her head in negation.

"Tika. There comes a time when the guilty have been punished enough, and we have to move on. This is that time. All the species involved in this damned war have been devastated. There are no winners. It's enough. We have to move on from this."

Tika got up from the table. She stood, glaring at Rita, for several seconds.

"It will never be enough for me. As long as one Stree remains alive in this universe, I will hunt them. Hunt them and kill them. The Stree feared us because we were different. Let them fear us now for a better reason."

And with that, Tika turned and departed the room. Hajo followed her. As the hatch closed behind them, Rita stared at the lone bodyguard still in the room with her.

"Maybe it would be best if the *Armidale* fails. If all the Stree here on Stree Prime were killed. Then Tika and her Goblins could hunt down the rest of them and wipe them out. Maybe the Universe needs to start with a clean slate."

The bodyguard stood, staring at Rita.

"They killed our planet, Rita. They deserve to die."

"No, Jim. They don't."

Jim Carter glared at Rita.

Rita had refused to leave Stree Prime without her husband. But she had also needed Jim to be aboard the *Armidale* to help the prisoners escape. In the end, Jim had done the only thing possible to be in two places at once.

There were now two copies of Jim Carter in the universe.

Turning and departing, he left Rita alone in the conference room. Rita closed her eyes and bowed her head, her thoughts swirling, and began another prayer.

CHAPTER THIRTY-FOUR

Stree Prime
Corvette *Armidale*

"There's two of you?" Bonnie asked incredulously.

Jim nodded. "Yeah. I didn't want to tell you at first. I thought you'd probably freak out. But yeah. There's another copy of me on the Stree battlecruiser with Rita."

Bonnie shook her head in disbelief.

"I..." she stopped, at a loss for words.

"Rita insisted one copy of me had to stay with her. But she didn't trust anyone else to get you and the other prisoners out. So there's two copies of me. One here, and one on the battlecruiser."

Bonnie looked at him in awe. "Which one are you?" she asked.

Jim, puzzled, cocked his head. "What?"

"Are you the original or the copy?"

Jim grinned. "Your question makes no sense. Both of us are copies. The original was my biological body. Or I guess you could think of the data that's stored somewhere in the electronics of the scanner as the original. But both myself and the one on the battlecruiser are copies. Two copies of near-perfection, of course."

Bonnie sniffed. "A long damn way from perfection, bub." She grimaced, thinking it through. "But...what do I call you? Jim? Or Jim 2? Or Jim Prime?"

The fat Stree face that Jim was currently wearing wrinkled in a huge smile. "How about Lord Jim?"

Bonnie bowed her head, trying to hide her grin. It was hard to be pissed at Jim when he was like this.

"I think I'll just call you Jim and we'll leave it at that. But wait - how long are you gonna stay in that fat fucker's body? Did you bring the bodybuilder along?"

"No. Rita needs it worse than I do. But Hajo and Luda already made an android copy of my bio body. It's in the cargo area. I can switch back into it anytime."

"Well, the sooner the better. I really don't care for your new look. But...Jim; what will you do? If Rita has the other copy of you...Oh, hell, this is gonna be such a mess for you. I'm so sorry."

"Well...don't be sorry. I did what I had to do to save you and the rest. I'd do it all again."

"But Jim...you know we can't follow that battlecruiser to Aslar. As soon as we finish pushing the impactor, we have to make a break for it."

Jim lost his smile. "Yes, I know."

"That means you won't be with Rita."

Jim shook his head. "No, I'll be with Rita. Just not this copy of me."

"But Jim..."

The creature across the table from Bonnie stood up. He raised his palms, a gesture that was universal. A gesture that meant, *there's no fixing this problem.*

"I'll be fine, Bonnie," he said. "When this is all over, I'll go find something else to do."

"You...you could come stay on Phoenix. With Luke and I and the rest..."

Jim shook his head in negation. "No. That's the last thing I could do. It would cause nothing but trouble. Either Luke would be jealous of me, or I would be jealous of Luke. If I can't have Rita, and I can't have you, then I don't want to be anywhere near Phoenix."

Over the PA system, they heard Captain Stewart call everyone for the attempt to deflect the third impactor.

And with that, Jim/Cotrapi turned and shuffled off toward the bridge of the *Armidale*.

Phoenix System
Outside the Jail

"Mark Rodgers," said the tall, gray-haired man. He pointed to another man, younger, even more bruised and battered. "This is Luke Powell. We're mighty glad to see you, son."

Mac nodded, glancing at Luke. "Tatiana's father?" he asked.

"Yes," said Luke. "How is she?"

"She was good last time I saw her, sir," Mac replied. "This morning about 1 AM. She'll be with the group attacking from the west."

"Outstanding," said Luke. "So what's next?"

"We'll take you folks out to the west a bit and secure you in a location away from danger," said Mac.

"Bullshit," said the female, who had introduced herself as Zoe DeLong. "No way. That sonuvabitch Turgenev will be around here somewhere. We're gonna find him and kick his fucking ass," she continued.

"No, mum," insisted Mac. "My orders are to secure your safety. We'll find a safe place to wait this out."

The third man - introduced as Rick Moore - had not yet spoken. Now he interjected. "You can go find a safe spot for yourself, if you want, but we're going to get Turgenev." And with that, he picked up a rifle from one of the dead bodies on the floor, grabbed the ammo belt, and headed for the door.

Zoe DeLong and Luke Powell mimicked his actions, taking the other two rifles and ammo belts. Mark, Luke, and Zoe headed for the door.

"No, wait, please!" yelled Mac, at a loss. "I can't disobey my orders!"

Mark paused and looked at him.

"Son, I'm the Governor of this colony. My orders supersede those of Tatiana Powell. So we're going to get Turgenev. You can come or you can stay. Up to you."

The four slammed the door open and went outside. Mac looked at Olivia and shrugged.

"I guess we have new orders," he said. Olivia smiled. Together, they followed the civilians.

Outside, they found the four huddling, discussing their next steps.

"Where would you be, if you were Turgenev?" Mark asked.

Rick Moore scratched his forehead, thinking. "I think I'd be right in the center of Central Park, protected by a ring of troops."

Zoe shook her head. "Nope. Too much chance of something going wrong, being caught in the middle of a nasty firefight. Turgenev's not going to take a chance on that. He'll be in one of the apartment blocks, probably up on the roof where he can get a good view of things."

Mark looked at Luke. "Well? What do you think?"

Luke grimaced, looking around in the darkness. "On balance, I think I'd go with Zoe's idea. I think he'll be up there somewhere, watching things play out below him."

"But which one?" Mark thought out loud. "There are fourteen apartment blocks now."

"One of the unfinished ones," said Zoe. "That way, he doesn't have to worry about people getting in his way or coming in behind him."

"OK, one of the unfinished Blocks," said Mark. "There's four of those in work. Which one?"

Mac had a thought. "The one closest to the center on the west side, sir," he said. "He'll have picked up on Battalion East coming in through the forest on the east side first, so he would have taken the block opposite that."

Mark smiled at the young militiaman. "By George, son, I think you're right. That's what he would do."

Mark turned back to the others. "That would be Block

Eleven, then. That's the unfinished one closest to the center on the west side."

"What are we waiting for? Let's go get him!" said Rick.

"Wait," Luke spoke up. "We need a plan. It doesn't do any good to go in guns blazing and get shot to hell."

A silence fell over the group as they thought. Rick spoke up again. "We could go steal a shuttle and drop in on him from above."

Zoe reached over and touched Rick on the cheek in a loving gesture, but - as women have a talent for doing - a gesture that also admonished him in some undefined way.

"Hon, we'd have to fight our way through the main part of his troops to get to a shuttle. I don't think I want to do that."

Rick shrugged, nodded.

Mac threw out another idea. "We have climbing ropes in our packs. We could climb up the outside of the Block."

Mark looked at the young man. "The outside of those Blocks is as smooth as a baby's ass. Nothing to secure the ropes."

"Then," Luke said. "We just have to walk right in like we own the place."

"What do you mean?" asked Mark.

Luke gestured back toward the jail. "We've got three bodies there with Turgenev's militia patches on their shirts. Three of us put on their uniforms. We go report to Turgenev that his prisoners have escaped. I'm betting he'll want to know the details and have us brought right to him."

Mark nodded. "That's reasonable. I think I like that. But...he knows all of us."

Mark turned his gaze to Mac. "Son, are you up for this?"

Mac nodded. To his surprise, all his fear had dissipated. He had never felt stronger in his life.

"Yes, sir," he answered.

"And me too," added Olivia.

Mac looked at her, protectiveness overtaking him.

"No, Olivia. Stay here."

"In a pig's eye," Olivia spat back at him.

Stree System
Corvette *Armidale*

Captain Stewart had brought the ship to battle stations. Commander Brady sat at the XO console, with Lieutenant Hodges at Helm. Jim Carter and Rachel Gibson entered the bridge, Rachel moving to the Tactical station and Jim to Comm. Both had just returned from the cargo bay, where Luda had assisted them in switching back to their default android bodies. The rest sat or stood behind Stewart, out of the way.

"ETA to intercept?" asked Captain Stewart.

"Four minutes," called Brady. "On course. We'll nose right into that little crack on the near side of the asteroid as gently as possible. Then we'll start to push."

"Captain, message from Rauti. He's warning us off," called Jim.

"Or what?"

"Um...he says if we don't get clear, he'll turn the pusher missile toward us and ram us."

"I was afraid of this. OK, Rachel. Take him out."

With a nod, Rachel fired a spread of four missiles at the pusher behind the asteroid. They ran straight and true directly toward the huge missile. The pusher disappeared in a fiery explosion.

Stewart sighed. "So ends Commander Rauti." He turned to Luda and Liwa standing behind. "I'm sorry, Luda," he spoke.

Luda shrugged. "He had lost his mind, Captain. It is well."

"Two minutes to intercept, Skipper," called Brady.

Stewart turned back to the Goblins and Humans behind him.

"It might be best if you went to your cabins and strapped in. This could get a little rough."

Bonnie shook her head in negation. "I'm staying right here, Captain."

The rest joined in with Bonnie, refusing to leave.

"So be it," said Stewart. He turned back to his work, dismissing the fate of those watching. He had bigger fish to fry.

"One minute to intercept," called Brady.

The *Armidale* was now traveling at 30% light speed - 89 million meters per second. 201,073,619 miles per hour. She would cover the remaining 75 million miles to Stree Prime in only fourteen minutes.

But other than the obvious problem of impacting space dust at near-relativistic speeds, or running into the stray chunk of debris from the planet, the intercept was not particularly difficult. There was no apparent motion relative to the impactor. It hung in space before them, a huge oblong rock, nearly motionless to their view as they inched up closer and closer to it. The impactor was mostly white, covered in ice; but there were a couple of places where the underlying rock showed through. One of those places was a small crevasse, a shallow crack in the surface of the asteroid. That was the *Armidale*'s target. Carefully, Lieutenant Hodges began nosing the *Armidale* into the crack, trying to bring it up against the asteroid without damaging the integrity of the hull.

Everyone on the bridge held their breath as second by second, Hodges pushed the *Armidale* up into the crack. If he approached too slowly, they would not have enough time to push the rock off-course and cause it to miss the planet. If he approached too quickly, he'd crack the hull of the *Armidale* like an egg.

"Just a little bit quicker, Lieutenant, if you please," called Brady, watching the countdown clock on his console. They were running out of time.

Hodges gulped and nodded his head. He tweaked the maneuvering jets a tiny bit. Sweat poured down his forehead.

"Ten meters," called Brady. "A bit too fast now."

Hodges tweaked his maneuvering jets again, and the *Armidale* began to slow down.

"Five meters, still a bit fast," called Brady.

Hodges nodded, worked his controls. Then with a great

"clunk" the *Armidale* hit the asteroid, bounced back a bit, moved forward again and settled into position, its nose pushed firmly into the crevasse on the rock.

"Hull integrity?" Stewart called out.

Rachel, working the Tac Console, replied quickly.

"No evidence of hull breach. Pressure is holding."

"Excellent. Good work, Hodges. You are now fully qualified to poke ships into asteroids."

Hodges gulped again, nodded, and wiped the sweat from his forehead.

"Aye, sir. Ready to push," he responded.

"OK. Give us a gentle push at first, let's see if we've got a firm contact."

"Gentle push coming, sir."

Displayed in the lower right corner of the holotank, the assembled group could see the *Armidale*'s engine thrust and the pressure on the nose. Now the thrust number slowly increased from 1% to 2% as Hodges gently tweaked the main engines.

"So far so good," called Brady. "We seem to have a firm position on the rock, and hull integrity is still good."

"Bring us slowly up to 10%, Hodges," called Stewart. "Easy does it."

"Aye, Skipper," called Hodges. The thrust on the display moved slowly but steadily to 10%. The hull pressure indicator moved as well, rising to 20% of maximum.

"OK. Looks like the pressure on the nose is going up by twice the thrust level, at least so far. Bring us up to 25%, Hodges."

"Aye, Skipper."

The display moved slowly to 25%. The pressure on the nose moved along with it to 50% of maximum.

"45%, Hodges."

As the group watched, the thrust increased slowly to 45%. But the pressure on the nose spiked suddenly to 99% of theoretical maximum. Creaking and groaning noises could be heard from the front of the ship. The *Armidale* was clearly indicating her displeasure at so much load.

"Brady?" called Stewart.

Brady shook his head. "Not enough, Skipper. It'll still hit the planet. We've got to have at least another 10% thrust to move it off the line in time."

Stewart looked grim. "I don't think she'll take another 10%, XO. She's already groaning like an old woman."

Stewart turned to the group behind him. He said not a word, but looked straight at Bonnie, holding her eyes.

Bonnie knew what Stewart was asking. Except in the minds of these few Human survivors, the EDF didn't exist anymore. It was now just a warrior's memory, on this little corvette in the middle of the enemy.

But in the mind of Captain Stewart, Bonnie was still the senior EDF officer on the *Armidale*. Stewart was asking permission to endanger both his ship and the lives of everyone on board.

Bonnie nodded silently at Stewart. Without a word being said, Stewart turned back to his console.

"Hodges. Increase thrust to 55%. As slowly as you can, but still fast enough to push this damn rock off course before it hits the planet."

Hodges took a deep breath. Slowly, carefully, he tweaked the thrust controls. The *Armidale* protested, loud groans coming from the front of the ship as composite and metal compressed in a way never envisioned for a spaceship design. A loud pop made everyone jump in their seat as something gave way up front. Rachel, eyes glued to her console, lifted one finger in the air, a visual indication to everyone that they still had pressure. All eyes were glued on that finger as the *Armidale* continued to creak and groan, with occasional pops and bangs coming from forward.

And then Hodges raised both hands from his console, as if he were afraid to even touch his controls again for fear of breaking the ship.

"55%, sir," he called.

On the front display, the hull pressure indicator flashed red numbers at them, standing at 125% of maximum. Warning chimes went off on every console on the bridge. Everyone froze, afraid to move.

Every so slightly, the curve of the impactor's trajectory on the front display began to change. Slowly, the projected curve shifted, moving at a snail's pace, changing from its original target on the surface of the planet. First only slightly, then more, then it curved until it showed an impact on the edge of the planet. Then the projected curve cleared the planetary surface - a trajectory that would streak through the lower atmosphere. Ever so slowly, the curve raised away from the surface, higher into the atmosphere.

"Out of time!" yelled Brady. "Back us off, Hodges! Get us the hell out of here!"

"Aye, sir," Hodges yelled in response, his adrenalin high. "Backing off!"

The *Armidale* withdrew from the asteroid as fast as Hodges could work the controls, the hull once again popping and creaking as the load was removed. Rachel continued to hold up her finger, showing they still had hull integrity - and pressure. As soon as Hodges had room, he fired the mains at max, streaking past the impactor on a vector to get them clear of the planet - and the massive amounts of debris that swirled around it from the first two impacts.

"Are we good?" called Stewart.

"I think so," Hodges responded. "Give me a few more seconds..."

Hodges was bent over his console, pushing keys to analyze their vector, watching for stray junk from the planet and selecting a course that would keep them clear. Stewart, impatient, unbuckled his harness and rose from his seat, walked to Hodges' console, and put a hand on his shoulder. Silently, he watched as Hodges worked, saying nothing but giving the young lieutenant encouragement.

After a long minute in which nobody said a word, Hodges

leaned back with a sigh.

"We're clear, sir," he said, looking up at his captain. "Decelerating down to normal speeds and clear of the planetary debris."

Stewart nodded. He turned to Brady.

"And the impactor?"

"It missed clean, sir," replied Brady. "Not by much, but... well...horseshoes and hand grenades. It missed by enough. It's on its way back out-system now. At that velocity, it'll depart the system. We'll never see it again."

Stewart turned in his seat to look at Bonnie behind him.

"What next, boss?" he asked.

"Let's get the hell out of Dodge," said Bonnie. "We've got a good gap between us and the battlecruiser now. They couldn't catch us even if they wanted to. Find a vector that'll keep our distance from them and head us back to Stalingrad."

Stewart looked grim.

"Are you sure you want to go to Stalingrad? Nothing there but...wreckage."

"I'm sure," said Bonnie. She looked around at Luda and Liwa. They nodded solemnly. She turned back to Stewart.

"We may only find wreckage. But by God, we'll not abandon them without trying. We'll search that system for survivors for as long as it takes."

Phoenix System
Turgenev Headquarters

Turgenev was almost ecstatic. He had been certain his plan would work - but it was actually working better than his wildest dreams. His Northern Force had roared in, taking Misha's Battalion East in the flank. Pushing Misha south, the pressure was off his Central Force as Misha fought for his life from this new and unexpected attack.

That freed up Central Force to turn on Tatiana. As they brought the full measure of their firepower around to face the west, they had stopped her in her tracks.

As soon as she was fully engaged, his Southern Force had attacked. They came into Tatiana's flank like a prairie fire. She was now fighting for her life, caught between a rock and a hard place. She was retreating, moving her troops back into the jungle, as Turgenev's militia pressed her from two sides.

Another hour and she'll have no choice but to retreat all the way back to her landing area, try to survive long enough for the shuttles to come pick her up.

This is almost over.

***

Mac, Olivia, and Mac's assistant squad leader Frank Masters walked resolutely toward Block Eleven. They wore the uniforms of the three guards they had killed, and carried their rifles. They had made a valiant attempt to wash out the blood from the uniforms and cover the bullet holes. It was a quick patch job, but they had arranged bandoleers of ammunition over the worst of it and crossed their fingers.

They knew, without looking, that the rest of their team, along with Mark, Luke, Rick, and Zoe, were shadowing them a hundred yards to the west, hidden in the shadows of the tent city.

It seemed they had guessed correctly; there was a constant stream of messengers coming and going from the Block.

"That's his HQ, alright," muttered Olivia.

"Yep," said Frank.

"Here we go," Mac added as they approached. There was a table set up in front of the building, with an officer sitting behind it. There were a half-dozen guards lounging nearby in what appeared to be lawn chairs.

Acting as naturally as he could, Mac marched up to the building, centered himself in front of the officer, and snapped to attention.

"Sergeant Davis reporting, sir, and the prisoners have escaped from the jail. I thought I should let you know."

"What?" roared the officer, slamming to his feet. "You let

the prisoners escape?"

Mac hung his head, his demeanor one of shame. "Yes, sir. We were attacked by a large force, and they freed the prisoners."

"Where'd they go?" yelled the officer, highly agitated.

"Into the jungle to the west, sir," said Mac. "I think." Mac held his head as if in pain. "I was knocked out, sir, but that's what I was told."

The officer, clearly disgusted with Mac, turned to one of his nearby guards.

"Corporal! Take them up to Command HQ and have them report to the adjutant!" he yelled.

The guard jumped up, waved at the three of them, and headed for the door. Mac, Olivia, and Frank followed. In the darkness, no one seemed to give them a second glance.

Climbing the dark stairwell to the top of the unfinished building, Olivia wondered if their ploy would work. Turgenev was no dummy; many of the colonists hated him and would kill him in a heartbeat if given the chance. He had to know that; so there would be tight security around him. And surely, they would take away their rifles first.

Other soldiers went by them, some running for the top of the stairs, some running downward, as Turgenev's messengers came and went to the various combat units of his militia. Slowly they climbed, Mac still holding his head from time to time, pretending to be injured.

Olivia felt for the pistol tucked deep into her pants, the butt just barely reachable under the top of her waistband. That pistol - and those of Mac and Frank - might not be enough. Or they might be searched at the top of the stairs, and those pistols taken from them.

She knew Mac and Frank had combat knives, tucked into the back of their pants. She didn't have a knife; but she had one more weapon, one that she could use as a last resort. If all else failed.

And then, suddenly, they were at the top of the stairs. At the other end of the hall, she heard the drone of an electrical generator. Lights were hung from the ceiling, wires running down the hallway. There were dozens of people moving about, tables set up in the hallway, security guards. It was the chaos of a military headquarters in the middle of a battle.

Two burly security guards came to them and gestured for their rifles. Mac and Frank unslung their rifles and handed them over. Then the guards gestured to Olivia. She unslung her rifle and gave it to them. They began patting down Mac and Frank, looking for other weapons. Quickly they found their pistols and combat knives and removed them, tossing them into a large box to one side.

Then one of them moved to her. He leered at her and began patting her down. He clearly was mostly interested in touching her - roughly, harshly, he roamed her body as she stood stock still. He quickly found the pistol in her waistband. After searching for other weapons, he stood back and waved them through.

Olivia exulted. *He missed it! He missed the other pistol! He was so busy feeling me up he missed it!*

Then the thought sank into her, the thought that felt like a cold wind on her back.

Then it's up to me to get Turgenev. I'm the only one that can do it now.

Their original guide led them forward, down the hallway to a large double door on the left. Rick Moore had told them that each apartment block had a large rooftop garden, and that this building's garden would be unfinished, leaving a large open space on the roof.

"That'll be the most likely place for Turgenev to set up his HQ and Observation Post," Rick had said. "It'll be double doors about half-way down the top hallway, on the left."

Looks like Rick called it.

They were led through the double doors and immediately fetched up against a row of desks blocking their way. There was one desk in the center and two to each side. The light here was dim, just barely enough to make out faces. Past the desks, Olivia could see the darkened roof. There was just enough dim light for her to see a row of officers at the edge of the roof, looking over a tall parapet wall with binoculars and night vision equipment. They were talking among themselves, gesturing, pointing to the battle going on to the south of them.

And the one in the center was Turgenev. Olivia had seen pictures of him. Even from the rear, even in the darkness, she could recognize him. He was a good two inches taller than anyone else on the roof and had the broad shoulders and bull neck she had seen in the photos. She estimated he was only twenty yards from her now. Could she get to her gun and shoot him before his guards killed her?

No, she decided. *I have to try to get closer.*

"What?" snapped the officer sitting at the middle desk, glaring at their escort.

"These are the guards from the jail, Major," said the corporal. "The prisoners have escaped."

The officer shot to his feet. "What? How?" He snarled at Mac, who was slightly in front. "How could you let this happen? Idiots!"

The officer turned and went out to the roof, went up to Turgenev and whispered to him quietly. Turgenev turned, stared at them, his face an impassive mask. He gestured to them to come forward.

This is it, Olivia thought. *If I can get the pistol out. If I can shoot before they shoot me. If I can hit my target - I've never been that good of a pistol shot. Maybe I should toss the pistol to Mac.*

But...no, I won't have time for that.

I'll have to do this myself.

Steeling herself, Olivia stepped forward toward the tall Russian, her hand already drifting backward, where she had stuffed a small pistol right up the crack of her ass.

***

Kim Geun-shi was ecstatic. He had assembled hundreds of people - mostly Asian, including Chinese, Korean, Japanese, Indonesian, some few others - into a tightly knit yakuza gang, helping Turgenev take over the colony. But those yakuza also allowed him to blackmail Turgenev; he might only have a few hundred adherents, but they were the most ruthless ones in the colony. Removing their support would seriously weaken Turgenev's position. Turgenev knew it and didn't dare cross Kim at this point.

So Kim had forced Turgenev to make him a colonel in their militia. And now Kim was in charge of Turgenev's Southern Force.

And Kim was happy. Beating back the initial charge of Tatiana's Battalion West, he had fought them to a standstill. Now his troops advanced on them, pushing them back into the jungle.

Even better, his radio messages told him that the Northern Force was doing the same to Misha's Battalion East.

They were winning. It was just a matter of time now. Within a couple of hours, they would have eliminated the last threat to their rule. They would hunt down the stragglers of the Ukrainian bitch's army and kill them to the last man.

But not to the last woman. Kim had other plans for the women. Turgenev had given him the slave concession for the colony.

The women would be captured and sold on the open market.

Except for a choice few. The choice few that Kim would keep for himself.

And maybe - if he were lucky, if he were really lucky - he could capture that Ukrainian bitch, Tatiana Powell.

Kim would make her his personal slave. He practically salivated at the thought.

"Sir!" came a call from his Chief of Staff, "something strange down south!"

Kim snapped out of his daydream. "What?"

"We have reports of rifle fire coming in on our flank, from the south!"

"Show me!" snapped Kim. He rushed to the map on the

desk."

The major pointed to an 'X' marked on the map. "Right there, sir, about one klick south. There's something...wait..."

The officer clutched his earpiece, obviously receiving another report. He looked up at Kim, distress visible on his face.

"An assault from the south, sir. A large one. They've managed to flank us somehow. They're attacking from the south!"

***

Turgenev was standing at the edge of the roof, looking over the parapet toward the south. He had been shocked by Kim's report of a fresh assault on his flank.

Another assault force? From the south? How? How did that bitch do that? She doesn't have enough troops!

Looking through his night-vision glasses, though, Turgenev was forced to admit reality. He could see heavy enemy fire to the south. More, in fact, than he was seeing from the jungle to the west.

Somehow, Tatiana had gotten a large force around to Kim's left flank. Turgenev realized Kim was in trouble.

It doesn't matter how she did it, he thought. *All that matters is how to counter it. I'll have to pull troops from the Northern Force to help Kim.*

"Major!" he called to his Chief of Staff. "Order Cerutti to withdraw one company from his assault on the east and turn them south to help Kim. Quickly!"

"Yes, sir," called his Number Two.

Turgenev fumed.

That damn Ukrainian bitch. She's tricky, all right. But not tricky enough. I've still got her. With a company from Cerutti, Kim will have plenty of troops to push her back. We'll still have the bitch dead by noon.

"Sir," came a voice behind him. Turgenev turned. His aide behind him was pointing to three troopers by the entrance. He didn't recognize the three at all. And something about them looked a bit off, he thought. It struck him instantly.

"The prisoners have escaped from the jail," his aide said. "These three came to tell us."

Turgenev waved the three closer. When they were a dozen feet from him, he gestured to them to stop. They did, pausing behind his aide. "Report!" he barked.

One of the troops stepped forward one step and began speaking.

"Sir, we were attacked at the jail. I was knocked out. When I came to, the prisoners were gone. We searched for them, but we can't find them."

Turgenev nodded. He saw the female standing at the rear of the group moving her hand. She was moving it toward her ass.

And he knew. A lifetime of survival in the Russian underworld sent up flares of warning in Turgenev's mind. He grabbed for his pistol, and at the same time the female moved quickly, diving to one side and reaching deep into the back of her pants.

It was an old trick, and Turgenev had used it himself on occasion. Men tended to search women in a certain way. They would focus on the front of their bodies, because - well, because they were men. They would often not search their rear very well. This woman had taken advantage of that.

Even as he saw her hand come out of the back of her pants with the pistol, Turgenev was firing. He dove to the side, taking shelter behind his aides, sacrificing them for his own survival, firing at the woman as fast as he could. He saw the muzzle flashes from her pistol, the barrel tracking him as he moved. She was lagging him, though. He had moved just fast enough. She was firing a bit behind him. One round went close to him, so close he felt the buzz, felt the tug of the bullet as it pulled at the sleeve of his shirt.

In front of him, his adjutant went down like a sack of potatoes, a bullet in his chest. Turgenev continued to roll to the side, the bitch tracking him, firing, the noise deafening even on the open rooftop.

And then it was over. Turgenev lay on the roof, breathing hard, trying to accept that he was still alive. In front of him, two of his aides lay dead. Beyond them, the woman also lay dead, his last couple of shots taking her out. Around them his staff stood frozen in shock.

Turgenev stood and stared at the two other troopers who had come on the roof with the woman. He knew both of them were the enemy. Both were now held tightly in the grip of four of his security guards, who had finally reacted.

"Take them out of here!" he yelled. "Lock them up! Idiots!"

CHAPTER THIRTY-FIVE

Phoenix System
Cerutti's Northern Force

Cerutti shook his head. He had received the order from Turgenev to detach a company and send it south to reinforce Kim. He had done it; but he didn't like it. His attack to the east, into Misha's Battalion East, was encountering strong resistance.

Once they had entered the thick forest, the enemy had gone into some kind of guerrilla warfare mode. They hopscotched back and forth in front of his troops. First a group would appear on his right, ambushing his troops from an unexpected direction. And then, just when he got his forces re-directed to assault into them, they were gone. Another group would appear suddenly on his left, another ambush taking out one or two dozen of his people.

His troops were getting shy about moving forward in the thick forest. Every time they did, they got waylaid from an unexpected direction. His Northern Force was not that large; losing a couple of dozen people every fifteen minutes was whittling away at both his numbers and the morale of his troops.

A couple of hundred yards behind his lines, Cerutti was moving forward when the new attack hit him. One moment, he was gazing ahead in front of him in the darkness, trying to determine where he wanted to direct them next. The next moment, tracers were flying all around him, not from the front where the enemy should be, but from the rear, from the northwest.

From a place where there should be nobody. No enemy could be there. They had watched so carefully with their drones.

Nobody can be there. It's not possible!

It was his last thought as a bullet smashed into the back of his head.

***

Tatiana looked at her makeshift battle map in satisfaction. It showed Cerutti's Northern Force falling back in disarray, his troops running in panic as their left flank was rolled up. The end-run she had sent around to the north had caught Cerutti by total surprise. His troops ran toward the west, throwing down their weapons and making for their apartment blocks, hoping to hide from the onslaught that was killing them by the dozens now.

To the south, Kim's Southern Force was not much better off. Even with the reinforcements Cerutti had sent, they were also being pinched in between opposing forces. Tatiana's second end run to the south had come around Kim and attacked into his left flank, pushing him back to the north, pushing him into the center of the colony.

And Tatiana's Battalion West - only a skeleton force now, after she had taken most of the troops for her end runs to the north and south - was still strong enough to keep Kim penned up, prevent him from moving farther west. Kim was in a bottle. Outnumbered now, his troops flailing to hold their positions, the only place he could go was back into the open area of Central Park.

And that did him no good. Once Cerutti's force had collapsed, Misha's Battalion East had no opposition to speak of in front of them. Misha had left one company to mop up the remnants of Cerutti's Northern Force; the rest of his troops were now attacking into the center of the colony, pushing

Turgenev's small Center Force back. Misha had already taken the center of the park and was holding the shuttle parking area.

It was all over, Tatiana realized. There was no way out for Kim, and no way out for Turgenev. She had them. Sooner or later, they would realize it too, and they would surrender.

Or she would kill them all.

Tatiana sighed.

Always so much death. Why did I have to be so good at this? Why couldn't I just be a nice, quiet mother, with a couple of kids to raise, a nice quiet husband, a nice quiet life?

But…somebody has to be good at it. Somebody has to be good at killing our enemies.

You just have to make the best of what Fate doles out to you.

She glanced over at her aide, Major Granville.

"Tommy, I think it's about over. See if you can get a message to Turgenev and also to Kim. Offer them a surrender. Remind them it'll save a lot of lives. And Major…"

"Yes, milady?"

"Point out to them the alternative is that I'll kill them both."

"Aye, milady," Granville smiled, as he went to carry out her orders.

2,885 Lights from Stalingrad

The *Darkstar* had settled into the dull routine of a long voyage. Captain Ostend sat at his desk. A good simulated whiskey - the best the AI of the *Darkstar* could produce from the synthesizers - sat in front of him. Across from him, Commander Woh sat, a glass of the same concoction in his hand. Behind them, back toward Stalingrad, lay light years of nothingness as they bored on toward the center of the galaxy.

"To distance," said Ostend, his words slightly slurred. Woh raised his hand and grunted.

"Distance," he answered.

They drank, and then pulled their glasses down. Ostend

shook his head.

"Tagi said go at least 10,000 lights before we start looking. So we've got another 7,115 lights to go. Another 148 days."

"Yeah," Woh answered glumly. "A long damn way."

"But..." Ostend mused. "We did our duty. We followed orders."

"That we did," agreed Woh. "We followed our damn orders. I really wanted to punch holes in Stree ships, though."

Ostend broke a grin. "You realize, with this old tub, they'd have punched a lot more holes in us that we would in them."

Woh shrugged. "I guess."

"But still...," said Ostend. "I wish we could have given it a go."

They sat in silence for a bit. Then Ostend raised his glass again.

"To orders, even when they suck."

Woh nodded. "To orders."

Far in the back of the cruiser, in the cargo hold, thousands of small crates sat. And in each crate was a well-padded electronic device containing thousands of dormant scans.

The children of the Goblins sat unaware in their electronic storage, waiting for a time when their Human guardians could find someplace for them to live without fear.

Waiting for the day when they could live again.

Phoenix System
Colony Headquarters

Mark Rodgers sat at a conference table in the command tent, the strain of the last hours still evident on his face. Around him sat Gillian, Tatiana and Misha, Luke, Rick Moore, Zoe DeLong, and several members of their staff. All of them were shell-shocked, dirty, and exhausted. The air of the camp stank of gunpowder and death.

"How'd you do it, Tat? How'd you flank them like that?" asked Mark.

Tat smiled. "I split my Battalion West into three forces early this morning. I sent one force wide around to the south, and the other wide around to the north. I kept a small decoy force with me, just enough to present the appearance of the main attack coming from the west as Turgenev expected. As soon as we got Kim engaged, we started falling back into the jungle again. He fell for it and came after us. That opened up his flanks. That was the beginning of the end."

"Remind me never to go up against you in a battle," growled Rick Moore from the end of the table.

"Well," said Mark. "It's over. We have to move forward now. Somehow, we've got to get this colony back on track." He glanced around the table. "Luke, what's the status of the mop-up?"

"All enemy combatants have surrendered," Luke replied. "We've converted Blocks Eleven and Twelve into temporary prisons. We had no trouble finding people willing to serve as prison guards - in fact, the only problem we've had so far is preventing our enthusiastic prison guards from taking their prisoners down to the forest and hanging them from the nearest trees. I guess Turgenev's people were pretty brutal."

"And what's next with the prisoners?" asked Mark.

"We're going through a process of identification now. We'll identify the die-hards and the thugs and criminals - any that committed major crimes during their rampage, things like rape, murder, and so forth. Those will remain locked up until we decide what to do with them.

"The rest of them - the fellow travelers - will be identified, then released back into the general population for now. We can decide what to do with them later."

"OK," said Mark. "Sounds like a plan. And how about our colony resources, Zoe?"

"We took a lot of damage to the crops out East," Zoe responded. "I've already got crews out trying to save as much as possible. I think we can recover most of the damaged crops without too much loss."

"Water systems?"

"No damage to the water systems. We're good there."

"That's a miracle," said Mark. He turned to Luke. "And you've already restarted the shuttles to bring down the rest of the colonists from Transport Five?"

"Yep," said Luke. "They're on their way down right now. We'll have the rest of the folks down by late tomorrow night."

Mark leaned back in his chair. He passed his gaze around the room.

"So. One last item for today's agenda, before we go get some much-needed rest. Turgenev and Kim."

There was a silence. Everyone looked at Luke. He was still considered the de facto Supreme Court of the colony. Luke realized they were throwing this open question into his lap. He leaned forward.

"Does anyone think a trial is necessary?"

Everyone shook their heads, some of them smiling at the very thought.

"Then I'll pass sentence now, if that's OK," Luke added.

Mark nodded at him.

"Turgenev and Kim are sentenced to be scanned. Their bodies will then be destroyed. Their scans will be held in storage until we have the technology to build new starships."

Luke looked around the table.

"And from that point, they'll drive a starship for one thousand years."

CHAPTER THIRTY-SIX

Stalingrad System
Dyson Swarm

The surviving ships of the Stree fleet spent the next days methodically hunting down and killing every Goblin warship in the system. Thirty-one Goblin ships had survived the last stand at the Dyson Ring; twenty-four hours later, all were destroyed. Admiral Sojatta's replacement, Sub-Admiral Jisellat, was as efficient as Sojatta when it came to fulfilling his mission parameters.

Standing off from the Dyson Ring, he spent the next ten days blowing it to pieces. Any fragment bigger than a few square miles was pushed into the star by remote-controlled rockets.

When that was over, Jisellat turned to the hundreds of other, smaller Dyson squares orbiting the star. One by one, his tugs de-orbited each one into the star, until none were left.

Stalingrad was dead.

Finished, Jisellat turned his remaining ships and headed for Aslar. He knew there was no point in returning to Stree Prime. His home world was as thoroughly destroyed as the Goblin system. In the end, mutually assured destruction had won out. Two species, hating each other beyond all reason, had finally succeeded in killing the majority of their citizens.

Two Months Later
Phoenix Colony

The shuttle landed gently in the grass of Central Park,

just outside Council Headquarters. The pilot waited a minute for excess gases to exhaust from the vents, then lowered the ramp. In the opening at the top of the ramp, figures appeared, stepping one by one out of the shuttle and into the waiting arms of loved ones and friends.

Luke waited patiently at the back of the crowd. He knew Bonnie would be last out of the shuttle. And he was right. A dozen Humans stepped off the shuttle before he finally saw the love of his life appear at the top of the ramp, shading her eyes in the bright sunshine.

Stepping forward, he waited as she let her eyes adjust. Then she saw him. Her face lit up and she ran forward, down the ramp and into his arms. And for the next few minutes, the universe disappeared for both of them as they folded into each other, oblivious to the stares and smiles around them.

Later, in their apartment, they sat on Luke's makeshift couch intertwined like a couple of teenagers, still unwilling to let go of each other. Bonnie's head was on Luke's shoulder, and she had a drink in her hand - the first locally made alcoholic beverage of the colony.

"How on Earth did you get liquor?" Bonnie asked, swirling the drink in her glass.

"First of all, we're not on Earth. We're on Phoenix," laughed Luke. "Second, there was a family rescued from Tennessee that knew how to make a still. As soon as we had some corn and potatoes growing in the fields, they made a midnight raid and collected a bunch of the crop and started making moonshine. Mark decided rather than try to fight it, he'd just embrace it. So he told them to take one of the empty storage areas in Block Fifteen and turn it into a moonshine factory. Viola! Instant cottage industry!"

"You know, Mark's a pretty smart cookie," said Bonnie. "If he had tried to suppress it, there would've been nothing but trouble."

"Exactly. Now, instead of moonshine wars, he collects a small percentage of the product as tax. He exchanges that for food and other things needed by single mothers, the elderly, injured people who can't work, that kind of thing."

"So everyone benefits."

"Well, not quite. We've been rationing it pretty strictly to prevent alcoholism. But there's already a black market springing up around it. We're gonna have problems with that. But you know, any approach has its problems. At least this way some good comes of it - although the people fighting alcoholism will suffer. We'll try to help them somehow. It's not the best solution, but it's all we've got right now."

Bonnie took a sip and grimaced.

"Well, all I can say about it is that it's wet and it burns going down."

Luke grinned. "Yep. It has all the essentials."

There was a short silence. After a while, though, Bonnie spoke.

"I guess we should talk about Rita and Jim."

"I guess so."

"First of all, there's two Jims now. Rita made two copies of him."

"My Lord!" exclaimed Luke. "Two copies of that madman?"

Bonnie smiled. "You know he's not a madman. He's just a man of action. And when we needed him, he was there for us. So don't say anything about Jim Carter. And besides, I know you're just jealous."

"Not really. I just like to get a rise out of you when I get the chance."

"Yeah, right. Well, anyway. Rita made two copies of him. One copy went with her, and the other stayed with us on the *Armidale*."

"So where is he now? That other copy, I mean?"

Bonnie shifted in her seat, a bit uncomfortable. She bit her lip before she continued.

"He stayed at Stalingrad. Refused to come with us. Said he'd be a third wheel here. He took the *Armidale*'s shuttle and said he was going to stay there at Stalingrad for now."

"And you just left him there? You didn't try to stop him?"

"I did try, hon. But has anyone ever succeeded in stopping Jim after he's made up his mind to do something?"

Luke shrugged. "Yeah, you got that right. So...you think he'll be OK?"

"I guess. I told him we'd send Duncan in the *Armidale* to check up on him every six months until we're sure he's OK. He told us not to bother. But I'm going to do it anyway."

"So what about Rita and Tika and the other Jim?"

"They decided to remain in Goblin form and go to Aslar - to continue their charade as Videlli and Tarilli. Along with Hajo and the other Jim."

"I guess I don't fully understand why they would do that. What do they hope to gain?"

"They know the Stree establishment will keep going at the Goblins until there's not one Goblin left in the Galaxy. Rita is hoping they can somehow find a way to prevent that. It's a long shot, but she's going to try."

Luke took a long drink, thinking through what Bonnie had told him.

"And Rachel and Ollie?" he asked at last.

"Well, it took them a while. But they finally decided they love each other. But they didn't want to come here. Since they're both Goblins now, they thought there was too much chance of bringing trouble down on us here at Phoenix."

"Bounty hunters, you mean..."

"Yeah. Ollie thinks after what happened, the Stree - and other bio governments farther out toward the Core - will put up large bounties for Goblins. Ollie said that a year from now, there'll be a hundred bounty hunters out chasing Goblins down, trying to collect the bounties. They just didn't want to bring that kind of trouble to Phoenix when we're still getting our colony going."

"It's a damn shame," said Luke. "They didn't have anything to do with the destruction of Stree Prime."

"Preaching to the choir, babe. Preaching to the choir."

"Where will they go?"

"Four of them - Ollie, Rachel, Luda, and Liwa - are heading out of the Arm. They salvaged a corvette at Stree Prime. They're going to point it toward the Core and keep going until they find someplace where nobody ever heard of Stree or Goblins."

"Or Humans," mused Luke.

"Or Humans."

EPILOGUE

Stalingrad System - 1,275 Lights from Earth

The little packet boat had once been called *Donkey* - a joke by its pilot. What had started as a joke had stuck, though, and the packet boat had been known by that name since.

Despite its name, it had done yeoman service. It had carried two young EDF officers - Rachel and Paco - to the distant Dyson Swarm called Stalingrad, where the first contact between Humans and the androids called Goblins had been realized, and a treaty agreed. It had carried a Goblin called Tika to Dekanna, where she played a role in saving Humanity from the onslaught of the Singheko. Lastly, it had returned Tika, Jim Carter, and Rita Page to Stalingrad, to begin Rita's life as a Goblin.

Then it had been relegated to an obscure dock on the Dyson Swarm, no longer needed. There it had been, a remnant of a brighter day, when the Stree entered the system. And as the Stree blasted apart the Dyson Swarm, ending the Goblin civilization, the little packet boat had somehow survived. It had been blown off the Swarm to drift away into an elliptical solar orbit, missed by the Stree as they methodically destroyed every remnant of Goblin civilization they could find.

Forgotten, the little packet boat might have stayed in its lonely orbit for centuries or even forever - if not for a quirk of coincidence. A shuttle passed in the vicinity, searching for usable debris in the system. A sensor beeped.

The android inside the shuttle had the general appearance of Jim Carter. It had his tall, lean body, his flashing blue eyes, his salt-and-pepper hair. It had his quirky, goofy smile as he saw *Donkey* again, for the first time in a long while.

But the Goblin inside the shuttle was only a copy of Jim Carter. His original biological body was long since turned to ash, on a distant orb known as Stree Prime that no longer existed as a viable planet. And his other copy was with Rita Page, somewhere in the black, headed to Lord Knows Where.

This version of Jim Carter had sardonically changed his name, at least in his own mind. He called himself Nemo now - an old Latin word for 'nobody.' It was his little joke – and another part of the reason he carried the strange smile.

For the last year he had made the destroyed Stalingrad system his home, a hermit roaming around in the debris, looking for things that might interest him.

Donkey interested him. He made a course change and vectored to the drifting boat, pulled alongside, and gave a remote command to *Donkey* to open its docking port. To his surprise, it did. With great delight, he realized the little boat still had power. He docked and made his way over to it. Entering, he found it nearly pristine, hardly damaged by its ordeal.

Moving to the cockpit, he paused for a moment, remembering. Remembering the last trip on this boat from Dekanna to Stalingrad, with Rita. Remembering the wife and lover he would never have again.

Because I'm not Jim Carter anymore. That life is gone, like a puff of smoke. Now I'm just Nemo. No matter how real it seems to me, I'm just a cheap imitation of the real Jim Carter.

The bitterness came back to him again, as it sometimes did. But he tried to suppress it. He didn't want to go there today.

Not today. Rita did what she thought was right. It was the only way to save Bonnie and the others. I guess I'd do it all over again.

Checking systems, he found them all functional. Only a little light maintenance would be required to bring the boat to normal status.

After some thought, Nemo made a decision. He had been

in the wreckage of this system for quite a while now. There wasn't much he didn't know about it. It was time to move on.

Twenty-seven days later, the little packet boat settled to a landing at the old Deseret Airport in western Nevada. Through some miracle, it didn't fall over in the soft sand. The ramp came down, and Nemo stepped out on the old Earth.

Visibility was poor; the dirty, low-hanging clouds were only a few thousand feet off the ground, and the wind was blowing sand around. Nemo ignored all that; he had eyes only for the crumbled ruins of a white aircraft hangar a few dozen yards from him. He moved around it until he found what he was looking for - an old World War Two fighter - a P-51 Mustang - its nose poking up from the fallen tin roof of the hangar. It looked remarkably intact, considering what it had gone through.

His internal radiation detector had been going off since he landed; Deseret was roughly between Reno and Las Vegas. Both cities had been thoroughly destroyed, and the entire state had taken a pounding, as the Stree ensured they obliterated all the military bases in Nevada. And Nemo knew his android body was not impervious to the radiation fleeting through him.

But he could sustain it for many days, maybe a month. And that would be enough. He turned off some of his bio-feedback mechanisms, so he wouldn't feel the pain and nausea caused by the radiation. He could repair himself later.

He cleared away the debris from around the Mustang, found his tools under the rubble, and started checking the airplane. He found and repaired a half-dozen items. He scrounged parts and sheet metal from other wrecked airplanes on the field, until at last - six days later - he was satisfied with his work.

He found some av-gas in one of the tanks on the field, stale but maybe usable, and fueled the Mustang. Then he spent another half-day clearing debris off the runway, until it looked reasonably safe to use. At last, he strapped into the cockpit, fired up the engine, and taxied out.

He pushed the throttle up slowly. The Merlin engine

coughed and backfired, unhappy with the old, stale gas. But once it got into its power curve, it smoothed out, and he released the brakes. The Mustang rolled down the runway, gathering speed. As he got rudder authority, he increased the throttle. The tail came up and he lifted off, pulled up the gear, and bored into the sky toward the mountains to the west.

He had been lucky; the dirty clouds had actually thinned above the airport today. He could see patches of blue sky for the first time since he arrived. It was a happy feeling.

Maybe this old Earth will survive after all, he thought as the Mustang climbed proudly into the sky, a fierce bird released again from the bindings of Earth. *Maybe there's a bit of hope. Someday people will live here again.*

After a few minutes, he was in the Panamint Mountains of California. He went crazy then, flinging the Mustang around the peaks and through the valleys, looping, doing hammerheads, throwing it around the sky, reveling in the freedom and joy of being in the air again. He made a turn around Telescope Peak and then, for the sheer hell of it, turned around it once more.

Finally, he just climbed, up and up, until the old Mustang had nothing left to give with the weak avgas in her tanks.

At thirty thousand feet, he leveled out and headed east. At this altitude, he could see well over 150 miles in any direction. But he saw no signs of life anywhere. No smoke, no movement, not a thing to indicate Humans had ever lived on this lonely planet.

He flew to Las Vegas and made a pass over the crater where once there had been a vibrant city. The crater was larger than others he had seen; the Stree had used one of their bigger bombs here, he realized. Probably a fifty-megaton.

Then he turned and headed back to Deseret. He did the classic World War Two landing break, coming in at high speed, flinging the Mustang up into a long climbing curve, letting the g-forces help the gear come down as he laid it over. He lined up on final and did a reasonably good wheel landing, the mains touching while he held up the tail, working the rudders, letting the tail settle in when it was ready.

Taxiing back to the ruins of his old hangar, he turned the Mustang to face west, toward the mountains of California across the state line. He let the engine idle for a bit, then shut it down. Climbing out, he chained the Mustang down, as securely as he could. Standing back, he inspected his work.

His eyes fell on the registration number painted on the side of the airplane.

N16CAP.

It was a tribute to his friend Jim "Capone" Calderone, his Weapons System Officer from his F-16 days. The friend he had killed on his last combat mission.

I didn't kill him. Not really. That was the biological Jim Carter.

But...the memories are just as real. You are a faithful copy of Jim Carter. So, are you just as guilty?

It sure feels that way. There's no escaping that.

You stupid SOB. Why did you have to go back for that last firing pass? Cap was yelling at you not to do it. But you just had to try, didn't you?

Shaking off the memories - true or false though they might be - Nemo reached out to the plane and put his hand on it, caressed it one last time, the touch of a pilot for his plane.

Then he covered it with a half-dozen tarps he had liberated around the field. He knew it was a hopeless gesture; it wouldn't survive long outside, in the wind and sand and rain. And even if it did, the chances that anyone would come along in the next fifty or a hundred years and find it before it crumpled to rust were virtually zero. But he did it anyway, because it was his to love, and it was the only thing he could love at the moment.

Then he stepped back and looked around. The ruins of the hangars surrounding the runway broke his heart. He looked at the corner of the airport, to his left. A large red hangar had stood there once. It was long since gone, dismantled by Mark Rodger's federal agents now more than five years ago, when they were looking for clues about the sentient starship *Jade*.

But he remembered.

This is where Bonnie and I fell in love.

This is where Rita came to life.

This is where it all started.

Finally, he walked back to *Donkey*, entered, and pulled up the ramp. A few minutes later, *Donkey* lifted off the planet for the last time, and headed out of the atmosphere.

Nemo smiled. Someday, maybe Bonnie or Luke or Rita or even his daughter Imogen might come to Deseret. And they'd find the Mustang, and they'd wonder who tried to preserve it like that.

And maybe they'd think of him.

###

AUTHOR NOTES

Thank you for reading Book Five of the Broken Galaxy series. This series has been a joy to write, as I have long since fallen in love with most of my characters. That's an occupational hazard of any author, but I'm especially prone to it. I make no excuses; though I've been told lately that I should kill off more of them. Ah, but that's hard to do when you like them so much. Maybe next book...

Don't forget to check out the preview of Book Six right after these notes!

Finally, don't hesitate to contact me with thoughts / ideas at the locations below!

Sci-Fi, New Books, Hard Science, and General Mayhem
www.facebook.com/PhilHuddlestonAuthor

Author Page on Amazon:
www.amazon.com/author/philhuddleston

Special bonus - if you have not already signed up for my newsletter, sign up now and get one of my books for free!
www.philhuddleston.com/newsletter

PREVIEW OF NEXT BOOK

Goblin Eternal

Kaeru System - 2,678 Lights from Earth

The bounty hunter delivering the two unconscious figures into the jail was - at least on the outside - a Human female. But not too many Human females could pick up an unconscious two-hundred-pound Kaeru thug under each arm, take them out of the back of a truck, and dump them on a handcart like two sacks of potatoes. Pushing the cart into the foyer of the jail, the hunter smiled at the clerk as she slid the cart to a stop in front of his desk. Speaking Kaeru like a native, she gestured to the two prisoners.

"Here you go, Alin. Two more for your lockup!"

The clerk leaned over the counter, staring at the two unconscious figures slumped on the cart. "Oh ho," he smiled. "Poir and Rang! You'll make some good money off those two!"

The female had been using the name Loen here, on this backwater planet on the edge of the Orion Arm. Now, with a large grin, she nodded. "Excellent. I need it, believe me. Pickings have been slim lately. My poor ship is about to turn to rust. I'm not sure it's got another trip left in it!"

As the clerk shoved a tablet toward her, Loen moved to the counter. She signed, transferring the prisoners to Alin's care, and waited as he countersigned and transferred upwards of ten thousand credits to her account. Taking her receipt, she turned to depart when he spoke up again.

"By the way, someone was asking about you last night."

Loen froze, then unfroze, casually turning back to the clerk. "Oh, really? Who was that?"

"Some big-ass Singheko. I was a couple of chairs down from him at the Slightly Wounded Bar & Grill; but I heard him asking about a female Human bounty hunter."

Loen had indeed once been a Human female - twenty-one years ago. But she was far from being Human now, even if she passed for one on this planet. She displayed a lack of concern, smiling broadly.

"It's not hard to overhear a Singheko, eh? Even their whispers sound like a *meshar* growling in the night."

Alin nodded. "Yep, that's for sure. He was trying to be discreet, but I could hear him. He was asking the bartender if there was a Human bounty hunter working this area, a female one."

"And what did the bartender say?"

"It was Bain. You know him. He wouldn't give one of those seven-foot-tall bastards the time of day. He told him to take a hike."

Loen gave a brief nod, a gesture of indirect thanks.

"I doubt he was looking for me - but give Bain my regards when you see him."

"Why don't you tell him yourself? He's on duty tonight, I think. And you just got paid - I'm sure he'd like it if you'd spread some of those credits around!"

"I may do just that, Alin. Sounds like a great idea."

Not.

With a wave, Loen departed the jail, moving back to the rented truck outside. She got in and left, driving slowly back toward the shuttleport, thinking.

Another damn Singheko, come to hunt me down and sell me to the Stree. Let's see, how many of those damn Lions is that now? Five? Not counting the dozen-odd other species that have come after me...

Loen pounded the wheel of the truck a couple of times

and cursed somewhat creatively in a rare language known as English. Then she settled herself and calmly drove the truck back to the rental facility. Turning it in, she walked to her beat-up ship parked on the dark pavement of the nearby port, entered, closed the hatch, and moved to the galley. Tearing off her gun belt, she slumped into a chair, splayed out her legs, and smashed her fist on the tabletop in frustration and anger.

Why can't they leave me alone? Why? Just leave me alone for once!

This Goblin in Human form was tall - just an inch short of six feet. She was of indeterminate race, her original biological DNA assembled from random bits and pieces when she was cloned by a semi-insane sentient starship named *Jade*, those many years ago on Earth. Her hair was black, short, military-style. When she was younger - when she was still a Human, and before the Singheko War - she had worn long, curly black hair, taking meticulous care of it, viewing it as a prized legacy of her unknown DNA parentage.

But that was a long time ago. As an officer on the starship *Merkkessa*, she had cut off those curls. And when she had been scanned into Goblin form, that short military-style haircut had stuck.

Of course, she was a Goblin. She could easily transmit herself into any of a dozen other physical bodies she kept in her cargo hold.

But this one - an exact model of her original biological body - was the one she preferred. She rarely changed out of it.

Now, smashing the table again, hard, hard enough to leave the surface ringing in response, she let out another string of curses in her native English, a run of words that would have left any old-Earth Marine in awe. Then, subsiding, she shook her head, calming herself so she could think logically.

I really need to run. Just run. Now. Don't even hesitate. Get the hell out of here while I still can.

But...I want to say goodbye to Jianna. I wonder if I can take that chance. Those damn Lions are good trackers. I don't have much time. But maybe...maybe I can say goodbye to her...

Deciding, Loen jumped to her feet and grabbed her pistol belt. Strapping it back on, she hurried out of the ship, trotted to the terminal, walked through and out the other side to the transport station. In five minutes, she was on a train to downtown. Using the embedded comm in her head, she sent a quick message to her Kaeru family. She had taken a room with them two years ago. Their relationship had blossomed; now she felt part of their family, staying in their home when she was between trips.

Leaving would hurt. Leaving everything she had cared about for the last two years, during her time on Kaeru. Leaving the family she had grown to love. But she had no choice. To stay would put them in extreme danger. She had to run, and run hard, never look back.

Just one quick goodbye. That's all. Then I'll go.

Taking a seat in the end corner of the car, she stayed alert for anything unusual, but nothing happened. The car was nearly deserted anyway - a Delphi couple with their luggage, a couple of Kaeru workers from the port heading home after their shift, and one Tilvex businessman who looked like he'd experienced a long day.

Changing trains at Kaeru Central, she took the express to the suburbs and within fifteen minutes was at her destination. She walked the two short blocks to a small cottage and quietly keyed the door code, stepped into the house.

It was quiet. It was much too quiet. She knew instantly the Singheko had beaten her here, was already in the house. She had just enough time for that thought to register before the EM pulse hit her, knocked her to the floor, her joints frozen, unable to move.

Her brain should have been frozen too - knocked offline, blacked out, leaving her unconscious. But she had long ago paid a Taegu black market medic a shitpot load of money to add additional shielding to her android brain. She was still conscious.

She wished she weren't. Her eyes focused on a clump of something down the hallway, a bundle of clothes. But more than that. Oh, much more than that, as she realized what she was looking at.

A child.

A dead child.

A satyr of old Greek myth, two budding horns just starting out of her skull. Four toes instead of five, but still a foot. Four fingers instead of five, but still a hand.

A Kaeru satyr, but still a child.

And now a dead child. Her lovely adopted sweet happy satyr daughter lay dead on the floor in front of her. No more bedtime stories. No more pajamas. No more kisses goodnight. And just beyond, she could see another body. Jianna's mother. Her lovely adopted sweet happy satyr sister. The Singheko had left nothing for her, nobody to call family anymore. No witnesses.

With a clump, two huge, booted feet moved into her view from the side room. Though she couldn't lift her frozen head, couldn't turn her frozen neck to see higher, she knew what she was seeing.

The feet of a Singheko "Lion." A seven-foot-tall creature that looked much like an upright, old-Earth lion, hence their nickname. Standing tall instead of walking on all fours, they had the upright pointed ears of a predator, on a head that still showed a trace of a muzzle, evolution slow to wipe out the last vestiges of a lineage that had hunted for blood on the hot savannas of their planet a million or more years ago.

The most dangerous creatures in the Arm. Mercenaries, shock troops, bounty hunters.

Killers.

Zimra zu Akribi stood over the crumpled figure on the floor, holding the EMP pistol steady on her in case he needed to fire again. But Loen lay motionless, frozen, not even twitching.

"I hope you can hear me, you Goblin bitch. I hope you know who I am. I am Zimra zu Akribi. You killed my uncle. You killed my planet. Yes, I know who you are, Admiral Rita Page. You ran far and fast, and you sank deep into the culture of a dozen planets. But always I pick up your trail again. Now - it ends. Now you go to Aslar. And there, the Stree will kill you as slowly and painfully as possible."

Continue the story with Goblin Eternal on Amazon!

WORKS

Imprint Series

Artemis War (prequel novella)
Imprint of Blood
Imprint of War
Imprint of Honor
Imprint of Defiance

Broken Galaxy Series

Broken Galaxy
Star Tango
The Long Edge of Night
The Short End
Remnants
Goblin Eternal

ABOUT THE AUTHOR

Like Huckleberry Finn, Phil Huddleston grew up barefoot and outdoors, catching mudbugs by the creek, chasing rabbits through the fields, and forgetting to come home for dinner. Then he discovered books. Thereafter, he read everything he could get his hands on, including reading the Encyclopedia Britannica and Funk & Wagnalls from A-to-Z multiple times. He served in the U. S. Marines for four years, returned to college and completed his degree on the GI Bill. Since that time, he built computer systems, worked in cybersecurity, played in a band, flew a bush plane from Alaska to Texas, rode a motorcycle around a good bit of America, and watched in amazement as his wife raised two wonderful daughters in spite of him. And would sure like to do it all again. Except maybe without the screams of terror.

Printed in Great Britain
by Amazon

62575551R00188